# Truth To Be Told

HATTY SWIGGS

**D'Go Man Publishing**

This is an original publication of D'Go Man Publishing

This book is a work of fiction. Names, characters, incidents and dialogues are either the product of the author's imagination or are used fictitiously. Any resemblance to actual persons, living or dead, are entirely coincidental. Characters in this book have no existence outside the imagination of the author and have no relation whatsoever to anyone bearing the same name or names.


Cover art by Katlyn Oman
Cover layout & support: DYD Publications



First Edition: June 2011

ISBN: 0615310842
ISBN-13: 9780615310848

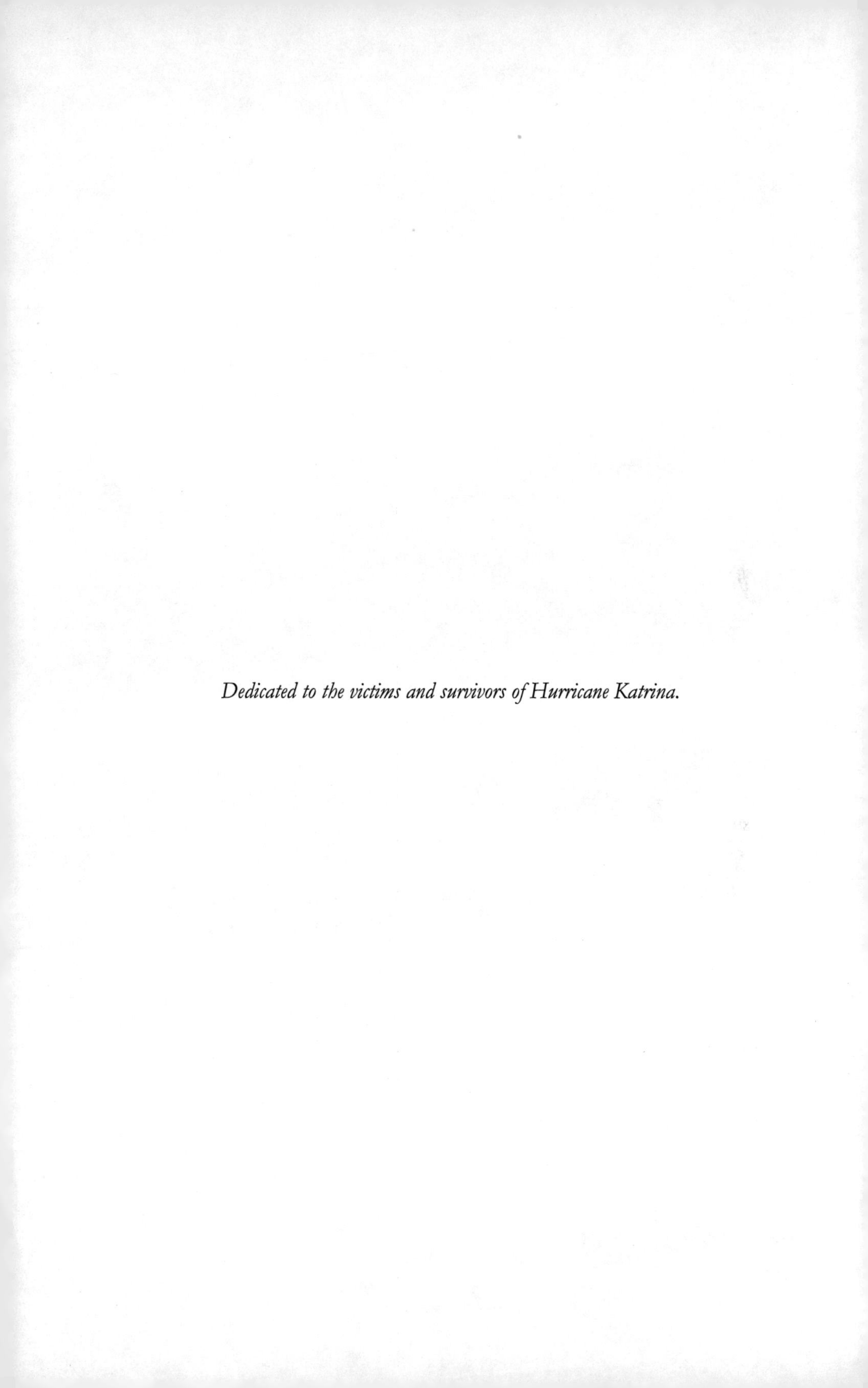

*Dedicated to the victims and survivors of Hurricane Katrina.*

Likening love to be as that of a fine, delicate, so purely fragile a crystal - one bestowed on each of us at creation. None seem spared the embrace of inflicted damage.

We set about our smudges and smears, tarnishing the very foundation it has been set upon. We put forth cracks unto its surface; with so many names being shattered into unrecognizable pieces.

*There being one shown through. Capable of embracing this crystal love with clearness of heart, she polishes gleam to glistening fullness.*

He being the intent of these writings - *the truth belongs to her.*

# PART I

## CHAPTER 1

Somewhere between the half-chewed lemon roll and a scrambled deck of cards, my thoughts of him kept returning. Those inconceivable moments, the things he had said. A smile filtered in, tipping my face with the recollection of how I came to be Hatty Swiggs. Just as suddenly, the moment was stolen away. I turned sternly toward the window. A serious memory ignited; smile erased. Why had he asked this of me? Through the glass I could see old "Beulah", the name I had christened my truck. She was covered with snow, parked almost impatiently.

"All right then," I said aloud as I brushed the cards aside. I didn't bother to gather them up to put them back in the pack. Maybe I'd be shuffling them again in a minute or so. I went to find some paper and a pen, then I sat back down.

At times, an over-the-road truck driver tends to believe he's seen it all. Yet deep inside, he knows the road ahead is less predictable - less patient than the planners of pavement intended it to be. Like the weather that can never really be forecasted past ones nose, it was the weather indeed, that brought all of this about. No dream, ever in my mind's eye, could have been farther out there than the truth that was preparing to beset me. A moment that grabs you between a breath and a heartbeat, one that makes life stand still by catching the troubling realization that what you had always thought to be true, was not.

Friends simply think of me as some kind of guitar-pickin' gypsy trucker. But mine's a story filled with career changes, bringing me at long last to a comfort zone that seems to suit my soul. This is an occupation of solitude. There are few restrictions on how one chooses his or her appearance. It's my place to wear long hair, contrary clothing styles and this dangling Kokopelli earring that tends to bring second glance sparks from the common eye. It's the way I am. Although I'm college educated, it's this gypsy state of mind that lures me — never knowing which direction I'll be routed to next or what state or province my body will rest in at the end of each day.

This job takes me away from home eleven to twelve days straight, covering the lower forty-eight states and all provinces of Canada. The time back to my wife Kathryn and our cabin in the Wisconsin woods is usually a short, highly valued, two or three days. It's mostly drive and sleep, with the short time in between spent strumming my guitar, singing her love songs over my cell phone, and writing I-miss-and-love-you postcards with pictures from places she may never see. Kathryn, whom I long ago nicknamed and always call Kat, has no interest in traveling around in a big truck. She works in an office. During her two-week vacation, she won't go with me while I work. Although she keeps saying "someday," it hasn't happened yet, and I'm doubtful it ever will. She'd much rather go to an island somewhere for her vacation, and I never argue with that.

My passion has always been music — from the first guitar I received from my brother on my tenth birthday, to the somewhat absurd collection I hold today. It has gotten to be that every time I set foot in a music store, I'd see the 'axe' of my dreams, the one I've needed all my life and just can't live without. Kat says I'm fickle, and finally cut me back to one purchase a year. She said it must be my midlife crisis, but conceded it was better than a blonde bimbo and a red corvette.

## CHAPTER 2

It was late August 2005 when this story began. It's my birthday on the twenty-eighth and Kat called to wish me a happy day. It was a Sunday morning. She asked where I was, and where I was heading.

"Got a load going down around Mobile, Alabama to deliver mid-day tomorrow," I told her.

There was a brief silence on the line, broken by a startled, "Wait a minute, doesn't the company know there's a hurricane coming that way? It's huge!"

I never listen to the news or watch television, let alone converse with many people while I'm on the road, and I only use my CB as needs require. This was the first I had heard anything about a hurricane.

"I guess the computer don't know that," I replied. I remember smiling, as I was referring to the satellite-tuned keyboard in our trucks. "What's it called?" I asked her.

"Katrina!" Kat blurted out.

"Oh, a Russian hurricane," I replied, jokingly.

"It's not funny! You need to call in and get out of there right away!" I could hear the alarm in her voice; she was nearly crying.

"Now that you mention it, I'm noticing heavy traffic coming north," I told her.

"You need to turn around! They're saying it's a category five. The winds are at 170 miles an hour! It's gonna hit by tomorrow morning right where you're going! They say it could weaken a little, but radar shows it covering the whole Gulf of Mexico. And after it lands, there'll be tornadoes!" Her voice had risen considerably.

Our conversation had a sudden unsettling, disconcerting effect on me. I'd been looking forward to my time down South in hopes of finding a baby alligator for my grandson TJ. Although they're illegal to own as pets, I had promised him I would try to get one, chancing the law for the love of a boy to whom I'd been a hero since day one.

"I'll call in and find out what's up and get back to you," I assured her. I thought about what she was saying. The call ended with, "I love you."

This changed things and my senses heightened. It wasn't more than ten minutes farther down the road, between Montgomery and Mobile on Hank Williams Memorial Lost Highway (I-65), when my Qualcomm, the on-board computer system, flashed a message for me to re-route north. I was to drop my trailer in Monroeville for a relay, then hook up to a load in the drop lot there; my destination would then be Kansas City. I took the next exit, pulled safely to the side, and applied the airbrakes. Kat will be relieved, I thought, as I brought out my atlas to trip-plan the next move. I can steer this small side road north and save a little time. It'll get me there, I figured, as I studied the map. It's not a truck route, but it's not shown as restricted, so I'll take it, and zigzag if I have to. A driver can be innovative that way.

After a call back to Kat to allay her fears, I pulled back onto the freeway. Eventually, I found my back-road exit heading northwest; taking a turn onto what quickly would become a trucker's nightmare, what I call a white-knuckle ride. My hands gripped the wheel, as it shook to the relentless pounding on Beulah's suspension system. My body was bouncing up and down in the driver's seat. Her tires tortured their way in and out of rutted pot holes, disintegrating asphalt, and assorted clumps of displaced tar. Our path wound back and forth. It was all I could do to stay out of the ditch. It was the kind of road that seems to narrow as you drive farther along, with grass growing out of its deteriorating cracks. It was a road nearly abandoned, years overdue for repaving, lined by crumbling shoulders and broken chunks of flung tar rocks lying about in the ditches. There were sharp blind turns that put the rear end of my trailer precariously on the wrong side of the road. Will I get out of this? Will this road just die out somewhere? I was talking out loud. I remember nearly praying that some Nascar wannabe, or inattentive driver on a cell phone, wasn't coming around each next turn.

After what seemed a lot longer than it probably was, I slowed for an approaching intersection somewhere outside Uriah, Alabama, and to a road that would take me north. I remember hoping it would be a more eighteen-wheel friendly ride from then on. As I came to a stop, I noticed a small building off to my left, with a sign that read "Gas and Groceries." There was another small sign near the road that had been hand painted. It was on a cheap piece of plywood, nailed to a wooden stake that had been pounded into the ground. The sign simply read "Bait." That got my attention. I had heard baby alligators were sometimes sold as bait. There appeared room for a semi in the gravel lot behind the building, so I steered old Beulah in, letting her, and my nerves, take a much-needed break.

As I walked around to the front of the station, I noticed a single vehicle with dark-tinted windows parked alongside a set of outdated gas pumps. A smartly dressed gray-haired man was filling his tank. I approached the wooden entrance door. There was a sign hanging by string, draped over a nail that simply read "Open." Stepping inside the quiet store, I hardly took notice of the customer with his back to me, looking through the glass doors of a beverage cooler. A musty smell, blended with that of smoked fish and stale cigarette smoke, hung in the air. There were swirls of sticky yellowed tape, half-covered with dead flies, dangling from the water-stained ceiling. An overhead fan, loose and wobbling in its bracing, revolved slowly. The roughly worn wooden floor moaned and creaked to my footsteps as I approached the counter. A young man sat behind it reading, or maybe he was just looking at, a worn and, by all appearances, outdated girly magazine. It seemed a real effort for him to lift his eyes when I asked, "Do you sell baby alligators for bait?"

Before he could respond, I heard a voice behind me say: "You don't want no gators son, they'll bite yer guitar-pickin' fingers off."

A bit startled at who this might be, I turned and light-heartedly replied, "I wouldn't want that; my guitar's been my best friend since I was ten years old."

The stranger now standing before me, with a warm half smile, holding two bottles of juice and a bag of peanuts, was an elderly, scraggly bearded gentleman. Vagrant in appearance, he was wearing a beat-up old fishing hat. He was thin in stature, with glasses resting low on his nose. His hair, probably once a sandy or chestnut brown, was now well graying and fell past his shoulders. He was loosely dressed in a wrinkled off-white pullover shirt and caramel-colored khaki pants. I guessed he was in his late sixties or so. He had that familiar look, like someone I'd seen before. You know the face; we all bump into them now and then.

"Yer a guitar player then?" he asked.

"Never leave home without one," I quipped. "I live and breathe music."

"You oughta play me something," he said casually, yet almost daringly.

Now, I'll play for anyone that'll listen — in small roadside bars, coffee houses, truck stops, and even rest areas, but I recall wondering why he'd take the time or interest. "We should get movin', there's a storm coming," I replied.

"Ahh, we got time; how 'bout it?"

"I guess so," I said with slight hesitation. "It's in my truck out back."

"No gators 'round here," the kid behind the counter at last responded.

"Name's Marcus," the old man reached out a steady hand.

"I'm Grant," I said quickly as my hand met his. He then paid for what he had, and we walked to the door.

Once outside, he said, "Be right with ya," then headed over to the car parked at the pumps. The windows were half down and I could see two medium size dogs jumping about inside.

As he handed the bag and bottles to the driver, I could hear him say, "Pull around back by that semi, will ya?" He pointed to Beulah, then to me. "I'll meet you back there," he gestured to the driver. Then he and I walked around the store, back to my freightliner.

I unlocked Beulah's driver-side door, climbed up, and retrieved my guitar that was strapped in the top bunk. I set it on the passenger seat, opened that door, and climbed out, then reached up to grab the Gibson J-45 that I'd had since my band days in the '70s. I closed the door and walked around to the front of the truck where Marcus stood waiting. I was able to glimpse that the car still hadn't moved.

"It's my 'car guitar'. It don't matter if it gets dinged or scratched anymore. I leave my clean guitars at home," I explained. He didn't say anything, just looked at it, then smiled at me. Finally the car slowly pulled behind my trailer and I noticed there was someone in the back seat. I then put my foot up on the step of the cab and strummed a 'G' chord to hear if it was in tune. Good enough, I thought.

Since the stranger was later in his years, I thought for a moment, then surmised that an old Everly Brothers tune would be to his liking, so I played and sang, *Let It Be Me*. When I finished, he still wore that smile.

"That was really good, son, really good!" he said. His face was beaming. And with sincere blue eyes looking into mine, he reached his hand over and placed it on my forearm. "Can ya play me another?" he asked.

I thought for a moment, then replied, "Sure, one more, I guess." Choosing one of Kat's favorite Elvis songs, I started to play, *Can't Help Falling In Love with You.* It was when I began singing the second verse that it happened. He started singing along, and things began to seem mysterious. I can't recall the exact moment or the last words that were sung, but I abruptly stopped playing.

I've tried, but to this day I am unable to find the words that would truly describe the dreamlike out-of-body sensation that pulsated through my entire being. As if by the speed and force of lightning, my mind raced in and out of denial. An avalanche of goose bumps ran up and down my arms, back, and thighs. I could feel the hairs standing up on the back of my neck. Then that curious smile returned to his lips, like that of someone recognizing my thoughts. Now peering through those scruffy un-groomed whiskers was a dimple. My eyes plummeting into his gaze, a clear blue shown through. His expression was that of now being recognized, and in a complete focus, I realized who this man was.

All previous images were at once unscrambled. I knew those eyes for sure, and now I could see so clearly. "It can't be!" I heard myself exhaling aloud. But there were no doubts now that would contradict my adamant instincts. He was not the same man you would envision, if you were to attempt aging him from past memories; quite the antithesis. Covered over in wrinkled age and rendered this other character, he vanquished all of the old conceptions. Indeed very much alive and in the flesh, he appeared physically well.

"Guess we'd better get going," he said, snapping at my sustained trance. It felt much like that of a muted rattling crack that can instantly run across a windshield. Maybe only a mere moment had passed. I couldn't tell. But it broke the deafening, pounding sound my heart had been sending into my ears. There probably existed an endless silence for him. He said, "I want you to meet a couple people," as he motioned toward the car. He began to walk to it. I followed in a zombie-like fashion. The back door opened. Two dogs jumped out and started running about, sniffing at the ground, and at me. A woman of slim, medium stature and slender facial features glanced at me from the back seat, then she delicately stepped out. Her jet-black hair was nearly waist length, with swirls of hinting gray intertwined throughout its waves. I still had not muttered a word. The front door opened, and the man who I'd seen at the pump stepped out. He was middle aged, maybe in his late fifties. Stocky, somewhat overweight, he had short-cropped graying hair. His attire was that of a casual, yet clean-cut professional.

The woman, on the other hand, beamed gypsy radiance. Exotic in her beauty; imposing; wearing a long dress of many colors that cascaded to her ankles. She stood emboldened by intricately beaded leather moccasins, and plenty of adornment — earrings, bracelets, necklaces and fingers full of rings. As a leaf meets the wind for a first time, fervent in my eyes, she was a wonder to gaze upon, and I did. Pedestal-like to my eyes, she stood in the light, sublime, stirring at my emotions.

"This is my wife, Juliette, whom I affectionately call Jewel," Marcus said, as he tucked his arm around her waist, nudging her nearer to him.

I nodded, finally finding my voice long enough to say, "I'm Grant". She looked at me with early morning dew eyes, as though she'd just awakened. They were of light hazel, soft topaz to mossy green, and much more than that.

I was acutely aware that I was staring, and how I was totally intrigued. "It's nice to meet you," she replied in a soft, haunting voice. A tint in her smile gave way to grand enchantment. Her presence had become, well, ineffable. My mouth may have been lapsed open.

"This is our good friend, Credence," Marcus added.

The man responded with a simple, "How ya doin'?" upon which I turned to the gentleman and nodded.

Now I couldn't stop myself, as my voice seemed to gush out in dubious question, "And your name is Marcus, you say?"

I saw Credence look at him sharply. Obviously bothered, he held a bitten frown, a furrowed brow. Jewel, flashing a mischievous smile, glanced up at Marcus from the side for a mere second.

"Has been for years," was his grinning reply.

"But," I started to say, trying to focus a thought into words.

"Marcus," he repeated, insisting.

I pursued no further. There was overwhelming confusion settled in the moment. It was too much to absorb in such a short space and time. My poor mind!

"This kid can play," Marcus announced to them, almost bragging. "I like his rhythm and finger-pickin' style, even with those driving gloves he's got on; good voice." Then he turned to Jewel and made a remark that I didn't understand at the time: "This is him," he told her. There was a pause as they stared at each other, then they both looked back at me. "I'd like to hear you play again sometime. I play some too," Marcus said. "You should call me after this thing blows over, and maybe we can get together next time yer down this way?" As soon as Marcus said this, Credence reached into the front seat, retrieving a pen and a small pocket notebook.

"I'll give you my numbers too," I responded, still impounded in zombie. Credence gave me the pen and book. I wrote down my cell and home phone numbers. I couldn't chance not seeing him again. "Can I get your number then?" I wishfully requested.

"Sure," he said, taking back the notebook. He jotted down a couple names and numbers. Tearing the page from the notebook, he explained, "These are friends of mine that'll relay messages back to me. I don't have a phone myself." The names he had written were Burton and Clay, with corresponding phone numbers for each.

He seemed to examine me again and said, "We should get going. Sure good to meet you." He then reached again to shake my hand. Jewel, with a smile, nodded. Credence simply got back into the driver's seat without a word.

"Same here," I managed to utter as they were getting into the car. With my head numb, providing me with nothing more to say, I turned toward my truck and began walking away.

Over my shoulder I heard him say, "Like yer hat!" With a half turn I looked back, smiled, then I continued on.

## CHAPTER 3

When I reached Beulah, I picked up my guitar that I'd leaned against the left drive tire. I then walked around to the passenger side, opened the door, and set the Gibson upright on the seat. While walking around the front toward my driver's side, I saw them pull away; they headed north. I started to feel some semblance of normalcy returning, and it occurred to me I could have asked them where they were going. For sure, we all needed to put distance away from the approaching storm and without losing anymore time. I climbed up into my driver's seat. Still a bit dazed, admittedly confused, I pulled onto the roadway to move ahead with the assignment I had been given. I made a quick call to Kat that evening, and all I said regarding this event was that I had met someone interesting, and would tell her all about it when I got home. I didn't consider it to be an over-the-phone topic for conversation.

It was midmorning the next day when I tuned in the Fox News channel on my XM radio, something I rarely do. I was on my way to Kansas City now with this new load, and the news machine was just beginning to rev up, as Katrina was hastening toward landfall. Shepard Smith was broadcasting from what seemed to be the epicenter of an impending disaster. I was completely riveted to the news coverage. I knew that much of the world was also tuned in, following an event that would sadden our hearts and minds for some time to come.

The day was filled with ongoing accounts of unparalleled destruction in the Gulf. America will never be the same, I was thinking. We're losing New Orleans, and the whole Gulf coast is getting wiped out. It had been an astonishingly awful, and wonderful, two days, I told myself.

How could I have met him? How could this be? Could it really be him? My mind began spinning again. "Don't matter," I thought, "nobody will believe you anyway." I joked inwardly, almost talking aloud to myself. That's something a trucker should watch out for. Then I began leaning toward doubt. I thought that someday I'd look back on all of this and be convinced that I couldn't distinguish my dreams from reality. Then I laughed out loud. It was something I needed; a release of sorts. And what am I gonna say when I get home?

The rest of this trip was routine, but for the constant updates on the hurricane and its toll of human tragedies. Now I was eager to get home, catch the television coverage of what I had, up to now, been only picturing in my mind — the flooding and destructive force. How can the I-10 freeway be wiped out? I tried, but couldn't imagine.

A driver tends to space time and distance differently when he's heading for home. Adrenaline seems to kick in; miles disappear in the push. The next thing to captivate my attention was simply pulling into my own driveway. It's one of my heart's favorite moments.

Mid-afternoon now, Kat was still at work, which would give me the time I needed to unload a few things, and maybe get at my dirty laundry. It would be nice to have these things out of the way, allowing my time with her to be more dedicated. As I tried to control my anticipation until we would be together again, I turned on the news, but I couldn't sit still. I started thinking about him again. Wait till I tell her about this! What will she say? What would the world think if it only knew?

Our favorite thing to do when Kat and I are together, besides the obvious, is to find some music somewhere, a band or juke box, and dance. Sometimes we dance at home to the music of the stereo, but often we enjoy going out with friends, having a few drinks, and busting out our pool cues for a rousing game of eight ball. We have our favorite restaurants. Above all, we try to relax because the time goes by so fast.

Her timing was usual; as I watched from the kitchen window, the Camaro pull into the yard. I met her on the porch, in what seems to be our traditional lovers, "welcome home, missed-you-so-much," moment. We let our celebration begin.

As evening neared, we freshened up for a night out. "Is anything bothering you?" Something must have shown. She knows me too well.

"No, why?" I replied.

"Nothing, you're just quiet."

"We match," I said, referring to what we'd chosen to wear. She smiled. We were ready to rock.

Our small town is just another sleepy 'burg nestled in the heart of America. It has a population of less than two thousand, and that includes the countryside farms, and us "stick people" who dwell in the vast surrounding woods that cradles our modest cabin. We whimsically refer to the town as "Jetsburg" because it's so fast-paced. It does have hot spots, and decent meals. This night we elected to go Oriental. We would top things off afterward at Smoky Joe's Bar, for pool. There were some new tunes I hoped to locate on the jukebox that I had heard on my XM radio while I was on the road. We like to say the juke box gets drunker than we do, with all the money that primes that pump. I always jot down the titles of new songs that I can't wait to share with Kat. And besides, I can't play decent pool without good musical inspiration.

As I recall, we danced to its music around the pool table later that evening, the highlight being a "three-step," to *Think About It, Darlin'* by Jerry Lee Lewis. With the clacking sounds of other players' pool balls; we dance for all the tomorrows when our arms would be empty.

I'd wondered earlier, as we were preparing to go out, when might be the right moment to bring him up? Relax I told myself, it'll just happen. There probably is no perfect time.

So it had been during our dinner, as our conversation turned to the Katrina news, when I suddenly found myself almost blurting, "Guess who I met down south?"

"Oh, I don't know, someone famous?" she assumingly asked with a half-hidden and somewhat dismissive smile.

"Yeah, somebody everyone thinks is dead!" I responded.

When I told her what had happened, and who he was, her response was an unbelieving, "yeah right," as she bit into her spring roll. The whole story was screaming inside of me to come out. I elaborated on all that had happened, and how shocked I was. "Oh, Grant, you worry me sometimes," she sighed, managing a smile.

I retrieved from my wallet the names and numbers that he had given me and showed them to her. "If only we could find a sample of his handwriting to compare," I thought aloud.

"Why are you talking like this? You worry me!" she scolded, now seemingly annoyed.

"Some things can't easily be explained," I said.

"It wasn't him!"

"It was, though," I muttered back softly.

"Don't talk about this to anyone! It sounds crazy," she insisted.

I shrugged my shoulders, agreeing to drop the subject then, and I spoke no more of it, but my thoughts would not be still.

The weekend sped by, as my time at home always does. In between seeing the kids and grandkids for too brief a time, there was my thankful repose of how blessed our lives are.

Monday, my departure approaching much too fast. From my regular checklist on that Sunday afternoon, I hurriedly picked up the groceries at the store that would be needed for this next trip. I finished packing Beulah on Sunday evening.

That old truck seemed ready to go. I can't recall all of the places we've been together, yet for some unexplainable reason; I believe she remembers every mile. Sometimes I know she gets as weary as I do when I glance from her side mirrors at the black plume smoke pouring out of her stack. Lately her cruise control refuses to work. It's almost as if she's telling me she wants to rest for awhile — take a break. After I do stop and turn the engine off for a time, the cruise seems to mysteriously work fine when we return to the road again. These little quirks remind me how very much alive Beulah is to me and what a partner she's been. Our pulses run together. That's why I catch myself sometimes saying things out load like, "Oh c'mon, why do you have to do this now?" Or "C'mon baby, c'mon baby" when we're trudging up those stiff mountain grades. She knows I'm not just talking to myself.

Once again, all was ready for the morning. There would be that warm kiss from her lips to my heart for days to come, her unending embrace for me to recall. And she will say, "See you after work" — never goodbye.

# PART II

## CHAPTER 1

Yes it's true; a driver's prevailing wind is ever-changing, never predictable. It can be inclement weather, flat tires, mechanical breakdowns of all types, traffic delays, road construction and a real push to make on-time delivery. On the other side of that coin are sunny skies, fair sailing, and "you have all the time in the world to make it, kid." With unforeseeable combinations of everything in between, it truly is a minute-by-minute scenario each and every day.

This time out went smoothly enough. During that first week I found myself pulling into our operation center in Laredo, Texas, with a load to drop for relay, destination Mexico.

Having completed this assignment, I waited for the next one to come across my Qualcomm. Time seemed to stand still in that hot and dusty parking lot. I decided to grab a quick shower and a sandwich machine-microwave lunch, all the amenities this facility had to offer.

While sitting at a table enjoying a mostly tasteless, rubbery burger, I overheard two drivers talking about another hurricane on its way. When I got back to my truck I turned on the news channel, and sure enough; this one they were calling Rita. She was heading for much the same area that just got devil-kissed by Katrina — the area seared with scars that will always burn an enduring pain.

A new work order was coming across now. Hook up to trailer number such and such already located in the lot where I sat. It was a relay, with its destination Florida. While I listened to the radio news, my street-level directions came across. I was to take I-10 all the way. Wait a minute, from what I'd heard, parts of that interstate were gone, I reminded myself. Then came my call to the trip planner, aka dispatcher. "Parts of I-10 were destroyed by Hurricane Katrina," I explained.

"The computer doesn't have that programmed in," he acknowledged. I had to smile, another computer routing oversight. It was pretty much the same thing I had told Kat a few weeks earlier. "I'll change your routing points to Dallas and from there take I-20 across and reroute south once you get past the damaged highway. You should be alright with that; stay safe," were his closing words.

I would need to keep tabs on this storm, as I considered that we could still be crossing paths farther on up the line. It was early afternoon, Saturday, September 24. I was between Tyler, Texas, and Shreveport, Louisiana, when this hurricane introduced herself. It had once been a category four, with winds around 140 mph. Now it was a category one or two with wind gusts coming in at 80 mph plus. I was heading into another real "white-knuckler." My load was light, 17,000 pounds of paper towels. I had to laugh. You go, Grant! Save the day running paper towels into a hurricane. I hoped they were super-absorbent!

Even having been rerouted on I-20, things got serious too fast. Cars, vans, and pickup trucks lay in the ditches. Most were tipped on their side or were upside down. It was getting hard to hold Beulah on the road. I saw a fellow company driver's rig jackknifed in the trees. An ambulance and rescue squad were on the scene, a lot of flashing lights. I could offer no help. I had to continue on and find a safe place to stop before I ended up in the same situation. I had to let this thing blow through.

It was near Longview, Texas, where I spotted the turnoff to National Truck Stop. As I managed her in, everything there was dark. The power was out.

I found a space between two rigs, pulled in, and planned to hunker down. I let my cab sway back and forth to the wishes of the wind, while watching debris and tree branches sail past my windshield.

My thoughts turned to Jewel and Marcus. I wondered where they had come from. Was it their home they had to leave behind? Had it been destroyed like so many others? Was this one going to bring trouble for them?

Remarkably, I was getting service on my cell phone, so I quickly called Kat to let her know my situation. She was relieved to hear I had stopped.

Although I had not kept her up-to-date on my whereabouts to conserve her worries, she had somehow felt I might be in harm's way, in the wrong place at the wrong time. I'm sure she guessed I had more sense than to knowingly put myself in danger, but then again, I've been known to leave her with elements of doubt.

She understands the concept of a trucker's psyche, that when the wheels aren't moving, you aren't making money. I assured her now; my wheels were not moving anywhere, unless I got blown over. I think I felt her smile over the phone. After our call, I reached into my wallet and retrieved the paper from Marcus. Out of concern, I felt a need to try to reach him. I dialed the number for Burton; there was no answer. A brief recording asked that I leave a voice message. Since I had never been in contact with him before, I declined the offer temporarily. I tried calling the number for Clay and the response was a recorded message relating that the line was temporarily out of service. I figured I'd try again later. My nerves were recognizably worn. I lay down in my bunk and let Rita rock me to sleep.

Around sunset, I awoke to things having noticeably settled down. I walked to the building that housed a convenience store and restaurant. When I stepped inside, the atmosphere was eerily subdued. Still without power, it was candlelight that half-illuminated the slow activity. A few people were sitting around the lunch counter. The apparent waitress, cook, and two others were seated off to the side, conversing at a table. I purchased a soda and returned to my truck. My dinner that evening would consist of sandwich spread on crackers and a can of beanie weenies, a most delectable combination.

It was time now for my usual evening call to Kat. She would be home from work. In all probability she would have fixed herself supper by this time. I was eager to play her a new song I had finally finished composing. This one took over a month to write. Sometimes they come easy. Sometimes I have to pull them out kicking and screaming from my inner most self. This was one of those highly paid dues songs; I titled it *High Test Love*. I've dabbled in song writing much of my life with no wish of becoming a so-called "star." I never tried to pursue any calling in that direction. I do like to write, play guitar, sing and entertain, but as I've heard said, "no autographs please."

Seeing my caller I.D., Kat answered the phone with a sweet, "Are you still on the ground?" I could tell she was smiling. She's such a cutie. I quickly gave her my updated situation, and I sensed much relief in her voice. We then reviewed the day's other events, fulfilling the need to share with each other our lives. The usual "how was your day, what's new, talk to anybody?" type of chat. I could tell she was in the middle of dinner, so what better time to lay this new tune on her. When I'm at home, it's often her wish to have me play guitar while she cooks. She says she loves that; I think it's part of my personal romantic structure to swoon her with song. She always inflates me with, "that was wonderful," or "you're so good!" And so love goes around and keeps the circle churning. I could tell she really loved this one, so later on, just before she went to sleep, I scooped my guitar up and sang the last words to her again. "Pretend it's just us, and the promises our kisses bring." Then we said goodnight.

## CHAPTER 2

It was well into the following day when all company drivers received a memo. These messages are referred to as "macros," with some having appropriately assigned numbers given regarding their content, and others are simply called freeform. This particular one, going out to all drivers, was the later, requesting any volunteers willing to bring relief efforts to the stricken Gulf Coast region. My company, arguably the largest in the nation, felt an obligation to dedicate a portion of its van fleet to this mission.

While driving, I thought about the probability of seeing Marcus and Jewel again and how the chances would increase if I were to respond to my company's latest request. I did so without another moment of hesitation. For the most part, I would have expected the utilization of our southerly located drivers to be accepted for this work, but I also considered the fact that much of the aid may be coming from the north. This, coupled with the fact that I am a category one driver (meaning as high a rank as exists with the company), might give me an edge at getting south more often, thus increasing my chance to see where this dream might take me.

But, I was heading for home now with a load bound for Oconomowoc, Wisconsin, a suburb, so to speak, of Milwaukee. In just a few days, Kat and I would dance again. Once more, I retrieved the folded paper with numbers from my wallet. I was approaching the Wisconsin state line when, bingo, someone answered.

"Is this Burton?"

"Yes, who's this?"

"My name is Grant, and I…"

"Oh yah, he said ta grab you if ya called. He wants to talk to you. When ya comin' down?"

"Well, I don't know, I'm up north headed for home right now," I explained. I asked that he convey that I had signed up for relief efforts, and would expect to hear something in that regard within a week or so, but I had no idea where it would take me, or when.

"I'll let him know; call me when you get a fix on that. We'll see what we can do," Burton said.

"Where would I need to get to?" I inquired.

"Houma, Louisiana would be your best target, but right now it's a real mess down this way. I'd guess within a couple hundred miles of there and something could be arranged; I don't know, just keep in touch."

"I'll do that. Talk to ya soon then."

I was so excited to get this response that I realized, in hindsight, I should have asked about them. I had so many questions piling up in my head, I could hardly breathe. OK Grant, there's time, take it easy. I was thinking an adventure was about to begin. I felt so ready, and man, was I right!

A driver has nothing but time to sit and think. We run the gamut of thoughts up and down, inside and out, from the obscure to the obvious. Emotions pull from absolute delight to the deepest blues, often without apparent cause. Thoughts can make us oblivious to things around us at times, daydreaming at its utmost.

I found myself now seven hours from my home and questioning reality. I know who he is. I think he knows that. What's he thinking? Are these things really happening as they appear? Am I making much more of this than what will be? These things I think I know now, so different than what I thought I once knew. Is a door about to open? I'm crawling out of my skin to find out! Am I chasing a shadow no one else sees? Questions were hemorrhaging.

The ride home seemed longer for me this time. My mind contested where I should be with all of this. I concluded I would not speak of it during the weekend unless Kat did. I have little solid ground to speak on. It would only prove to complicate the matter, even in casual conversation. Can this just be danced away for now? That's where this weekend would need to go.

And so it was. We danced and dined. We joked with friends who always ask where I've been. I play a guessing game with my favorite bartender when he asks that question. I tell him what road kill I had seen, and make him guess which parts of the country I had gone through. Rattlesnakes and tarantulas equal deserts of mostly Arizona and southwest Texas. Armadillos and coyotes, well that's not fair, they seem to be nearly everywhere! I tell my tales of the road and take them to places in their imagination that they may never see in their lives. Its entertainment for them and a release for me from the tensions those miles pile on my muscles and bones — therapeutic to all.

We spent time with the grandkids. I told a few grandpa stories and gave them treats; generally spoiled them good, then sent them back to their ma and pa. Kat has come to best describe our weekends together as crazy whirlwinds. And they always seem to be.

## CHAPTER 3

Back on the road again, and admittedly, I was losing sleep over him. Call it haunting, how something like this can grab hold of one's life, make you ready to abandon your road for one not clear, yet beckoning your every nerve. Unable to verbalize, no one to tell, that's how it was for me.

It was late September now. Birds were beginning to flock south, cascading in waves across the sky. They cut and swerve in their dance-like fashion. One could swear they often number in the thousands.

The news was still of the hurricanes. The catastrophe had a double punch. That part of America was tattered by these two successive, horrific and unprecedented, murderous storms. Then I got dealt a player's hand.

After having just delivered a load in Romeoville, Illinois, a neighbor of Chicago, my orders came to drop my empty trailer nearby at our operating center in Gary, Indiana. I was to pick up some pre-loaded Gulf relief freight there, staged for relay, destination Opelousas, Louisiana. It would be a drop-loaded operation for later distribution where needed. The content was 37,000 pounds of battery pre-packs. My pay would remain the same, although my TAH (time at home), might at times be somewhat compromised. It may be shortened, or off by a day on either side. I would be getting information sent to my home, explaining all details for future involvement with this operation. At last, I felt I could do some good. I studied my maps, and yes, this delivery would be within the range of Houma, as Burton had suggested. I can make the call. I calibrated my route and timetable. It would be mid to late afternoon on the twenty fourth if all went well. With an explicit number of legal hours that the D.O.T. allows a driver to run each day, those hours would be nearly run up by the time I made the drop, so the rest of my day would consist of finding a nearby truck stop to take my break.

I relished my excitement to the bone. It was all I could do to keep from grabbing my cell phone now to try to make it all happen. Yet the driver part of me knew to hold back. Nothing is even close to sure until you're hooked up and headed down the road toward your destination.

After I reached the Operation Center (O.C.) with a quick search of our lot, I located my assigned trailer and hooked up. I gave it a visual inspection and opened the doors to view the cargo placement. Filled to the very back were boxes labeled "Hold For Hurricane Use Only." That moment I felt a surge to my being. My smile must have had a glow. I sealed her up, went back to my driver's seat and let out a long, deep sigh. I updated my log book with all the appropriate information. It was time to go.

Once on the road, maybe ten minutes down the line, I reached for my wallet and my phone. Burton would be my first call. He answered. Would things fall into place?

"Hello?"

"Hi Burton, this is Grant."

"Oh hi, how's it going?"

"Pretty good, I'm coming your way." I quickly explained my assignment and the time element involved.

"That's good, I'll let him know, and see what he says."

"I'll be staying at a truck stop on I-49 at exit 23," I told him.

"Sounds good, I'll call you back, or maybe he will. Things have been really hectic down here, but he is anxious to talk to you."

"Looking forward to hearing from you," I told him. With that, the conversation ended. Now my mind raced. I have to find out. I have to get the chance to ask him how things actually happened. How all this can even be possible. It is him, isn't it? I know it is! Of course it is! And if it is, why is he letting me in? This had to be one of the best-kept secrets the world had ever not known. What's going on here? I was confused in my thoughts, at the same time, convincing myself I was on target. "I'll soon find out," I said aloud. Then I began wondering what I would ask him if given the chance. I may have limited time, so I'll need to make the most of it. I have to get my thoughts in order. I have a couple days of driving to do it. Don't get so bent out of shape, I told myself. I elected, once more, not to say anything to Kat about this until there was something substantial to say. I would call and update her later.

## CHAPTER 4

It was the middle of the next day when my cell phone rang. I didn't see a caller I.D., so I answered with, "Hello, this is Grant."

"Hey there, this is Marcus."

That voice came back to me. Yes, it's definitely him!

"Hi, how are you?" My voice may have sounded excited.

"Doin' good considering all that's happened and all the things we're in the middle of down here. Heard you're on your way down; that's good!"

I explained my route, including when and where I intended to spend the night.

"We're coming up for supplies, so I was hoping, maybe, we could do a lunch or something," he suggested.

"Well, my truck stop guide shows they have a place to eat right there, and I'll be out of hours to do any further travel," I explained.

"Good enough, we can meet you there. Grab a table, if you get there before us, and I think we'll have some time to chat. I have to go now, though, 'cause I'm in the middle of a dozen things," he said with a short laugh.

"I understand, I'll see you then," I said, thus ending the most fleeting moment of my life. It's him alright, I told myself convincingly. This is great! Wow! My mind felt the numbness sometimes felt after experiencing a great fireworks display. I'll wait until this plays out before I tell Kat. In fact, I better wait until I'm with her. This isn't something I can throw at her over the phone.

I know that when you try to hurry time, time stares you in the face and slows way down. Minutes can feel like hours. I had to keep reminding myself to calm down, to take it easy; don't let this climb on you, just drive the truck.

That evening, as I closed my day at another obscure rest area, I made my goodnight caress call to Kat. I told her of my assignment, and she seemed proud of my dedication and the help I would be giving, even with the probable sacrifice of my home time. If she had any thoughts of me meeting my famous dream, she gave no sign. I would tell her my story only after the fact, I decided.

## CHAPTER 5

The only delay I experienced was on the morning of delivery. Traffic had come to a complete stop due, it turned out, to a fatal accident ahead of me. This was one of the times I turned on my CB to channel 19 for details about which lane to use, and what the problem might be. Rubbernecking is usually the main issue, people slowing down to look at the wreckage. It's one big drawback of this profession, having to witness far too many of these crashes. Too many times I've viewed sheet-covered bodies on the roads or in the ditches. Too many times I've seen the stunned faces of survivors.

Sadly I witnessed one such incident, a weeping and frantic young girl, desperately running back from her stopped car, cell phone to her ear, reaching for a man who was lying in the road. She had apparently side-swiped his motorcycle, which lay a hundred or more yards ahead. As I maneuvered my trailer cautiously past them to make room for medical assistance that had yet to arrive, I could plainly tell that he had expired. Images such as that sear the memory. With the miles we cover, these become all too frequent. As drivers, it serves to remind us to not relax our attentiveness. I imagine some people get numb to these accidents. When I pass those crosses that have been placed on the sides of the road, I often catch myself reflecting of those in my life I've lost.

When I plan my trips I make a habit of being on the cautious side, with regard to timing. Although early with many deliveries, I am rarely late. This day, I seemed well within the window that I had given Marcus. Still nearly 100 miles from my drop site, I began seeing elements of the hurricanes' aftermath. Trees were uprooted and flattened on the ground, or they were half broken off in the middle. I started to notice a phenomenon I'd be seeing all too often in the future: roofs of homes and businesses covered with blue tarps — used to different degrees depending on the damage, scattered about the countryside in all directions along my route. There were signs of devastation everywhere.

My load having been delivered without a problem, I sighed in relief. My mission was complete. I was now pulling old Beulah into my planned truck stop and taking a parking space where I would spend this night. A quick glance of the cars in the parking lot showed nothing recognizable. By now the palms of my hands were sweating as I settled back to complete my log book. I would probably need to run the engine to keep the air conditioning going later, but for now, I shut her down. It may have taken a little longer to complete my logs, as I continually glanced up, trying to spot him. I was eager, yet trying hard to remain calm.

It was time to go inside the building. I needed a moment to breathe. One needs to take a deep breath or two when you get this way. That's what they taught us at the academy, when I learned to drive truck. I found it to be a useless tool in many instances, but would it help me now? My emotions were roaming and incomplete, indefinable in their disguised nervousness. "It's now or never," I told myself aloud. Oh wait, I remembered that's the name of a song! I smiled, as I stepped down to the hot asphalt. Briskly, I crossed the lot, head down, no thoughts. I found myself reaching for the handle at the main door trance-like, then I walked inside.

The restaurant was off to the right. There was a clear view from the entrance, where I stood, to the horseshoe lunch counter and the tables beyond. I picked him out right away. He was seated, facing me with two other men, one sitting on either side of him. The chair facing him was empty. He was wearing nearly the identical clothes he wore when we first met. He spotted me as I made my way to their table. He gave a smile, as the others turned to look in my direction. I recognized Credence now, dressed casual, yet clean, with a wrinkle-free shirt tucked into wrinkle-free pants, and polished wingtips.

"Different hat," Marcus proclaimed rather loudly as he stood to greet me. He seemed excited.

"I'm a man of many hats," I explained.

"I really like that one!" he said. "Good to see you!" He shook my hand, while putting his left hand firmly on my shoulder in genuine affirmation. It settled my senses. I was surprisingly calm now, and at ease with that moment.

"Grab a chair. We were lookin' to get some lunch," he said, as he sat back down. I noticed, they each had open menus in front of them. The gentleman I had not yet met closed his, and slid it over to me with a smile.

"This is Jewel's uncle, Clayton. If you come to our place, Clay will be the one to get you there," Marcus explained. This was a man in his late 50s, I guessed, with a deep tan, strong and handsome in appearance, though unshaven with tasseled hair that hadn't seen a comb. His presence came on with ardor, in a jovial manner. His arms were muscular and full of tattoos, mermaids mostly. He was wearing a tank top, with what appeared to be oil stains in front, and shorts. He wore a bandanna tied around his neck. It was frayed, with sweat stains where it rode against his skin. A baseball cap with a swordfish emblem on its face lay in front of him next to his glass of water.

"Hi, glad to meetcha," I said.

"Comment cava," he replied genially, as we shook hands.

"You remember Credence?" Marcus asked.

"Sure, good to see you again," I said reaching to shake his hand.

"You too," was his reply, extending his hand.

"Been here long?" I asked, as I turned to Marcus.

"Not long, had some coffee, but now we gotta eat. Afterwards these guys are gonna go get some of the supplies we need, and you and I can talk a while." Marcus said.

The waitress was hovering over me now, so I made a quick study of the menu.

"Would you like some coffee?" she asked me, as she went around to refill their cups.

"No thanks, had plenty already today," I told her.

"Are we ready to order?" she asked.

Clay and Marcus glanced at me. "Yep," I told her.

Clay ordered first, in an accent unfamiliar to me. Sounded like he said cheeseburger, and a coke, with indistinguishable words between. The waitress seemed to understand. Marcus ordered chicken Caesar salad and apple juice, while Credence ordered a rueben and milk. I went with a steak sandwich, fries and a coke.

"Did you weather the storm alright? Is your home in that area?" I asked.

"Our place has been there for generations. Handed down to Jewel over 30 years ago, but no, not so well, yet I have to say a lot better than some folks. We're survivors," Marcus said. I thought abstractly for a second and said to myself, "you sure are."

"Wha dat dere tattoo?" Clay asked, as he placed his finger on my left forearm.

"Clay can't stand tattoos!" Marcus said with a smirk and a wink.

"Jamais, ah cane — ah taureau, t'ink ah ge anudder diable," Clay exclaimed with a hearty laugh.

Credence just smiled and shook his head.

"I guess they call these jailhouse tattoos," I said. "Handmade, self inflicted, with a needle and some thread wrapped around in a ball near the tip, dipped in India ink as ya tap away. It was suppose to say 'ennui'. That's Latin for discontent, dissatisfied, annoyed, bored, vexed, and the like. It has a lot of meanings." Clay smiled widely. So did Marcus, in a soft way. Credence just looked at it with a sober face I was almost getting used to.

"I was doing it while talking on the phone to my girlfriend at the time. Only the 'u' and the 'i' turned out right. She thought that was special," I explained.

"Jewel says hi," Marcus said.

"I'll miss seein' her. Her scenery is celestial," was my response. Boy, I don't know how that came out, or where it came from, but it made him smile and he winked again at me. "Are you picking up some things for your place?" I quickly added.

Marcus sighed and leaned back in his chair for a moment, took off his glasses and placed them on the table. Leaning forward again, he rubbed his face up and down with both hands and then he began to explain at length: "We boarded her up in a hurry as best we could before we left. We sent everything of value to Jewel's cousin up north." He paused to take a drink of coffee, then he went on, "Our place is set back from a main bayou, and up on a slight hill overlooking a small lake. We're on an upgrade, which is rare in the area. I think that's why it's sustained the place for as long as it has, but it was still inundated by a water surge; flooded all around us. It hasn't receded much. And there was wind damage; a tree took the porch. The outhouse is gone, but it was about time for a new one anyway. It was both these hurricanes added together that have pretty much kept us from getting things cleaned up till now. Rita got us good! Jewel is staying up north with her cousin. I have to say she's taking this pretty hard. She fears normality has been lost forever, and we've never been apart this long. I need to kiss her so hard my lips will forget to breath," he sighed wearily. "We need to focus from gray to clean colors again. Wonderin' if this old body is gonna clear the wreckage this time. But I'd guess it's as simple as finding one another's hand as you cross between your dreams in night's darkness." He managed a smile. I wondered what he meant.

Perking up just then, he said, "Jewel and I would like you to come and visit once we get the place back in order. It shouldn't be too long. Maybe stay over and do some pickin'. I've got some songs I want you to hear, and see what you think,"

"I could maybe do that. I'd sure like to," I responded with contained excitement. I then explained to him the Department of Transportation, (D.O.T.) 70 Hour Rule for truck drivers, which states no driver can be active over 70 hours in eight consecutive days. If one gets close to using up those hours, he can elect to take what's called a 34-hour restart. In such cases we park the truck. Our tires are not allowed to move during this time. With the GPS units attached, the company can tell where we are within 15 feet at all times; modern technology. After we stop for that period of time, we wipe the slate clean and can start over. Drivers with a lot of experience can often arrange to get these 34 hour breaks in the most desired places: Vegas, Malibu, New Jersey. Did I say New Jersey? Well, to each his own. Anyway, this scenario would allow me to spend an overnight sometime. He was glad to hear it.

Now the waitress was giving us our plates. As we ate I didn't want to waste any of this time." I had so many questions spinning in my head. "So you play guitar much?" I asked Marcus.

"That and I read a lot," he replied.

"Yah, me too. I write a lot of poetry and dabble in song writing. I'm a writer fighter," I explained.

His eyes lit up, and with an expression changed to delight, he proclaimed, "I was right about you!"

"How's that?" I asked.

"Can't explain instinct. That earring of yours set me off. God of music isn't he?

"He brought music to the people, but I guess he was also known for fertility," I explained. "From what I've heard, virgins would run from him, and barren women would seek him out," Having said that, Clay let out with a loud, almost embarrassingly abrupt laugh. The rest of us just smiled.

"I did know, after hearing you, I'd like to pair up," Marcus said.

"Whattaya wear dose gloves? Ya wear dem oil de time?" Clay interrupted, referring to the driving gloves I wore.

"I have burn scars on my hands and it used to make me very self conscious, been wearing them for years. Never really think about it now. They're like a second skin to me, so to speak, and with the fingers cut out, I can do most anything with them on, even play guitar." As I explained this, I glanced over at Marcus, and he gave an approving nod.

I asked Marcus why, of the millions of pickers out there, he would want to pair up with me.

Then he looked deeply into my eyes again, and asked, "Do you believe in destiny?"

"Never really delved into that," I smiled.

"I don't believe in coincidence. I'm a strong believer in fate. Have you heard the word 'predestination'? It's used in the Bible in several places. What is destined to be, gives nothing left to chance. I think there's a reason for everything, including why we met the way we did." he tried to explain.

It was an odd moment for me. From the corner of my eye Clay seemed to be observing me in a hard-to-describe, unusual way. My appearance is a bit flamboyant, I admit, but it was a deeper stare, as though he knew something about me that I didn't.

"Can I get you anything else, dessert?" the waitress asked, as we were finishing up. None of us were interested, so she laid our bill toward the center of the table and bid us a great day. Credence told her the same as she was turning and walking away. "Merci beaucoup," Clay blurted loudly.

"I'll take care of this," Marcus said as he pulled the check in front of him. "You guys want to meet us back here when you get done? Look for us in an orange semi out there."

As they stood to leave, Clay said, "Dis coonass ge ever't'ing den. See ya ween we t'rough." Then he turned to me and added, " See ya ageen if ya ge fudder sout."

I smiled and nodded with a, "Yah, see you soon I hope."

"Yea ye righ," Clay said as he walked away.

Credence walked away with just a nod to me.

## CHAPTER 6

And now Marcus and I were alone, and that realization tweaked my nerves; once again, I was a bit on edge. Having previously thought of all kinds of things to ask and say, I was now momentarily tongue-tied. There was an uncomfortable split second of silence, then he looked at me. From my deepest depths without thought or hesitation, as if he were pulling them out of me with his eyes, came my words: "I know who you are."

He winked at me once more. "I know you do. I wanted you to know. Now you've joined but a handful." Then he added, "There's a reason for everything, remember? That's why rivers bend."

"But how; what's…" My speech was stumbling now. I had to catch myself. "There's so much I need to know!" I said.

"And I want to tell you," he responded with a warm smile, that distinguishable lip now so pronounced and recognizable to me. His smile had a way of calming me.

Awkwardly, I exclaimed, "But I saw the grave in Memphis, and…"

"No you didn't," he interrupted, again with a smile, but with that added smirk.

He stood up now and took the bill in his hand. I got up and followed him to the register counter, where a young lady met us with a rehearsed greeting.

"Was everything alright?" she asked.

"Real good," Marcus said.

As he paid the bill, the young lady was oblivious to the identity of this stranger before her.

"Could you see that our waitress gets this?" he asked, as he handed her a five and some ones.

"Sure thing!" she replied.

As we began walking away, I remarked, "It's amazing no one recognizes you!"

"I was sorta recognized a few times, years ago; thought I could blend in with shades and a mustache when I ventured out. Then I lay low for a long time and changed my appearance the best I could. The beard helped a lot; so did letting my hair go back to its original color and letting it grow in a different style. As you can tell, I lost a ton of weight. I owe that, and everything, to Jewel," he confessed. "When her eyes look into mine I'm branded by love."

"But really, how did you believe you could get away with it, I mean you being you?" I was going down my question list.

"Have you ever noticed birds on a telephone wire, how they almost always seem to all be facing the same way?" Then he added, "People are very much like that."

It was just one of many things I would hear him say that would make me scratch my head more than a little. It's a wonder I'm not bald.

We were stepping outside when he said, "Anyway, no one expects me to still be alive, although I heard a few years back there was a rumor going around that I had been put in the witness protection program." He laughed, and so did I. Just then he spotted a truck with a horse trailer attached, and the subject quickly changed. "There's one thing I do miss, though. I used to love to ride. Had some fine horses. Had a golden palomino that I still dream about sometimes," he said.

Marcus spotted my truck and walked straight to it. "Like to see the inside of one of these newer beasts," he remarked.

I unlocked the passenger door and told him, "Grab those handles and climb on up." As he did, I went to the other side and did the same. We were like buddies now, that was the feeling coming over me.

The heat of the afternoon had made an oven of the interior. I quickly started her up and turned on the AC. "It'll cool down in a couple minutes," I said apologetically.

"That's alright, I'm used to this kind of heat. Hey, this is really nice! You a hippie or something?" He gestured at my tapestries, oriental pillows and design decals I had adorned my sleeping quarters with, not your average trucker décor.

"Gypsy at heart, I guess. Nomadic gypsy, just happens to be driving a truck. Or that distant gypsy soul, stuck in a today's trucker body," I lightly laughed.

"Maybe that aura about you got my attention," he said.

"I gotta ask," I said curiously, "what is that accent Clay has, 'cause he's a bit hard to understand."

"He's Cajun all the way! Only they pronounce it, 'Kiyan.' Use to be a shrimper in his earlier years, but he's worked steady for us now since Jewel and I've been together."

"There's my biggest question," I blurted. "How did all this happen? How did it come about?"

"That's simple: I fell in love, could say I was bewitched."

"When? I mean…" I tried to formulate the exact question to obtain the true answer, but he interrupted.

"We met in Green Bay, Wisconsin, shortly before my so-called demise. I was on tour, and she was there for her mother's funeral. She got tickets from her sister, and they both came to see me. Her sister knew someone, and was able to get backstage. It was love at first sight. I never knew any kind of feeling like that before in my life. She put a spell on me, and I've been under it ever since," he explained.

"But how did it come to this? You had everything going with the star you were. You had achieved so much!"

"Achiever of chains since it began in the '50s, even before my first album, even before Sam and Sun Records," he confessed. "She saved me, that's all I can say. I fell under her spell, and she healed me. Our worlds met when my mind said it couldn't take anymore. That's when she became my only truth. All I could see from that night on was myself, forever following myself into her arms. It was that way and still is."

I wish I could remember all he said during that conversation. He spoke of this love so profoundly; his words seeped in poetry. It was clear how truly and deeply in love he was, and all that she meant to him. But I was still wondering how it had all come to this. "So now you live down here and the whole world thinks you died a long time ago?"

"That's it," he acknowledged. "I arranged for her to see me in Memphis, she came up, but didn't like it at all. She was totally uncomfortable, out of place. It was a crazy time. I was getting engaged to someone else at the time, even had a ring done up. But everything changed in a heartbeat. I was going through a lot then. I wasn't a kid anymore. I think I was really getting serious about life for the first time. She had settled in a place she had inherited from Clay's older sister, and she talked me into coming down. It was all so secretive back then. After that, I knew what I had to do. It didn't take long to orchestrate a new beginning, money can buy almost anything."

"It's all too hard for me to fathom," I said in bewilderment. I had to ask again: "How could such a secret be kept from everyone, and for so long? How did you think the world would take it?"

"I guess I didn't care about that. There was a desperation inside of me that had been building for so long, and now I just wanted a life for myself, and Jewel gave me the reason to get it."

"What about your past life, the ones so dear to you?" I asked, somewhat in amazement.

"They've kept this secret, too. I'm worth much more dead than I ever was alive. They see me sometimes. They're actually happy for me to have found this. We have a good relationship; it all worked out. We all have the money we need," he added.

"So Jewel is Cajun?" I asked, trying to piece it together through my sporadic confusion.

"Half, and half Ojibway, which is a long story. I'll let her tell you. And what about you? Whatever happened to that girl you were talking to on the phone when you made your tattoo?" he asked.

"I married her," I said with a smile. "And it occurs to me now that we have something in common. We've both been with our ladies about the same length of time. I remember that day well, when you supposedly died." He and I looked at each other with goofy expressions on our faces, then laughed. "Your lip still gives you away, you know. If one looks close enough so do your eyes and dimples."

"I keep it all hid as best I can," he said almost shyly, "I've had a lot of time to practice. Actually, to tell you the truth, years have slipped between the days and I can't conceive how much time has really gone by. So that's her then?" he asked as he looked up above me, referring to a picture I have above my door."

"Yep, her name is Kathryn, but I call her Kat, and she's got a spell on me too," I said.

"So how did you two meet?" Marcus asked.

"She was a close friend of a girl across the alley from where I lived in Saint Paul, Minnesota. She first saw me out in the street, hot doggin' with a Frisbee and a couple of my buddies. I was a real hambone with the tricks I could do. I spotted her, too, and said "hi" from a distance. It was on the lower east side, kind of a rough neighborhood. There was a street down the block we called, Pain and Agony Avenue, and a bar called *The Salty Dog*. I drove some friends there one night in my cherry '49 Plymouth. We were playing foosball; had a bunch of quarters up, and feelin' no pain. Those guys went to the can or to get drinks or something. A great lookin' blonde came up to me, and she asked if I'd like to get kidnapped. I said, "Sure!" Evidently she and Kat had been in the bar a few minutes earlier. Margaret, the blonde, had a date but Kat didn't. They were planning on going bar-hoppin'. She asked Kat if there was anyone in there she'd like to take along, and she pointed me out. Margaret told her to wait in the car, and that she'd take care of it. When she escorted me outside she had me jump in the back seat of this black caddie, and there was Kat. It wasn't many miles down the road before we shared our first kiss. She said then, I'd need to work off a million dollar ransom. Haven't been able to do that yet!" I laughed.

"That's almost as good a story as mine!" he chuckled.

"That's not all," I added. "I left those guys at the bar. They had no idea what happened to me. My car sat in the parking lot for three days. I did call my sister who eventually told them I was alright, but they weren't real happy with me. When I got to Kat's place that first night, she had parrots flying loose around the house, didn't believe in clipped wings or cages. The place was an exotic garden land, with plants everywhere, and a small indoor pond with a fountain. As the night turned to a dream in each other's arms, her record player was on 'repeat' and it played *Moonlight Mile* by the Rolling Stones all night long. I knew my life had changed forever then, and for the good."

It felt like Marcus and I had been friends for a long time now. We sat in the truck, explaining our lives, letting our feelings be known. There truly was something special going on that I had not experienced before. Friends come and go in life. Some take time for us to recognize, while others just have a way of stumbling into our day-by-days, then disappearing. But this one was like out of the pages of some mystery comic book, with my character now seated next to the super hero. As strange as it sounds, that's kind of how it felt to me. My spirit was being tossed and turned in this new reality. But I really liked where I was going.

"Can I see yer guitar?" Marcus asked.

"Sure!" I stood up between the seats and reached up to the top bunk and retrieved the old Gibson, handing it to him.

"I'm having trouble with this Marcus thing." I confessed.

"You can call me anything you want, except my real name." he advised, as he lightly strummed on the guitar strings.

"Maybe I should just call you L?" I remarked.

He smiled at that. "That'd be OK, been called that before. But now I owe you one," he said as he gestured a threatening forefinger in my direction. Then he continued strumming and started playing a song. I sat there in amazement. His voice came through in stunning recognition of the past. There were those chills coming on me again. It turned out to be a song that he had written, *A Lot of Room for Lonesome*. It was astounding to hear that voice again! The song was wonderful.

Again, I really wish I could remember all we talked about that afternoon. It seemed to me there was so much pinched into such a short time. He said he wanted to read my writings, and that I should bring some with me next time. I remember him asking what I did for fun when I wasn't trucking. My answer was somewhat off the wall, but accurate. "You mean besides guitar and music? I got a Gibson on my 10th birthday from my brother. Music has been my life pretty much ever since. I write a lot. I'm also a people watcher. I know that sounds stupid, but really, humanity is interesting to me. I am a beach comber though. Love vacationing on islands. Love serenading Kat with my ukulele. Wherever I can capture a beach, my toes will be squeezing sand," I said wistfully.

Just then a rental box truck pulled up in front of Beulah — it was them; they were back.

"Guess I gotta get going. There's a lot needs to get done. I'm working to have my Jewel back. The pulse of her never leaves my side," he said with a smile, and that pronounced dimple. He leaned the Gibson against my writing desk behind the driver seat. "There'll be another day for something." He nearly whispered. We both got out of the truck and stepped over to greet Credence and Clay. They were standing near the rear of their truck. Credence had a piece of paper in his hand.

"Couldn't get the stain in exactly that shade," he immediately explained. "So we picked up one that's close. If she likes it we'll use it. They didn't have the corner pieces like she wanted. We'll have to get them someplace else. Got all the lumber and shingles. I think we got all the hardware." Credence was going down the list. "This stuff should get us well into where we need to go," he concluded.

"Good, good," Marcus acknowledged.

"Deen ween de battle, but ah t'ink we take de war," Clay chuckled.

Marcus turned to me as I was smiling at Clay. "You keep in touch with Clay or Burton. It's not always that easy for me to reach a phone but I want to hear from ya soon," he urged.

"I'll do that. Hope I can visit you soon!" I said resoundingly.

"See ya ween ya ge don dere," Clay added. "Take ya on mon boot." He shot a strong, jocund smile at me.

Suddenly we were all smiles; even Credence gave a rare grin. We all shook hands. Marcus put his left hand on my right shoulder, again, meaningful to me. They got in their truck, and with a wave from Marcus, they pulled away and out of the parking lot, toward the freeway entrance going south. I stood there for a moment. I said, "Wow." The afternoon was swiftly giving way to the sunset. Boy, do I have my story to tell, I muttered as I climbed back up in my cab. I sat behind the wheel staring out over the parking lot. I took a deep breath. How was I to keep this secret to myself?

## CHAPTER 7

A new day and a new direction. I had mentioned nothing to Kat about that previous day, only telling her I'd been on an amazing adventure. I'd fill her in soon enough. She had grown accustomed to my tales of the road, and I suspect she thought this to be just another one of those. But so different was this one to be, it would dramatically transform our lives into a most riveting, unforeseeable treasure. Even today I find it hard to fully comprehend, as things continue evolving.

It was toward home now that my assignment was showing. In a few days I could re-warm my heart in the place it longed to be. Would she take this crazy news more seriously this time? Would she be upset, or join me in these newly forming revelations? My thoughts gave way to jarred emotions, as I neared my weekend with her. I got ahead of schedule, which sometimes occurs, and returned home early Friday morning. Kat had left for work only two hours before. I had the day to do my turn-around cleaning and restocking of old Beulah. The hours passed quickly, and again, it was the porch meeting that we so looked forward to.

She'd had a draining day, and it showed in her tired appearance. "My brain feels sucked out. Can we go get something to eat and have an early night?"

"Sure babe," I said consolingly.

We didn't bother to spiff up. She just fixed her hair a bit and said she was ready to go. I had cleaned up earlier, in anticipation of a longer night out, but I gladly followed her lead.

We decided on dinner at a place we simply refer to as, "The Hill." It's located on the highest ground in the area, and offers great sunsets. There was the usual crowd of locals there, and we lightly chatted with the folks at a few tables before finding one of our own. It had a window with a great view, which I guess some people just aren't that interested in. As crowded as it was, we had the best spot in the house. I could tell Kat was tired. As we sipped our pre-dinner cocktails, I had to give her the news.

"I met with him again, this time for lunch, after I delivered that relief load in Louisiana," I confided.

"Oh yah, what did he eat?" She was looking out the window.

Was she toying with me? That was my first thought. I didn't answer her question. "He wants me to come down to his place and maybe spend the night next time. He lives in the bayou somewhere. Wants to play guitar with me. Says he's written some songs."

She turned to me, expressionless. "Don't get lost down there and never come back. I've heard that happens to men sometimes." Her response was nearly emotionless, yet I caught sight of a grin.

Now I knew she was just humoring me and not taking this seriously. "I wish there was some way you could believe me on this," I said with a resigning breath, beginning to feel exasperated. "He's real, and I'm not making any of this up," I now cautiously whispered so no one else could hear. She looked at me with a blank stare. "I just want you to share in my excitement. Wait till you meet him and Jewel," I said. Kat seemed uninterested.

"Don't you want to talk about me? All you think about is him!" she suddenly snapped. "You're so gullible, so easily influenced. It's not him! It's just somebody pretending to be him." It felt like she let it all out in one response.

"When you meet him, you'll know," I responded. "He's not the hip-shakin' rock star all the girls went gah-gah over. He comes on more philosophical, almost trancelike, poetic, an intellectual. And anyway, when you look him in the eyes, you'll know," I insisted. But I could see this conversation was heating up, and she was visibly strained. She was close to crying; I know her that well. I quickly changed the subject and asked her if she'd had a chance to let the kids know that I was home early. She knows how much I look forward to seeing them, and the grandkids, when it can be arranged. There would be another time and place to bring up Marcus and Jewel again. Or maybe it was just best to let it lie and see if she asked anymore about them. I was in a quagmire over it at the moment, and her.

When we arrived at home, it was settling just to cuddle on the couch and watch the nothingness of our television. Channel surfing our satellite stations always reminds me of that Bruce Springsteen song, *Fifty Seven Channels and Nothing On*. But it was just great to be home and giving in to the jet lag of the road. This weekend would fly by, as they always do, no matter how I tried to grab hold of it, try to rein it back. The road is one long day; my time at home, one short moment. Can there ever be a way to harness the time that holds your heart, make it surround you as if at a standstill?

# PART III

## CHAPTER 1

Thoughts spin in circles, how these roads take me everywhere, in every direction, then always back on that sweet road home. One would think the country would get smaller with familiarity. More often, the opposite is true. When you get to know the sights and landmarks, time seems to drag between them. Only when I am occupied in daydream or music do these places have a way of slipping quickly past.

Here again, I was headed on the same northeasterly path taken countless times before. Another humdrum run from Chicago to Detroit, across the Ambassador Bridge, through Windsor, Ontario, then Toronto and on to Montreal in Quebec. There are so many border-crossing regulations, dealing with paperwork and brokers, just to get these loads across. Then it's back to the U.S. with even more red-tape ordeals. I love Canada, except for this.

It was on to New York state, and westward again through Pennsylvania. But this time would prove to be different. It was near Erie, where I had stopped at a Pilot truck stop for the night, when I started feeling under the weather, scratchy throat, fever. By the next day when I reached our operating center near Akron, Ohio, I was becoming severely ill, with a cold quickly developing in my lungs, apparently heading straight toward pneumonia. I was beside myself.

I sent a message, explaining my situation and my need to be routed home as quickly as possible. My dispatcher Darin responded immediately with a load relay, already sitting in Akron, to go back to Gary, Indiana. There I was to drop the trailer to be relayed again, and for me to pick up another load, staged and ready, going to Minneapolis. From there, I was dispatched to bobtail home, just me and my Beulah.

I set up an advanced appointment with my doctor, scheduled within hours of my arrival back home, half expecting to be hospitalized. I was going down fast, and was taking all the cold medications truck stops had to offer. I knew I was definitely in trouble, and it would take every ounce of effort I could muster to get back home. By the grace of God, I made that turn into our driveway. All of my energy was spent. Unpacking would have to wait. Kat took time off work, waiting intently to bring me to the clinic. When my exam was complete, including X-rays and a white blood cell check, it confirmed what I had feared.

Some relief came when I was told this could be treated at home with antibiotics and high-volume fluid intake, together with complete rest. The convalescing would go on for almost four weeks, with doctor revisits and white count rechecks. The wind had been taken out of my sails. Listless and weak, time had no element. My thoughts and senses felt stuck in quicksand. Without energy, days and nights blended together in a haze. I did nothing but sleep. I had no interest in television or stereo, time felt bleak. Kat has such an optimistic outlook on life, but even her attempts to make things lighter were to little avail. I just had to let it clear itself out with time. I don't recall ever having been so sick in my life. It was one mean germ!

Around the third week, daylight began to slowly filter back into my world. There were sunbursts to my mornings. My life was taking root again. Each day let a little hope sneak through my window. I started finding things to do around the house. When I did, I discovered, in some of my unopened junk mail, amongst all the benign company newsletter updates and pep talk waste of paper, a letter containing two decals saying "Hurricane Relief." Included were instructions explaining how they were to be placed on each side of my truck above the current permits. The letter went on to explain how some of the loads would require a classification of top priority, with the possibility of a Louisiana Highway Patrol escort upon reaching that state line. It would be coordinated as needed. I interpreted upon further reading that this appeared to be a somewhat generic letter. Patrol escort was referring to flatbed drivers and the transportation of heavy equipment. For my part, it went on to explain how some loads may be well over the weight limit by D.O.T. standards, but the weigh stations would just flag us on by.

I guess this information got my blood cooking again, because I felt markedly improved after that day. It brought back all that was stored, resting in the back of my mind, about when my life had climbed aboard a rollercoaster. It had been well over a month since I last spoke with anyone down South. Here it was approaching mid-November now and I was once again feeling ants in my pants.

## CHAPTER 2

The day came at last with a final doctor visit. I was given the release form enabling me to return to work, under the precaution to take it easy for the first couple weeks. "We don't want a relapse on this thing," were the doc's words.

When I arrived back home, I was on the phone, calling my Driver Business Leader within five minutes. Before the afternoon was out, I was cleared to be given an assignment the following morning. One phone call remained to be made: I dialed Darin direct. He was glad to hear I was back.

"Any relief loads going on?" I asked. After a computer search, he responded.

"Yah, looks like there's one out of Menomonie, Wisconsin, slated for a drop at the National Guard Distribution Center in New Orleans — it's toilet tissue and the like. They've been needing a lot of it down there. You want the assignment?"

"I'd be glad to. I'm anxious to get back in the saddle and help out."

"I'll set it up for ya. Should be coming across your Qualcomm shortly." Darin assured me.

"Thanks bud, I'll head out first thing tomorrow." There was excitement caught in that instant, like an electrical recharge. I was me again, or the new me, the one I was just beginning to discover before I got knocked off my feet. It was almost as if I'd lost a month of my life. It couldn't be made up, but I couldn't look back. There was so much new about to occur in my tomorrows, I could feel it. I bet I don't much sleep tonight, I thought to myself. I was right.

The rest of that afternoon I would concentrate on packing. I gave old Beulah the once-over pre-trip inspection; then I called Kat at work and asked her to stop on her way home and pick up a few groceries that I'd need. She was relieved to hear I'd be returning to work in the morning. Short-term disability pay was but a fraction of my regular earnings. Like so many others, we live from paycheck to paycheck. It has always been a struggle to get ahead while raising kids. We are true middle-class Americans.

While packing my clothes, I looked at my collection of hats strewn across the homemade racks in our foray. The hat I was wearing the last time I saw Marcus, the one that he had commented on, stood out. When I find a hat that seems to suit me, I usually buy more than one, in different colors. I've always been into color coordination when it comes to my vagabond wardrobe. Even as a trucker, everything I wear matches, although, I imagine it's a bit unorthodox to the average driver's eye. The hat I was wearing was black. I also had an identical one in dark blue, hardly worn; it would be my gift to him. I placed it in my bag on top of everything else, in hopes and anticipation of seeing him soon. I also gathered together a collection of some of my writings he had requested, and placed them under the hat. It was mid-week, but yes, I was more than ready to hit the road again.

The next morning, Kat once again served me a hearty breakfast of steak and eggs. I didn't seem to be getting started as early as usual; part of me wanted to be at home and with Kat a little longer. I put it off as long as I could, but now we were exchanging smooches at the door, where I always tend to say, "Hold down the fort." Then I feel her watch me as I stroll to the truck and climb inside. As I turn onto the road out front, I always pull the air horn two short bursts. I look over and see her wave; my window comes down and I reach out with a longing wave back to her, standing out there on our porch. I confess, there are times I feel a tear well up in my eye as I run through the gears and realize she's hearing me fade into the day.

I've always been a softy. The kids would tease me when I couldn't watch a single episode of *Little House on the Prairie* without using up a couple of tissues to clear my eyes. I've come to rate the movies I watch in much the same manner. One to ten — the number of tissues I need to get through it.

## CHAPTER 3

The phone call to my southern friends would have to wait until I'd cleared my assigned load and knew that all was as it's supposed to be. Sometimes there can be a mix-up and the load might be taken by another driver, or the trailer somehow might be unserviceable for a number of reasons. The wiring for the running lights could be malfunctioning. There could be a flat or badly worn tire needing immediate replacement. With the weather turning colder, most common up north in winter months, there could be frozen brake drums or plugged air lines. In addition, there have been occasions when, if the load has been sitting in a relay drop lot, a break-in or vandalism of some sort has occurred. I've even seen all the tail lights stolen, or the wiring pulled out and destroyed. Nothing in this regard surprises me anymore, and one has to be prepared for these possibilities, even if they are not that common.

Upon arrival at the lot, I located and thoroughly inspected my trailer. The back doors having been previously sealed, there was no way to inspect the contents. It was a relief to see that the paperwork appeared in order. I found it in the relay box attached to the outside front wall of the trailer. It was complete, with appropriate seal number, content description, and weight. When things go smoothly to that point, one can think about heading out.

So it was, with my anticipation building to a roar, I started dialing numbers. First Burton's with no success. Then Clay's, whose line was seemingly back in service, yet there was no response and no opportunity given to leave a message. I had a sinking feeling, but down the road I went.

I was jumping the gun; I began to align my thoughts. As yet, I hadn't even calculated my ETA, (estimated time of arrival), let alone arrange a time to see them. It's a long ride. I'd have time to get this worked out. I would try calling later in the day, or perhaps I'd wait until tomorrow.

At my first rest stop break, I took the time to develop a trip plan. For the most part, it's based on average miles per hour, coupled with required D.O.T. breaks. When I calculate the number of miles to my destination, I can get a pretty accurate timetable. I always allow a few extra hours in a long run like this, for unforeseen traffic delays, or in the winter, bad weather conditions.

This was working out well. I could deliver by mid-afternoon and get away with not showing myself as available to run again until noon the next day. That's acceptable in our company's scheme of things. It would not be as good as the 34-hour restart, but it could be enough time to possibly visit Marcus and Jewel; my fingers were crossed.

Four hours farther down the road, I made my calls again. This time Clay answered. No mistaking that voice. I gave him the details of my time and destination.

"Eey brudder, dis time we git t'gedder n de playree! Call back win ya ge fudder sout'. I see my bon poonah tnight. Oui, he be gld ta see ya ageen. It bin a mont o mo ey?"

"OK, call ya back." I ended the call and wondered to myself, what in the world he just said? It sounded positive, so I felt upbeat. I would make another call at the same time tomorrow.

Now I was getting back in the groove of things. Being away from the road that long makes you wonder if you're gonna mash the gears a lot, or maybe forget some fundamentals. But as it was, I was riding a bike again. No problem with my abilities that I could tell; sort of like I never left.

Into the next day, things were running smoothly. The temperature was becoming markedly warmer. I stopped for lunch at a TA truck stop, and after that, took a short walk to stretch my legs. Sometimes that's pretty much all the exercise a driver can get. Back on the road, it was air conditioning time. That's when you realize that you're really heading south.

I was right in my designated timeframe, and I felt assured I'd be on time in New Orleans tomorrow. Make the call, Grant, you're dying to know. No one answered on Clay's line. Shoot! It was time to let time stand still again.

Now it was nearing supper time, my hour to check in with Kat. But first I just had to try Clay again.

"Yah, ever't'ing bein' set. Credence w bee der ta ge't'yah. Ye stay oar. I tink dis b'goood. Ye se dese bayas ba mon boot!"

"I will need to be back to my truck by noon," I reiterated, just so there would be no confusion — yah right! Every time Clay said anything, I was confused.

"Dat'll be OK, cuz he want ta ge togedder fer t'ings."

He sounded excited. If I understood him correctly, it sounded like a "go." I was jumping out of my seat; it might be hard to sleep again tonight.

As I checked my truck stop book listings, I found one to my liking just 20 minutes ahead. I'd have a warm dinner there and then turn in early. I would try to get a daybreak start in the morning, if sleep didn't elude me; that was the plan. I called Kat and told her I'd be seeing him again, and it looked like I may be staying at his place tomorrow night. She greeted the news with an uncomfortable silence.

"Are you sure you wanna take that step?" was her reply. I wondered then what was going through her mind. Was she just confused over this whole thing?

"I think he wants to play guitar with me."

"I have to go. I ordered some Chinese take-out and I'm outside the restaurant right now. The food's probably ready," she said.

"I'll call you back. I'm going to bed early. You can tuck me in," I replied. The call ended distantly. Was all of this going to cause unforeseen problems I might later regret? I had unabated confusion, blurred thoughts.

There are moments in life when one feels the need to step back and question the direction he might be going. This was one of them. Those few miles before the truck stop found me dizzy. What had happened thus far, I ventured to believe, had been clear to me. I'd always been the adventure type, but really now, what was happening here? Where was I really going? I shouldn't have to be concerned; it appeared I was flowing into it naturally. Yet, I confess, when trying to get a view of the big picture, I had flashes of the supernatural, or even perhaps, the unnatural. And that was the aspect causing me unease; how was it making Kat feel? How could I smooth this out? I reconciled I'd follow this through no matter what. Everything would work itself out. No regrets.

The call to Kat for my goodnight hug came earlier than usual. Her mood seemed lighter now. Maybe a good meal helped.

"Will your cell phone come in down there?" she asked.

"I'm not sure, but Clay has a phone," I assured her. I gave her his number.

"Just be safe. Don't get lost and never come back. Don't fall under some spell. Maybe it's a trap and he knew you'd go there if he told you about guitar playing. I guess I just have a suspicious mind," she said. We laughed together. Now she was coming around, more opened up. That's the girl I know and love. The call ended with twice the warmth in my heart. She was with me. It made all the difference.

## CHAPTER 4

On the day of my intended arrival I chose to wear a beret. Some say it makes me look like Dr. John, especially with the goatee I grow for these approaching winter months. So I was thinking, Dr. John's from down this way, might as well flow with it.

It was hours to go before I'd reach New Orleans, the "Crescent City" of my memories, and now destruction began appearing everywhere. Blue-tarp roofs dominated. The closer I got, the more intense the battlefield, a true war-zone atmosphere. Homes were piles of rubble, or where homes and buildings once stood proud, now ghostly in vacant frames. Moaning plots of land blotted my view, only hinting where vibrancy had once contently reigned.

I imagined the remnants of cities, towns, and the countryside in Europe from the evils of a world war. I had to compare what I was taking in to what the history books, film documentaries, and photographs had depicted of those times. I no longer had to imagine what it would be like if bombs went off indiscriminant. Yet, as I presume happens in wartime, baleful perdition created a numbness in my mind that closed out the magnitude, not wanting to envision the terror. All of these images dulling my heartbeat, I feared time would not give me long enough to forget.

In the portions of New Orleans through which I was allowed to drive, there was not the city I remembered. The places I recalled were indistinguishable, roughly and dingily removed. Stray, skinny dogs scavenged through phantom streets of mud, where signs showed the asphalt was now being scraped clean by bulldozers and heavy equipment. It had really been such a drastic and abrupt moment, hard to understand. Changes like this should take place in terms of years, not in a single, dramatic day, not so dismal and indescribably sad. How will they ever bring this city back? I found I could not force a tear, I felt mad. Why, in God's Mother Nature, did this have to be? I had questions where there were no answers. I had to turn from dwelling on what I saw, to the promises that had brought me here. I forced myself to feel wonderfully lucky. This was the blinder that would keep me open and upbeat. I knew I needed to make this a great experience in my life.

I was pulling into the entrance of the distribution center. There was a lineup ahead of me with over a half dozen trucks like mine, several fellow company drivers, all slowly being directed to their designated areas. It was then that I noticed the parking lot area for autos, and saw Credence standing outside the car he had been driving that first time we met. It was a dark blue Chrysler 300. He had someone with him, and they appeared to be conversing casually. He noticed me behind the wheel of my freightliner. A uniformed National Guardsman was waving me in. When I approached the small guard shack, I was asked for my paperwork, then directed to a drop location. Credence and the other fellow watched as I backed the trailer in. After I unhooked, I walked over to a guardsman nearby, inquiring as to where I could park Beulah for the night. I was told to park off by the side of, or behind the building. I could see several delivery vans, some bobtails like mine, and military vehicles parked in the area. I found a spot between them and shut Beulah down. Much of the area was restricted. The orderly calm amongst the chaos seemed impressive, hard to explain. There was no mistaking the serious dedication. Determination was definitely in the air.

I quickly grabbed my guitar and my bag, placed them on the passenger seat and floor and then climbed out of the driver side. I locked that door and went around the other side to retrieve them, having been preparing for this moment for days. I rounded the building and the guys awaiting me watched with smiles as I approached their car. A smile on Credence, rare.

"You made it," he said.

"Been waiting long?" I asked.

"Not long," the other gentleman answered.

"This is Burton," Credence explained, as he introduced me to a tall, thin man, maybe around 60 years old. He had short black hair and was clean shaven, but for a finely trimmed black mustache. He was wearing a Hawaiian shirt, casual pants, and loafers.

"I should have recognized your voice," I smiled. "Glad to meet you!"

"You too," he acknowledged. "S'pose we should get going. You're on a limited time-frame I understand."

"Yah, wish I had longer…maybe next time."

Burton opened the back door, and I threw my bag and guitar to the far side and climbed in. "I'm excited," I confessed aloud. They looked across at each other without a word and then Burton smiled back at me.

"Marcus told us where you stand with him. I think he's kind of excited, too," he responded.

As we drove through the streets, we were all quiet, looking from side to side at the piles of a mess that could be described in no other way. Nothing was said. As we left the city, everything we saw was in much the same ruin. I dialed Kat at work.

"Hey Hon, I'm in. I got picked up and we're on our way to their place now."

"Be careful. Will your cell phone come in down there?" she asked.

"Will my cell phone have reception where I'm going?" I inquired.

"Hard to say, maybe not very well. Clay has a phone and lives close to them." Credence assured me.

"Maybe not, babe, but I can probably get to a phone later. I'll call when I can, love you," I told her.

"Love you, too," she quietly repeated. We ended the call in short order; I knew she tries not to tie up her line at work for very long.

We were heading south on US 90, very rural, past Raceland, then on through Houma. The trees we saw left standing were shredded, limbs and branches broken, split grotesquely from their original forms. On many, the bark had been stripped completely off, leaving naked skeletons. Even these trees seemed to have screamed during their last moments of life — nothing they could cling to. There was water everywhere. How much of this area was flooded previously, I did not know, it seemed surreal. I had never before been this far down in the bayous.

"Has there always been this much water?" I asked.

"Land's been disappearing for some time now," Burton acknowledged. "It's all sinking into the gulf. Those storms just hurried it along is all. Don't know how much of this water will recede and give it back."

We must have traveled for more than an hour and now we were in back county, taking roads with no signs or names. It wasn't long and we turned left into what seemed to be a pasture of marsh grass — a two-rutted path in a long field leading toward a grove of damaged, yet surviving trees. As we entered the shade, I thought how lucky these trees were, indiscriminately saved from the plight so many others had been left to bear. There had been so many taken by their roots — splintered to bits, gone. And what of the lives of so many people? I had to stop thinking.

I caught sight of a house then, just off to the left, back behind thick underbrush. It had the appearance of a cabin, though larger, with a satellite dish and two tall antennas on the roof. Credence stopped the car, facing a canal some 30 yards ahead. I could see the top of what appeared to be a small tugboat of some sort. The figure walking toward us from that house was unmistakable. As we all got out, I heard Clay yell, "Ah don lak ta say, but ya kicked ah ala a skeets." Dressed rather oddly to me, in a loose sleeveless top, bathing trunk-type shorts and tall rubber boots, he came straight up to us, saying, "Aye padnat," and shook my hand with a wide grin. It was true; the insects got bothersome in that instant. Having lived in the woods much of my life, the bugs didn't get to me as much as they do some folks. "Le g un de wadda n g wh from dese," he said to me. The others seemed in a hurry to get back in the car. I retrieved my things from the back seat and laid them on the ground.

"I'll see you here tomorrow, around 10," Credence said.

"See you then; thank you," I replied. Burton just gave a short wave as they closed their doors, and backing out to a small turnaround cut away in the trees, they pulled away, out of sight.

"Des tempetes mh fer des bugs," Clay said sourly.

"At least in Wisconsin they know their season. None around this time of year. That's one of the blessings of snow and ice," I said half-heartedly.

He smiled and said, "Viens avec moi, I sha ya mon boots." He turned and started walking toward the water. I picked up my things and followed. "Das mon shrimpin' boot, we go tagedder sm time," he was smiling, as he pointed to the one with a tugboat type design, anchored slightly offshore. It had multiple tall masts made of metal framing, with bright green fishing nets dangling and entwined along the poles. There were red cages hanging from her side.

"We tah dis one up ta dem doe," he pointed, referring to an aluminum, flat-bottom type john boat, roped to his wharf pole to my right. It had a small gas-powered outboard in back, plus an electric motor attached to the side, with connections lying near to what looked like a car battery. The boat appeared equipped with a depth finder, and some sort of GPS unit. It had a large searchlight permanently attached on steel rods in the front, with chords also running over, and lying next to the battery. There was a long, wooden pole strapped and hanging out to one side.

I saw a regular Sears-type fishing boat tied on the other side of his dock. There was another flat bottom, with a large propeller in the back, nestled in the weeds, near the shore, behind the fishing boat. Along the bank rested a pontoon. It had no motor or seats, just tie-down hooks attached to the floor running along each side. Load straps lay loose, thrown about on her deck. It appeared to function as a trailer, to possibly be pulled by another boat.

Clay climbed in the flat bottom that was tied to the dock and motioned for me to do the same. There was an open cooler of beer and ice next to his seat. I laid my bag and guitar between the seats. Once in and seated, I was instructed to "tie loose de boot." He started the motor as I pulled the rope from over the dock pole. He handed me a can of beer with a grin, then eased her out and headed what felt like upstream, though there were no decisive signs of a current. As I looked around, I saw trees broken and downed, much like I had seen everywhere else. Yet I was surprised to see how many were still standing, some virtually untouched, though partially under water. Of those left stripped to skeletal corpses, tendrils of swaying Spanish moss, ripped and torn about, were still straggling off of them, giving way to the breezes. There were oaks and some overhanging willows. I could see tangled vine canopies, creeping, attaching themselves with insistence to gnarled, long since fallen hardwoods. Where resilient vines could, they stretched to grasp hold of that which, once thriving, now gave them a faint promise to survive.

Just moments from the shore, we circled to the right around a bend, chasing up a small flock of mallard ducks. As they skimmed the water, Clay exclaimed, "Greenheads!" I nodded yes.

"How's shrimping been since the storms?" I asked.

"Mos de boots er gone, sunk, wiped aut!" He responded almost angrily. "Ah, boo dem coonass ga ala'a la grue. Dey're na t'rou, jus nee sm bonheur." He had a rough grit to his voice then. "Ala'a ilans gon t da wadder," he added. I tried to decipher what he had said.

Off to my right I heard a loud splash, then another. I immediately thought alligator.

"Gator!" I resounded.

"Cocodrie? Pas du tout, garfish," he explained.

I guess I was a bit on edge, not knowing what to expect. It was this somewhat strange surroundings I'd never experienced. The thickness in the air, the sounds and the lack of sounds. I have been on many rivers. In fact, our cabin is located near the banks of one. Kat and I find many occasions for summertime casual floats. Leisurely, we'll cast our fishing lines to the bank, then reel in with the current, back to the boat as we drift. We quest for the smallmouth bass, walleye, northern and muskie, or maybe just to enjoy a bottle of wine. But this was not a river I was used to, more like a lagoon. At times, it seemed like a cul-de-sac, even though I knew it wasn't.

I saw a muskrat swimming near the shore among the trunk remains of what I now recognized to be old cypress trees. We circled once again to the right. I counted nine trees, cypress and tupelos, all leaning in the same direction — an island type of oasis. In stark elegance, the compelling blessing of a nearing sunset shone its slanting light as their backdrop, casting dancing sparkles over the darkening, murky water. As if on a painter's canvass, soft and unfocused, clouds billowed their proposals to a cerulean sky. The remnants of today's light now splashed our horizon bright with blue-orange to purple-black. The days were becoming discernibly shorter. I seem to always long for more time. A snuggling silent moon, bending twilight, was already pulling in its shadows and greeting the stars — light breezes were promising the night.

Clay cut the motor and untied the pole. The water seemed to whisper as we approached the shoals of these shallows. In a spot along the bank, indistinguishable at first, lay barely visible, there was an opening to a small inlet. Clay pushed with the pole and the boat veered quiet and smoothly to the left, being captured, then swallowed into a weeded covering away from the main channel. The ride seemed merely minutes. Amidst the faint sounds of frogs and crickets, his was the silhouette now standing before us on the bank near the edge of this water's darkness. All else was silence but for our boat whisking upon a marshy shore, resting in gentle repose. He stepped quickly into moonlight and clear view.

## CHAPTER 5

In what now had become a familiar voice to me, he said, "You made it." He reached out his hand to shake mine.

"Sure did L," I replied, as I threw my bag onto the land. He pointed, motioning for me to hand him up my guitar, so I did.

"Jus fil du courant don der," Clay laughed.

"Yah, right," Marcus replied.

Climbing from the boat, standing on the shore in that brief instant, I felt as if in a dream. It may have shown in my face.

"Hypnotized by greeting stars?" Marcus asked. And I may very well have been. It was like I was looking down upon myself from somewhere above.

"Just in time for dinner on Clay," he then added proudly with pleasure in his voice.

It was getting hard to distinguish detail as the moon seemed to push at the extinguishing darkness, blurring our images. I heard Clay securing the boat behind me then climbing up to join us.

His left hand holding my guitar case, Marcus put his right arm around my shoulder for a brief second and simply said, "Follow me up."

I picked up my bag and walked beside, slightly behind him, as Clay followed a short distance back. Our moon was now dimly lighting a small path as we climbed a slight grade. Soon, I could see flickering light coming from three windows a short distance away.

"Where in this world are we?" I half whispered to myself.

Dogs began to bark, and I could sense them running toward us.

"Don't worry," Marcus comforted. "They're barkers, not biters."

As they seemed to bounce around us I felt assured it was the two I had seen jump from the car that first day. As soon as Marcus called them by name, their barking stopped. Clay was jousting around with them while we walked. "Ye couillons!" I heard him exclaim.

We reached what appeared to be a porch, somehow appearing incomplete, with two steps leading up. Separated in parallels of broken moonlight, and giving way to the lantern lights from the windows, one could see that a side of the porch was partially missing. I saw boards leaning against the wall of the house. There were sawhorses and a tool box on the floor nearby.

When he reached for the handle of the front door, Marcus turned to me, and with a smile said, "Welcome to our home." Then he opened it. The dogs pushed their way ahead and we followed them inside. Clay closed the door behind him, leaving the busy moon to struggle with those shadows. We were now in a spacious open living room attached directly to a brightly decorated kitchen to our left. By candlelight, it exuded a cozy warmth.

It was in this calm and quiet radiance, illuminated by the combination of soft candle and lamp light, standing near a table between the two rooms, she took on an iridescent glow. In dancing colors, as sparkles are between shadows, the stillness of Jewel's smile, ardent; she was gem under glass. I stood enamored, admittedly amorously smitten.

"Well hello there." Her voice, to me, was a breath of splendor. She turned to Clay with a familiar nod, an elegant smile.

"Hi Jewel," I caught myself sheepishly reply.

"I hope you're hungry." She pointed to a rectangular-shaped table that was set for four. Plates of simmering prepared food had been placed in the middle, separated by three lit candles. It was a tantalizing setting. The smells were a combination of unfamiliar spices, baked fish and a mix of some kind of vegetables. Aromatic like nothing this nose had ever encountered before; my taste buds were reeling.

"W'er!" Clay burst out.

"Sure am," I gladly added.

"I'll show ya your room. You can drop your things," Marcus said.

The dogs seemed to be calming down, close at heel, as we walked to the far end of the living room and to an open door on the right. There was a door just before that, and it had a tarp draped over it. As I entered the room they had offered me, I saw a single oil lamp burning on a stand beside a double bed. Thereupon I laid my guitar case and bag on the bed, then turned to join him at the door. He was smiling. Clay was already seated at the table when we joined him there.

"Ga'a ge dose udder guys te'r bot sun'p," Clay said.

"We've got our guys working on the place," Marcus explained to me as we sat down at the table. Jewel was seated next to Marcus and across from Clay; Marcus was across from me.

"You look like an artist, a painter in that hat," Jewel said to me.

I smiled. I was having trouble finding my voice, but I managed, "This is nice."

"It's speckled trout that Clay brought. He's really our grocery store. I made them into trout puppies," She giggled after she spoke.

There was cornbread, red beans and rice that I could tell…a bowl of lemon slices and a large bowl of blackberries.

I noticed now the tiny flowers in Jewel's hair were complemented by small braids with intricate beaded jewelry intertwining. They were attached somehow in the waves. Fully composed living art in its highest form, I thought to myself. I'd never seen anyone like her, yet she was, in so many ways, reminding me of Kat.

"This is okra-laced gumbo," she said, pointing to a plate. "And we have pecan pie for dessert."

I heard myself say, "Wow!"

Marcus laughed lightly, and Jewel gave a slight hint of a smile. Clay was already comfortably digging in. I sensed he'd done this many times before.

We were all eating quietly for a time when Marcus remarked, "New sparks, new fires." This probably brought a confused look to my face, and our eyes met. "Days have flown by unsung, in unnoticed moments. I've courted the winds, trying to keep them on my side, howling winds, kicking up dust storms of frustration and waves that have been unescorted as they passed back out to sea." After a second he added. "You feel like singin'?"

Whew! I thought. "Ah yah. I guess I always do." was my response.

"I'm going back to where chance begins. Got some songs I want you to hear," he said enthusiastically.

"Got a couple for you too," I replied, glancing over and into Jewel's twinkling wide eyes.

"For years I've been trying to write a song to tell the world goodbye but haven't been able to do it. Gave up tryin'. Guess I came to the realization that maybe I just can't do it," Marcus concluded.

The energy in the air was heightening. This would prove to be a night never forgotten.

"To deny music in one's life would be like never having been alive at all," Marcus remarked, and he took another bite of food.

Clay looked up from his plate with that broad smile of his and then resounded "I'wu dance te dat!" Jewel tilted her head to the side and gave Clay a fresh smile, her eyes clear and bright in the candle light.

Marcus looked over to me and said, "When you told me you live and breathe for music, that's when things attached, ya know?"

"It's the way I am, L," I confided.

"L? Wa dat?" Clay asked.

"That's my old, new nickname," Marcus explained, pointing a finger at me and smiling.

"Mon Dieu," Clay muttered and with slight hesitation, "mon" again as he scratched the back of his neck.

"I've always believed in the power of dream. It's taken me everywhere I've been. It's taking me now," Marcus said, looking back to me.

I stared intently at him, not fully understanding what he meant, saying nothing in reply.

As I looked around, their dwelling seemed simple — nothing elaborate, nothing extravagant. It gave one a feeling of bayou life as it may have been in the past: humble basics, like a two-chord song. There was an artist's touch of elegance, Oriental rugs on the wooden floors and paintings on the walls. Due to the lighting, they couldn't be made out in detail. The walls were of a dark wood. The furniture looked hand-made, comfortable. In the kitchen was a wood burning cook stove, pale yellow enamel. It looked to be antique. The walls and cupboards were a light cream in color, there was a faint smell of fresh paint when I stood near them later on.

"Did you have many repairs to make after those storms?" I asked, as I glanced at Jewel for her reaction. Her face instantly grayed a little, lost its glow. As if transfixed, staring blankly into the candle light, her movements hesitated, like she was recalling a bad dream.

"Yah," Marcus quickly replied, "It'll all turn out with improvements when we're done though. Jewel will get her greenhouse attached to our bedroom. The old one was out in the yard, but it got torn apart. It used to have tame birds flying around in it all the time. Hope I don't end up with birds flyin' 'round our bedroom." He winked at me, trying to lighten the moment. "We have a modern outhouse now," he added. Clay laughed. It worked: Jewel smiled again, all those colors began to return.

Clay finished his dinner before us. “”Ever’t’ing reel gooed, yea ye righ,” he complimented as he rose from the table. “Bah ah t’ink ey bedder ge ba.”

“Thanks for bringing me,” I told him. He looked up from petting the dogs, giving me a warm smile.

“See ya bright and early,” Marcus said energetically.

Clay nodded, turned to Jewel and said, “Merci,” then walked to the door, both dogs following at his feet. He opened the door and walked into the night. The dogs instinctively stayed inside, perhaps for the unspoken promise of leftovers.

As we were finishing our dinner, Marcus talked about how they had weathered many hurricanes over the years, but how these last two were so different. He told of a great flood, way back in 1927, that he heard had changed the area, and how afterward, they built so-called un-breachable levees that changed the course of the Mississippi River. He had heard this and many stories from Clay and others, whose ancestry dated back to the Cajun’s first migration to the area. He explained how the oil companies came in and built canals that further imposed on fragile balances, causing land to steadily disappear into the water.

Jewel listened quietly watching him with swooned, loving eyes. Though so utterly flamboyant, she seemed to be a woman of few words.

Our plates were now empty and I couldn’t take another piece of pie. I admittedly gorged myself with as much dignity as I could muster. I’m sure I ate more than both of them put together. I did have a bit of a trucker weight problem, with an appetite to match. “That was wonderful!” I exclaimed.

“Lemme show ya something,” Marcus said to me. He got up from the table, and I followed him to the living room. He retrieved a guitar that was leaning against a wall in a dark corner, reached out, and handed it to me, saying, “How ‘bout this one?”

It looked incredibly old, considerably beaten up. There were cracks running along the front, and what seemed to be little indentations all over the surface. It was as if it had been tapped repeatedly by a ball peen hammer. It was darkly aged, with weather checkering and spider-webbed miniscule cracking all over where the finish had once been applied. It seemed delicate, like it could fall apart in my hands. I was almost afraid to handle it, and not initially impressed. I gave it back to him.

“It’s been around the swamp a few times. Been through more than we’ll ever know. It’s a ‘41 Martin. Got it years back, from a local yokel,” Marcus explained. “No, try it out.” He reached it back over to me. “I can see old Carvel with it in his hands right now,” he added, although I didn’t understand. Again, the steadiness of his arm, so close to me, brought incendiary impulses to my heart, and I politely received back his offering.

Somewhat reluctantly, I sat down on a chair and was about to play when Jewel walked in and sat down on the sofa across from me. There was a wooden coffee table in front of her that was the full length of the sofa. It looked to be handmade. There was a Bible on one end of the table, a notebook and pen on the other, with two lit candles in-between. I smiled a boyish smile over to her and began finger-picking "*Air on a G String*," by Bach. This is the intro I haphazardly use when I do the song, "*Whiter Shade of Pale*," made famous by Procol Harem back in the late '60s. I wasn't more than 10 notes into it when I was overcome by a most gentle and the sweetest of sounds. It was like nothing I had ever heard come from any guitar I'd ever played. It can only be described as the sound of pure bells. I looked up in amazement. Marcus and Jewel were both smiling in my direction.

"Unbelievable," I sighed. "I'm astounded; never heard anything like it! Take it back, 'cause I'm afraid I'll break it," I joked. I stood and handed it back to him, saying, "Let me go get mine." He nodded with a smile. As I got up and walked to the bedroom door, I glanced upon another guitar, much brighter in appearance — a classical type, leaning on an opposite wall. A small banjo with a strap was hanging by a nail just above it. I reached in my bag and took out my writings, then the hat I had brought for him. I opened my guitar case, pulled out my old Gibson, and brought it all back into the room.

"This is for you," I said as I handed him the hat. His smile showed delight, and he put it on.

"Looks good on ya," I admitted.

"It does," Jewel said, somewhat excitedly.

He grinned. The dimple appeared in his cheek. "Thank you," he said, and added, "I'll wear this one out!"

"Here's some of my writings you asked to see. I call this collection *Very Serious Spaghetti*," I said, grinning, as I handed him the folder.

He laughed with amusement and asked, "Can you leave it here for us to read later?"

"Sure, I'll be glad to. Let me know what you think."

He strummed the Martin and said, "Got some songs I'd like you to learn."

"Cool," I replied. Then he started playing in earnest.

The song turned out to be called "*Stealin*." I followed his chord progressions with my own, somewhat unique, finger picking patterns. My notes took on overlapping, harp-like nuances. His voice rang out as true as it had in the days of old. More goose bumps came upon me as our strings blended together magically. When the song was finished, he said, "We did it right." We decided to play it again. It was a fresh, new style of song to me. It broke into changes, very different from any I had heard before, with the most fascinating lyrics. Lines like: *"I'm stealin' away from you / all the colors deep in blue / all those colors lost from sunshine / for the color that is mine / I'm your wine, and I'm reaching."*

Jewel sat comfortably now, on a short love seat type of sofa, listening contently — a priceless, perfect audience. My heart was floating. I played *High*

*Test Love*, the song I had just finished writing about a month earlier. Marcus strummed rhythm to the fingering style I had created for the song. Once again it went the way it seemed meant to be played. We were now making our music complete, and we knew it. There was a confined, yet robust joy in the air, happy fulfillment that has no words. We were discovering the enticement of our new friendship.

Throughout the course of those quickened hours, in between conversation, we had one stretch break, where I asked to use the bathroom.

"There are a lot of trees out there," Marcus said.

"Spoken like a true woodsman," I replied.

We must have played 30 or more songs that night. Some of his, some of mine, and songs we just happened to know and love. Some of the songs I played by other artists, they had never heard before. I like to change songs sometimes, slow them down, re-constructualize them, so to speak, often to a classical format. I do so with "*Against the Wind*" by Bob Seger. I also did a slow version of "*I'm a Believer,*" made famous by the Monkees, but I think it was written by Neil Diamond. I made my voice sound like Waylon Jennings for that one, and they got a real kick out of it.

We were winding down. I could sense it was getting late. I didn't have a wristwatch. We were in relaxed conversation, still holding our guitars, sipping on the tea Jewel had provided during this little musical extravaganza.

Recalling how he had once shared with me his comparison of birds on telephone wires, I was reminded of a song. Without introduction, I played and sang, *Bird on a Wire*, by Leonard Cohen. He said he had heard it somewhere before, and I could tell they enjoyed my performance.

"My fingers are sore," I whimpered.

"Mine too, I'm not used to playing quite this much," he said.

"Don't you miss performing in front of audiences?" I had to ask.

"My feelings of those years are numb and sore as these fingertips. Some of my memories had nowhere to stay. I got kinda burned out on all of that, I think. What I do miss and remember well is driving. Man, I had some great cars! Had a black Stutz and I still dream about that one too. Still have it under my car port, in fact. Man, I don't even have a car port!" He laughed with excitement. "Had a fine Continental; used to love my motorcycles," he added.

It was time for another song. "Let me lay this one on ya," I interjected. I re-tuned my strings in a special way, to what I believe is called Malagassy tuning, and put my capo on the third fret. Then I did the song, *1952 Vincent Black Lightning* by Richard Thompson. It effectively blew them away. They actually applauded when I was finished.

"That was wild, Grant! I never heard anything like that, it was great!" Marcus exclaimed.

"I loved it," Jewel said in earnest. Her face was aglow.

"It's easy to do music here. This is a ponderer's hideaway," I boasted, knowing what I meant, but not sure it was conveyed correctly.

We were contently letting our relaxation shine, like a blessing that had been bestowed upon us. We shared the same realm; it was obvious — a priceless time, like nothing to compare it to and it filled us. Our smiles were of that awareness, warmed complete by our company. Marcus came back with a lighthearted number he'd named, *Sugar Cookie*. It was a fun winding-down to the evening. We then decided we would call it a night. I left my guitar on the sofa as we stood up together.

"Thank you for all of this," I said, gratefully.

"It's our pleasure. It was real fun," Jewel replied, then began walking to the front door, stepping outside. Marcus smiled, leaning his beat-up beauty of a guitar back against the wall.

"She went out to read the moon and stars. The color of Mars no doubt twinkles bright in her eyes tonight. Get some good rest," he said. "If we have time, I want to show you around tomorrow, before you go."

We went our separate ways into that astonishing night. I knew then, it wasn't fate, but providence that had overtaken us.

## CHAPTER 6

My head reeled as I lay in bed. It took a while, but my body relaxed enough for me to doze off. It had been a long, exciting day, yet somehow it seemed all too short. I must have slept deeply, because the next thing I remembered was opening my eyes to the light of day seeping through a slim crack in the window curtain. Indistinguishable sounds were coming from what seemed to be far away. I arose quickly and got dressed. When I opened the bedroom door and stepped out, I saw Jewel with her back to me at the kitchen window. She must have heard or felt me.

"Well good morning," she said, as she turned with a smile that could light up anyone's day.

"Good morning," I replied, smiling back at her. "I'd like to discover your modern outhouse if I could," I added with a grin.

She pointed through the window, outside, and off to her left. "Coffee is on when you get back."

"Sounds great!"

When I stepped outside, I could see Marcus, Clay, and two other men, about a hundred yards down a small hill directly in front of me. They were standing next to what appeared to be a small cabin near a large shed. I saw what had to be an outhouse, to my left, in the direction she had pointed. Walking to it, I found I was on a pathway of various sized wooden circles. They looked to be cross sections of trees inlaid evenly with the ground. Each had unique geometric carvings in theirs surfaces. Many were stellate, arranged by carved-out pieces forming star-shaped designs that radiated out from their centers. I was impressed by the unique craftsmanship. The wood trim on the outhouse was equally impressive, like nothing I had ever seen. Once inside, I had to admit, it really was modern. There were painted designs on one wall, in what appeared to be a work in progress. There were two holes with new wooden seats, and two of what looked like hand-carved toilet paper holders on each side.

When I returned to the house and stepped inside, Jewel and Marcus were seated at the table. He was wearing the hat I had given him last night.

"Ready for coffee?" he asked.

"Sounds good," I replied. "I just visited your new outhouse. You two really do everything together, don't cha?" I said with a smirk. They glanced at each other and grinned. From Jewel once more came her enchanting giggle.

She stood up and walked toward the stove.

"I left water in your room to freshen up," she said to me.

"Thank you," I replied.

Marcus was sipping coffee. "Did you get some rest?" he asked.

"Slept good," I replied. I walked back to my room, still not feeling fully awake. In the bedroom I saw a bowl of water on a small table, with a towel and a wash cloth lying next to the bowl. There also was a glass of water on the night stand. This is nice, I thought. I freshened up and brushed my teeth, ready now to see what this new day would bring.

When I returned to the table to join them, there was a plate of scrambled eggs, toast, a small bowl of jam, a glass of orange juice, and a cup of hot coffee waiting for me. It turned out to be a crawfish omelet, and the taste was magnificent! Jewel and Marcus already were eating; everything was so casual.

"Jewel had painted the walls of the old one to look like the walls of my old billiard room," Marcus laughed, referring to the outhouse. "Did you notice she's art-deco designing it?"

"Yes, I can tell; it's gonna be great!" I complimented.

Marcus ate quickly, stood up, then said to me, "See ya outside when you're finished." He walked to the door and stepped out. I noticed the dogs were nowhere around. I figured they were down there with Clay and the others. Jewel was seated across from me. She had finished eating and was sipping her coffee.

"Can I see your hands without those gloves?" she asked.

I looked up from my food. "Sure, I guess so," I replied courteously, as I took the gloves off and reached my hands across the table to her. She took them in hers, closed her eyes for a moment, then opened them again and she turned my hands palms up, staring into them. She then guided my left hand back on the table and released it from hers. Still holding my right, she gently squeezed it and ran her fingers along my lines, intently studying them. It became apparent that she was reading my palm. She showed herself mystical to me in that instant, as though she could see into my heart.

"He's been looking for you for some time," she casually said to me, as she traced my lines with her finger. "In you he sees a fulfillment; you'll understand," she said. She was smiling as she added, "I've had dreams of you. We met in a darkness that was slowly to become light." Then she gently released my hand. "We need to get your health back," she said, staring deeply into my eyes. Those soft, golden beacons, half hidden within a leafy mist, launched my ship. "He hasn't done music with anyone except me since we've been together," she quietly added. A chill ran up my backbone, and I felt tear well in my eye. What she said had, for some reason, gotten to me. I didn't know what to say; I smiled. She had never stopped smiling.

With a couple more bites, I had finished my breakfast. I took a last drink from my coffee cup and set it down. I figured Marcus would be waiting. Jewel reached across, picked up my coffee cup, and looked into it as intently as she had done with my palm. She gave a brief sigh. Had something been told to her in those few remaining grounds at the bottom of my cup? I had never had an experience like that. I had no idea what she was seeing or thinking.

"Thank you, breakfast was great," I told her, without asking about that which I had just witnessed with the cup. I put my gloves back on and stood up from the table. "I better catch up with those guys."

"I'll see you out there," she replied.

I walked to the door, venturing out, once again, to meet the day. When I stepped down from the unfinished porch, I took a long look around. There were panes of glass stacked in a row against the finished porch wall to my right. Alongside them were several tall boxes marked 'Solar Panels'. Building materials were scattered on the ground nearby. The new greenhouse had been framed in, attaching to the side of the house where evidently, their bedroom also was located. I took a few steps into the yard, turned around to view their home. It had cedar siding, stained a light gray. I saw it as a hermitage, partially built within a hill or knoll, with vegetation covering the roof and growing along the walls. It was almost like a camouflaged blanket. There was a black tank on a tall wooden platform that grew from somewhere behind the house. As I later learned, though I never took one there, it held the water for their showers. It had a gas-powered, motorized pump that filled the tank, which was heated by warm days and sunlight. It was then gravity-fed back down to a small closet located next to their bedroom. The water drained through a hole in a wooden floor, and out of a long pipe that extended down a slope from the house to a culvert.

Turning back to that small hill, I saw Marcus walking toward me. Down beyond where the others stood, between some palm trees and low bushes, I could see what looked like a lagoon, a backwater pond. I glanced to my right, near the house. There was another circular wooden walkway leading back around to the other side and what appeared to be a well-aged barbeque. I took a few steps in that direction. There was an attached oven on its one side, and a chimney, all made of rock and cement. There appeared a tinge of green, layered, almost as if painted, with coated patterns of moss and lichen upon the rocks and embedded in the cement between. There were vines anchored and climbing up one side of the chimney. It was like a picture on a calendar. Directly behind it, only a few feet away, stood a small screened-in building. It had a table in the center, and a bench on the right side, with a sink and hand pump built into it. I could see a large bucket directly under the sink, which I imagined was used for draining. It had the appearance of what one might call a summer kitchen.

"What do ya think of all this?" Marcus asked as he approached.

I turned to him. "It seems so peaceful. There's so much mellowness," was my instinctive reply. "It's even a bit mysterious to me, like no place I've ever seen. It makes me feel somehow different. I don't know, it's very cool."

"Got a favor to ask ya," he said. "Clay's a Harley rider. Can you play that motorcycle song for him?"

"Sure," I told him without hesitation.

"Believe it or not, he could use some perkin' up," Marcus began explaining. "For the most part, Clay's place was spared from the storms, their sense of direction showed no reasoning. A lot of his friends lost everything — their homes, boats, and their livelihood. Some of them lost their lives — the so soon of forever — stories yet to be told. There are no steady predictables. He's so close with it all, almost overly personable to a fault, having a tough time over it — that which was and is no more. It's breaking his heart. He's been trying to help those he can. He has a hurt he'll never show or tell. He used to have what the locals call a 'joie de vivre', a joy of living. He's not that old Clay. We want him back. I know he'll find his way with the healing of time, but we're missing him. We need to see and feel his real smile again."

Marcus' look, so sincere, with deepened, concerned lines surrounding his eyes, as he imbued Clay's inner struggle to me, it wrenched at my heart. I had no idea what Clay had been going through. For him to be any more jovial was hard to imagine, but as I thought about it, I could sense a hurt inside his sun-wrinkled face. He did seem introspective at times. Anything I could do, I would. All three were heading up the hill toward us now. The dogs appeared from out of nowhere, jumping around them as they walked. Clay was again rousting about with them.

"You should know, the fulltime occupations of these guys are Jewel and I. There are a half dozen folks in all, they're dedicated," Marcus confided in a subdued voice. "Lately, we've kept them all pretty busy."

I was at once curious. "What's Burtons' job?"

"More than anything, he's security. He knows a lot of people. Believe it or not, there's far more security here than meets the eye, he's to thank for that."

"I guess I know what Credence does," I said.

"He covers things for us. They're all our dear friends, sisters and brothers, have been these many years. Their gift is letting me live what life had forgotten to give me before. They're steadfast in the secret, done everything they can to make our lives normal. The young kid you see coming has no idea who I am," he warned. "We don't want him to. He just helps out on weekends, still in high school. Clay calls him, 'bon a' rien,' (lazy). He reminds me of myself at that age. All he thinks about, or wants to do, is play swamp pop on his electric guitar."

Clay, the kid, and the other fellow approached. Each of them had a can of beer in their hand. Clay had two, and with a warm smile, handed one to me without a word. The kid, tall and thin, in a dirty T-shirt and blue jeans, looked a bit out of place, uncomfortable. The other man was short and stocky.

"Got the boards cut to length," the older one said to Marcus. Just gotta get 'em up." He had a brusque voice, a tough edge about him, burly and overweight, with overtly hairy shoulders. In a sleeveless, ragged shirt and baggy pants, his appearance was unkempt. He had a sullen, ornery look on his aged face. He was 60 years old, or older.

"This is Elbow Jack and his grandson, Eddie Bergeron," Marcus said to me. "This is Grant," he told them. I nodded and shook the kid's nervous hand.

"Do I call you Elbow?" I asked, reaching out to shake hands with this inimical, stocky fellow.

"Go 'head, see where it gets ya," he growled with a sparring gesture and a muscled grin. He then clasped and shook my hand too heartily, almost painfully. He was holding an old soup can in his other fist, his lower lip bulging from the tobacco between his teeth and gums. Allowing a stream of juice to spew from his pursed lips into the can, he then wiped his chin with the back of the same hand with which he just shook mine. This antic I would come to witness countless times when in the pleasure of his company. When he dumped that can, I could only surmise, was when he urinated in the brush. I later noticed his teeth were extremely tobacco-stained.

"Jack was a brawler. He used to use his elbows in fights. That's how he got the name. Could knock a man out with them, did a lot a damage," Marcus explained.

"When fightin' was fun ya mean," Jack snorted with a bolstered bark of a laugh. "Dems sparin' gloves yer a-wearin'?" he asked in feigned confrontation.

"Nah, just drivin' gloves," I told him.

"Jack's retired. Now he's a raconteur — a story teller," Marcus explained.

Jack would prove to be one of the most warm-hearted men I'd ever met, although one would never have ventured that guess. He carried such a malign scowl to his face. I had to rename him Mad Jack, because of the look he always held. I would never dare call him by that name to his face, even to this day.

"Grant's got a song for y'all," Marcus told them enthusiastically.

"I'll get my guitar," I said in response. I turned, climbing the short steps of the porch. Jewel was washing dishes at a sink under the kitchen window to my left, as I walked in. There was a hand pump, apparently well water, connected to the counter next to the sink. When I passed by, the stove felt warm from the small wood fire that had been burning itself out within its side bin. She gave me a smile, and I gave her mine; I went to retrieve my guitar.

"He's got me doin' that motorcycle song for those guys," I called to her, as I picked up my Gibson from the far room.

"I want to hear it too," she said brightly, spinning around to look at me directly.

I half turned to somehow thank her for everything with my smile, opening the door to go back outside. In that split second, with a somewhat perky bounce to her step, the instance of a smiling dance, I'd swear her eyes gave a luster, almost a spark, as they met mine. Once again she appeared magical, reminding me of Kat in some way. I must admit, it set me sailing.

You could say I floated out onto the porch. I saw all four members of my audience were standing up there now, dogs at their feet. The men seemed to be conversing in the far left corner about that unfinished section. Except when Clay got them riled up, the dogs were well behaved; they appeared old. One even had gray whiskers around its nose. Upon seeing me, Marcus turned, quickly snatching up a small bench seat near him, placing it down in front of me.

"Ya'll gotta hear this," he turned to tell the others.

I sat down and carefully re-tuned for Richard Thompson's song. They loomed silent above and in front of me. The door opened, and Jewel stepped out to join us. I saw Marcus smile at her without saying a word. She was looking at me, they all were.

I sang and played that song with more vigor than ever before. I gave it feeling, like the main character was me. I gave it everything I had, and with a bit of a Celtic accent. When finishing it up, I even gave it the extra twist a player sometimes discovers when performing so enthusiastically; then I looked up.

"My land!" Mad Jack exalted. The kid stood rangy and smiling — restive, acting like he had the jitters. He gave nervous, darting looks, back and forth at everyone, as though he didn't know how to react. Clay had a smile on his face from ear to ear. Marcus beamed proudly at me. As did Jewel, blushing, gazing down at me seated on that chair. I had an unwound, almost relaxed feeling, hands hugging the guitar. She, on the other hand, seemed charged for that instant, like penned-up high voltage. It was like she was awaiting a switch to be flicked on so she could explosively react in some way. I think she wanted to hug me but held back. It's hard to explain, such intensity wrapped within that peaceful aura of hers.

Clay came over, and without a word put his arm around my shoulder, giving me a few rapid and very hearty squeezes. He had love in that arm, I could feel it. They were all intermittently applauding. You done good, I told myself. I must have been smiling broadly. I had won the audience.

"Fel lak ridin' naw!" Then Clay yipped like a prairie cowboy into the morning air. I imagine it riled the ducks. I looked at Marcus and he gave me a wink.

"That got my day started," I heard Mad Jack say.

"Yea ye righ!" Clay quickly added, still grinning widely at me.

Eddie must have been the silent type. I never heard him say a word the whole time. But, in a nervous way, he knew how to smile.

Mad Jack was now rummaging in the tool box on the porch floor. He was ready to get back to it. The pesky midges (up north we call them "no-see-'ems"), started to become a bit bothersome. Everyone seemed to be swatting at them.

"Grab that wood plane," Jack told the kid. They started back down the hill; work was on his mind.

Clay looked at me and said, "Dat wh sumt'ing! I lak ta'ear anudder, but tink ah cane. Jack'll break bot dese coonass arms, Is' pose I ge don dere." He smiled wide, he was shining. I gave him an understanding nod. He turned and headed down to join them.

Can there ever be another time like this? I asked myself. I stood up and leaned my guitar against the house, then stepped down off the porch to take a stretch. As I looked around, again the water everywhere grabbed my attention. I turned to Jewel and Marcus on the porch.

"Us Wisconsinites call Minnesotans "swampees," but you guys really are! I said. I was trying to be funny. Jewels eyes welled up immediately, there were about to be tears. The smile instantly was gone. Marcus cast a blank expression. She turned and walked back inside. The mood turned to a blackness. I was taken aback. "I didn't mean…," I ruefully started to say.

"It's alright. She'll be fine," he consoled me. "It's just that since the storms, she sees this like a swamp for the first time in her life. It's devastating her on the inside. She's been here most all of her life. Things changed almost overnight — may never be the same again. The time it takes to calm the waves from wind and storm are what she's living through now. It hurts, we all have separate sighs. She's told me she wants to move on; to get out of here. We're trying to brighten everything back up again. Don't think it's working."

"I need to tell her I'm sorry. I was only trying to be funny; I feel terrible!"

"You watch," he said, "she'll be back to her old self in a minute. You won't need to say a word. It's okay."

I felt bad. It sure took the pizzazz out of that moment. Standing dumbfounded, I helplessly did not know what to do. "I still don't know why you chose me. Why I'm the one," I told him, now half pitying myself, frustrated.

His smile reappeared. He seemed to light up. "I told you." He started singing; "He's got you and me brother, in his hands, he's got the whole world in his hands."

That voice, the way he's able to sink it in, got a smile back out of me. "The more I think I know, the less I find I've learned," I sighed to him, remissive.

I could tell he wanted me to shake it off. "Next time I'll show ya around out here. Need to watch for snakes, though. I've been hit twice. And spiders! Jewel took care of my snake bites, or I wouldn't be here.

I looked at him in awe. "Gators too?" I asked.

"Not so much as you'd think. Not here anyway. Soon, I can get you that baby one you've been lookin' for if you want. Mama gator won't like it much though," he laughed.

"Naw, you talked me out of that one," I replied with a laugh.

"Grab your axe. Mornin' is goin' by. We got time for another song or two," he told me as he turned to the door.

Feeling somewhat drained, I picked up my guitar and followed him back into the house. Jewel was seated at the kitchen table. She was reading the collection of my writings I had brought to them. I gave her a lost puppy look. She mustered a warm smile for me. It brought light back into my morning. There was a brown paper bag on the table. "This is for you," she motioned to it with her hand. "Something to tide you over when you're thinking about those cheeseburgers and French fries," she said lightheartedly. She was back! I almost felt like crying. In fact, I did inside, as I opened the bag to take a look. It was assorted nuts and seeds, mixed together with, apparently, dried berries. I later found the crunchy taste to be sweet and with a hint of mint.

"Thank you," I said gratefully. "So you think there's hope for me yet?"

"Can't give up on you, you're too important." She gave me a wink.

"I agree with that," Marcus chimed in.

"You guys are great. I hope I never outstay my welcome here," I said with an apologetic tone.

"You kidding? We're lovin' yer hide!" Marcus said; Jewel gave a sugary laugh. It sounded angelic to me; again those goose bumps — one of my many character flaws.

I sensed the morning could not give us all we wanted, but like The Rolling Stones sang, we'd "get what we need." Besides, I knew in that moment, there'd be days to come for us to share.

## CHAPTER 7

As we walked to the living room, my curiosity regarding that tarp draped over the door of the room next to mine made me ask, "Was this room damaged?"

"That'll be one of our last fix-ups," Marcus replied. "Here, I'll show ya." He lifted the tarp and hooked it to a nail on the door frame. I leaned my guitar against the wall and followed him inside. It was a somewhat dark room, with no windows. From what I had seen outside, it probably was located more under the hill than the other rooms. "This room brought in more water than we ever thought it could," Marcus said. I glanced up at the ceiling. Almost pattern-like, it was water-stained pale green to light brown swirls, bleeding from a surface that once must have been completely white. The wall to the left, the other side of the wall to my room, where the headboard of my bed would be was completely stripped down to 2x4 bracings. The wall behind us had recently been sheet rocked. It was still unpainted. On the right was a bookcase covering the entire length of the wall. It still held remnants of silty water and dirt upon the wood surfaces of each shelf. There were things laid out intermittently on them. "This was filled with our books, they're in a dry storage now. Most have been water-damaged. We still haven't gone through them to see how bad they really are," Marcus said.

At eye level, I noticed jars with labels on some of them, reading: Hibiscus, La Pre 'Le, Citronella, Mamou Root, Ginger Root. "What are these?" I inquired.

"Those are Jewel's," he responded proudly. "She's a healer, what locals call, Traiteur. Uses these and a lot of remedies to help people. Learned the ways from her daddy, and him from his mama before; passed down from generations. You'd be surprised what healing secrets she knows. Her daddy always told her that her eyes were hued with mystical stars."

At once my mind ignited — inner thoughts proclaimed loudly to myself, "That's what it is!" I stood there flabbergasted for a moment. I couldn't say a word. I wondered to myself, "Had she actually learned all of these things? Had her father really taught it all to her, or was it in part a cosmic, very special gift?" Maybe both. I couldn't fathom the depth of her mystery, and probably never will. I stood staring at those jars, many without labels, speechless at this revelation. "I've never heard of it," I finally caught myself saying aloud, fumbling at some sort of acknowledgement. I stood peering into those glass jars, trying to decipher what I was actually viewing. Marcus just stood there smiling.

"This was our library, slash, art room. It will be again." He was holding such promise in his words. "We have a huge collection of great books. Wait till you see. Let's go play a couple quick ones," he said, motioning to the door.

We stepped back out into the living room, and Jewel walked over from the kitchen. In seeming anticipation, she took the same seat she had when we finished off the night before. He was picking up his classical guitar that had not yet been played. He handed it to me. "I think it's tuned," he told me. "Play us one."

As I sat down, something inside of me wanted more than anything to apologize to Jewel to cheer her up, to erase that earlier blunder I had made. A song by John Prine, titled, *Clocks and Spoons,* a song about yearning to get back to the country, would be perfect. It tells of fond memories of those things that used to be and about getting back to them. I sang and played it, especially for her.

I could see it held her captivated, and I must admit, it sounded surprisingly good, performed on that classical guitar. Her eyes revealed a love as she looked into mine. I believe I may have blushed a little. Her presence, so rare an experience, personifies love.

I took a moment to examine the instrument. It appeared to be handmade, with the usual nylon or gut strings. There was no name on it anywhere, or any indication as to who may have built it, just a "JD" crudely carved into the headstock.

"Where'd ya get this one?" I asked Marcus.

"Jewel's had it in her family for years. Don't know who made it, or even whose initials those are. Plays pretty sweet though, don't it?"

Jewel beamed, yet not saying a word. "It's a real nice axe," I told him. "Got another one I'd like to try," I said, eager to hear how the guitar would sound on another John Prine tune, *Angel from Montgomery*. As with the last song I had played, Marcus and Jewel showed their appreciation. He, with a grateful look on his face while Jewel was radiating as a fresh blossom does for its first light.

"Man, I love that song!" he proclaimed. "I'm gonna wanna learn that from ya."

I was surprised he had never heard it. I handed the guitar to him with an agreeing smile. (That one happens to be on my top 40 list of songs to play.) I stood up, went over and picked up the Gibson, and we continued, seated in the same places we were the night before. Marcus, still holding the classical, began finger-picking a song he had written, called, *Intoxication Avenue*. It was a bluesy tune, again different than any style I had heard before. It was the first time I had seen him finger-pick in such a manner. Up to that point, he had basically strummed the previous songs. This was a wonderful song about getting out of a soul's blackness. The best way I could describe it: poetically deep.

"Wow," I said, shaking my head in amazement. Suddenly, Clay was at the door. My time was done.

"We gotta ge brudder, cuz Creed'll b'dare," he informed us. Marcus concurred, and so sadly, it was time to wrap things up. Clay smiled and stepped back outside.

"Man, this went too fast!" I exclaimed.

"You get back here as soon as you can. We've got a bunch of music to do," Marcus said, as we all stood up.

"I will." I wanted to hug them both; it felt that close. They made me feel that way, and I didn't know how I could thank them. "I can't begin to tell you…," I started to say.

"It's been a great beginning," Marcus interrupted. "I'm lookin' ahead. Bigger notes will hang longer," he proclaimed in an excited tone.

"Come back to us soon," Jewel added. "We'd love to meet your wife."

"Kat ever travel with you?" Marcus asked.

"No, she won't. I took her for a ride around the block once and all she could say was," "It's too big!" "It made her nervous. She'd drive me crazy that way. It would be worse than a back-seat driver, and that would make me WAAAY too nervous! I hope you'll get a chance to meet her. She doesn't believe any of this. She thinks you're just some Joe, pretending to be who you really are." Both Jewel and Marcus laughed.

"Maybe we'll just have to go up there," Jewel said to me with a twinkle in her eye. Marcus turned to her with an inquisitive look on his face, but didn't say a thing.

"Guess I better get my stuff," I said with regret. With guitar in hand, I walked back to the guest bedroom to collect my things. I rejoined them, still standing in what I will fondly remember from then on as our music room. I was holding my guitar case in one hand and had my bag strapped over my other shoulder when Marcus quickly stepped over, and with his right arm around both my shoulders, gave me a tender squeeze. He smiled widely across to Jewel, and she was smiling back at me.

"Got a-lot-a get ta knowin' when we meet next time," he said brightly. How illustrious his eyes were to me then, or perhaps it was my adulation. It touched me, a deep feeling I can't say I'd ever felt before — one that made me feel I'd almost give my life to. What was this?

"Ok," I managed to say back, walking now toward the door.

"Don't forget this," Jewel called out, reaching across the table for the paper bag. She handed it to me in almost a ballet curtsy, intentionally being cute. I couldn't help but return my warmest smile. A heart recognizing indissoluble family love. There had been so many special moments; I couldn't begin to recall them all. But the most memorable moment came next. Jewel moved close, resting both of her arms across my shoulders. She nearly whispered, "I don't believe in saying goodbye." Like a valentine bouquet, sweetened, as by such an aroma's promise, she gave me a tender kiss on the cheek. Pressing forward, she wrapped me in a warm hug.

Now I knew it was time to go. I couldn't stay another second. I wanted to hold onto their cloud, yet Jewel had made me miss Kat in that instant. "I'll try to be back soon," I told them. I turned once again toward the door. Marcus and I both moved in that direction. As he opened it, I paused and gave Jewel one more smile. She timidly smiled back then stayed behind, as he and I stepped outside.

Clay was outside mulling about, looking at the building scraps on the ground. I could see the other two guys down the hill, hand-sawing on something that was lying across two sawhorses. Mad Jack saw us and waved in our direction. Eddie merely looked up at us, then went back to what he was doing.

"Ready den?" Clay asked.

"I gotta lot of work back at home. Still need to get more wood up for winter there," I explained, half hoping to identify with them as being a backwoods man. They simply smiled.

The three of us began walking to the inlet where Clay's boat lay moored. The dogs came running to join us as we walked. Clay started rousting with them right away, as he always did. It seemed to be a game they played together. When we reached the secluded shoreline, I threw both my overnight bag and the brown bag onto the floor of the boat between the seats. I turned to Marcus and asked if he'd hold my guitar case until I got in. We paused and looked each other in the eye. He took the case from my hand.

"Loved it, son," he then said to me.

Clay and I got in the boat. Marcus put the case in my outstretched hand. "Stay alright," he said. Clay was already pushing us onto the water with his pole as I settled into my seat.

I called back to Marcus on the bank. "My dad used to tell me it's a great life if you don't weaken." Marcus stood there, half slouching, hands in his pockets. His body language told me he was sad to see me go. "See you soon!" I called out.

We watched each other as the space between us widened. He turned, and with a brief wave from behind his back, began walking away. Clay and I reached the broadened daylight of open water in what felt like a single breath. After one final strong push out, Clay set the pole against the side and strapped it down. He took his seat and, in one pull, started the motor. Then he tossed me a beer.

I found myself reflecting on some of the things Marcus had said, as I stared down at the water lapping along the side of our boat. Some of what was said was lost to my memory. Between our songs the night before, he had, at times, gone off on poetic tangents, their meanings undecipherable. What was it he said? What was he trying to say? Oh, I tried so hard to remember, but I couldn't make myself understand. The time had gone by like lightning, like a dream — that somebody pinch me thing.

I started looking around, trying to focus on this new moment. I noticed what looked like shells scattered along a stretch of one shore bank. "What's that?" I inquired.

"Dey're oyster shells. Dey puh'm dere ta save de lan. De playree, she sinkin' in de wadder." His face exposing a sadness then, the face Marcus had tried to tell me about earlier. "Dere's yer M'su Cocodrie!" He pointed to the opposite shore.

"Gator!" I exclaimed with trepidation. I was in true Captain Hook paranoiac form. I could see it clearly on the bank; had to have been more than 10 feet long!

Clay laughed heartily when seeing my alarm. "Yea ye righ, dey're nuttin' brudder." He was entertained, but trying to console my nerves. I watched the alligator as we passed. It didn't move, but I could tell it was watching us. My spine must've been straight up and down; my nerves were tangled between each paralyzed muscle. I couldn't help myself. These things were new to me, strange to my comprehension. A foreign world not remotely close to the one I was used to.

I was pleased to glimpse the familiar snapping turtles along the way, their heads popped out of the water and then they'd disappear. We rounded a bend. There were ducks, and again we startled them to flight. I saw a pelican on a dead tree stump, oblivious to us. A rabbit was running on the shore between the trees. I pointed to it. "Lapin," Clay said. Nature was in full show as if just for me. This part of the world seemed teeming with Eden's creations.

Too soon, we were turning in at Clay's wharf. He cut the motor and we drifted, floating perfectly to the mooring place alongside the dock. I grabbed onto a post like an ambitious sailor and tied a rope to it. This had to be humorous for him. Once on land, I took a long stretch, and a last drink from my beer can. That gator experience still had me tightened up. An overweight, low-to-the-ground dog joined us, wagging its tail lovingly. "Eey Woogie," Clay acknowledged, as he threw his empty beer can near the stump of a tree. He bent low and gave the dog a couple pats. I threw my can next to his.

"Yer dog?" I asked.

"Yeh, des pauvre chein, she's ol't'mer. Creed musa le er aut," he replied.

A few more yards and there was the Chrysler, Creed was behind the wheel, seated patiently. I sensed we were running late, but he seemed alright about it. He's hard to read, almost emotionless, few expressions, but he gave me the feeling that he was genuinely content as we approached.

"How'd it go?" Credence asked.

"It was great!" I excitedly replied. "It was wonderful!" I resounded, as I threw my things into the back seat of his car.

Clay stood smiling, as I turned and gave him my sincerest thanks, then shook his hand. "Fare thee well brother," I told him. "See ya soon. We'll catch a shrimp!" He laughed, and took hold and shook my hand a second time.

And so I was back in the car, sharing the front seat with Creed as he drove us from that grove and into the clearing. Once again we were in view of the devastated world that, defying reason, brought all of this into my life. The ways in which destruction can create anew will ever astound my mind. I can somehow come to grips with the understanding of change as the true force of existence. I resign myself to the fact that I will never fathom the phenomenon of bad bringing about good or good causing bad. It's not for man to know, I reckon.

I found Credence to be anything but a conversationalist. Any words I was able to pry from him were brief. "Do you live around here?" I asked.

"New Orleans."

"You married?"

"Wife and two daughters."

Now that intrigued me. Could they know about Marcus? I had to ask: "What do they think of what you do. Do they know who Marcus really is?

"I work for Burton. His offices are based in and around New Orleans. He's a security analyst and architect. That's what they know I do," he explained with a rare smile. That was the gist of our conversation for most of the way back.

I dialed Kat; she would be at work. "Hi Hon, I'm on my way back to the truck. I had an unbelievable time; wait till you hear!" I told her, trying to spur excitement.

"I'm glad," she responded blandly.

"I'll call ya back when I get on the road."

"I'm glad you're alright," she quickly added. "I was worried when I didn't hear anything from you."

"Sorry, the time got so absorbed," I told her, trying in my best tone to be apologetic.

"So it doesn't sound like he burst your bubble. I thought you might have found out who he really is," she said.

I couldn't respond. I had gained not an inch of her belief in all that was happening. I knew then, it would be a daunting task. I didn't feel I could argue the point sitting there next to Creed. I would take this up later.

"You'll have to explain things to me," she said, upset now. I guess my pause in our conversation got her sparked. She blurted, "Who are these people!" It wasn't said in the form of a question. "Does she have a sister?"

"Somewhere in Green Bay, I think." It was a startled response to a loaded question. I needed to end this call.

"We're there, I gotta let you go. Call soon. Love ya, babe." She let the call end without further friction. I had lied. We were still 10 minutes from the National Guard center.

I sat blankly quiet, choosing not to ask myself questions I couldn't answer. I felt a sad loss of some sort. I know Credence sensed something was amiss. When we got to the center, he pulled into a slot in the parking lot and turned the motor off. I guess he felt he had to ask.

"Everything alright at home?" He does get right to the point.

"My wife just doesn't believe any of this. I don't know where she thinks I've really been. I guess I don't blame her; does seem pretty far-fetched," I told him.

"It'll work itself out. Marcus has opened up his world to you. I'll bet she'll become a part of it when the time comes; it'll be fine." He tapped his hand on my thigh. It was the first time I gathered any form of emotion coming from this man. I realized then how aware of an individual he probably was, and thanked him for the support. We parted with a handshake. He didn't bother to get out of the car.

"See you next time," I said, as I stood outside his window.

"Sounds good," he simply replied. He gave a short smile, then pulled out of the parking spot and drove away.

I walked back to old Beulah, threw my things on the passenger seat, and climbed up inside. Putting things in their assorted places, I then turned the key to accessories. My Qualcomm lit up. I was to pick up the same trailer, now empty, that I had brought in yesterday morning, and drop it at a shipper location near Alexandria Louisiana. There I was to pick up a preloaded trailer to be delivered to Bloomington, Illinois. Darin was working me back toward home.

# PART IV

## CHAPTER 1

I was thinking back to when I first learned to drive an eighteen-wheeler, likening it to be a military boot camp. I attended our company's training academy for three weeks with an additional two weeks on the road with a training engineer.

It was up every morning at 5 a.m. seven days a week. We were taken by bus from the motel to the academy grounds at 6:30. Half of our day was spent in the classroom, the other half behind the wheel. We were driven back to the motel at 5:30 p.m. We would need to fend for ourselves regarding supper. On average, there would be two or three hours of homework each night, with testing to follow the next day. It was a grueling schedule, but the training our company provides is considered the best in the business.

Of the 64 who attended orientation that first day, only 19 graduated. Some had been told by the second day that they would not be considered. For many, the job requirements were more than they had anticipated. Three or more were packing it in each day that first two weeks, dropping like flies! One minute next to you in the class, the next they've disappeared.

Those of us who stuck it out and "made the grade," so to speak, were given a short ceremony and dinner that last day. Our instructor was going over some of the company policies, explaining in detail how the time at home process would work. Every other weekend home was standard for van drivers, such as myself. There were other categories: flat bed, team drivers, dedicated accounts, etc. We were told that two holidays a year, everyone, without exception, was to be guaranteed time at home. That would be on Thanksgiving and Christmas. I remember one fellow raising his hand and asking if he could stay out all the time — said he didn't want to go home. He was told that something could be arranged through his service team leader, but he would still be dispatched home for those two holidays. "But what if I don't ever wanna go home?" the driver asked sincerely. The entire room burst out laughing! Here was a married man with children. I thought to myself, "You poor sap, maybe she don't want you to ever come home. Just keep those checks rolling in to the bank account." I'll never forget that guy, or the inanimate look he had on his face. I wonder, even now, what became of him. Is he still out there, homeless somewhere?

Now I had my commercial driver's license, (CDL), completing the hiring process and assigned my own truck. I named her Old Betsy. She had over 900,000 miles on the odometer. I guess they wanted to see how hard I was gonna to be on her. I happened to be good to her. Nevertheless, she was sent into retirement within three months. My second truck was Daisy Ann. I was able to put nearly 600,000 on her before I was blessed with Beulah.

These were the thoughts occupying my mind as I pulled into our driveway. Ah, home again, and it was Thanksgiving! All I cared about was being with my family.

Kat had taken a vacation day to prepare for the dinner. According to plans, we would have a house full. She and I reunited in usual fashion on the front porch, all kisses and smiles. When I stepped inside, I could see the kitchen in fully dedicated, labor of love disarray: turkey thawing in the sink, pie crusts formed in pans on the counter, and varying degrees of food preparation going on all over the place. I dare say only she could understand this organizational process — busy girl. I decided it was best for the moment to stay out of the way. I went to the closet, retrieved my favorite guitar, and tuned it up.

I sat down on the kitchen stool near the telephone. "Tell me what you think of this," I told her, as I began playing what I could remember of Marcus' song, *Stealin'*.

Her back was to me when she remarked, "One you learned down South?"

"It's one of L's. I can't remember all of it."

"It's really nice, really different," she commented.

"Kinda like poetry set to music. It evokes a painting in my mind," I told her. "It's almost a jazzy blues, wouldn't you say?"

"That's what you call him, L?" I smiled as she turned to look at me, then she shook her head in that way she does when she thinks I'm a bit overboard. "Does she play too?"

"Hasn't yet; don't know. She wants to meet you."

"Don't see how that's ever gonna happen," Kat muttered back.

"Maybe they'll have to come up here." I had a half-sinister grin.

Her reply, an unbelieving "Ya, ok."

I started playing again, although I don't recall the songs. I played the whole time she did her kitchen work. Nothing more was said about them. I didn't bring it up, nor did she. Maybe she was waiting for me to say more; there'd be time. I was going to be home for four days. With the holiday season upon us, coupled with the fact that I still had six days of vacation I needed to use up by the end of the year, there was little likelihood I'd be seeing Jewel and Marcus again before January. While I sat there, I wondered what it would be like singing Christmas carols with him. I smiled. It was an amusing thought.

Later, after brief snuggling on the couch, our night ended early. Tomorrow would be a busy, and I'm sure, a hectic and blessed day, and it would begin early.

## CHAPTER 2

There are many reasons for an old trucker like me to be thankful. It reached a heartfelt peak when cars began pulling in our driveway. First came Laura and her husband, Jim, with our three grandkids: TJ, Mindy, and Collin. Within minutes, along came our youngest, Lacey, and her boyfriend, along with her three dogs Dex, Star, and Lola. Our son Nathan was in Chicago for his job, and would be unable to attend. Then, like clockwork, came our sophisticated, career-oriented eldest, Lynn, with her husband David and their two dogs; Jake and Hank. Five dogs running in and out of the house under everybody's feet, together with three small children filled with energy. "Barrel of monkeys," Kat remarked. I just smiled. Let the fun begin.

With so many there for dinner, we needed to add two card tables to our living room table. When it came time to serve the food, Kat's creativity with tablecloths made it look as if it were one long table.

Lacey said grace. Light conversation ensued as we filled our plates. Then came the hammer: Kat tapped her glass with a spoon for everyone's attention. "Your father has a delusional announcement to make," she remarked. "Go ahead honey; tell them about your famous new friend. Dad's been visiting and playing guitar with someone we all know and love." I looked at her sourly. "Go ahead babe, tell them," she insisted. All eyes were on me now. It felt like a hot seat.

I recall beginning with, "Well, it so happens," then starting to relate the story of how I met Jewel and Marcus. After a brief description of the circumstances, I told them who he was. The girls laughed immediately; the guys, evidently realizing it was alright to do so, did the same. The grandkids, not knowing what it was all about, laughed along. It only lasted a painful minute. Thank goodness for my witty son-in-law, Jim. He alleviated my suffering momentarily.

"I didn't tell you guys, Marilyn lives right across the alley from us," he said. "Man, did she get fat; must be 350-plus! You wouldn't recognize her!" Everyone was laughing now, including me. "I can't stand it when she takes out the garbage. She's always singing something about a candle in the wind. It probably wouldn't sound so bad if she'd take that pipe out of her mouth!" By now, no one was eating. The laughter became more of a roar, and I recall the dogs barking outside.

"Alright, alright already! Stop it, you're hurting my cheeks!" I shouted.

"Is he related," TJ asked sincerely. The laughter didn't stop.

"Yah, he's your uncle Marcus," Lynn said.

"When can we meet him?" TJ innocently responded.

"Yah, when can we meet Uncle Marcus?" Lynn insisted.

Even as the patriarch of this family, I had no control over the situation.

"Food's getting cold," I said, almost desperately. That calmed things down briefly, everyone realizing this was true.

"I have the perfect Christmas present for you now," Lynn said. "You need a journal so you can keep track of these escapades. Maybe you can get him to autograph it." More laughter; I only smiled. I had been beaten into submission. I looked around at everyone despairingly.

"Oh, leave Dad alone. He can see who he wants," Laura remarked.

Even more laughter. Laura then gave an irritated expression.

"I don't know who these people are, but they've got him convinced," Kat said.

"Can we just eat and talk about something else? Next time I'll take his picture," I told them.

It was at that moment our six-year-old granddaughter Mindy piped in and saved the day: "I boogied in the kitchen. I boogied in the hall. I boogied on my finger, and put it on the wall."

Now everyone was in hysterics. My cheeks really hurt!

"Who taught you that?" Lacey asked.

"Grampa."

I just snickered, and so went this Thanksgiving dinner, more light-hearted than any I could remember from the past. When the laughing had subsided, the food was eventually enjoyed. To my surprise, no one said or asked anything more about it. No one seemed interested in any specifics. If they had, there may have been an ounce of belief somewhere. I sensed, with an inner sigh, that there was none. It was like a joke told, laughed about, then forgotten. They just moved the conversation to life's other little attributes. I can't say I was hurt; I guess it was more relief. I had never even considered the rest of the family in this thing with Jewel and Marcus; maybe I should have. I knew from that moment that I may need to. Thus far, my family had shown no belief in anything I'd said in this regard. It was becoming all too important for me that Kat, at least, realize the truth. Up until then, the consuming excitement was all mine. My impatience was taking hold. I needed to speed up whatever it would take for her to see. The question was how it could be done. This consideration, rumination, would haunt me.

We were finishing the meal now. Kat had to surprise us once again. "I was watching a show on, I think it was the Discovery channel," she began explaining. "From what I can remember, it was about two girls and a boy somewhere up in the mountains of Spain in 1904. The Virgin Mary appeared to them and gave them prophesies. One was about Hitler, and there were other things that came true. I remember it was something called Fatima. One prophecy said that God would send a king dressed in white and the whole world would know his name. It was within the same time-frame of Pope John, and he thought it would be him, but God never revealed anything like that to him, and it's said the Pope was quite disappointed that nothing ever came of it. After that the girls ended up living their lives in a nunnery. Want to know what I think? I think it was supposed to be Elvis; he wore white! He was the king and the whole world knows his name! He got his start singing gospel, but somehow things got whacked out and God must have thought this was not what he had in mind."

Everyone just sat there in silence. What could best be described as dazed amazement had filled the air. You really could hear if a pin had dropped. I looked at Kat as if she were from another planet. She sat there with an innocent smile. What could anyone say?

"That sounds possible," David finally remarked, almost as if to appease his mother-in-law.

"Whatever," Lynn added, and that was pretty much that. The topic died.

After dinner, it was time to enjoy the kids, yell at the dogs, yell at the kids, and enjoy the dogs. The girls helped their mother clean up, while us boys drank beer and watched football on television. I could care less about sports, but the atmosphere was family love, and again there were moments I fought back an appreciative tear. It was wonderful, and I dare say, over too soon.

My time at home once again had flown by. It's like time sneaks out minutes, and even hours, to the point where it seems to cheat a person from what they're fully due. I had chores that needed to be done: clean the chimney, re-insulate the well pump, check the heat tapes, and polish off the wood pile by making it a few feet taller. My grandson TJ stayed over for a couple of days to help his Grandpa clear the way and make brush piles. We cut and stacked enough wood to ensure our heating needs for the coming winter would be met. Better to have too much wood than to run out in March, and to have to trudge through snow drifts to go out and cut more. That's a miserable prospect, and one I've had to face more than once in the past.

The other two grandkids stayed over just to keep Grandma happy, giving their parents a break, and providing Kat and I our quota of hugs, kisses, and oh, just a touch of tension. The night before I was to leave would provide the next relaxing moment Kat and I would be able to share with just each other.

We had a quiet dinner under candle light. I told her more of my visit with them; how Jewel had read my palm, and of the healing she does for people. I described their place to her, and told her about Clay, Elbow Jack, and Eddie.

She listened intently enough, giving me little sign of skepticism. The only comment she made was, "And you still think it's him?"

"I know it is," was my sincere reply.

We needed this unwind time. I think she could tell I was fascinated with Jewel but it didn't seem to bother her. We were in a slow down moment, to be sure. The atmosphere was cozy close, warming our hearts. We took the time to dance for a short while to the songs of Sade on our stereo. There was so much love going on in our cabin in the woods that last evening. The family foundation showed stronger than ever in this place where we had raised our babies and struggled throughout our years. A thanks for the giving that couldn't be denied.

## CHAPTER 3

It would prove to be true, that through these holiday weeks, my time on the road would be in short bursts, mostly local assignments. True to her word, Lynn's gift to me that Christmas proved to be a leather-bound, very fine, and probably quite expensive, journal, with the accompanying comment: "Get that autograph!" Was she half-wanting to believe me after all, or just daring me to prove her wrong?

It was 2006 now, and I was back to the steady routine of earning a truck driver's living. The first two weeks out, I was sent through states directly to the south, culminating at the farthest point in Houston, Texas, with loads working me back in the direction of home. To have not gone farther east was disappointing, to be sure, but at the same time, I couldn't expect to always be able to go where I desired, just because I desired it.

The next time out found me headed east, with a load going to New York State, my dismay was only human. Yet after that delivery Darin came through for me once again. Another load of paper products, to be picked up pre-loaded, not far from my last delivery. It was destined for a place called Warehouse Specialists, located in the southern section of New Orleans. This time, if I calculated it right, I could manage a 34-hour restart for a visit with Marcus and Jewel. I was more than excited. It was a feeling, I imagined like the prospect of seeing a long lost family. Again, I would not make any of the phone call arrangements until more certainty prevailed.

The pickup turned out to be as smooth as it gets, no hitches. The time element would allow me the opportunity I was hoping for. Providing there would be no breakdowns or flat tires along the way, I could be there by Sunday afternoon, and not have to run again until Tuesday morning — a little dream vacation that I hoped would come true. I called the warehouse where I was to make this delivery. I inquired as to a safe location to leave my truck.

They assured me it would be safe on-site. One more day down the road and I could dare to make the anticipated call.

My preference now was to try Burton first, only because he was easy to understand. I was having trouble with the language barrier between Clay and myself. This arrangement would need to be understood by all, with no room for those questionable moments when I don't understand a thing Clay is saying. I needed more exposure to that Acadian dialect before I could find any real comfort zone. I did hope that it would happen, that I would have the time to adapt to his way of speaking someday. A day out from my destination, and the time to call came at noon on Saturday. An unfamiliar voice answered.

"Could I speak with Burton please?"

"He's not expected back for a couple hours," was the man's response.

"Thanks, I'll try back then."

"May I ask who's calling?"

"Yes, could you tell him Grant is trying to reach him?"

"I sure will. Is there a number he can reach you at?"

"I'm in and out of range right now, but if he'd like to try." I gave him my cell number.

"I'll give him the message," the gentleman assured me.

I thanked him "kindly," which is the way it's done down South.

It's funny how, when I'm down that way, for some unknown reason to me (especially in Texas) I pick up that southern drawl within a couple days. So noticeable it seems that when I get back home, it's still easily detectable as to where I'd been. Kat says it's just because I'm so impressionable. I can't explain it. It's that south-of-the-Mason-Dixon-Line thing that gets me.

My thoughts now returned to my family's doubts. How could I make this truth somehow incontrovertible to them — find a point where they could not deny? What could I do to relieve these controversial speculations that might go on every time I visited Jewel and Marcus? A solution had to be conceived. It just had to! I've always hated dark spots in my mind like that; call it a cloud. It even tends to make my dreams go bad.

The cell phone rang. It had been less than an hour, but the caller ID told me it was Burton.

"Well Grant, it's been awhile," came his recognizable voice.

"I'll say! How's everything with everyone?"

"Real good! They've come a long way since you've been here last.

I explained my timeframe for a visit, the location of my destination, and my estimated time of arrival.

"Good, Marcus will be glad to hear it. Give me time to relay this and I'll get back to ya."

"Shaw nuff," I told him, trying to spark with the lingo. What I really needed was to get my ears ready for Clay.

After that call, for some reason my ride seemed lighter. I was more awake compared to many afternoons when I tend to get groggy, and more often than not have to stop at a rest area for a 45-minute cat nap. Now I was barreling to the delivery.

I didn't hear back from him at all that day. It was a bit of a come-down to my anticipated rush. I didn't sleep well that night — too much on my mind. I remember making my first journal entry:

*"Jan. 21st, 06. Headed back to see them. Hope to be at their place tomorrow. Have been working on a new song. Maybe he can help me with it. I'm excited!"*

Around 8 a.m. the next morning, I got the call. "Everything's set. Credence will be there to pick you up. I won't be able to come along. I have appointments to keep. I'll have to catch you next time through maybe," Burton said.

I thanked him for everything, and told him I hoped to see him again soon.

"Marcus is excited. It's good to see him in such high spirits. You do something for him, I can tell. He really likes your company," he added.

"The same goes for me too! I can't begin ta tell ya," I replied.

"Drive safe," were his closing words. Once again I had that goose bump thing going on. This was going to be great. I could feel it.

## CHAPTER 4

I knew I had again reached the battle zone. Absolutely nothing had changed. In fact, now it seemed to look even grayer. For many miles before I reached the city, dungeon scars, as if wrought by the very hand of evil, bragged their presence. It was hard for me to hold my composure. Total devastation, no, annihilation; everything was laid to waste. Nearing my delivery location, I saw cars on top of cars. Rubble covered every square foot in many areas. Cleanup efforts showed no progress. Overwhelmed? Or I guessed that, perhaps, this hadn't been a priority sector.

Arriving at my destination, I brought my paperwork to the warehouse, whereupon I was directed to a place for my trailer drop and where I could safely leave Beulah. There was no sign of Credence. I finished filling out my logbook information, then sat as patiently as I could behind the wheel, peering out of my windshield for any sign of the Chrysler.

My overnight bag sat on the passenger seat; my Gibson leaned against it — "please let this happen" I was saying to myself aloud. Then, almost immediately, I saw that familiar dark blue car pull into the lot.

I scurried out of the driver's door and around to the other side. I reached in, grabbed my stuff, and locked her up. I had a smile on my face as wide as a kid going through the gate to a fair, when I turned to see Credence behind the wheel. I got to the car in about two leaps!

"You know how many warehouses these guys have in this town? I'll bet twenty," he said. "Believe me, I found out!"

"Good to see you too," I laughed. "Other than navigational problems, how ya doin'?"

"Good, good. Good to see you."

As we drove from the city, I asked him how their place was coming along, to affirm what I had already heard from Burton, but seeking more detail.

"Good, I guess. I haven't seen it. I haven't been out there since they first came back after the storms. Don't like the water much. I'm a city boy. Don't really see why anyone would want to live in all them weeds and bugs," he smiled.

I could tell he was getting used to me. He was opening up more. I think we were becoming friends. It was a nice departure from my first impressions of him. We were able to talk now.

"How's the home front? Does she still think you're on some mysterious venture?" he asked.

"She doesn't know what to think. And now my whole family thinks the jam slipped off my toast."

He laughed. "It'll work out. Marcus will find a way to clear things up for you. Let him know what's going on," Credence advised.

"I'll talk to him about it, 'cause right now I don't know what to do."

Pulling into the grove at Clay's place spurred my anticipation. Another out-of-this-world adventure was about to take place. Clay was down by the boats with his dog. They walked up to greet us when they saw us pull in. Woogie never barked, she was a tail-wagger. I think that dog was always smiling. That's the impression I got. As for Clay, he was wearing a languor smile, as if tired. He seemed sluggish, although his greeting to me was no less animated.

"Ey brudder, bot' time. T'ought ye gh lost!"

"Too long," I replied with a grin, and I gave him a hearty handshake.

"Yer bon poonahs'r waitin'," he said.

"Wait! I do believe your English has improved," I joked.

He came back with a "Yea ye righ."

"I gotta get you up north, meet you some of our northern girls. Get ya some of a that yankee sweetness." I was hassling him.

"Qui qui, buh ah don lak ta leave dese bayas ur ma playree."

"You will, once ya get a taste of some of that warm northern comfort," I told him.

We were getting a brotherly thing going on. It was a good feeling, the camaraderie we were building between us.

"I'll leave the two of you, and this great debate," Credence interrupted.

I thanked him earnestly, asking if he could be back early on Tuesday morning to give me a ride.

"Be here first thing; see ya then. Have a good time." We shook hands and he got back in his car and then lickety-split, drove out of the grove.

"Hi ya Woogie!" I squatted down and scratched her head and ears. Clay looked down at us sullenly.

"Gah a fvr ta ask ya. Les talk on de boot."

I looked at him mysteriously. What could this be?

The boat ride to their place took on a somber tone. Clay wasn't drinking beer today. He began to tell me how Woogie had been diagnosed by a veterinarian to have tumors, with not much healthy time left. Clay would have to face the day when she would need to be put down. He went on to explain how this was a dog that had been with him for almost 16 years — his protector and his best friend. She had traveled with him everywhere. She had gone shrimping with him a thousand times. They had been together on every bayou you could name and most of the one's that have no names. Then his question came: He wanted to know if I would write a song about her. I didn't have to take time to think about it. I told him I could, that I would be glad to, and that it was the least I could do for them. He smiled in relief, like a load had been lifted. More color appeared back in his face.

We entered the inlet — arrived already. No gators this time, though I guess my focus had been strictly on Clay. I did see a snake slither across the surface of the water. It always amazes me how they can swim. But now we had banked along their shoreline and I was climbing out of the boat. There was no one there to greet me this time.

"Yah knw ah tah ge dere, ah cane stay. Dis coonass ga udder t'ings at ga'a g' ta."

"Sure nuff, I'm good," I assured him.

"See yah ageen wheen'm t'rew."

"Ok bon poonah," I told him. I had asked Credence, and he told me it meant, "good friend."

He smiled widely at that, a smile that beamed with life's light. God, I hoped I could do him good, I remember thinking. His hand gave a strong wave, an undeniably strong man.

As I turned to walk the path toward their house, Jewel came in sight, walking in my direction. The dogs were with her and they saw me at that same time. She stopped their barking almost immediately.

"How are you?" she asked softly, as she approached.

"Real good! Sure glad to be back."

"Did you eat those snacks I gave you?" she asked as she leaned and kissed my cheek.

"Sure did, they were great. Kept me away from a burger or two," I smiled.

"Marcus is taking a nap. I didn't want to wake him just yet. He's been working so hard. He's been anxious to see you. We're excited you can stay longer this time."

With the bag over my shoulder and the guitar case in my hand, we started walking up to the house. When we reached the front porch, she turned to me and quietly said, "There's someone I want you to meet. He's down at the cabin." She half turned, and pointed down the hill. I nodded, and set my things on the ground. "What's your favorite color?" she asked, as we began walking along side each other.

"That's easy, I would have to say the color of my wife's eyes; steel-gray blue."

She stopped in her tracks. Turning to me, she said, "Really, her eyes are that color? They sound enchanting, beautiful!"

"They are, but you should talk," I told her, looking as deeply as I could into hers. She blushed.

"What's she like?" Jewel asked as we continued on.

"I hope you can find out. She's usually the optimist in the family; sees good in everything, but this thing about you guys has her doubting." I tried to explain. "It's not in her nature to be this way. She's my angel on earth — low-maintenance love. Sometimes I know I just don't do all that I should, but she sticks to me like glue; always tries to bring me up."

She stopped walking again. Jewel showed a concern to her lips. "Marcus and I have been talking about it. If Kathryn won't travel with you then we need to go up there or something." She broke into a reassuring smile and turned to walk again.

Now I noticed a fellow sitting on a chair on the porch of the cabin. He was an older, short, rotund black man. His hairline had receded, leaving a round global shining head, which, as we neared, I could see contained beads of perspiration from the top to his brow. He had one of those cross sections of a tree, like those I had seen on the ground, resting on his lap. He was carving on it, using a chisel-type tool, tapping lightly with a small hammer. He looked up at us as we approached. He had big eyes and a wide smile for Jewel, holding that look when he began to ponder me. My first impression was that his head seemed big in relation to his overweight body. A harmless sort — diffidence, a bashfulness emanated.

"Grant, this is Hershel. Hersh, I'd like you to meet our good friend, Grant."

With a smile covering wide across his face, and expanded cheeks past the realm of average, he said nothing.

"Good to meet you Hershel," I told him, reaching out my hand. He looked at my glove, and didn't extend his hand to shake mine, only sat there smiling.

"Hersh has been making our walkways, he's an artist," Jewel explained.

"I saw them up there; they're really great," I told him.

"You'll have to see some of the wind chimes he's done," Jewel said. Turning to him, she said, "I'll be bringing supper down in a little while." He looked up at her and nodded, still holding a smile. In fact, it never left his face.

I gave him a nod and a smile as Jewel and I turned to begin our walk back up the hill. Along the way she explained how Hershel was a "special needs" person, mentally challenged since birth. He could not speak, but understood everything we had said. Jewel explained to me how she had cared for his mother toward the end of her life, and that his mother had asked Jewel if she could care for him just before she passed away. He had been more or less discarded by the rest of his family. She and Marcus were happy to have him here. He gardened for them, their groundskeeper so to speak.

"How come I hadn't seen him till now?" I asked.

"The last time you were here, he was in his little boat out on the marsh. He feels safe there. The truth is, he's scared to death of Jack — full of trepidation. We can't seem to make him feel otherwise. Jack calls him Grunt, because of the sounds he sometimes makes when he tries to talk. Jack can come on mean sometimes, even though he doesn't try to. Anyway, Hersh has been with us over fifteen years. He's Marcus' best audience when it comes to music. He's diabetic, and it's hard caring for him sometimes," she added. Then she sighed.

We were nearing the house now, and there was Marcus, standing on the porch, leaning against a pillar at the top of the steps. He was wearing the hat I had given him and he was smiling. "I see you're wearing another new hat," he said to me.

"I see you're wearing an old one," I joked. It had a band now, made of beads and fabric around the rim. "I like that band," I remarked, pointing to it.

"Jewel made it. Pretty fancy huh?"

"Very cool," I replied.

He came down the two steps and reached out his hand to me. We shook, and again he put his arm around my shoulder, giving a quick, warm squeeze. I looked to my right and saw the greenhouse had been completed, with plants already inside.

"Man, it's good to see you again," he told me.

"You too. The holidays kept me homebound. Got birds in your bedroom yet?" I asked, motioning to the greenhouse.

He laughed. "Wait till ya see what she's done ta the outhouse!"

I glanced over to it, and from where I stood, could plainly see that Jewel had flower beds placed behind rocks piles that circled the ground near the approach. Designed wooden planters had been attached, chest high, on both sides of the door. They were filled with blooming red and white flowers.

"Can't wait," was my reply. God, it was good to be there with them again. I should have said it out loud.

"I see you met Hersh. He's my biggest fan; maybe my only one," Marcus said.

"That's not true," Jewel piped in.

"Where was he the first time I met you guys?" I didn't want to bring up the words, "during the storm."

"He was with Clay, at Clay's brother's place up north. It's a safe haven for all of us sometimes," Marcus explained.

"I'm starting to explain to my family about you guys," I told them. "They want to meet you. They don't believe a bit of this."

"Likely they will soon enough," Marcus replied. "Grab your stuff and bring it in. Man, I'm glad you've got longer this time! Been writing any songs?"

"Workin' on one I'm calling, *Old Ways to Remember*. Wanna help me with it?" I asked.

"Sure, if I can," Marcus smiled.

"I was hopin' you'd say that. Know how sometimes ya get stalled out? That's where I'm at," I explained.

"I've kinda been like that off and on for nearing thirty years," he joked. Jewel looked at him, smiled, turned to me and shook her head. At that, we climbed the stairs of the porch and walked into the house, dogs again at our feet. Something cooking in the oven smelled awfully good. It most assuredly had a way of making me immediately hungry.

"Leave them out," Jewel told Marcus, pointing to the dogs. He re-opened the door and told them to go. They obeyed without hesitation.

"Your room's waiting for you," she told me.

"I'll go put my stuff away," I replied.

"I put the writings you left us on your bed," Jewel added. "I really love what you see and how you say it."

"It was all very good, more insightful than you may realize," Marcus said.

I thanked them for that, then went to the bedroom and set my things on the bed. When I returned to our music room, their living room, Marcus was standing there waiting for me. I saw Jewel with her back to us, busying herself in the kitchen.

"We've got some time, let's go outside," he said. He walked to the door and I followed him out. As I was taking a look around I noticed the porch work had been completed.

I had been to Marcus' birthplace in the past. There was a wooden swing hanging from the porch ceiling there. Now he had one here also, almost a replica. The dogs were hyped, jumping up at him as we stood there. I was sure that they could smell the cooking. "Take a walk with me, will ya?" he asked. I nodded.

We stepped from the porch and headed down the hill toward the cabin. The dogs followed. Hershel wasn't in sight. We veered to the right, just before we reached the work shed near the right side of Hersh's cabin. We came to a thin path between the shrubs. It led further down an incline.

"Watch for snakes and spiders," he instructed.

I followed him between trees and brush, neither of us saying a word. After around fifty yards there became an opening, a clearing of short marshy grass. It stood sparse, with trees that were filled with Spanish moss. Creeping vines were entwining their way through a plethora of vegetation. There were palm trees interspersed through this, almost a "park-like," veritable garden. It appeared to have been well groomed during a prolonged period of time.

We walked past a wooden bench that sat under the umbrella of a willow tree, facing a small lake or pond. Its surface, layered in duckweed, was filled with cattails and huge water lilies, celebrating their way up from the water. There was a small island off to our left. I saw an egret; just like the ones we have back home, standing in the water near the island's shore. A falcon darted past us low. The sound of songbirds, and the deep, low bellowing of bull frogs, coupled with the sharp chirping blends from tree frogs or crickets filled the surrounding air. It was almost deafening. I followed him farther along the bank, then he walked up a few paces from the water's edge, where he abruptly stopped.

"It's beautiful here — a wild specter celebrating itself!" I proclaimed exuberantly.

"I'm glad you think so," he replied. He was looking over and above the tree line at the sky. "Here I watch new sunrises, with clouds that appear and disappear on their translucent voyage." Then he looked back down at me. "This is where I really want my bones to rest," he said, reclining his shoulders. He was apparently referring to his gravesite.

"What? Where?" I quickly interjected.

"Yer standing on it," he casually smiled.

In reflex, I bounded back. Evidently appearing comical, It made him laugh aloud.

"Come, will ya sit with me awhile?" he asked, as he walked a few yards farther up to where two worn and weathered folding chairs were leaning against a tree. He opened them and motioned for me to come and have a seat. I obliged. We sat there without a word, facing the water, just listening. It truly was an enchantingly beautiful and secluded place. There was thunder off in the distance. In that instant, observing the full scope of it, it felt as though I had traveled back 10 million years. I half expected to see a Pterodactyl fly by at any moment.

"It's a slow wind blows through here; mostly moans in blues and greens — laughs in silly yellows sometimes. Cold shadows will mark this spot," he confided with a sigh.

"It's a wonderful place," I assured him. "Does it have a name?"

"Yah, I guess so. It's the place with no name," he grinned. "Here I speak to my God in silent churches, where the only sound is the life breath of my soul." His voice had quieted while he spoke, reining with a soft calmness. It showed that all credit of his faith went to a higher entity. I'll never forget those words; I felt that he had somehow, at that moment, defined his religion for me.

"Is this where Jewel wants to be?" I asked.

"Yes, of course, in the garden of belief. We've both known it for a long time."

I told him my plan had always been to have my ashes scattered on the waters of the St. Croix River, near our cabin. Then they would flow down to where the river flows into the Mississippi. From there they would flow down to the gulf, dump into the ocean, only to circulate around the world and eventually come back to where they started. He just grinned at me without saying a word. Then I had to express to him how his plan was too secret, so hidden — how no one would know.

"Where does a lot of tears over your grave getcha?" he exclaimed. "Our poetry will always rhyme here in the end." He sighed. Then he turned, and with only a slight hint of hesitation, looked at me with an anxious expression. "I need you to do something for us," he said softly with the most sincere look on his face.

"What's that?"

He took in a deep breath. His voice again softened while he exhaled. "We need the truth to be told. We need you to write about it, a book or something, what really happened and who I am now. I guess that's what I'm asking."

I stood up immediately, almost leaped, as though my leg muscles repulsed. I took a few steps toward the water. I felt odd quakes in my knees. I don't think I was breathing. "What?" I managed to convulse, as I faced the lake.

Turning, I looked hard at him. "You know, Clay asked me to write a song about his dog. That I think I can do. Are you saying a book? No, I can't do that! I've only read a handful in my life and they put me to sleep. In truth, I could count the number of books I've read on one hand. I wouldn't know the first thing!" Standing resolute, I found myself reacting sharply, in jagged remarks. A light rain was beginning to fall. Evening was settling on us, and on this place.

He stood and walked over to me, smiling. He looked up at the sky. "Rustic clouds standing in the way of arrogant thunder," he said. Looking back down to where our eyes met, he gave me such a hard, enduring stare. "Jewel and I've perused your writings and your style transverses our needs. We talked about it, you can. We've thought long and hard, and neither of us wants to pass in obscurity — giving all our best occasions to the memory of the wind. She wants you to be the one. We both do."

"But I can't. I'm sorry, really. No, I can't," I implored him, my expression trying not to appear to be retreating from my stance. I was attempting to hold onto strong resolve. I felt a fissure to my heart. "When I read a book, it puts me to sleep," I reiterated. "That's how I'd write one, too." Trying hard, I bared a half- dissolving smile, not intending to be so sternly disobliging.

He put his right hand on my shoulder, assurance in his touch. Faith shown through, in his eyes wide opened. "Just write what you're going through right now, and it'll tell its own story. If it becomes a book, it'll be a book. Just look deep into the edges of belief." He now seemed, as if with concern, to almost be humbly asking.

"I wouldn't know where to begin. Why don't you write it?" I asked, trying in that desperate moment to make him stop. How could he be so brazenly presumptive? I could sense I had a weak hold on my persuasion.

He kept a deep, calmly dimpled smile as he said, "Just start at the beginning. Look at us and stretch a crazy way. I'm the pirate gonna be chasing your dreams back and forth on your sea. Gonna come all the way across my ocean to make the waters roll."

What in the world was he talking about, speaking in such confusing discourse? It felt evermore crazy, an uncomfortable place. We were getting wet now. I felt cold. He had to be realizing this awkward discomfort.

"You know, we can't even hope to catch a glimpse of our tomorrows. All we can do is let our beginnings be," he said. "Just think it over awhile." He then turned toward the path. "If it's God's will," I heard him mutter. I walked behind him with a numbness that defies words. I couldn't even think. I was just stumbling along.

"There's a hot bed simmering on this earth tonight. The noises in our storm will cross over it," I heard him say, not turning his head as we walked. We were starting to get really wet now. It drew my senses back to me. I was thinking, he brought me to this esoteric position for what? I wasn't angry, more like stunned. I tried to humor myself. Here was the most praised character ever to walk the face of this earth, under Jesus, Muhammad, Buddha, the saints and prophets. And now he wants to go naked before the world? I laughed out loud at the thought of it. He slowed, cocked his head in a half-turn and winced at me. I asked myself, "Think he's wondering what that was all about?" I smiled mischievously. He noticed, but said nothing. Thus I entertained myself with more thoughts, examining the peculiarity of this moment. "I think he's worried now that I won't do it. He has a right to be. Besides, is he impervious to the shock waves it would cause?"

We reached their front yard. He stopped and turned to me. "All our supplies come by boat now. Before, there was a way by land, sort of a Robin Hood path through the swamp woods." I could tell he needed to move my mind away from what we had just gone through.

"That must be hard," I warmly expressed back to him.

"You hungry? I think she has supper ready."

"Excitedly so," I told him, trying to bring us back to a level of comfort. I needed him to understand that I wasn't upset; just not confident. My self-esteem about such an endeavor was low; convinced for the moment that it was something I could never do. My temperament had eased. At the time, I sided with the idea of it being more of a joke.

As we neared the porch we could see Jewel appearing through the kitchen window, disappearing, then reappearing again.

"She paces like an unanswered queen," Marcus said.

## CHAPTER 5

Dinner was served in much the same elegance as it previously had been. A setting of candlelight and warm food — again fulfilled by her exquisite presence.

There were brown shrimp in a white gravy sauce. "This is 'la grue' (cheddar cheese grits)," she explained. "These are Creole onions, and collard greens," she pointed. And there was French bread.

All through the beginning of our dinner, we sat quietly. I was filled with repose, relaxed in their company. I felt sure she knew he had asked me. She, too, was silent now. In fact, no one made a peep. It felt a little strange. I had to break this silence. "Could use your help on that song," I reminded him.

"Sure, if I can. Be glad to. You got writers block?" Marcus asked, breaking into a grin.

Jewel giggled impulsively, but continued looking down at her food. Marcus had a dumb smile while looking over to me. It was instantly infectious. I laughed, and then we all did. I composed myself briefly.

"Yah, now that ya mention it, I guess I do!"

We all seemed, once again, to be comfortable with each other.

"It's kind of a song about you, ya know?" I informed Marcus.

"Really not sure I can help you out with that then," he continued to smile.

"It's funny that you asked me what you did out there, now that I think about it. I mean, especially with me writing a song like this."

"Can't wait to hear what you've got so far."

"That makes two of us," Jewel added.

I had known for some time that I couldn't finish this song by myself. The inspiration came from meeting him. The secret was, he had to open up and add the parts only he could tell. I figured there was no other way to finish it. It was meant to draw him out, try to discover things I did not yet know. I hadn't planned it that way; it's just how it happened. It had the makings of a good song, and I couldn't let this opportunity pass by.

Maybe he had an inkling when he asked, "You get stumped like this on many songs you write?"

"Not usually," I said. "But some take months. Others I can do in one sitting. The song about Woogie shouldn't take long."

"It's sad; she's been his best friend for so long," Jewel said.

"Yah, she's outlasted all his other girls," Marcus added.

Jewel looked at him and smiled. "He'll miss her more than any of them too!"

"There's a lot of songs I'd like to cover with you," Marcus said to me. "Got a bunch up my sleeve."

I was excited to hear that. Who knew where all of this was going? Yet again, I wondered about what he had asked of me out there. He wouldn't settle for my definite "no," and I don't do torment well. There had to be a resolution, and sooner than later. I'm also not good at dishing out disappointment. This was a quagmire that wasn't about to let me relax until I could close the topic.

Dinner was now finished, and he just couldn't wait to get to the living room (our music room), and commence with the goins' on. By the time I had unpacked my guitar from its case, he was already playing, *Waitin' On A Blue Moon*, one of his originals. I hadn't even been given time to tune up.

When he finished the song, I said, "Man, I like that one. Why haven't you tried to go someplace with this stuff?"

"I do, straight to my lover's arms," he replied.

Again, I could hear Jewel's cute little giggle. We were once again warming to the place that can, so often, be hard to find. It's the place that makes musicians click instead of stumble. I wanted to get right to it. "I call this one, *Old Ways to Remember.* It has an introspective approach. I'm trying to make it bounce back and forth from the then and now. That's what's so hard for me," I explained.

He reached across the table for a pen and paper. "Play me what you've got," he instructed. Jewel was at the kitchen sink, washing dishes. She turned and looked at me, then smiled. I went through the first verse and stopped. He had been writing. "Can you play that again?" he asked. I did so, only to continue on to the second verse, and up to where the song had stalled out. I hadn't accomplished the bridge or final verse. "This is good, but I need to hear that last part again," he said. I ran through the whole thing once more. "Okay, give me a little time with this; it has good makings. I wanna run through it alone for a while," he explained. "I've got some ideas poppin'."

"No problem, take whatever time ya need," I told him.

"It sounds serious, but good. Seriously good," Jewel remarked, walking toward us. "It's not a love song though, is it?"

"No, I guess it's really not a love song, but I don't mean for it to be a heartbreaker either. Just a thinking song," I tried to explain. Marcus smiled over at me.

"You got time for one babe?" he asked Jewel.

"In a minute. Let me finish up," she replied, then turned back to wipe off the table.

He started playing another song I didn't recognize. I tried finger-picking along to his chording. It was a country number through and through, lively, with a fairly quick tempo. It turned out to be called, *Bust My Britches.* I don't know if he intended it to be humorous, but I found it to be. I followed that one up with one I had written many years ago, meant to be a spoof on trucking and country music, called *Tears in My Gears.* I could tell they were starting to have fun — so was I.

For a short while we were trading numbers back and forth. I'd play any old song that would pop into my head and I think he was doing the same. We were warming up. The dogs lay calmly on the floor by our feet, half sleeping, just as they had the time before. I lost track of Jewel, until she reappeared holding a fancy light green glass bottle topped with a cork. She set it on the table in front of us, then went to the wall and pulled down the banjo. Marcus and I were between songs while she strummed, turning its tuners, finding a perfect open 'G' chord.

"I didn't know you could play," I remarked to her.

"I'm just a baby banjo player," she said, with a shy expression.

"Have a pull off this," Marcus said, as he handed the bottle across to me.

"What is it?"

"It's my home perfection," Jewel said. "I call it, Thin Ice."

I pulled the cork out and took a cautious sip. It had the taste of honey and licorice, along with some flavors unrecognizable. It smelled of flower blends, and fragrances I couldn't put my finger on. It was sweet, melting on my tongue leaving little to swallow. That is until, as I later found out, your tongue gets drunk and has its fill. "Ooo that's good! What's in this?" I had to inquire.

"Absinthe for one thing and other secrets; don't be shy, have another," Marcus insisted. And so I did and passed the bottle to Jewel. She followed my lead and passed it on to Marcus. He actually took more than a sip.

"Shall we do one for him?" he asked her. She nodded.

They began their song together, *As the Waves Roll Out,* he on guitar, her on the banjo. He sang the first verse; *"Feel the way you rise and fall, by the drumbeat of your heart / Holding to this magic kiss, you caress the tinder spark / Flaming strings on some wild guitar, pull your spirit from the edge of doubt / Oh how your eyes run deep, when the waves roll out."*

I sat astonished, stupefied you might say, by this mysterious, deep melody. Its lyrics pulled me in. She began singing the second verse. There came a swirling spell — her voice, entrancing, mystical, bewitchingly beautiful, haunting each word. There are those rare moments when you hear a song for the first time and it slams your chest like a sock to the heart. You know right then and there that it'll be a favorite of yours for the rest of your lifetime. How should I explain, it was prodigiously enamoring. I was besieged by the beauty of her moment. So much so, that I wasn't concentrating on the words, more on their delivery.

She had sung something about falling into a dark-end street where silence holds their vow. And something about an alluring breath connecting a dream that brings kisses with a deliverance mouth. I don't know, I don't exactly remember. Maybe I have it wrong. There was a line where she finds him where her soul desires the drumbeat of his heart. The last line went something like, *"the seed knows when the moon will glow, so the waves roll out."* It flabbergasted me! Unable to contain my exuberance, I had to tell them that it was the best love song ever written.

"No it's not, but I have one that might be," Marcus teasingly replied.

"Hard to believe you can top that!" I resounded. "Man, how can there be better? When the top of the summit is reached, then there it is." He handed the bottle back to me. "Sure, I'll have another swig off that," I said.

"You're playing on thin ice now, son," he laughed.

I had to admit, my senses were going light-hearted — that "dance the night away" feeling. It was turning into some real fun. The night was rearing it's beautiful head. Jewel played along to almost everything we did after that. We were passing the bottle between songs, and I'd keep saying, "Alright, I'll have another swig off that," and "Yah, give me one more swig." That's how it happened. Marcus stood up suddenly, so abrupt it somewhat startled Jewel and I. He leaned his guitar against the side of his chair.

"I've got it now!" he exalted, as he sat down, leaning back and putting his hands behind his head. "Your name's gonna be, Hatty Swiggs!"

I had just taken a drink and almost blew it out of my nose. My eyes bugged out. "Nail on the head, Marcus," I managed to say, half-choking.

Jewel laughed loudly. "You've got it," she exclaimed.

"I told you I owed you one," Marcus emphatically said, looking across at me and grinning.

"Have another swig there Hatty." Jewel told me, laughing again.

"Let's go, you guitar-pickin' maniac," I replied back at him, and I began playing, *Gotta Travel On* by Billy Grammer. He knew the words. We shared the verses. Jewel played along exuberantly. We laughed together at the end. Our night flew by. Songs shimmered their dance with the candle light.

I realized it was time to retire, after I stood and fairly floated outside to find a tree. I had no idea what time it was, for I had laid my watch on the bed stand earlier. The sky had cleared and the stars were swirling like a Van Gogh painting. I looked up at the show for I don't know how long, then found my way back inside. It was clear to each of us that this magical night had been spent. There would be a tomorrow. We left our instruments where they were, and bid each other a warm and touching, "goodnight."

Once alone in my bedroom, exhaustion tried to overtake me, yet I felt unsettled. It was hard to just lie down, but I would try. Attempting to focus on things around the room, it wasn't working very well. I reached for my journal and a pen in my bag, put my feet up and leaned into a comfortable position on the pillows.

Journal entry: early a.m., 1/23/06:

*He has asked more of me than I am. My spirit will be laid asunder to rock these waves home! What am I supposed to do? They're asking to be exposed, brought back to life in some remittance dance they want to give to the world. I don't see it. They should leave this peace be, this place where cloaks and daggers lay more stilled than they know. It'll only be trouble out there. My soul longs now to be an awakened sigh.*

I fell back low in the pillows. Through the window screen, I made out the hooting sound of an owl, way off in the distance. In the middle of a deep breath, I closed my eyes.

## CHAPTER 6

The sun was high in this winter's sky when next these eyes re-opened. I had left the shade up and everything was too bright. The lantern was still burning on the table beside my bed. My journal lay open beside me. I had slept with my clothes on. Now it was an effort for me to sit up, and could hear myself groan. I was blurry-eyed and off-balance. My mouth was cotton dry. Objects seemed obscure and out of focus. The colors of things were a tinge different than I had ever seen. "I feel snake bit," I moaned a half-whisper to myself. My head fell back on the pillows like a rock. I lay there awhile, opening and closing my eyes, trying to clear the fogginess. "Man!" I said, then left them closed and fell back asleep.

When I opened them again, I stretched across the bed, in what felt like slow motion, to retrieve my watch — 11:40. Everything was quiet. I sat up a little easier this time. I managed to lift my legs over the side of the bed. Slowly, cautiously, I stood up…not as bad as I feared. I sat back down, reached for my boots and slipped them on. I had to go out and see what was happening.

Marcus was just outside my door, seated at his guitar-playing chair and reading a book. I found myself holding the door frame. He looked up at me and said, "I once had trouble with sleepwalking, but never sleep dancing like you."

"What?" I uttered.

"Just kidding, how ya doin'?" he replied.

"Whoooow." I put my hand on top of my head.

"That rough, huh?" he smiled.

"No, I guess not really, but what hit me? I ain't never had this before."

"You'll get used to it. It's just whirlwinds of the ever after," he grinned. "Let's step out for some air. Grab a cup of coffee." I was glad to. I went over to the kitchen counter and helped myself. He waited for me by the door.

Once outside, I noticed it had rained during the night. Everything was wet. The air smelled fresh with the fragrance of clean vegetation. It held a clear sweetness. My focus was coming back. I was lightheaded but my stomach felt fine. I just wanted to stand there and breathe for a minute. The dogs were quietly meandering around the yard. I could see Hershel sitting on his cabin porch.

"Let's go say good morning," Marcus said, when he saw me looking down the hill. He started walking in that direction.

"Just a sec, I need a tree," I told him. He stood waiting while I walked around to the side of the house, and behind a large old tree. After a minute, I scurried to rejoin him.

"Where's Jewel?" I asked, as I trailed in his footsteps.

"Clay picked her up awhile ago. They'll be back soon. Some people needed her help. She goes out a couple times a week like this, on her rounds, so to speak. She's my little medicine girl," he said proudly. "For her, it's a blessing and a curse," he added.

"Why do you say that?" I asked.

"Sometimes she learns more about people and their lives than she really wants to know, a precursor to the dark side of things. It takes more than a little out of her when she gives that much. She says it's her lot in life, her heritage to do this. It saddens her to know she'll be the last one to carry it on. After her, there's no one else in the family."

I had nothing to say in response, as we approached the cabin.

"Jonah in the belly of his whale," Marcus said, pointing up at Hershel.

Hersh stared at me with those wide-open round eyes and that smile as big as his face. He was carving on one of his wooden circles. "Good morning," I said to him. He just kept looking at me. There were chairs nearby him and Marcus grabbed one, pulling it up alongside Hersh, then sat down. I followed his lead, pulling a chair up next to Marcus that faced them both. I took a seat.

"We seal and varnish these when he's done before we lay them in the ground. He re-varnishes them about once a year. They hold up really well, aye Hersh?" Marcus smiled at him. Hersh smiled at him, expression unchanged, then back down at his work. He continued to notch away on his design, with the tap of a small hammer and his tiny chisel.

"You do great work," I told him. "These designs are outstanding!" He didn't look up. We sat there, quietly relaxed in the moment, Marcus and I sipping our coffee.

In that silence, thoughts were breaking through to me. I felt a need to explore aloud, questions he had evoked in me. "About this writing thing. There's really not much to write about," I told him, trying to negate this whole matter. "I don't really know nothin'."

"You know where you've been, that'd be a start. We can fill in the blanks as you go," Marcus responded. He wasn't going to let me off the hook.

"And that'd be a book?" I asked.

"I think so, once it all gets told," he said.

"I don't see how, I tell ya. I would need to know a whole lot more. You'd need to tell me so much more."

"Does this mean yer willing to give it a try?" he asked.

"I don't know, no, I mean I just don't see how. I need time to think. Besides, I doubt any publisher would be interested, I mean, what makes you think anybody's gonna believe this? I don't even believe it half the time," I laughed.

"All I know is that my spirit won't rest unless this gets done — needs to come full circle. It doesn't matter how long it takes. There really is no hurry. I'm not even concerned if it ever does get published, or if anyone reads it, let alone believes it. But I do have faith that it'll all come to pass. Right now, all I know is, it has to be told. All we would ask is that there be no cursing or swearing in your writings. You wouldn't be able to give out this location or Jewel and Clay's last name. Oh, and not the names of our dogs, either."

"Why's that?" I asked.

"They're great little watch dogs, but when you call them by name they stop barking. Maybe you've noticed?"

"Oh yah, I have." I said.

"We need them to bark if anyone were to come around."

Again, we sat quiet for a time. Hersh never looked up, but somehow I felt he was gathering in all that we had been talking about.

"I would need a tape recorder to help me to remember," I finally remarked.

"That'd be good! We should record the songs, too!"

"What about a camera?" I asked.

"No, I don't think we're really ready for that," he replied without hesitation. "I'll talk to Jewel about it, but I'll tell you one thing: You'll never be able to take a picture of Clay. In fact, to the best of our knowledge, it's never been done."

"He's never had his picture taken? I can't believe that," I declared.

"You bring out a camera and he'll disappear. Maybe it's that old Native American thing about stealing the spirit. I just know he acts scared to death of them. He's never let it happen and he never will."

"Wow!" I exclaimed.

"I'll bet I've had a million pictures taken of me, but I can tell you with certainty, there are no known photographs of Clay."

"I guess I've never heard anything like that before," I said.

"He's a one-of-a-kind, all right," Marcus replied.

"So what would you want out of this book endeavor? I mean what do you really expect of me?" I asked, trying to sound sincere.

"I just know it needs to be done and I'm quite sure that I can't do it myself. Jewel and I have talked about it for a long time. It needs to have an outside perspective, to be told right. You're perfect, God sent. I guess the best way for me to try to explain it is that my soul has told me its need to come full circle. Jewel understands, and that's why she's willing to sacrifice whatever it takes to get it done. She knows that it's you too. So I'm asking you to try. We're asking you to try." He looked at me then with sullen eyes, a look that I hadn't actually seen from him before. It reminded me of a look my dad once gave me when he asked if I was on drugs. I lied to him then, and said that I wasn't. I still regret that lie. I believe it was the only one I ever told him. And that lie tarnished my life more than the truth ever would have. But now, as Marcus looked at me, there was no lie to tell. I couldn't even muster up a good excuse. I remember leaning back and tilting my head to the side, biting at my lip, and not smiling.

"I don't take many things haphazardly," I told him. "This is serious, what you're asking of me. You can probably tell, I'm torn. I can't bring myself to say yes."

He lightly slapped my thigh. "We're gonna pull your spirit from the sand and the sand from your spirit, m'boy," he smiled. Great! Now he was even sounding like my dad.

Just then the dogs that had been lying at our feet stood up, both looking toward the bayou's main waters. A split-second later I could hear the faint sound of a boat motor.

"That them?" I asked.

"At'd be my guess," Marcus replied. He looked in my eyes. "I can understand your concerns about this thing. Just don't start out so serious. Silver bullet words will come. You're gonna surprise yourself."

I was still not smiling. He doesn't even know me, I thought. Why was this happening? I was having trouble piecing together how all of this had, indeed, come about. I heard the motor shut off. "Let's talk about this later. I've got some thinking to do," I told him.

"Shaw nuff," was his simple reply.

Again we sat there in silence. You could hear the sounds of blending wind-chimes off in the distance. Hersh had never looked up during any of this conversation. He appeared engrossed in his creation. I noticed his tongue was half hanging out.

Just then the dogs ran off the porch toward the inlet. Within seconds, Jewel came into view, followed a few seconds later by Clay. Now Hersh stopped what he was doing and looked up. As they walked into the yard, I noticed them both carrying beer cases, which later turned out to be filled with grocery supplies. They set them down, turned, and walked toward us. We stayed in our chairs as they approached.

"Aye Atty," Clay called out to me, with a big grin.

"Word travels fast 'round here," I shouted back to him. I turned and smiled at Marcus. "Guess it's set in stone," I said to him.

"Shaw nuff," he repeated with a grin.

As they came near, Jewel's flowing radiance overtook all space. She wore beadwork embellishing across her forehead, stunningly beautiful. She was wearing a pearl necklace with a matching bracelet that encircled her left wrist three times. She had an intricately beaded and brightly shimmering cloth bag on her left side that was strapped around her neck and under her arm. Around her waist, on her right side, attached to a woven multi-colored belt, was a matching smaller bag. It was hanging low over her hip. I noticed from that moment forward that she always had that bag hanging there. A bright yellow butterfly was fluttering about her. "She's always a new and exciting sight to behold," I was telling myself. Yet I couldn't help but notice her tired smile.

"Writin' a song bot dis cabane galerie?" Clay asked.

"Good idea," Marcus retorted. "Where'd you step?" referring to the mess all over Clays' boots.

"Yah ye righ," Clay said, looking down at them.

"He's been in boue pourrie," Jewel responded, adding; "He's not comin' in the house with those, and his socks probably smell just as bad!" We all laughed. Hershel smiled as though he understood. She reached up and handed Hershel a small brown paper bag. He opened it slightly, tilting his head to the side, peeking in with his right eye. Then he looked up at her and they both smiled. Jewel nodded, and he nodded back. "Have y'all had breakfast?" she asked, still looking at Hershel.

"He didn't get up till lunch," Marcus said, referring to me.

"I still ain't up," I replied.

"Just tryin' ta bring him 'round with coffee," Marcus laughed.

"I'll put together some crab patty sandwiches; that'll snap him out of it," Jewel said.

"He's gonna do it," Marcus said to her, motioning with his head toward me. She looked at him, then glanced at me, smiling. Without another word, she turned and began walking back to where they had set their beer cases down. I turned to Marcus and gave him a look like, "where did you get that?"

"C'est bon," Clay said. I had no idea what that meant. To this day, I can't decipher half of what Clay says.

"If yer stayin' for lunch, I guess you're gonna eat outside," Marcus said to Clay, then looked over at me, adding, "Let's come back down here with our guitars, eat lunch, and play a few for Hersh."

"Sounds good," I told him.

"Mais qui," Clay said.

"Be right back," Marcus said to Hershel as we rose from our chairs. He didn't respond — just kept tapping. The three of us started walking up the hill. Clay went over and retrieved the other beer case as we were heading toward the house.

"M'ungry fer mudbugs," Clay said.

"What?" I said.

"Those are crawfish," Marcus explained. "Squeeze the head juice on corn, mix it with a little butter and pepper, mmm."

"Whoa," was all I managed to say. "What's next?" was what I was thinking. Every bit of this seemed like a new lifetime.

## CHAPTER 7

Walking onto the front porch, Clay turned to me and said, "Ha ya lak dis galerie?"

"He means the porch," Marcus had to explain.

"It turned out great!" I exclaimed. "I can't help but notice the porch swing. It's nearly identical to the one you had on the porch where you were born," I told Marcus. In truth, it looked identical, but I didn't say that.

"That was more Jewel's idea," he said. "I do love it though. I don't remember any swing way back when, just chickens, and oh yah, a cow. I remember a lot about Mom and me. She picked cotton, ya know?"

"No, I didn't know that," I told him.

"She was older than Dad. She gave everything to me. I tried to give it all back to her too."

I saw reminiscing take shape in his face. I could sense he was going to go on and on with this, maybe not in a positive way. I felt like changing the subject.

"Your greenhouse looks finished. It sure turned out nice."

"She's already growing her remedies and favorite flowers," Marcus responded.

Clay took a chair, a can of beer in hand, and leaned back. The dogs lay down right up next to his feet, probably thinking he had food, but they were cautiously sniffing his boots.

"Is it really part of your bedroom?" I asked Marcus, referring to the greenhouse.

"There's that door you see on the outside. It's our outside bedroom wall. Come on, I'll show ya." He motioned for me to follow him into the house.

As we passed Clay, I looked at him with a smile. He just shrugged his shoulders and smiled back. I think he was finding it humorous that he couldn't go inside. I know I was.

It was an immediate turn to the right once we were inside. He opened the door, showing me a rather simple bedroom, brightly illuminated by the glass wall of the greenhouse connection. There was a large, antique wooden bed with an intricately carved headboard, probably hand-carved. There were matching night stands on each side. Both stands had oil lamps on them. The one nearest to us had a small jar on it, which he picked up, extending it out to me in the palm of his hand.

"My drug of choice these days," he said. "She rubs it around my temples each night before bed — soothes my sleep. Haven't had a headache or bad dream in all these years." Jewel appeared in the doorway just then. A poignant glare of laxity spun across her eyes. It was as if he had just divulged a secret. He didn't seem to notice her there, and just as suddenly, she vanished. He set the jar down on the night stand, never having handed it to me. I continued to look around the room.

There were two dressers that matched in wooden design. But one had a mirror attached, with a chair tucked under the middle, between the drawers. It was located against the wall to my left. An open closet was located to the far right. The other dresser simply had four drawers, and was located against the wall by the foot of the bed. There were three oil paintings on canvas, simply framed, two above the headboard and a larger one hanging on the wall above the second dresser, near the door right next to us. The two paintings above the bed were of swirling flowers, as though they were being blown by the wind. The one nearer to me was that of a small lake. There were grasslands surrounding it. It looked very much like the place with no name. It also had the swirling-wind movement to its painting style, and a clouded sky. They resembled a combination of all of the impressionists — dotted patterns, brilliant colors, and bold brush strokes fading to soft imagery. Everything in the room seemed immaculately clean and tidy. Nothing was strewn about or out of place.

"Who's the artist?" I asked him.

"Jewel. She likes to paint a living earth that knows no suffering. In fact, that's all she'll ever paint."

"I could have guessed these were hers; they're wonderful," I said.

"We could have birds in here if we left that open," Marcus chuckled, motioning to the glass door that opened to the outside. "She had them in the last one, and they were quite tame. They would land on her shoulders and her hands. She fed them by hand. They'll be in here soon enough. She insists that they tell her things. They sure won't talk to me. She can hear a broken branch scream. Flowers bring her music."

"These paintings tell me that would be true," I said to him.

He smiled, putting his hand on my shoulder for a brief second, he turned, stepping back out to the kitchen. I followed. He stood by the table for a moment watching Jewel preparing sandwiches. Turning toward me he said, "Let's tune up." I nodded, and we walked back to the music room. He sat in his same chair. He's become a creature of habit, I thought. I passed my tuner to him and he started tuning that old Martin. I tuned to each of his strings as he went along. We were on the money in less than a minute. I was about to be stunned.

Looking over to me, he said, "Here's the one." Then he began to play and sing what would turn out to be called, *The You in Me.* It was the most fantastic love song I have ever heard in my life. Jewel stopped what she was doing, turned, and looked at me with a smile. I think I was expressionless, unless my mouth was agape. The melody was astonishing, words blazoned with passion. An inextinguishable fire presented itself. His voice ignited, like nothing I had ever heard from him.

Grasping at the words with all the memory I could muster was challenging, confounded by the most excited moment in my life's musical recall. Maybe seeing The Beatles live in concert when I was a kid was almost as impressive, but this was over the top. I could touch it. It was touching me, like nothing I can express in words. Somewhere in the song, I remember these words; *I want to run my fingers along your face / where the shadows capture amazing grace / and the moonlight filters its loving trace / on the raptures perfect hiding place.* On he sang, asking his darlin' to put her hand in his, and how they would go dancing with all new rhymes for her, just for her. The song swelled with romance as it went along, and I couldn't believe a song could be so strong. When it ended, I couldn't say a thing. I just looked at him. He knew it had an impact. I wonder if he knew I was knocked out.

"We're gonna run down and play a few for Hersh," he called out to Jewel from across the room.

"I'll bring lunch down," she called back.

"Thanks, babe." He told her. It was exactly what I would have said to Kat.

But there I was, motionless. What had just transpired was a mystical experience. I knew right then what had to be done. I would need to begin writing. There would be no more hesitation. I was overwhelmed with the need to capture all of this. Without any doubt in my mind, the power struck my being like a moth to a flame. There's no other way to describe it, only that

I had the need to record all of this in any way possible. That realization encased me. It took over my destiny. Looking back, I wonder if he somehow knew that playing that song for me would be the convincing factor. I can't help but believe he did. Nothing in music before, or since, has ever felt so strong, so affecting. The world has to hear this, I thought in my excitement.

He got up from his chair and looked down at me, smiling. "Ready?"

"Ah yah, sure." I was in stunned adoration, realizing again, as I looked up at him, who it was that now stood before me. I had become settled in a comfortable space. Idolatry had been all but erased. It had simply been a familiar atmosphere of friendship. But this moment had reminded me, no, shocked me, back to the fact that I was in the presence of greatness. It gave me an out-of-body experience, once again me looking down on myself and wondering how in the world I had gotten there. I slowly stood up, guitar in hand, and numbly followed him to the door. I glanced at Jewel as we walked by. She looked into my eyes. Her eyes were twinkling; she completely understood what had just transpired in me.

We walked out on the porch. Clay was still sitting there. I know he had to have heard that song through the screen door. I turned to look at him and was greeted by that grin of his. I figured he knew everything that was going on. He got up and followed us, dogs underfoot, as we made our way down to where Hershel was still sitting, carving away. He looked up, that same huge smiley face greeting the three of us as we sat down around him. Marcus and I started strumming our guitars without any real focus, just searching for a trigger.

"I jus gotta play this," I said, breaking from my trance and starting the song, *Jambalaya*, by Hank Williams. Marcus joined in and we shared verses. Clay even joined in the chorus, although he seemed to be a little tone deaf. We all sounded as "hick" as we could. Hank would have been proud. It was a real warm-er-upper. Now songs started clicking in my head. Sometimes my mind goes blank when I pick up my guitar. I can't seem to think of anything to play. That hasn't happened around Marcus. He invokes music to the point where I can't seem to play enough. I started running down my memory list, playing songs, some old, some fairly new, with Marcus strumming and adding vocals to what he knew. This went on for a half dozen songs or more. We were out to entertain Hershel. Then Marcus played one of his originals called, *Guess I've Got to Know*.

"I need to record these," I said to him when he had finished.

"I need you to record all the ones I've written, and to learn them too," was his reply.

His comment surprised me a little. I wondered why he felt that way, but I didn't say anything. I think Hersh was enjoying our jam session. I know Clay was.

"I needja ta play ageen dat sickle song fer mon be'be'," he said to me.

"Which baby is that? You've got a dozen," Marcus scoffed, glancing over at me with a wink.

"Yah ye righ, ah cane elp mon gris-gris," Clay replied. "Oil dem filles' belle!"

Marcus just looked at him, slightly shaking his head. I saw Jewel come out of the house carrying a beer case and heading our way. I had no idea what time of day it had gotten to be. When she joined us on the porch, she opened the case, producing a large glass jar of lemonade. Next came grapes and sandwiches, then glass cups for our drinks. She set everything on a low wooden table that was in front of us along the porch wall, then pulled up a chair next to me.

"Help yourselves," she said, then turned to me. "This should cure your ills Hatty."

I looked into her smiling eyes, then reached over and picked up a sandwich. Marcus and Clay were doing the same. Hersh actually placed his carving at his feet and followed our lead, timidly helping himself. I had never eaten a crab patty sandwich before. I had to compliment the taste, although my appetite didn't seem to be on normal ground. I knew it had to be near mid-afternoon, but I didn't feel that hungry. The sandwich and a few grapes were more than I needed. The ozone feeling I had awoken with that morning was fading, slowly being replaced by normalcy. I was first to pick up the guitar again. I had found that Marcus eats much slower than I do. Clay, on the other hand, inhales it.

"Maybe you've heard this one before," I said, as I began *Waiting on a Friend*, by the Rolling Stones. After I finished, I was surprised to find they hadn't. Clay nodded that he had. Marcus expressed how much he liked it by slapping my knee with an accompanying grin. He really shows his dimples when he smiles like that. I immediately followed that song up with another, more recognizable Stones song: *Wild Horses*. This one they had all heard before and Jewel said she appreciated my slower acoustic rendition. I was tired inside, knowingly not giving these songs "my all." Still, we were relaxed, fully enjoying each other and this special moment. Marcus would rarely initiate someone else's work, nor any of his old material, yet he enjoyed it when I did, always adding his own special spice to what was being played. It goes without saying how much flavor he added when he sang them with me. For the most part, we played everyone's stuff except our own that afternoon.

Now had come the time of day I would learn to recognize as Marcus' nap time. I learned that he did this for an hour or so, almost daily.

"What say we pick this up when the sun sinks a bit?" he suggested to me.

"At'd be good," I responded. "I could use a good stretch and a walk around."

"Merci beaucoup," Clay said to Jewel, referring to lunch and throwing his used napkin in the beer case. Then he nodded a thanks to Marcus and me for all the entertainment. I hadn't actually found his boots to be too pungent. "Dis ol Carencro t'inks a ga ge dis pauvre ass fadder un. Ah see ya an de morn brudder," he told me.

"Kinda early," I responded. He nodded that he understood.

"I have a café au lait made up for you before you go," Jewel told him.

"Sure," he replied as he rose from his chair.

All three of them stood up then, but I remained seated with Hershel.

"Think I'll play a couple more for this guy," I told them, as I briefly put my hand on Hersh's shoulder. He had finished eating and was back to doing his carving, but he looked up at me with an authentic smile. I knew I had a friend.

"Sure, good," Marcus said. "I'll catch up to ya in a bit."

I nodded to them and smiled, as they went their way. Marcus looked tired. I came to find him to be in that state on most of our days at around that time. They all went up to the house together. Jewel's arm was wrapped in Marcus' while they walked. Their dogs were running circles around them. I had noticed they never fed the dogs at the same time we ate. As much as those dogs hinted, I'm sure they had come to expect their feeding time was to be a separate event. They were always well behaved, never out of control, although sometimes they were more excited around Clay.

After a brief moment, I saw Clay re-emerge from the house with a cup in his hand. He gave us a wave with his arm and turned toward the inlet. I waved back wholeheartedly. Hershel never looked up.

Now it was just Hersh and me. It was very quiet, but for the slight chipping sounds of tiny wood pieces giving way to the light tapping of his small hammer. He was in a relaxed, trace-like state of concentration, his tongue sticking out of his mouth. Then I heard the faint sound of Clay's boat motor revving up in the main channel. As I sat there, nothing came to mind to play during this shared silence. Then all at once one came to me. I sang and played the song, *The Circle Game,* which I believe is a Joni Mitchell creation. Then I played, *Wonder Where the Lions Are*, by Bruce Cockburn. I had to drop the low 'E' string to a 'D' for that one, and while I was tuned that way, I followed up with *Harvest Moon*, by Neil Young.

Venturing to guess, I'd bet I know a thousand songs. If only my memory would help me to think of them once in awhile. What'd I just write? Did it make any sense? I'll try again. There in my brain somewhere, are the songs lost to the time in between, where I have forgotten that I know how to play them. There, any better? You don't need to answer that. But once in a while I surprise myself with a song that pops up that I haven't played in twenty years, yet there it is. I remember all the words, chords, and finger picking patterns — riding high on my musical bicycle.

## CHAPTER 8

It was a short while later when Jewel came back outside. She started toward us, looking down at the ground as she walked. When she got to the bottom step, she looked up at me.

"Did you want to take that walk?" she asked.

"That'd be nice," I warmly replied.

I stood up and laid my Gibson on the floor by the side of my chair. "See ya in a minute," I told Hershel. His pose and expression remained unchanged. He continued tapping. I stepped down from the porch and joined Jewel. Her smile, so warm and welcoming, as I stood next to her. She turned, walking toward the path that Marcus and I had taken the previous night.

"I kinda get the impression Hersh sticks pretty close to his cabin. Does he?" I asked.

"It's his comfort zone, that, and his garden and little pond behind the cabin. He hides out whenever Jack's around. Jack scares him so."

"No offense, but Jack does look a little scary," I told her. She laughed. I wanted to get her to open up to me. When Marcus told me about her being a "Traiteur," it made me wonder. I had never heard of it. I had heard of voodoo and how that was supposed to be practiced and perhaps prevalent in places down this way somewhere. Pins in dolls, crazy wild frenzied dances, monkey feet stuff. So I asked her about it. She assured me there was no voodoo in what she did, that she was more a back road country doctor, using old natural herbal remedies, coupled with her ability to uplift people's spirits in the things she says and the ways she treats them.

"So, in a way, you do magic," I played on words, chuckling.

"I don't do magic, magic does me," she laughed demurely. "Watch for snakes," she added with a smile as we walked.

"You seem so naturally a part of all of this," I mentioned.

"These are dwarf palmettos," she said, as she ran her small, delicate hand along some leaves while we walked. She pointed, "And those are tupelo gums." I smiled as I looked at her. She looked back at me. "I thought you'd like that," she said. "And honey locust," she pointed again.

"Is it true birds talk to you?"

"I talk to them, too; they tell me things," she said softly. "I converse with all you see around us."

We reached the clearing where the willow hovered over the wooden park bench. Again, I was overwhelmed by the teeming sounds of birds, frogs, and the assorted unknown. I saw the most beautiful colored birds with pinkish-orange feathers. I pointed to them.

"Roseate spoonbills," she explained. She had to have noticed my almost startled amazement at their presence.

"It is an Eden isn't it? It almost feels like Mother Nature's place of residence, her home address. It literally blushes in her glory." I told her. Ok, so maybe I was overemphasizing. Maybe I was just overwhelmed at the peace this brought to me. She simply smiled, turning to step under the willow, then taking her place on the bench. She motioned for me to come and sit beside her. I gladly obliged. We sat silent; looking at all we were surrounded by. I gazed for a time at the small island. There were a lot of wood ducks circling around, bobbing under the water for food, seemingly untroubled by our presence.

"Marcus said you wanted to know more," she said.

"I don't know anything, and he wants me to write about that," I explained in a half-desperate tone. "Somehow the blanks would need to get filled in before I could even think of starting something like this. I'm lost on how to go about it. It's not something I have ever thought of doing and I'm not sure that I can. In fact, I'm pretty sure that I can't, but maybe I'd be willing to try," I admitted.

"I'll help in any way I can," she told me reassuringly.

"Good, 'cause you are so much a mystery to me." That made her smile in the way that only reinforced what I had just said. "You're like no woman I've ever met," I had to add.

"That's good, I hope."

"Oh, it's spectacular," I said. She had a distant look in her eyes then, as if staring out at some far-away realm. Turning back to me, she gave a grateful sigh, then smiled. "Marcus said you're Cajun and Ojibway?" I then asked.

"Yes, I am of the Anishinabe and Cajun people, that's true."

"Were you born here?"

"Yes, not far from here."

I was trying to fit pieces together. "There are Ojibway here?" I questioned. I was sure their origin was in the North.

"No, these are Houma and Chitimacha peoples," she said.

"Well, there ya go! Can you see where I'd be confused here? And if you're Cajun, how come you don't talk at all like Clay?"

She laughed a dainty little girlish laugh, then began telling me an abbreviated story about her life. First she tried explaining things about the Acadian culture, how Creole was a mix of Native American, African, and French, That Cajun was Acadian French. I confess, none of this I fully understood, although I owed it to myself to further research this subject someday. At the time, it didn't seem apropos' to question information.

She continued by telling me about her father, Clay's oldest brother, how he had been in the Merchant Marines during World War 2. After the war, he sailed on the Great Lakes for a private company. It was during a shore leave near Green Bay, Wisconsin, where he met her mother. She said a whirling love affair ensued. They were married, and not long after, he moved them back to Louisiana. That was where she and her older sister, Lorraine, whom they nicknamed Rainy, were born, four years apart. Her mother's name was Mary. During their childhood they lived in several places around Terrebonne Parish.

She seemed quite vague about her childhood recollections, not bringing focus too much detail. Then came the reason why. When she was 14 years old, her father and his crewmate drowned in a shrimp boat accident during a bad storm. It was a real turning point in her life. She had been close to him, while her sister was closer to their mother. Her father, too, was a Traiteur. He had learned the ways from his mother. Ever since Jewel was a young girl, he would take her with him when he practiced. I envisioned she was his darling. She would learn much from him at that early age. I guessed he was priming her to carry it on.

It wasn't long after his death that they moved back up to near Green Bay, close to her mother's relations, members of the Oneida Nation. That was where she spent her adolescent years. Later on she would attend classes in Stevens Point, Wisconsin. While she was there, her aunt passed away down here, leaving the house to her and her sister. Rainy was married and had a baby. Her husband was holding down a good job. They owned their own home and had no intention of moving down South. Jewel made the decision to quit school and move down here to live. She knew Clay as a child. They soon became as close as brother and sister.

As I was relating to her story, things quickly fell into place. She told me about how she had returned north for her mother's funeral; that her mother had died suddenly from a brain aneurism. It was during this fateful stay with Rainy, that she and Marcus first met. The way she expressed that moment was much the same as Marcus had told it to me — a chance, almost bewitching, love at first sight. Destiny, I'm certain, is the way he would put it. The way it went, Rainy and her husband, Bill, had tickets for Marcus' concert. Bill gave his to Jewel. He had a friend who was a manager where the concert was being held and was able to get them back stage. The rest, and thus hereupon documented, is history.

I sat there listening without interruption. This was by far the most she had opened up since we'd met. She paused then, looking off with distant eyes.

"Love knows you're here," she softly said to me, turning and looking deep into my eyes. It transfixed me momentarily.

"Marcus said I can bring a tape recorder to help me remember things," I was finally able to say.

"That would be good," she replied, turning again, staring off so far away.

"What about a camera?" I asked. There was a moment of hesitation. She turned back to me. "I'll talk to Marcus. I know he's told me if we come out, he would want it to be pictorial somehow."

This was a surprising revelation for me. "He said he would talk to you about the camera idea. He told me about Clay too," I explained.

"Oh, don't try to take his picture; you'll lose a good friend."

"Do you know why that is?" I asked.

"No, I just know how he is about it," she said.

"Clay wants me to compose a song about Woogie, his dog."

"I think you'll do well," she replied.

"I'd guess he's pretty close ta that dog?" I wondered aloud.

"They've been everywhere together. Closer than any of his many girlfriends," she confided.

"Has he ever been married?"

"No."

"Ever come close?"

"Not that I can say," she again smiled. "He's a wild one, the real rebel in our family. Gave his father gray hair, I'm sure." We both laughed. "Did a little jail time in his younger days. Nothing big, but he was so untamable. That might be why girls like him so much. Besides, he's good lookin'."

It was at about this time that Marcus came into the clearing. The dogs chased ahead of him. As they ran to the bank, ducks took off at all angles of flight.

"She was just telling me what a wild and crazy dude you are," I told him.

"I'll bet," he said. "You could write a book." We all laughed. I was beginning to convince myself that, indeed, this could happen. Still, I was feeling the undertaking to be overwhelming, almost unrealistic in scope. I had not yet cleared the precipice.

"Yah, write a book about the Grand Canyon L," I said jokingly, trying to confess to both of them the enormity of such an endeavor.

Jewel rose without speaking, walked to the water's edge and stood there a moment. Marcus took the seat beside me. He still looked tired, like he hadn't really rested. Jewel began slowly walking the water's edge, following the bank to our left. She stooped down a couple times to examine something and continued walking for a distance, around a bend, out of our sight.

"She told me about her childhood and about her folks," I told him. He just nodded as if half awake. We sat quiet for a time.

"I thought I had been living out all of my dreams before she came to me," he said casually. He spoke in a soft, unusual tone. "Can hardly breathe without those moon-soft eyes. She kisses me in glances." Then, as if awoken from some trance, he looked at me with a smile and boasted, as if rejuvenated, "Maybe I'm hypnotized! Maybe I'm under a post-hypnotic suggestion of love!" I smiled at him without a word. Again we sat quietly for a time.

Finally, trying to get more depth, I found myself asking if he ever missed the old life, even though I may have asked it before.

"I miss the guys. I miss James. I miss the band. It's hard deceiving people you really care about. Others back then, I never can forgive. The bigger I got, the bigger my ball and chain. In a way, I had to set them all free — couldn't make one exception. Everyone had to believe I died, that it was me they buried."

"You mean they did bury someone?" I asked.

"How hard do you think it would be to find a bloated body of someone who kinda looked like me?" was his answer.

I looked at him in astonishment.

"I don't really talk about that, never have. It's all I'm gonna say on the matter." Then, almost as if it were in the same sentence, he said, "I used to have fun with fireworks, now I can't stand loud noises." I had to laugh. He turned to me smiling.

"So you just turned from your home in Memphis and never looked back," I said.

"You know, I lived there 20 years and was hardly ever home. Spent a lot of time out in California, hated it, mostly trapped in motels. I loved Hawaii though. You know, I hear they still light torches," he said with a reminiscing expression.

"Don't you miss the outside world? I mean, a lot of things goin' on."

"Clay keeps us informed. He tells us the big stuff, like when certain people die. He told us about Roy. He told us about 9/11, but mostly I don't wanna know."

Roy? I wondered, but didn't ask.

"When we came here, it was like running and hiding in the palm of God," he sighed. Then there was silence.

"Did you ever think of having kids?" I ventured to ask.

"Jewel can't conceive. She's a mother to so many." Again we sat in silence. Jewel hadn't returned from her walk. The lowering sun was giving way to new shadows.

"Does her sister ever come down?"

"She passed away a few years back. Jewel hasn't been in contact with anyone up there since the funeral." Again, changing the subject as if to uplift, he added, "Do you know she makes all her own clothes? She makes most of mine, too. Her friend makes all of our candles."

It was at that moment that Jewel reappeared. She had plants in her hand. Making her way back up to us, she said, "I'm going to start dinner." We both smiled at her, and she turned on the path leading back to the house.

"She likes to cook doesn't she?" I asked.

"I think so. She likes to take care of me." We looked at each other and smiled.

"What'd she have in her hand?" I asked him.

"Don't know," he said with a goofy expression to his lip. "Should we go play some music?" It was good to see him perked up a bit.

"Sure!" I resounded over nature's symphony.

We both stood, following her at a distance, making our way back to the yard. It was becoming familiar to me now. The plants, the trees, I felt settled in. When we reached Hershel's cabin, he wasn't around. I retrieved my guitar from the porch and walked with Marcus to the house. It's worth noting, the bugs weren't much bother then. And now I could feel that time approaching when I would need to leave again. It had to be an early night — no drinking of that "Thin Ice." I had to be on my toes and back with Beulah first thing in the morning. I would have much to think about in the days ahead. I knew I would be making my attempt at writing this thing. I was just unsettled about its consequence. It felt like a life-long endeavor, like climbing a mountain I was unfit to climb. And would it turn into an active volcano?

## CHAPTER 9

When we walked inside the house, Marcus wasted no time heading to the music room. He picked up the classical guitar. This song must have been on his mind. He sat down and began to play another original, *Duchess of Sin.* It was moody, foreboding. It didn't even seem to be a song about someone, more about an existing spirit of some sort. It was eerie, and told of spells being cast, of shadows from sources that could not be named — must never be named. It was some kind of hell he was trying to decipher and explain, but somehow he couldn't.

It left an empty, drained feeling within the listener, treading on and tiring the soul. It was painful, almost too powerful. There would come a time when I would regret not asking him where that came from and who it was about. Instead, when he had finished I just sat there spellbound. "Whoa, L," was all I could say.

I fiddled with a couple strings, turning their keys to bring them back in tune. "How many songs have you written over the years?" I asked him.

"I guess I have fragments of hundreds, but a couple dozen I'd call finished. I think you should know, I want them out there. I want them heard someday. That's part of this comin' round thing. They were a gift to me. I need them to be a gift to everyone else in whatever way it takes."

He was making sense, filling in some blanks in my head. I knew this was heading somewhere. I wanted to lighten things up again. I began playing *Love Minus Zero, No Limit,* by Bob Dylan. He was familiar with it, and chimed in where he could. Jewel smiled from the kitchen. "How 'bout a drink?" she asked.

"Oh, no thanks," I said unenthusiastically. She laughed. I think she understood my dilemma. "Mornin's gonna come too soon," I then added. She nodded, and Marcus smiled and changed guitars, grabbing his old Martin and strumming a chord to check its tuning. He played another one of his originals: *Baggage Handler.* It went, *Won't you pack your things up under my wings, and I'll take you on this ride.* It was sweet. And almost without stopping, he played directly to Jewel, that old Elvis standard, *Love Me Tender.* It was like one special moment after another happened when I was around them.

"Soup's on," she said to us. He looked to me with a nod. We stood up and headed for the kitchen.

"Sure's been smellin' great. Can't wait ta see what this is," I declared with anticipation.

We sat down to wild duck gumbo, which I believe, had been in stages of preparation before I even woke up. There were blackberry dumplings along with bread pudding. There were assorted nuts in bowls between candles that warmed this culinary offering.

"I'm hoping you'll be able to come back soon," Jewel said, reaching across and touching my hand. She then proceeded to pass the gumbo.

Astonishingly, it was the first time I took notice of the fact that they both appeared to have matching tattooed wedding bands. I reached across to Jewel and gently took her fingers in my hand.

"What's this?" I questioned, pointing with my other hand, and lightly touching the tattoo. Her sweet smile said all that was needed. Then I looked over to Marcus, and at his finger.

"It was a quiet ceremony," he conveyed with a wink. I returned a long smile to both of them, and inquired no further.

"I can never tell when I'll get back," I told her. Then I began thinking. "I have a bunch of vacation this year. Any way you guys could come up? Or maybe if I kidnapped her, Kat would come down." They laughed.

"We're planning on doing some exploring, haven't really decided when. I think we could pop in at some point when you're off work and around home," Marcus said.

This excited me instantly. I wanted it to be next week! "Kat really needs to meet you guys. She hears about all this, but I don't know what goes through her mind, how she's taking it."

"We'll get this straightened out," Marcus assured. Jewel nodded, and smiling, reached back across and lightly touched my hand. "There's only one way ta skin a cat," Marcus added. Jewel and I looked at each other, our eyebrows and lips demonstrating more grimacing looks. We shook our heads in unison at him.

"Sometimes, Marcus," she chided him, as if he had just stepped in something. I laughed. He shrugged his shoulders and smiled back at her.

Dinner was predictably delicious. The sun had long since set. Our night would become all too fleeting. We returned to the music room. I decided now was the perfect time for a re-warm-up number. I started right out by playing Van Morrison's, *Moondance*. This was, and should often be referred to as, "the best of times." I never had better friends, better moments so complete. As my tribute to them and to their true love for one another, I played *Waltz Across Texas*, by Ernest Tubb. Marcus joined in the chorus.

Apart from a couple of bathroom breaks between the trees, we played our night away. Jewel picked up the banjo and played with us a while. For the most part, I led the way, running through many of the songs I knew from recent memory. I played a light-hearted original I had written while on vacation in Mexico. Actually, it was written at Lynn and David's wedding on an island off Cancun, called Isla Mujeres (the Island of Women). We spent most of the week barefoot and taking in the Caribbean view. It was there on the sand that I wrote, *Let's Call This Love.* Jewel giggled at the words, "F*eel the waves touch our toes on the shore/ make ya crazy wanna touch some more*."

I could tell Marcus really liked the songs I had written. He enjoyed hearing songs he had never heard, and some he hadn't heard in years. We drank tea and ate shrimp pie. I told them a story about how, when we were on the island, Kat and I would stop in at this open-air bar not far from our motel. I believe we went there all of the seven days we spent on that island. We truly enjoyed the Spanish music on the jukebox while we had our midday martinis. It wasn't until the last day, as we were waiting for the ferry to take us back to the mainland to catch our plane, that Kat looked around and made the discovery.

"Do you know this is a gay bar?" she said to me with an enlightened grin. I spun around to take full notice, and sure enough, it became evident. All this time and we never noticed! They found the story as amusing as Kat and I did.

But now the night was about over. We had settled back to just sitting there, talking small talk. I had been saving my favorite song of all times for a moment like this. Without announcing it, I picked up my guitar again. It had been leaning against the coffee table in front of me. Fully primed and ready, I played *When Your Heart is Weak,* a little known and under-acclaimed masterpiece by a band named Cock Robin. It would be my final hurrah for this visit.

Jewel's face was glowing, her smile adoring. Marcus beamed and said, "Wow!" I had done what I came to do, I joked to myself.

"Oh, that was so good!" Jewel exalted.

"It's my favorite song," I admitted. "I mean, besides yers, L."

"Man, I can see why. That's a one in a million." he said. "Where do you find this stuff?"

"It's out there. I just like what I hear and try ta learn it. There's so much out there these days, but some of it will bore and put you to sleep faster than any book I could write." That didn't go over their heads. They looked at each other deeply, believing then and there, that I had committed myself to their book project. I clearly read their minds.

"Think my stuff could make the grade?" Marcus surprisingly asked.

"You kidding? Your stuff is on top, the best, the most original songs I've heard. I'm not just saying that. There's something going on with your music that the world has never heard. It needs to. Maybe it's because you've been in the 'sticks' so long. I meant that as a joke," I quickly added, while looking over at Jewel, having learned the hard way of her sensitivity to this swamp thing. "Your seclusion has brought you to a place of such creativity, that well, I can't explain how much it's worth, only that its worth is enormous. You're right, when you say you should share it with the world. It's gonna knock everybody for a loop! I feel like warning them ahead of time that they should sit down first," I said. They both laughed. The evening soon reached its close. We were all tired.

"See what you can do with my *Ways to Remember* song," I mentioned as I rose, about to walk toward my room. Jewel hugged me warmly as we bid each other goodnight.

"I'll have something for you next time ya come," he assured me.

I was bushed, yet still wrapped in excitement. When I finally lay back in bed and forced myself to relax, it hit me; I had nothing left. I had spent it all. Sleep came down on me in an avalanche.

## CHAPTER 10

Clay's voice was pretty hard to mistake. My eyes opened to a new, barely sun-up morning. I knew I needed to get going. From what sounded like the kitchen area I could hear Clay say, "Mais jamais" something and "boscoyo" something. Who knows? He was talking to Jewel. I heard her agreeing with him. I couldn't make out anything about the conversation. I scurried to get dressed and slipped on my boots. There was always a pitcher of fresh water and an empty glass beside a large bowl on the stand just inside my door. It was as though the water fairy had visited during the night. I hastily freshened up.

"Couche-couche with bananes," Jewel was saying when I stepped from my door and into their view. Both of them had a fresh smile for me. I smiled right back. Marcus wasn't around.

"Mornin'," I said with a sheepish grin, walking toward them. "Gotta visit the boy's room, or, I mean, unisex art gallery rest area."

"If you don't have time to wait, you'll have company," Jewel said. Clay burst out with a hearty laugh. I got the picture. I had time to wait. There was oatmeal steaming on the stove. She must have arisen early.

"Whattaya say we floot w'du courant wit us," he said to me.

"What?"

"Jes kiddin'," he answered. I just gave him my stupid look.

"Hungry?" Jewel asked.

"Will be after I take care a business," I reiterated. Just then Marcus came through the door.

"Hey, good morning," he said as he put his hand on my shoulder.

"Mornin' to you," I said with a smile. "Be right back." I hurriedly passed him by, heading out the door, down the porch steps, and briskly along the wooden circled walkway to the outhouse. Some things can't wait. It was worth noting, there were newly painted designs on the inside of the outhouse walls. Art exhibit material, I thought, as I sat there.

When I re-joined them in the kitchen, I had to comment on what I had seen.

"I could sit there all day!" Marcus joked back to me.

"Sometimes Hersh gets lost in there," Jewel added. We all laughed. I tried to imagine.

Breakfast was hot cereal, buttermilk biscuits, and bananas. It hit the spot. Jewel always seems to feed us right — always in her state of grace. As the four of us enjoyed breakfast, I could hear distant thunder. We had a boat ride to take.

"What do we do if it rains?" I foolishly asked.

"We ge wedt," Clay answered with a grin. He glanced at the others, looking like he couldn't believe I just asked that.

"I knew that. I was jes testin' ya," I responded with my dumb smile. He looked at them again with a shake of his head.

"Yah ye righ," he mumbled under his breath.

"When you come back, bring that tape recorder with ya," Marcus said.

"Sure will." I didn't feel it was the right time to press the camera thing with Clay sitting there. "Hopefully soon." I added.

"Hope so," Marcus said in a somewhat reflective manner, as if he thought I might be gone a long time or had already been gone too long. "Got a lot of stuff you haven't heard yet," he added.

"I have some too, if only I can remember," I replied. Jewel laughed, Marcus smiled. Clay simply continued feeding his face.

With breakfast finished up, I needed to hurry things along. Without saying anything, I retrieved my things from the bedroom and came back out, letting them know it was time. It really was. I knew there would be an assignment waiting for me on my Qualcomm when I climbed aboard old Beulah.

With a small hug, Marcus said, "Don't do goodbyes, just stay alright."

Jewel came over. She had a brown bag in her hand. With a hug, she handed it to me. I looked inside, and again there were nuts and dried berries. But this time there were little purple and yellow flowers.

"For me to eat healthy?" I asked.

"We'll get you there," she said with a warm smile.

"Les ge at da boot an ge wedt," Clay said.

He was right; it was starting to drizzle. As we stepped from the porch, I could see Hershel sitting on the porch down below. "Just a sec," I told Clay, as I raised my pointer finger in the air. Jewel and Marcus were standing just outside the door on the porch. I set my things on the ground, and in a moderately slow jog that only a chubby trucker can do, I sauntered down to see Hershel. He was smiling big as I climbed his steps and took his hand with a shake, saying, "See ya soon, buddy." He understood, I'm sure. The grip of my hand was met by the grip of his, eyes looking well into mine. I gave him my assuring smile, then quickly returned up the hill. I was huffin' and puffin' by the time I got back to my things. Boy, I thought, I hope Jewel can work some of her magic on me.

As Clay and I walked toward the channel, I turned and told Jewel and Marcus I would see them soon. They nodded but said nothing to me. Jewel had her arms wrapped around Marcus' waist. He had his left arm around her shoulder. They looked like a couple in love. It was a wonderful parting image for me.

The float back was swift, his boat motor revved loud; so much so, it would have been impossible to carry on any conversation. Could it be he didn't want to get wet either? We reached his place without getting the shower he looked like he could have used. Credence was there and ready.

"Member dat song fer mon chien, Woogs," Clay reminded me.

"I'll get workin' on it," I promised. We shook hands whole heartedly as we parted.

"The roads back to New Orleans seemed ever gloomier for me this time. All the damage, still so prevalent, couldn't help but deflate the soul. I dreaded going back to work not knowing when my next visit would come. Credence never cracked a smile, although it was something I had hardly ever seen him do anyway. We talked about the lack of change, lack of any progress after this major historical catastrophe. He had a hurtful look on his face, too many bad feelings. For some reason, I could tell he really hated feeling this way.

"You should take a vacation," I suggested. "Jewel and Marcus said they might try to come up and see me. You're welcome to visit us, too. Maybe they'll want you to drive?"

"He was noticeably grateful for the offer, but remarked, "To Wisconsin? I'd guess they'd fly." I wasn't sure what to make of that.

When we reached the warehouse lot I knew I needed to make up time. I saw Beulah as I had left her. "I gotta hurry off," I told him apologetically.

"I understand. Hurry back to us." He had a warm, brotherly tone. I shook his hand firmly and smiled.

"Take care," I said. He shook his head, indicating he would, with all he could do to muster half a smile. I turned to walk, and heard him pull away.

A funny thing about truck drivers: They get content with their trucks. It's their home away from home. It's always a comfortable feeling climbing back inside, everything exactly as it was when I left. Within minutes, I would be off and running, with new adventures around each corner, but nothing like the one I had been having here. I remember wondering, "Would there be better times — ever closer times with them?" It still captures me in dream-like fashion, whenever I ponder this "where am I in life" scenario. Sometimes it sticks to my thoughts like glue, taking up much of my waking hours, rolling in circles around my brain. Questions during those moments never seem to settle into answers. Every assignment, between Jewel and Marcus, seemed inconsequential, as if filling in valuable time with blank spaces.

There came — in the dead of a snowy wintry Saturday morning — one decisive moment. As fate would have it, or as Marcus likely would call fate, I was bowled over. I feel a need to blame the lemon roll breakfast I was fiddling with, and not seriously eating. Or I need to blame the aimless game of solitaire I was trying to play. Something should always be blamed for an epiphany. They don't just come along out of the blue, as some may have you believe. They are caused by something, even if the cause is never truly recognized. They are surely given as a gift, but they're not for everyone. Mine washed over me in a tidal wave when I looked outside the window that fateful morning. It was almost as if the snow covering Beulah made her ask me, "What's your life been about anyway?" I stared at her for what may have been a long time. "What's it going to take for you to find something important enough to give it everything you've got?" She was coming alive, scolding me. She probably knows me better than I know myself. In that moment she opened up a whole "would be" story. It became clear the way this book should be laid out — how it could actually be done. I was even more convinced, hit by her lightning. With certainty, I was going to follow this thing through.

## CHAPTER 11

Back home we used to always say, "If Ben Franklin downtown don't have it, we don't need it." That was before Wal-Mart came in across the river in Minnesota. This afternoon I would make my supply run to Pine City. Aside from purchasing the usual supplies needed for my two week run, I proceeded to walk next door to Radio Shack, where I purchased a battery powered cassette tape recorder. I bought a small pocket recorder as well. Since I was going to go through with this, nothing was going to escape me now. I would be recording everything, at all times. I would capture every word and every song. I remember Kat asking me what I was doing, as we walked there from across the Wal-Mart parking lot.

"Something God has given me a chance to do," I recall saying. "Something that needs to be proved to the world," I tried to clarify. She said nothing, faithfully choosing to let me do my thing. I dared not ask what she was thinking. I didn't want to slow my pace. The quest was in motion. I didn't find anything to be too expensive at the time.

While at home that evening, I was rummaging through our art supplies for no known reason, and discovered a box of assorted large, glass beads. Early Sunday mornings, it has become our tradition to lie in bed, drink coffee, and go over all we have missed in each other's lives since we'd been apart. It's one of our favorite times. We look forward to waking early so we can fit this moment into our otherwise hectic schedules. It was becoming a part of our stories, for me to include Jewel and Marcus, and all that was happening between us. Kat was fighting it no more, better described as humoring me. I told her all about Hershel, how he made wind chimes and stepping stones. I asked her if I could give him some of the beads I had found. She didn't object.

Weekends run through like no tomorrows, almost as if a dream that you're not really sure happens. The lingering warmth from her lips are my memory's only convincing factor.

This time the ache of my leaving would be relieved quickly. An assignment came through. I was to pick up a relay 60 miles away, in Blaine, Minnesota, going straight to New Orleans. As it turned out, the load was sections of corrugated seawall and accessories, to be delivered near the Ninth Ward. It was to be unloaded at the worksite there. This filled me with excitement. I would be helping in a direct way, to restore control of what had been taking on the appearance of a lost battle.

Every assignment provides phone numbers to the pickup and delivery locations. I hadn't even left our front yard when I called the Ninth Ward location. It was to be a slow unload when I got there, and yes, I could leave my truck parked over as long as I needed. I was swelling with enthusiasm. Kat saw in me what had to be a most convincing adrenalin. As we kissed, she gave me such a loving last look, almost as if to say, "I want to believe you."

It was starting to feel that way to me, as Marcus had once explained, this was indeed "all meant to be." It had been less than three weeks, and in a few days, I would be seeing them again. I couldn't wait to call, but again needed to hold off until this load was securely attached to Beulah. We would then be on our way.

As it turned out, there would be no glitches. I called Burton. He was admittedly surprised at this swift return, assuring me that everyone would be happy to hear it. He would have everything arranged after he heard from me next, when I could give him an accurate time of my arrival.

Once on my way, it was one of those times where miles seemed to drag by. Interstate mile markers seemed to be lying to me as I passed. "It's only been eight miles? I could have sworn it's been thirty!" I spoke aloud to myself. And so it went, until I allowed myself to calm down in assorted daydreams as I drove.

It was becoming my habit now to include journal entries each night before bed. They mostly consisted of wishes and ramblings. I even asked God not to let this dream awaken, always thanking him for my blessings in my prayers. I tried at times to imagine, in assorted ways, where indeed this life of mine was leading. In my truck cab at night, I bounced in and out of my journal world with whimsical thoughts and frustrations. I would then set it aside, seriously attempting to expound on the book I had begun to write. There again, I would push myself up against walls, only to return myself to an easier journal scribbling — my pen back and forth, always seeking to explore a next inspiration, some sort of guidance to a story direction. All attempts seemed novice, at best. Was I really going to get this thing off the ground?

Again I came into New Orleans on schedule. It was nearly noon. When I reached the delivery location, I was directed to a lot where several camper trailers and semis were parked. I could see the Chrysler in the distance, nearly a block away. The person who signed my paperwork told me everything should be unloaded by mid-morning the next day. I sent a Qualcomm message to that effect back to Darin. I opened my trailer doors for them, grabbed my things from the cab of the truck, and locked up old Beulah. I was scurrying to get to Credence. He was grinning when I approached. I think he may have found it humorous, the way I lickety-split from my truck to him.

"How ya doin', old timer?" I asked.

"Doing good, how about you?"

"Glad to be here," I confessed.

"Marcus was happy to hear you're coming. How long can you stay this time?"

"This one'll have at be short. Gotta get back at the truck before noon tomorrow," I explained.

"Better than nothing," he consoled me.

On the way to Clay's, we talked about the city and how disturbing things were. We talked about the displaced and separated families and how things would never be the same. We both shared doubts about this city returning to its former self, even though we knew that it would. I expressed how happy I was to be able to do what I was doing, but confessed how small this contribution really was in the total scope of things. Trying to be optimistic, I spoke of how governments build monuments from dust. We talked about the World Trade Center and how a monument of some sort would probably be erected. We both understood something would be built to teach the world of America's endurance.

"This city will come back greater than ever," I told him in a hopeful tone.

Each time we were together, more and more, we were sharing a brotherly connection. It had taken a while to break that icy shell he held around himself when first we met.

The ride seemed shorter each time, and now we were pulling into the grove, Clay's home in sight. As we stopped the car, there stood Elbow Jack and Woogie. Mad Jack looked thick-skinned and mean as ever.

"Hey kid," he said to me.

"Hi Jack!"

"What time do you want me back?" Credence asked.

"Let's shoot for this time tomorrow," I told him.

"Good enough; see you then," he said, giving a nod to Jack. Then he backed the car to the turnaround. He always seemed to be in a hurry to go, but I understood. He was, after all, a driver much like me.

"I'll be bringin' ya over," Jack said.

"No Clay? Hey, Woogie." I stooped and gave her a pat. She seemed slumped, her stature low, slow, and cumbersome, but she wagged her tail like she was glad to see me.

"Clay's off and runnin' for a few days. He's goin' to a Fais-dodo Friday."

"A what?"

"It's a dance — probably last most the night, a real party. Eddie's band will be playin' along with a bunch a others."

"Eddie's in a band?"

"It's a swamp punk band, not my kinda music."

"Man I'd like ta hear that sometime!" I exclaimed.

"To each his own," Jack replied. "I gotta put Woogie back in the house. Meetcha at the boat."

Under his hardness, he lets slip a warm side sometimes. Maybe he just has to like you to let that happen. At any rate, as we got in the boat, he gave me a smile, like he was glad for my company.

As we settled in and before he started the motor, I said, "Clay told me Woogie is pretty bad off."

"I gotta take care of that while he's gone," Jack explained without a flinch. "There's no reason for unneeded sufferin'. Lord knows I seen enough of it in my day."

"It's a sad thing," I had to say.

"Yah, it is," he agreed.

"He wants me to write a song about her," I told Jack.

In actuality, I had been toying with a couple of attempts that hadn't gotten off the ground. I remember telling myself, "Man, I don't even know the mutt!" I found it difficult to write about a subject I didn't really know — and had only petted a couple of times. Both of my attempts at creating a song, thus far, had been of a slow and forlorn nature. They didn't work out. I had admitted to myself I would need to try a different approach.

"That'd be good, he'd like that," Jack responded, pulling at the rope to start the motor. "Clay's a tough buzzard; he'll do alright with it when it's done," he shouted over the roar of the motor, louder than he would have had to.

Jack maneuvered slowly. He seemed slow-pace in nature.

"I'm still scared of gators," I shouted.

"Sound of the motor usually scares them under," he yelled back. "But not always," he added, then laughed.

"Great!" I thought.

He swatted a mosquito on his arm. "Skeets round here don't buzz, they flap," he said. That made me laugh.

I had noticed a large scar all up and down one side of Jack's right leg. I chose to ask him about it then.

"Got it in 'Nam, got strafed by friendly fire," he said with a sarcastic laugh. Then he pulled up his shirt to reveal the scar extending all the way up his side and under his arm. It looked like it had been badly burned. "One of our fighter planes dropped this on me; military's full a mistakes. Clay knows. He's a 'Nam vet. This one got me the Purple Heart and a trip back home."

"Wow," I said. "At least you both made it back." He didn't respond. I felt the need to change the subject. "Is the work finished at their place?"

"Never be finished. They always keep me busy," he replied.

## CHAPTER 12

The skies were overcast when we reached my favorite shoreline, the sounds of dogs barking resounded in the background. After we landed, Jack and I both got out of the boat and headed up the path toward the house. The dogs came running up to us. They stopped barking as soon as they recognized Jack. I think they were starting to get to know me. Right away, there was Marcus, walking toward us. As we reached the yard, he approached. Jack just nodded, then turned toward the cabin and the work shed down the hill. Jack had a pair of wading boots slung over his right shoulder, and a large notebook in his left hand. "Got a bridge ta build," he told me, turning with a smile as he walked away. Marcus stood beside me now, a gentle, calming presence.

"Brought a tape recorder," I told him, as I patted my t-shirt at the small recorder protruding from my pocket. I pushed the button through the shirt and turned it on. "I'm gonna do it. I'll write your book." Those were to be the first recorded words.

Visibly ignited, he gave the wide smile, that of someone who seemed to already know. "I look for the story, like waiting to swing on a new dance floor," he responded. He put his left arm around my shoulder and gave me a squeeze. "Anxious as a rack of pool balls waiting for their break," he added as we began walking.

I smiled happily, probably because the relief was mine. I had now espoused to move forward and complete a work that would be important to all of us. It felt good to be back, and within me was a gladness that I'd made the step to do this project for my friends. Now, for the record, it would be legitimized on tape. I had deigned the writing to be my lot, in keeping with this feeling of destiny that he had long since blazed unto my spirit. Yet deep down, I held concern that chronicling this could prove to be the biggest trial I'd ever encountered.

"Life has a way of revealing new, unannounced pages. I can't seem to ever say I have things figured out," I told him.

He stopped for a moment, still looking straight ahead. "What covers each curve and corner, what forms our time, is an un-losing gift," he responded, then he continued toward the house. "It's the soul of ourselves that can never take, always will give," I heard him say, as I meandered at his side. He extended his hand once again to my shoulder as we walked, then said, "Space and dust will float down to settle on all of the reasons."

As we neared the house, the door swung open and Jewel lightly, elegantly, stepped onto the porch. It took one of her ravishing smiles to instantly bring brighter colors to the day. Her eyes shimmered, hauntingly heaven-sent. It felt like they were prospecting all the gold in life when she looked at me, melting me once again.

"I brought something for Hershel," I told her, gleaming.

"He's out on his boat," she said. "He'll be back later. How are you?"

"Really glad to be here," I replied.

"How 'bout some coffee?" she asked, charming beyond her words.

"Yah, sure, sounds good," I told her.

We stepped up on the porch beside her. I set my things down and she hugged me gently. She had a sweet scent of flowers. There were always flowers in her hair. I noticed then that the outside of her right hand was covered all the way to the mid-fingers with a drawn Oriental-type design, burnt orange in color. It matched perfectly with the bracelet on her wrist.

"What's this?" I asked, as I lifted her hand for a closer look.

"It's a henna tattoo. I put it on myself. It's an ink that lasts a few weeks then fades away."

"Beautiful," I whispered.

"Pretty good, yes, considering I painted it on with my left hand and I'm right-handed," she smiled. I flirted a warm smile back.

When we entered the house, she said, "You know where your room is." I held my undiminished smile as I proceeded past her. I stopped to lean my guitar case against the couch in the music room.

After leaving my bag in the bedroom, I returned to open my guitar case and retrieved the small bag of beads that I brought for Hershel. I had placed them in a small compartment, otherwise reserved for extra strings and guitar picks. I brought them to the kitchen table. Jewel was pouring coffee. Marcus was standing beside her. I had heard him tell her of my intention to do the book as I was retrieving the beads from the guitar case. Her smile was inviting, loving. I walked to their table and placed the bag down next to her coffee cup.

"I thought maybe Hersh could use some of these for his wind chimes. Do you think he'll like 'em?" I asked. She opened the bag.

"Oh Hatty, you have no idea," she said with soft flourishing excitement. "Where did you get them?"

"They were some we had in with our art supplies. After I told Kat about his art, she said she'd like him to have them."

"They're beautiful! It'll really make him very happy," she replied.

Marcus looked at me and said, "When your heart tells you this is everything and you know right then that it is."

I tried at the moment to understand what he meant, but I didn't. I just gave him a smile. "Can we record some of your songs this time?" I quickly asked, as we sat down to drink our coffee. I looked up to see that the trim around the cupboard door edges had been newly painted in intricate floral designs. "Those are wonderful," I exclaimed, pointing.

"Keeps me busy," Jewel said modestly.

"My heart is softened by her ever-fragrant creations. I'm somehow tamed by these new beginnings," Marcus said. Then he added, "I'd like to start over. I want you to record them all," referring to the songs.

The revelation launched me into the clouds. They had to have seen me glowing, as I took a sip of coffee. It had a new, mildly wild taste I'd never had. I sounded out a subdued, "Mmm."

"Chicory," she responded to my reaction. I smiled back at her.

While we sat, I told them how I had purchased two recorders with extra cassette tapes and batteries. I explained how, to do this book, I would need to be recording almost all of the time. I confessed how my memory treats me, sorely lacking more often than I'd like to admit. I asked if they had any objections. They assured me they didn't. I voiced my concern that everything remain natural and that we should forget they were recording. This would eliminate any compromise to the quality I was hoping to achieve. I was going to be an author, I then proudly proclaimed.

"You had told me you needed to know more. Let's go out on the porch and burn some of that tape up for a while. I'd like to get you started with some answers," Marcus said.

I was glad to hear that. We stood up, as Jewel began refilling our cups. "I'll get the other recorder," I said with enthusiasm. I went to the bedroom and pulled the larger, table-top player from my bag, quickly returning to the kitchen.

"Good," Marcus said when he saw it in my hand. He turned toward the door. I followed him. In a glance, I smiled back at Jewel as we were leaving.

Once outside, Marcus and I took chairs. I put the recorder on a foot stool near him. I didn't hesitate a second.

"Ready then?" I was anxious to get right to it. He nodded yes, and I turned it on. I took a sip off my coffee, then said, "Tell me about back then, when you met Jewel, how you came to decide to pull this big deception on the world." I wanted to dig right in with the things that had troubled me since we met. He opened right up.

"At the time I was rusting in a mutilated fear," he responded. "There was a blind approach I felt like I was always going through. It was a cruel taunting, up and down. I was becoming an ever darker, wilder storm. Layers of me felt like they were folding, collapsing in that whimsical storm."

His eyes were darting around at things nearby us. I wasn't really comprehending what he was saying, but I didn't interrupt.

"I never told anyone this before, but in those days I likened myself to a black stallion, a rogue. Now I feel a little like Rip Van Winkle, I've been in this dream for so long. Back then I was disabled, encased in some deep freeze greed, a darkness with need for shadows." He paused for a drink. I didn't say anything, just kept looking at him intensely.

"At first, my disappearing didn't come quietly. It had its pathetic screams. As time went by, she made me see I had only given up small places, that I needed to say goodbye to it all. No more do-overs. My world had been in an ashtray. All the melodies were becoming rancid to me. For so long I had been letting my wants be mistaken for needs. It was a cold dream, no warmth inside. Intricate phobias heightened from each malignant wish." He paused a moment, taking another drink. I remember thinking to myself, 'Wow, I hope this thing is recording all of this."

He continued. "Crazy days of many currents. People around me were withering my soul away. I began to realize, to focus. Sloppy giving made me give up on them. They were taking everything they could. I needed to find some way to shut off their poisons, to throw up my life."

What was I hearing? I could make no sense of it. How was I to substantiate this into a book? Jack was walking up the hill to us now. He stopped below the porch. I shut the recorder off.

"Gotta get goin'. I'll get back here early in the morning ta get Hatty," he told Marcus, then gave a smile in my direction, and our eyes met.

"Come for breakfast," Marcus said to him.

"Nah, gotta get goin'," Jack replied.

"Thanks for everything, Jack," I told him. He nodded with a leathery smile, and began walking toward the canal, dogs at his feet. They had been following him around like lost puppies since we arrived. As he disappeared off in the distance, I reached over and turned the machine back on. Marcus set his cup down. He was acting jittery. One knee was bouncing up and down. He started fumbling with his hands. He seemed to reflect for a moment, then he resumed.

"I remember overhearing them discussing their hunches, a bottle of wine between their senses. I lost hold of any decent dimension of friendship. Days of haste, waste, and assorted pleasures." He laughed aloud at some memory. "They bounced their life games off of me. We all forsook each other in brave, careless opinions. Nothing stood to reason, petrified emotions." He paused again. "Nothing we answered for," he continued. "It was a real fine thread I was dangling on. The sun was racing to sizzle our seas."

He was making my head spin, trying to follow what he was saying, to understand. His speaking in these prolific, jagged and poetic-type sentences made me deduce that he so badly was trying to say out loud how he felt inside. He was desperately trying to make me understand what he meant. It was having an opposite effect; it was confusing, not understandable. I could tell he was frustrated deep inside about these memories. He was venting. His excitement increased, steadily heightened. And after what seemed to be another inner reflection, he again continued.

"Anything called love had turned to dust. Everything forgotten to the point where nothing was remembered. There was that unforgettable sound of recklessness. It festered my soul. My blood felt like dust running through rusted veins." He paused once more and took another drink. "Letting the power of life go to waste, spiritual penalties were burying any brink of happiness. It was me without, shivering. Convenience ruled, controlled my world. I was 'wow man' in retreat, a sunken hull sealed in time. I couldn't see that I couldn't see, and when I finally did, well, I would have sooner given my soul to the gutter than to have kept rotting in that rich man's fantasy. You told me you had lied to your dad once. I gave mine the ultimate deception. The best part is, I have no remorse over it. He was better off going to his grave believing what he did. We had grown apart. He had remarried — new wife and all. I didn't sit well with that. I liked the kid though. He stuck by me closer than most"

"Wow!" was all I kept thinking. The door opened and Jewel stepped out. I let out a deep breath that I must have been holding in — although I hadn't absorbed what just transpired, what he was saying, I felt an ego boost that indeed, I may be a pretty good interviewer. Jewel had a large pan in her hands. She didn't say anything as she brushed past us sitting there, and stepped from the porch, turning to our right, along Hershel's foot path. I stood and leaned over the side to watch, as she headed toward the rock barbeque.

"Don't get me wrong; the early days at Sun were great times — back when I was hungry," Marcus continued. "Those times still shine in my life. I remember the Louisiana Hayride. I remember all those great nights — my times with Wanda. I'm just saying how it got!" He probably had seen bewilderment in my face. He was trying so hard to make things clear to me, the way he felt. He appeared scattered as he was trying to explain.

I was watching Jewel. She had started a fire under the grill and was cutting celery on a table to the side that was built right into the rocks. I turned to Marcus and asked, "All of your fans at the time, what about them?"

"I sigh at the memories of how I lived just to fill the frames they hung on their walls," he responded briskly. I wondered if he had actually heard my question. Had it taken a long time for him to garner these thoughts. I felt it was time to re-route the subject. I was trying to piece things together plausibility.

"Jewel then, was she the real reason?" I asked. When I look back, it was a stumbling question, but it worked.

"Love's made a man of me," he began. "Her voice, her voice has always made my days dance to the beat my heart-notes know as love. She's my voodoo princess, no, the certain, all-steady predictably mysterious spirit angel."

"I remember walking backstage after that Green Bay concert. It felt like standing-room-only in my head. I was surrounded by my usual entourage, but somehow she was able to step up in front of me. I had to stop. Know what was the first thing she ever said to me?"

"No, what?" I asked. My head was numb.

"She said she was the beginning of what every happiness means. She said she knew what fantasy does, that she had been my long delicate search. Then she delivered the knockout blow. She said, Out of the hollow into the holy, your waves have kissed my shoreline: Do you believe that? I couldn't move. She was staring deep into my eyes. Her smile sent pulsating promises. It was as though the magnetic poles from opposite sides of the earth were calling our lips to be together. I had never met anyone even close to her! That moment brought hot twinkling flares to our eyes. I could see my eyes in the reflection of hers. I couldn't stop staring. It wouldn't stop. Those flares have stayed. They've never dimmed. I look in those eyes today and see all that is my existence. It's a peaceful warmth to us now. I wander always to her marveling light."

I was enthralled now, speechless, and he could see it. He finished his coffee and gazed off in the distance at the tree tops. I could hear the faint rhythmic bells of wind chimes dancing to the light breezes. He continued on in his euphoric proclaim.

"She came on like silk, the fabric of charm. I ride on hope's perfume, where the sun and the wind dance her hair. I've found her every caress makes all concerns disappear."

This was love like I had never heard spoken before. I was blown away. I understood what he was saying now. I'm sure he caught the pleasing look I must have had on my face.

"Forever in our arms we etch the tide," he went on. "Her kisses are the flavors in my dreams. I get the sweetest colors looking at her. With our every wish, we've made rainbows here." He looked over to me standing there and smiled. I wasn't about to interrupt his flow. He hardly seemed to hesitate long enough to breathe between his words. He didn't even have to think about what he was saying — it just rolled out. "These are the things that can only be given to true lovers, heartthrobs of closeness," he said.

Jewel was walking back. She came to the porch edge below from where I stood, then hesitated. She looked up, first to Marcus, then me. I felt certain she knew the conversation had been about her. She looked back at Marcus in a most sincere way.

"Ah, the luscious fragrance of wild-tamed eyes unhurried," Marcus proclaimed, glancing at me with a wink. Whoa, I thought, as I gave her a comfortable smile. She smiled back, warmly glowing, and continued around to the porch steps. She stopped and turned toward the cabin below. There, like magic, Hershel had appeared, seated in his chair as he always had been before. He was working on what appeared to be one of his carvings. He looked up in that same instant. Jewel waved to him and he waved back.

"I hope this is starting to help," Marcus said to me.

What could I say? I glanced back at to him. I was out of things to say, out of questions, as amateur an interviewer as I truly was. He just smiled at me. Jewel glanced at us as she stepped past.

"Dinner in an hour or so," she said, then turned to go inside. He stood up and stretched his arms. I could tell he had gotten uptight. I turned off the recorder.

"I have something I need to give to Hersh," I told him. He just kept smiling. I went inside to retrieve the bag of beads. It had been placed on a small table near the back door. I turned and exchanged smiles with Jewel as I walked back out. She was setting plates on the table.

Marcus was sitting in the middle of the porch swing now, slowly swaying it back and forth with one leg. His arms were outstretched along the back on each side. He seemed now to be relaxing.

"I'll be down in a minute," he told me, as he watched me step from the porch. I turned and nodded, then casually walked toward Hershel, who was grinning his usual, wider than his face grin, as I approached. He looked genuinely happy to see me. He pointed down to his right at the base of the steps. There was a high metal laundry tub. I peered in to it. I was immediately taken aback at the sight of two huge snapping turtles. I wasn't expecting that.

"Whoa! Did you catch them?"

He smiled proudly, glowing.

"Way to go!" I climbed the steps and patted him on the shoulder. "This is for you," I said, and I handed him the bag. He took it from my hands, opened it, and peeked inside with his left eye. An even bigger smile appeared as he looked up at me. I could swear his eyes were watery. Ever since we met, I'd recognized him to be someone instilled with deep feelings. It gave me a sense of pleasure to have found this warmth in someone who could only express himself so uniquely.

Marcus was walking down to us now. I stood next to Hershel as he approached.

"Check it out," I said to Marcus, and I pointed to the large metal tub. He stopped to look inside.

"Hmm, I was expecting a gator," he laughed. "Looks like soup to me," he added, as he looked up at Hershel. "These for Clay?" Hershel kept smiling and nodded yes. "He catches them for Clay to butcher," Marcus explained to me. "Never sure what I'm gonna see when I look in there. Wanna take a walk?" he asked me.

Uh oh, the last time he said that, I believe my life changed significantly. "Sure," I said without giving an appearance of hesitation. "Now what?" I was thinking to myself.

Hershel looked down at the circle on his lap, forever smiling. I stepped from the porch to join Marcus. He had already begun walking toward the path between the bushes that lead to his place without a name. "I wanna show you something," he said as we walked.

In a minute we entered the clearing. The place my mind's eye sees as a prehistoric park. He stopped on the side of the big willow, pointing toward the island. Short telephone pole sections had been placed at intervals, standing upright, and protruding from out of the water. They appeared to be footings that extended from the shoreline to the island.

"It's gonna to be a bridge," he explained. "You said Kat prefers vacationing on islands, well, there's her island," he pointed.

I smiled widely at him. Wait till she hears this, I thought.

"Bridges connect gaps," Marcus said, and he once again gave me his warm loving wink. "Let's go sit down."

We took our seats on the park bench, and sat there for a moment, taking it all in. I pushed the "on" button in my shirt pocket.

"Man, I hope Kat can get to see this place," I exclaimed.

"She will," he assured me, then turned his eyes upward to look at the tree tops. "Here I can see the tops of things. I know after these rags of skin are spent away, the spirit is the only true form. This place tells me all of that. Listen, and you can hear the sound of your soul beating against your heart here." I didn't say a word. He looked over at me. I think he may have wondered if I was understanding him when he added, "I disperse my

meanings in dark waters." I just looked at him, expressionless. Deep waters, was what I was thinking. I tried to become an interviewer again.

"Jack said Clay was at a dance." There was an uncomfortable moment before he responded. I thought I had botched what I was attempting to do, even though I wasn't quite sure what that was.

"It's quite a deal, lasts for days, really," he finally said. "Everybody campin' out. A lot of music. A lot of bands. I went once, stood in the back of the crowd, listening to Eddie's group. Not my flavor, but good I suppose. He does remind me of me. I was a pimply-face kid like him. I wanted to be an electrician. I went to night school to learn. I don't know about him being an electrician, but I think he'll get good with his music someday. I can tell he has that all encompassing love for it, like I do.

"What's the name of his band?"

"Last I heard it was The Patty Melts, but they've changed it a few times."

I just laughed. "Where do they come up with these names?" We were silent again for a time. My mind was peacefully blank. I couldn't really think of anything to ask — what direction I should go. We watched scenery compelled to change. An otter was playing along the opposite bank. "What are those?" I asked, as I pointed at two birds with long legs, standing at the water's edge to our right.

"They call those sandwich terns."

Again, I saw a pelican at a distance to our left, perched on a cypress knee protruding from the water. The sounds of life were loud all around us.

He broke the clamor. "Everyone was really quite helpful in my quest for this masked identity. It was easier to disappear then you might imagine."

"How did you disappear anyway?"

"I don't think it's time to discuss that. It could cause trouble. Someday, I'll tell ya all about it, but it's not something everyone should know."

I let it drop. This was his show all the way. I knew I was just his tool. I guess that's not a fair thing to say, because I knew I had fast become one of his good friends. For that I will be forever grateful. I had to let him take the lead on this.

"You know, you go through life, and does anyone ever really say goodbye?" I could tell he was reflecting again when he added: "She never said goodbye."

"Who?" I asked.

"My Mom." He hesitated for a second, then concluded, "I believe in the salvation of souls that don't know no better than to not hurt others. God chooses them as his justification for continuing life."

What could I say to that? He was getting extremely profound again. Daylight was beginning to rest her shadows against the trees.

"Pink clouds understanding a blue moon," he said, pointing just above the leafy horizon. "I blame the existence of loneliness for almost everything, even

if it's slight, even if it's only brief. Loneliness does a lot of damage. It's the worst feeling ever created. Everyone gets it. Some really get it. It was embedded in me so deep before Jewel."

I interjected: "I guess that's why I play and sing. I'm thinkin' that's why guitars exist, to stop the pain. It's somethin' ta hold and cry on, bein' able ta hug somethin' in a way. Doesn't everyone need that?"

"Music saves," he replied. "We that play are lucky. Our reasons to cry have a place to go. Some don't have that. Where do they go to cry?"

"Maybe no place," was all I could think to say.

He slapped my knee. "Best we get to supper. I'm anxious to hear what we sound like on your tape."

## CHAPTER 13

The table had been set, and dinner was simmering under a warm linger of smoke, hinting delectable. Jewel had to have seen us approach the house to have timed this so well. There was apple juice, French bread, two bowls filled with berries, white rice, beans, and a main dish of shrimp Creole sautéed in a vegetable mix, with onions and small slices of lemons on the side. There was some kind of peppers, sweet I think, and the celery I had seen her cutting up earlier near the outdoor grill. It nearly made my salivary glands spurt out of the underside of my tongue. If I had attempted to speak they certainly would have. I have to say the table setting defied description. The tastes, magnificent — candlelight charmed. An atmosphere so sublime, it felt healing. Like a deep breath that takes all troubles away.

"An island for Kat to vacation on," I quietly thought aloud as we sat eating.

"Think it'll work?" Jewel asked.

"I hope so, but first I need her to click those ruby slippers and say 'I believe' three times," I joked. They both laughed.

"When will you be taking your vacation this year?" Marcus asked.

With my job, it's mandatory to submit vacation requests by the first quarter of the year. We are allowed three possible choices for each eligible week we have coming. The company decides accordingly, balancing so many drivers with the projected freight. It has to be a logistics nightmare. My choices came back for the second week in June, starting on the ninth, and the middle of September, starting on the fifteenth. Thanksgiving and Christmas were chosen as my third and fourth weeks, respectively. I told them the dates. He took a bite of his food without looking up, and didn't respond.

"Think you guys could ever get away and come up?" I again asked. He looked to Jewel. She looked back at him without expression. He gave me another of his blank looks.

"I'll tell you something, we're toying with the thought of movin' for a while. Burton is working on scouting out some places in the country for us to have a look at. I want seclusion. Jewel wants a mountain."

I looked at Jewel with surprise. "You'd keep this place, wouldn't ya?"

"I'll never let this place go," she said fondly. "We just need some different atmosphere for a while."

"What about your patients? What about Hershel?"

"There's someone else who knows what needs to be done." He will manage these people for a time," she explained. "Hersh will always live where we live," she added. "He'll always need my care."

"Does he ever come up here to the house?" I asked.

"He rarely ventures past his comfort zone. We don't make him, except when necessary." I had noticed she always brought his food to him before the rest of us sat down to eat.

"How much does he understand when we talk?"

"He only understands rudimentary. He pieces things together, and that gets him by. I think he hardly understands any of the things Marcus says."

"That makes two of us," I proclaimed jokingly. Marcus had a funny, yet continued blank look on his face, and said nothing.

"He does understand music to a point. One can tell he enjoys it deeply. I don't believe he knows loneliness. He's never displayed it," Jewel added.

"We could arrange to come see you when we're out and about," Marcus interjected.

I was beside myself in an instant, bursting out from deep inside, almost exploding in my skin. "You mean it?" I blurted, almost too loud.

"If that would be alright?"

"Man, would it ever!"

"We'd probably be flying. Is there an airport nearby?"

"A small one just outside of town," I said. I could hardly contain this new excitement I was experiencing. Could it really happen?

"We'll just have to see what shakes out," Marcus added. "How close are you to the source of the Mississippi River?"

"You mean the headwaters? I've been there. You can walk across it. It's maybe three hours or so from our cabin," I told him.

"Jewel has always wanted to see it, experience it, I guess," he said.

I looked over at her. She was shyly smiling in my direction, then nodded her head. "That's true," she confirmed.

"It could easily be arranged. Kat has never been there either. I'm sure she'd like to see it too," I said, looking back at Jewel warmly.

We sat in silence for a moment. He let the subject drop for now. "Hope ya brought plenty of tape," he said, then he stood up from the table.

I crammed my last few bites down. Jewel was left eating alone, as I followed him to the music room. He had that old Martin in his hands in a flash. I pulled my Gibson from the case that I had left leaning against the couch. I looked across the room at Jewel when I took my seat. She was looking back at me with a smile. She shrugged her shoulders, as if to suggest that Marcus had a one track mind. Then she looked down at her plate to take another bite of food.

The large recorder had been moved from the porch to the coffee table in front of the couch, probably by Jewel. I reached over and turned it on. She was walking over to us now. She had that famous bottle in her hand, and three shot glasses in the other. She poured us each a drink without asking, without saying a word, then walked back to the table to finish her dinner. I more than suspected that the night would be "Thin Ice" all around.

"I've lost so many lyrics not remembering I would forget," Marcus said as he checked his tuning. I said I felt the same way. His Martin guitar was amazing. It always seemed to be tuned perfectly. "I worked out something for that song of yours, *Ways to Remember,*" he said.

"Great," I resounded, as I tuned up.

"There are reasons for beginnings and ends, it's not for us to understand," he explained, probably in reference to my song. "We just get to live it. How lucky we are. I'm thinkin' ends we can never know," he concluded.

"Yer a blast, ya know that?" I said. His philosophical altitude often seemed to catch me a little dizzy.

"Yah, I know; yer a deal too," he responded.

"Thanks, but if you really knew me, you'd see I'm always dropping out," I said.

"Dropping out of what?" he immediately asked.

"Of whatever there is," I said.

There was this pause; he was thinking deeply, then he said, "That might be a good thing. You're unsettled, and that's where all beginnings start, probably live that tattoo you've got." We toasted. "To the music," he said. Then the two of us drank the first one straight down, almost celebratory.

"Yer a blast," I repeated. He just smiled, poured another, and we toasted to the music again. This time I merely sipped. He drank that second one down without hesitation. Jewel remained at the kitchen table.

"Just don't drop out of this one," he said, setting his glass on the table. "There's a lot in it for all of us. I suppose you're gonna want monetary rewards?" he asked with a wide grin.

"Yah, a hundred percent," I laughed.

"You got it," he replied.

"I can't leave a lopsided ending with no answers," I quickly added. "I won't drop this."

Without saying another word he began playing a song, an original he would come to call *Back to Teary Eyes*. I again sat astounded for a moment. I tried to play along, but he was using chords and progressions totally unfamiliar to me. I pride myself on being able to play along with the best of them, but this was really different, and a true blessing to listen to. Noticing the song seemed to be based in, or resembling, the key of 'A' and remembering I had a harmonica in my guitar case of the same key, I quickly retrieved it. Quietly, as background, I played along to his song as decorous as I could. Admittedly an amateur, I think I held my own. I felt I had experienced something no one in the world had ever had the pleasure of experiencing. What a treasure I was living through. What a turn my life had taken. I was, moment after moment, coming to realize this story was fashioning itself right before me. When he finished, he pointed to the harmonica in my hand and nodded approval.

"It's my pirate harmonica," I told him. "It's in the key of AAHHRRRR."

He busted out laughing, and from the other room, so did Jewel. Then, without hesitation, almost as though that song had just been a warm-up to limber his fingers, he said, "Here's what I got for your song." He played what he had written, adding to my stalled-out version. I just sat there and listened. As he was finishing, he flubbed the last couple of chord changes. "The problem with getting older than I used to be," he said, embarrassed.

I was polite. "Good deal. I think you've pretty much hit it," I said. In truth, it was mediocre at best. I had been hoping for more revelation, more introspection from him. I think, in part, that it was my song and not his; that it was disappointing, nothing special. "I'll polish it up with my own tit-tats later," I told him with a smile.

"Can you play back both those songs? I wanna hear how that thing is picking up," he said to me, referring to my table recorder. Jewel came to join us then, sitting down near me.

"Sure." I rewound to approximately the designated numbers on the counter where the songs had started. "Yah, a hundred percent," I heard my voice say, and so on. We listened without a word. The tape had picked up everything. The quality was lacking in many respects, but the words and the music came through. He seemed pleased with the results. I pushed the record button to resume.

"God shoulda let us to live for 500 years," he said. "It would all seem so much more complete then."

"You think so? Then you'd wish for a thousand." I responded.

"Would that be so bad?" Jewel asked.

"I'm thinkin' there's only so much a single soul's gonna want to do, and a thousand seems too much," I told them, and I could tell I was feeling the 'Ice' now.

"Maybe you're right," Marcus conceded.

"I wouldn't pose that question to Clay," Jewel toned in. "A thousand years wouldn't be near enough for him. There's a guy who never wants to near an end of any kind."

"Bless him," I said, and raised my glass in a toast.

Marcus quickly filled his glass, raising it to mine. "Yah, bless him," he said. I sipped; he shot his drink right down. Jewel poured her first one, tactfully gesturing her approval for the subject we had just given toast to.

Marcus explained how he wanted to start over, to record all of the songs he had written. The remainder of that evening would entail only his originals, from *Stealin'*, all the way up to where we had progressed. He instructed our each step in his erudite manner. I went easier on my drinking, but still had my share. Marcus was feeling no pain. Jewel joined in on banjo and vocals as she previously had done.

I consider the recordings we did that night to be priceless, a labor of love if ever there was one. Marcus had us do re-takes on the ones he wanted to change around a bit. We traded suggestive lead-ins and fade-outs that we supposed could be more encompassing to what he was trying to achieve. We worked on adding some fancy hammer-ons and pull-offs. That's guitar player's lingo, meaning to fill in between the notes, adding flow to the melody. Working in rhythmical congruity, all in all, we were satisfied with what had been laid down. It wasn't recording studio readiness, but our conjunction held its own, giving promise to each song's future endeavors.

"I need you to learn these like they were your own," he said to me at the end of our session. His expression, warm, benignant, almost as a father to his beloved son. I was overtaken. My eyes could have been welling up when we gave each other our heartfelt, "goodnight."

## CHAPTER 14

I must have been o-zoning, floating, as I plopped on the bed. My journal entry that early morning reads,

*"2/16/06: It's a long, gray wind that holds me down to zero while I'm on this other side. I'm lost and simple in this place of no fears. My focus is overwhelmed, where waves can't reach the shore."*

What I was trying to say, to this day, I'm still not sure. I remember when waking up, how a moderate breeze was ruffling a dance on the lightened window curtains. I could hear the sound of what may have been a mourning dove, then the gruffness of Mad Jack's voice. I had passed out with my clothes on again. I freshened up quickly. I was feeling fine, no hangover, no snake bite. I walked out of the room to join them.

Jack was seated at the table, his back to me, eating breakfast. Marcus was sitting across from him drinking from his coffee cup. Marcus smiled when he saw me.

"Well, hello," he said. "Another dawning of an untouched morning."

Jewel turned from the kitchen counter, sending me one of her electrifying looks. "Tomorrows can always be a nice new place," she said. I smiled back, half unconscious. Jack turned to look at me.

"Hey Hatty," he said brazenly.

"I'll bet I'm late," I sleepily replied.

"Late fer what?" Jack asked.

"I don't know, I just feel late. Late for this, I guess."

Jewel giggled. "Need to get you fed before we send you on your way."

"Yer a gem," I told her, and I sat down.

We ate deviled eggs, and, guess what, alligator gar patties on fresh bread. I thought they were joking, but the taste was not that of any I'd tasted previously. I'd have to say it was good — an experience. Toast and jelly made it all complete. Orange juice and coffee washed everything down.

While we ate, we listened to excerpts from our recordings of the night before. Marcus said we had accomplished a lot. "My memories are musical notes, my rhythm, her beauty," he remarked, looking over to Jewel. The mealtime was family warm, but I seemed to always feel unsettled when the time to leave is close at hand. I excused myself and they understood. I hastily went to pack everything. Jewel had her usual goody-bag for me. She was going to get me healthy no matter what, and in spite of myself. We all stepped onto the porch.

"Come down to the cabin a minute," Jewel told me. Just the two of us walked down the hill. As we approached his porch, Hershel peered out from a crack in the door. With Jack around, he acted quite timorous. We climbed the stairs and he half-stepped out, over a thin, ruddy, reddish line of dirt that had been drawn across the floor in front of his door. I wondered about that, and later found out from Jewel that he was superstitious. The line was to "fix" him safely. If anyone meant to do him harm, they would not be able to cross that line. His mother had taught that to him. It became another one of my bewilderments.

He reached his hand out to me then. In it hung dangling shells and beads on assorted lengths of strings. It was a wind chime, and he was giving it to me. The rough outer coverings of the shells, opposite their pearly inside, had been freshly painted a steel gray-blue in color. I looked at them closely, then at Jewel. She smiled and gave me a wink. I put my hand through the doorway onto Hershel's shoulder and gave a squeeze. I smiled at him without a word; in truth I was somewhat speechless. I stepped back from the door, holding my gift, as it dangled and resounded lightly in tones that seemed new to me. It was a pleasing resonance against the backdrops of Louisiana's hidden and delicate sounds. It's a place on earth that few may ever know. Jewel and I turned to go back up the hill. I knew she could tell I was touched deeply by his gesture. There was a love being played out with highest regard.

Jack was raring to go when we rejoined them. Marcus was standing up on the porch near the top step. Jewel went up to join him. She put her arm around his waist.

"Stay alright," Marcus said once again to me. He always managed to say that when we parted. I nodded. Jewel just gave me that priceless smile, like she was giving me the world and she knew it. Jack and I turned and walked toward the inlet, dogs at our feet.

When we reached the boat, I laid the wind chime gently over my bag near the bow, and my guitar case against that seat. I looked over to the back of the inlet where the water ends. There was Clay's pontoon, laboring with lumber and boxes, pulled up snug against the shore by a thick rope. It was attached to a winch on a steel pole that was protruding from the ground near the shoreline. Jack must have towed the load up that morning. I hadn't noticed the pole and crank before.

We set off. There would come my last patting goodbye to Woogie. Wind chimes would be the first thing of substance I could bring to Kat. I played her excerpts from the tapes. I remember her say indignantly, "Sounds like him, but so do a lot of people."

# PART V

## CHAPTER 1

I would visit them three more times in the winter and spring of 2006. Twice were ice runs from St. Louis to the National Guard Distribution Center in New Orleans. These were not refrigeration trailer units, but simply 53-foot-long vans. Ice had been loaded to overweight capacity, enlisting the equation that several thousand pounds would melt and leak out during transport. The "Hurricane Relief" decals on each side of Beulah's accessory doors assured I would pass by all weigh stations without being subject to inspection. The object was to get to my destination as soon as safely possible. The third run would be a load of bottled water that went to another warehouse location within the city.

Marcus and I had been concentrating almost exclusively on his written material. Together we were enlisting our individual styles to achieve all that we could bring his songs to be. When it came to the stories I would bring home to her, Kat was becoming increasingly passive, albeit blasé. And even though I gave her the wind chimes Hershel had made, she was not as responsive as I had hoped she'd be. I don't know, maybe she thought that I had bought the wind chimes. Did she believe I was making things up? I held back on telling her anything about the island and the bridge that was being made. It was as if she was closing herself off with disbelief. In one ear and out the other, best described her attentiveness.

My journal entries were becoming more and more frequent, sometimes two or three a day. Many times I would awaken in the middle of the night. Writing now was causing many instances of interrupted sleep. I was taking more walks during my free time during the day. I sat on mountain crests. I struggled with the book, trying to remain convinced I could be a high-falutin' book writer. I had purchased a laptop to help with my endeavor, although my computer knowledge was almost nonexistent. At least I had retained some of my typing skills from college days. The progress with the book was slow, at times seemingly halted. I was attempting more than one approach at a story line, searching for the best way to tell what needed to be told. Trying to regain what had been reflected to me from Beulah on that snow covered morning.

My songwriting had become almost non-existent. My times with Marcus were concentrated on the effort to get his songs on tape and for me to dedicate them to memory. We were blending our styles more and more smoothly. Together we were creating comfortable and satisfying renditions of what he had written. Although it was a struggle at times, we managed to keep things fun, even adventuresome.

"I never used to write songs," he had explained to me. "She gave me this gift."

"And a gift it's been, indeed," I had replied.

It was during this time, having early morning coffee on their porch, that I actually witnessed a small bird land on Jewel's shoulder. I believe it was a chickadee. She had been whistling a faint song while standing in the yard, just off the porch steps. She turned her head gently to it, an enchanting moment. Then it flew away. I turned to Marcus with my mouth open. He merely smiled.

Upon re-examination of some of my journal entries from these times, I found I was telling myself how conditioned I was getting to Thin Ice, yet my next writing would contradict my previous line of thought, emulsifying the experience as if being born again. When actual ice was added to it, there appeared a smoke like opalescence, cloudy swirls. Any way I looked at this concoction, it gave me ever new ways to describe its effects. Every experience with it a unique and different opened door. It confounds me still, my attempts to conclusively define these almost mystifying presentations.

While trying to write a song about Woogie, as I had given my word to Clay, frustration had led to an angry hurt. She was gone now. Jack had taken care of that business. All of my songwriting thus far had been slow melodies, somber, and not really getting where I felt it needed to go. There had come to be many scrunched-up pieces of paper in my waste bag.

I remember drinking in a bar with a couple of other drivers during a long layover. It was in a town called Elm Mott, Texas. We were discussing the dogs we had in our lives. I thought about Woogie, and the last time I had given her that pat goodbye. It hadn't hit me at the time, but when I left the bar and that conversation behind, I found myself crying while walking back to Beulah. My journal entry that night read:

*"I'm cryin' and I don't know why. Little bit of this, and a little bit of that. Woogie was just a dog, as simple as that...but she sure could take a pat!"*

As it turned out, I would laugh out loud the next morning at what I had written. And, as it turned out, in the middle of that teary night at around 3 a.m., I had turned on my bunk light, and in a surge of inspiration, I wrote her song. The melody was in my head. I would pick it out on guitar when I got farther down the road. It was, as it needed to be, upbeat and fast tempo. It turned into a celebration of her and the close relationship she had with Clay. I named the song *The Waggin' Woogie Boogie*.

Once back at home again, I called my close friend, Rick, who resides in Minneapolis. Apart from being just about the best lead guitar player I've ever had the privilege of knowing and making music with, he was also accomplished in mandolin, and violin. I had once heard an old man describing southern textured music say, "There ain't no bad fiddle." Rick's inclusion with Woogie's song was set in stone to me. The design would be that of a quick, frolicking dance number. When I called Rick on the phone, I explained my endeavor. He hardly shared in my enthusiasm.

"A dog?" he said, yawning. I had gotten him out of bed.

"Yah, but not just any dog. And it's for a dear friend."

"Oh, I thought all dogs are just any dogs," he replied.

"I'm comin' down so you can give this a listen," I told him. Minneapolis was only an hour and a half from our cabin.

"I'll come up," he said, surprising me. "Mae and I are looking to get out of town. You guys got time for some company?"

"Absolutely," I said, almost rejoicing, and without asking Kat first. I looked over to her, and thank goodness, she gave me an affirming smile. I gave her an appreciative look. "When can ya make it, tomorrow?" Kat leaned over to my other ear and said she would make chili.

"Tomorrow yah, what should I bring?" Rick asked.

"Guitar for now, but we'll need to add mando and fiddle eventually. Kat said she'll make chili." It was a good choice, one of Kat's knockout specialties, coupled with the fact that Mae is a vegetarian, and Kat can make it with or without meat.

To make a long story short, after Rick sat down with me and we peddled through what I had written, his enthusiasm built to inspiration. We polished out and completed a version that could hold its own to a band setting. There would come to be additions and subtractions, a fact of the matter with songwriting. What we had come up with that afternoon was a fun little ditty. As we warmed up our play, the song took on the life I had hoped for. We even caught Mae and Kat in a moment of dance during our living room jubilee.

Rick knows people in the music business. His contacts had grown and remained strong over the years — unlike mine, which had diminished with time while living my backwoods dream. He would pull the necessary strings. He called me that very week when I was on the road. Rick let me know that he had set up some recording time in a small studio, not far from where he lived. It was arranged for the next time I would be home. Having taken this initiative without consulting me first was in Rick's nature, and I appreciated that. It was almost more than I could have hoped for. His brother, Don, also an excellent lead guitar player, had volunteered to help out — more like jumped at the chance. He tends to jump at every chance to play. Don contacted his friend Scott to play bass, and another strong musician, Paul, whom I had enjoyed performing with a number of years earlier. Paul would be on percussion. Rick would dub in fiddle and mandolin where needed. He just refers to it as a mando. All was set to swing.

It would be all the more a special homecoming this time. Kat was happy to get away from the peaceful solitude that envelopes her many days and nights in the woods. She hasn't driven in a big city for decades, but as long as I was driving, the promise of something new and exciting prompted her to be in an unusually heightened and upbeat spirit. We would stay overnight at Rick and Mae's place, located near the University Of Minnesota campus, in what is known as Dinkytown on the West Bank. It is said that Bob Dylan played in a coffee house there before he went to New York and became famous. It's a vibrant, bustling little community, with occasional old Bohemian and Gypsy, Greenwich Village flare. I had ventured its streets in my early youth, when Cedar Avenue more resembled Height-Asbury for a time. Music and art had their domain within the candlelit evening windows of those old neighborhoods. I was eager to get back. I found it now to have a very international flavor, yet not without those old pastel mixes I so loved about the area.

The studio was at a small record store, inconspicuously located in the basement. It was a project of Rick's friend, Jeff, servicing local musicians, but not being subject to anyone renowned. It simply gave experience and promise to the hopeful. Leave it to Richard to have found the perfect place for this endeavor.

In recounting that day, it took longer to set up than it did to complete the recording. It turned into a cramped undertaking with our equipment; amplifiers for guitar and bass, drums, and our ladies as groupies, it was an elbow to elbow ordeal. After a time, the ladies wisely decided to shop at the small stores around the block.

"There goes our fan base," Don remarked, when they walked up the stairs.

Although we were not being charged exuberantly for the time we were recording, the session took on a "let's get this thing done" atmosphere. We climbed to the seriousness needed, subscribing all of our musical profundities, and pounding out a final, credible version. With one good go through, the song was quickly dedicated onto a CD. We all seemed satisfied with what we had put down.

As we packed up our equipment, I thankfully gave Jeff $300, which was more than he had required. The pay to us musicians would simply be copies of the CD, with no one taking credit for its creation. We would all reserve the right to play it anytime in public, just to see where it would go. I wanted to take the initiative to gain a copyright under the band name, *The Fly By Night Outfit*, but I never did.

## CHAPTER 2

I will forever recall that special moment in my life, when I first presented the song to Clay. It was on the boat ride to visit Jewel and Marcus. By this time, I had gotten more familiar with alligator sightings, even having had the occasion to motor precariously close to one on the boat ride up that preceded this one. The weather was getting warm, spring was surging forward. When Clay cut the motor to pole us in, I asked him if he would drop anchor in the shallows. "I have something for you," I told him. He did so without question. I pulled my guitar from the case, and there, afloat on that calm water, I played for him the one man acoustic version of Woogie's song. For once Clay was speechless. He actually got watery eyes — they honestly welled up with tears. I reached in my bag and produced 10 copies of the CD, and raised them up to him in one hand, spread out like a dealt hand of cards. "Here ya go," I said. Still he said nothing, an unashamed tear rolled down his cheek. His lower lip was quivering. He turned and lifted the anchor. He stood up, pole in hand, and pushed for the inlet.

It wasn't until we stepped from the boat that he nudged up close to me. Standing on the shoreline, and still without speaking, he gave me the hug of a lifetime. I can still feel the strong arms of his love and gratitude. He even spilled his beer on me during this gesture of thankfulness. It was, indeed, a happy ending to a promise fulfilled. I handed him the CDs. When I later recounted the spilled beer to Jewel, she laughed louder than I had ever, or since, heard her laugh. That visit would have more than this one special moment to remember.

In the place with no name, where the bridge footings had earlier been shown to me, there was now a foot bridge with guard rails. It led to a wonderful gazebo near the center of the island. It had been trimmed in decorative wood framing and was fully screened in. It had bench seats around the inside walls, with a table in its center. Flower beds had been planted around its outside base and two porcelain bird baths were set up a few feet away on either side. It was another picture postcard from this paradise unspoiled.

"I await spring winds to press summer's lips against her heart," Marcus said, while he was showing it to me. He was referring to Kat. I could tell, both he and Jewel were becoming excited to meet her.

Throughout each visit, I would observe Hershel tending to his art and his garden. His newfound pleasure seemed to be keeping those bird baths clean and filled with fresh water. We sat together on his porch for a time during each of my visits. Always the sound of his wind chimes brightened the atmosphere. He too, may have sensed a newcomer to his world in this enticing preparation for Kat to somehow make an appearance. I was more than ever determined that she would. She had to become a part of all of this.

It was during this time, while strumming my guitar on Hershel's porch one afternoon, I first witnessed Jewel administer to him his diabetes medication. He seemed comfortable with me there. We had developed a brotherly kinship in our mutual love for his art, the contentment we shared in the music, and the tranquility of this world that surrounded us.

During my walks with Marcus he came to explain the days before Jewel and how he had been drowning in drugs. He spoke of a doctor who I will not name. "My health was failing fast. I would have died, had she not saved both my spirit and my flesh," he said. "God brought her to me in my most needed hour. My faith has flourished since then."

"Why are you banking your wishes on me now?" my taped recording reveals me asking.

"Who else should I? Who else could I?" was his reply. "You're bringing me to a new beginning that no one will deny. That great hurricane happened for reasons man can't see. We're a part of its story, a story unfolding and yet to be told. Far greater catastrophes will be cast that will set mankind to ashes," he then proclaimed in a raised voice. "The souls saved will be on that train." Then he added, "You and me, well, as a nail's head bows to a hammer's blow." There he went again. He had lost me. Another phrase, I to this day, am unable to comprehend. Why does he, so often, choose to speak with this translucence, and so deep. "Watch for snakes," he's heard telling me on the tape. We were walking. I don't recall where. I could tell he had again set about confounding me.

I do recall a different moment on an earlier visit. I was attempting to play interviewer again. I had asked him about the first time he had used "Marcus" rather than his real name, and how it made him feel. Surprisingly, he couldn't remember. The conversation spurred him to other recollections. It was easy for him to look back.

"I remember a time at Overton Park Shell. It was around 1955. I think it was Webb Pierce that may have been playing. They were calling me up to do a song. I distinctly remember I was wearing a lavender shirt and pink pants. A joke was made, asking what color lilacs were, and someone remarked, pink! It cracked me up so hard, the seam ripped out in the back my pants. It's why, this many years later, I wrote that song, *Bust My Britches*. I would tear the seat out of my pants all of the time."

"Do ya still have that problem?" I asked.

"Jewel makes my clothes now. She keeps them loose fitted. Besides, she had to make 'em for me. I hear all my old ones are behind glass in a museum," he quipped.

He spoke about someone who worked at a place called Goldsmiths. He told about how he would have his hair and eyebrows dyed black at least once a month. Marcus would buy people new cars back then. Then the recollections took on a bleaker tone, as he again recalled his mother. A friend had accompanied him when his mother was dying. Marcus told how he had later secured her favorite band for the funeral. I felt the need to turn the conversation. My mind seemed to tumult in search of a fast recourse. I needed this to stay bright. I needed him to stay bright. He seemed to have two personality traits, happy and mad. Although I had only caught a glimpse of the latter, I recognized it to be disturbing the wellness he had long ago been conformed to. It was this looking into his past, I feared, that could lead to a destructive venom he no longer needed. I tried to be careful with my questions after that.

"I know you had a red MGA roadster. I had one, too — a '56 — first year they made them, and the same color as yours," I said proudly.

"Yah? Mine was a '60. That was a fun car. Liked my Stutz best. I was a suffering sports car coolie in my spider-webbed time."

That was profound, I thought to myself. "I met a trucker who claimed to have stolen the dipstick out of one of your motorcycles," I told him. He laughed loudly.

"So that's where that went," he replied comically. This was the Marcus I hastened to indulge in conversation. This was where I truly wanted the designs in my writings to go.

It was around this time that I took the initiative to rent a safety deposit box. The tapes were starting to accumulate. I considered them priceless and secret. Spring had long since set in, summer pushing its coarse forward.

Kat had long ago gathered up that deck of cards from our table and put them back in their pack. Replacing the crumbs of lemon roll now were assorted post cards I had sent. One that lay across the top of this dispersed collection was the most recent. It read: *"Spring, almost a summer feeling here, though I know you still have snow. These flowers are telling of kisses going north, where buds yet sleeping, rest before their crazy affair. These buds are smiling as I walk by, and remind me to tell you of their time to come. Just a wink away and their blossoms will be in your hair. Truly, Your Gypsy Boy."*

The fingertips of my left hand drew across the card, sliding it from the pile, to reveal another. This one read: *"Cloud covered, so I just can't see, but I smell the moonbeams. They are being lured, invited by a fragrance. I hear them melting in the embracing ocean of your warm soft eyes. They are drowned in love just as chocolate gives its everything when placed upon the tongue."*

"My word!" I said aloud. It was true. Even Kat had remarked, around this time: "You're talking to me in riddles and rhymes sometimes!" His poetic nature was most assuredly rubbing off on me. Justifying to myself, that it was much the same as the way I catch a southern drawl every time I get below the Mason Dixon Line.

Kat was slowly becoming aware of the changes in me. I had lost some weight and seemed to have more energy. My language was being tinted by his. She had also seen the remnants of Jewel's goodie bags.

"You eat this?" she exclaimed.

"It's good," I responded. "Everything they eat is amazing, wonderfully great tasting."

These had been my first experiences with Cajun cooking, and I don't believe Kat had ever tried any. I recounted, in what detail I could, how these people lived on "des bayas," as Clay would called them. I tried to describe to her what their surroundings were like, what a virtual paradise they were in. At best, she seemed only remotely interested.

There was a story Clay had told me. He called it, "La be'ne'diction des bateaux." In down-home northern boy words, it means, "the blessing of the fleet." The last one he had attended was before Katrina. Turns out that it's a parade of shrimp boats, with crews and families motoring down the bayou in celebration of the opening of shrimp season. It's like a festival, complete with flowers, music, beer, and a ton of great food. Led by a priest on the first boat, the true meaning is to ask God for a bountiful harvest, and to grant safety to the hardworking folks that toil with the nets. This life can be cumbersome and dangerous, as Jewel would attest. Clay explained how Katrina had wiped out much of this local industry, but the hearts of these people would always remain strong. The ancestry of this culture shows it always comes back. History has shown them to have suffered grievously. They are of a strong bloodline.

"They must make God proud," I remember telling Kat.

## CHAPTER 3

June was dancing in full swing. My thoughts were on our vacation, making time for the grandkids, and getting things done around my "Ponderosa." We never plan anything our first week off. There are chores to catch up with, so travel never seems to be in the cards.

Then came a phone call. It was Saturday morning and I had just gotten off the road the previous afternoon. Kat and I were still in bed, pillows propped up, enjoying coffee and sleepy conversation. Kat answered the phone.

"Hi, this is Burton, is Grant around?" She had a surprise look on her face as she handed the phone to me. She had never spoken with any of them before. She may not have even believed Burton existed. She said nothing.

"Hello?" I said.

"Grant, Burton here."

"Hey!" I said, surprised. Now I woke up. "How ya doin'?"

"Fine, fine, how 'bout yourself?" he asked.

"Great, I'm on vacation," I explained.

"I know, that's why I'm calling. How'd you like some company?"

I only hoped this meant what I thought it meant. I turned to Kat as I responded. "Sure, what's up?"

"It's Marcus and Jewel. They want to come up and see you guys."

I sat straight up; I could have jumped right out of bed! Kat could see my surge of excitement.

"What?" she asked.

"They're coming up," I whispered in a soft roar.

"Who?"

"L and Jewel" I told her.

"Who? Where, here?" was her reaction.

"Ohhh yahhh," I said back to her.

As it was, Burton stayed quiet during that brief exchange.

"Of course," I told him, without waiting for Kat's approval. "When?"

"Well actually tomorrow," Burton replied. "If that would be alright. I spoke with them yesterday. They've been making plans to visit a few places that I've suggested, and they thought this would be a good time to see you. I've arranged my best pilot to fly them around. Marcus had once referred to Burton as "The Enforcer," At once I could tell where that came from. He was a man ahead of his game, confident in getting things done without wasting time.

"Well sure, yes! We've got no plans." By this time Kat was squinting at me. I know that look. It's the, "what are you getting me into" look.

"Good then, we'll seal their flight plans. He told me he would call you by cell phone on the plane when they get close to your airport. I would tentatively say by early to mid afternoon.

"Any idea how long they can visit with us?" I asked.

"They've got a couple days to spare on both ends. You'll have to ask them."

"Sounds good," I told him.

"If you need to get a hold of me, you've got my number," Burton said.

"We'll just plan on them stayin' over. We'll show 'em a good time," I assured him.

"Okay then, I'll talk to you soon. I'll try to see you next time you come down," he said.

"Yah, you take care. Thanks for callin'. We're excited!" I told him.

"I'd be willing to bet Marcus and Jewel are too. Catch ya later," he replied.

"Thanks again," I told him, and we ended the call.

I turned to Kat. "Oh boy," I exclaimed. I think I was in a minor state of shock. "They're coming."

Kat said nothing for, what seemed like, the longest time. I had no idea what was going through her mind. At last she would see for herself. At last she was going to become a real part of all of this.

"What should we do?" she finally turned to me and asked.

"Nothing," I had to reply. "Our guest rooms are made up. There's nothing to do."

"I need to cook. What should I cook? You told me she makes you fantastic meals. I don't know what to cook," she said, frustrated.

"Take it easy. Make goulash or chicken soup, I don't know. No wait, venison. Thaw those venison tenderloins and make that fabulous wild rice hot dish of yours. There, I solved the problem," I said with a warm smile in her direction.

"Do they eat meat?" she asked.

"They eat alligator," I laughed. "I know they eat chicken gumbo. Sure they eat meat."

She had a worried look on her face. Again she said nothing for what seemed like too long. I could tell she was deep in thought. Maybe the part of her that wanted to believe was beginning to take over. I broke the silence.

"Maybe if they stay a while you could make your equally famous beer cheese soup. I'll make my infamously famous cinnamon rolls for breakfast."

That put a smile on her face. She leaned her head back on her pillow and sighed, trying to relax. I leaned back, too.

I'm gonna make my Under the Viaduct Beans," I exclaimed. She didn't want to hear that.

"That makes you fart too much," she said, as she cuddled close to me.

I had long ago given the dish its name, because it reminded me of something the old hobos must have thrown together under those railroad bridges during The Depression era. My version actually takes a long time to prepare. The pinto beans need to soak for a half day, then you start boiling them. I throw in everything I can find after that — carrots, celery, bologna, leftovers, and any spices I can get my hands on. It boils down to a great tasting addition to most any meal, and yes, it does cause a good many gastric intestinal disturbances —almost dangerously terminal. Maybe I should forget that idea.

"You're in for the treat of a lifetime," I told her. "We haven't made our travel plans to see any of the kids yet, and our chores can wait. This is big — bigger than life," I tried to explain.

"I need to clean the house," she said softly.

"The house is clean," I told her. "I should cut the grass though."

"And clean the garage," she added.

"They're not going in the garage," I replied. "Even if they did, it's not that bad. All I think we really need to do is go to the grocery store for a few things, and maybe pick up some wine or something."

She was beginning to calm down now, from her heightened excited moment — as was I. Things were falling into perspective. We finished our coffee and rose from bed to meet the day. The weather forecast was for calm weather, with warm temperatures and partly cloudy skies. It was a "Godsend." As we shuffled around the cabin, in what still amounted to a half daze, we weren't really focusing on anything. More coffee would be the cure. I poured us each another cup.

"Yah know, Jewel expressed interest in seeing the Mississippi headwaters," I said.

"Up in Bemidji?" Kat replied.

"Near there," I told her. "It's in Itasca State Park. I went there once, years ago. It's pretty cool."

"Oh, I don't know, I gotta meet these people. Maybe they're just a couple kooks who've duped you all this time," she said with a grin. "Maybe I shouldn't let them in the house!" I grinned back, and I knew, deep down, she was starting to believe. Tomorrow there would be no more denying. I was jumping for joy inside, on the verge of that term, "screaming for joy."

We spent the day doing what we refer to as puttzing around the house. We tried to relax. I tried to work on the book, but couldn't seem to get a thought pattern going. I played a little guitar while she tidied up the kitchen and did some light dusting around me. She took our best candles out of the buffet drawer and set them on the dining room table. I tried to keep her entertained, but we were both nervous. We finally showered by early afternoon, dressed for an early excursion to the grocery and liquor stores, then we dined out. I recall having a couple of strong drinks after supper. Admittedly, we were both trying to relax. Still, it would prove to be a struggle getting any decent sleep that night.

## CHAPTER 4

I woke up far too early that next morning, the sky barely hinting of breaking light. I had been lying there for what seemed like the longest time, opening and shutting my eyes. I turned to Kat, and in that dim haze of an approaching sun, I could see her eyes were open too.

"Mornin' babe," I said softly.

"Mornin," she said back, as she nestled closer.

"Did ya sleep?" I asked.

"Yah right," she responded.

We both confessed to having had a "toss and turn" kind of a night. I put my right arm around her and closed my eyes. We needed more sleep.

"Ready for coffee?" she asked.

"No," I murmured. "I can't even see yet."

I peeked, as she tried to close her eyes. Again I closed mine. It may have been a few minutes, but when I looked again, there she was staring at the ceiling. We have a stained glass shaded light above our bed. We discovered some time ago that the image the cut glass projected was that of Jimi Hendrix in sunglasses with flowers in his hair, looking down at us. It was nothing the artist had intended I'm sure. More like when you can see distinct figures in clouds sometimes.

"Jimi's telling you to go back to sleep," I whispered. She smiled.

"I'm gonna make coffee," she replied, and slowly climbed out of bed.

That was that. Here was a new day. I propped up my pillows and turned on the small light beside the bed. I could hear a whippoorwill singing through the open window above my head. I gazed around the bedroom to gain focus. Our window faces east, and the sun was permeating its presence through the trees. I adjusted the pillows, turned and plopped my head back down, lying in a sleep position. I wasn't ready to get up, but there it was, a great day waiting for us to face it. Was it going to be all that I had hoped for? Would this really be a day full of wishes come true? All my thoughts were starting to gather. I couldn't deny the feeling that this was all too overwhelming for both of us. I found myself worrying, and for no reason. I couldn't even find anything to worry about, yet I felt I had to. I'm sure it was just tension from what uncertainty eludes to. We needed to get ourselves back in our normal mode.

Kat brought in coffee, and we lay there for a time sipping, without saying a word. Relax? Out of the question.

"You didn't get the grass cut," she finally said.

"It's okay. I'm not gonna make beans, either," I replied. She smiled.

As far as anything goes, we were ready for this special company. It would just be the four of us, which is what I had wanted. I needed Kat to share my dream of a lifetime. There had been an empty feeling without her included. I knew my writing would come much easier with her in the loop. Maybe she could even help me with the dark alleys my words had been groping through.

"Why doesn't he want to write the book himself?" she asked.

"We talked about that," I explained. "He said it needed an outsider's perspective. Besides, I don't think he could, maybe Jewel could, but he's too scattered. You'll see what I mean. He's not the same person that he was 30 years ago. I don't think he's able to even come to terms with his own introspection. His thoughts are loose, sometimes confusing. He thinks deep. I don't think he could manage his thoughts to complete a descriptive story. I'm sure he couldn't."

"How old is he?" Kat asked.

"Seventy-one, I think."

"How old is she?"

"Timeless," I heard myself say. "No, I guess I really don't know. Younger than him, I'm sure."

As the morning became day, we started to become energized, to actually wake up. We were ready to let this happen. I helped Kat make our bed.

"What to wear, what to wear?" she said. It's one of her favorite sayings. She was rummaging through her closet. I headed to the shower. Any further recollections of that morning's preparation would be scant, at best. I recall being seated at my writing (card playing) table, and eating a ham sandwich, again looking out at Beulah. It was nearly afternoon. It hadn't felt like the day had really begun yet. Then the phone rang. I turned to see Kat standing by our kitchen island. She looked across at me. She wasn't going to answer it. I smiled, walked to the wall phone, and picked it up.

"Hello?'

"Hatty, my friend." It was Marcus. I guessed he was in an airplane. There was a distinct, yet far-away, unfamiliar engine noise.

"Well hello there, L," I resounded. I looked over to Kat, and nodded. She just stared at me.

"I hope you know you're getting company," he said.

"No, who?" I replied, in my joking tone.

"I'm bringing the band," he joked back.

"Oh good!" I resounded.

"Joey said we were at 10,000 feet, and about seventy miles out a few minutes ago. Now he says we're at about 3,0000 feet and descending, nearing your airfield. I guess it won't be long," Marcus said. The airport is only a few minutes from our cabin. This was perfect.

"Oh, be sure to tell your pilot to watch out for bears on the runway," I told Marcus.

"Yah, sure thing," he replied mockingly.

"No, really, we sometimes have problems with that. Besides, they'll bite yer guitar pickin' fingers off!"

He laughed loudly and repeated what I had said to the others. I could hear them laughing. "We'll see ya soon," he told me.

"We're on our way ta scoop ya," I replied, then hung up the phone.

"You go," Kat said to me with a resigning tone. "I'm not ready."

"What do you mean you're not ready?"

She gave me a subdued look, a bit uncomfortable, shyly unconfident. I wasn't going to push.

"All right, I'll see you in a little bit then." I gave her what I hoped would be, a reassuring kiss, then scurried out the door and jumped in our Cherokee, hightailing it out of our driveway and toward town.

Our airport is small. No tower, one landing strip, and a couple of hangars. I could see two small planes when I pulled in. They were near the hangars, tied down with ropes from under their wings, to something on the asphalt. Their windshields and side windows were covered with cloth. Then I saw another small plane. It appeared it had just landed, or possibly was getting ready to take off. There were people inside, but no one I could recognize. It didn't appear as though their plane had yet landed. My cell phone rang. It was Marcus.

"You down there?" he asked.

"Yah, what's taken ya so long?" I replied, with obvious excitement to my voice. He laughed.

"We had to circle. Someone was landing ahead of us." It must be the one with those people still inside, parked adjacent to the runway, I thought to myself.

Now I could hear a plane approaching. There was a warm breeze. The doors on the hangars were slightly rattling. The temperature was in the low 70's, with partly cloudy skies. I could hear their pilot over my cell phone.

"Kilo-golf-tango-golf-traffic, n-eleven-thirty-five-hotel four miles south, to land on three-zero." My recorder, pressed to the ear piece of my cell phone, picked up what was being said. I was becoming a real recording hound, trying to grab every precious word from every experience. Then the voice added, "Thirty-five-hotel is a Cessna." There was a pause, then he said, "Three-ten."

Now I could see them. My excitement made my leg muscles tense. I stood near the hangars, shifting my body weight from side to side.

"See ya in a minute," Marcus said.

"I see you coming in," I told him. We ended the call without another word. It was almost like I hung up on him. Man, I was hyped.

Their plane landed smoothly, turned near the end of the runway, then taxied toward me. It was a twin-engine, very sleek looking, with the numbers N1135H on the side. The engines shut down, and in what felt like a long time, a door finally opened and a two-step ladder unfolded toward the ground. Marcus appeared first. Seeing me, he gave a short wave, turned, and climbed down. Next Jewel appeared in that ever-present rainbow of excellence. She held out her hand to him, in a Cleopatra sort of way, as she daintily stepped down. I didn't know who else to expect. He did say he brought the band. As I began walking toward them, he stretched his arms briefly and arched his back. They were both smiling when I approached. Next from the door came a younger man, I'd say in his 30's. He was wearing sandals, shorts, and an opened dark-patterned shirt with the tails hanging out. He practically jumped down, maybe touching only one step. As I neared them, the man was looking over the plane, paying no attention to me.

"Surprise!" Marcus said to me, happily raising his arms in the air. "We made it up."

I gave him a wide grin, and Jewel reached out with both arms, embracing me warmly.

"Every time I see you it's as fresh as a rose whose petals have just opened," I told her. I don't know, it just came out.

"You're always my instant love," she winked, playing along with my mushiness.

I turned to Marcus and hugged him in much that same way. There was genuine affection between us. It was thrilling to have them there.

"This is Joey," Marcus said, introducing me to the pilot. The man then turned and acknowledged me.

"Hi," I said in response. We reached out and shook each other's hand.

He was a man, around five foot ten, very thin, yet muscular, with a thin face and long nose. He had a shaved head except for maybe a two-week growth. He was clean shaven except for maybe a three-or four-day shadow, rough around the edges, to be sure. He had a great tan.

"What kind of plane is that?" I asked him outright. It was really impressive to me.

"It's a Cessna 310; the J model," he replied.

"How fast does it go?"

"We cruised at about 205."

"Sure cool lookin'; is it yours?" I inquired.

"Naw, I fly a lot of 'em, Pipers, Beech Craft, but this one's sure got sexy tip tanks," he replied.

I smiled in agreement, if they were what I thought they were. "Burton told me you're his best pilot," I said.

"Ah, I just fly in the middle of the air, never on the edges," he responded modestly. "Most useless things to me are the runway behind and usually the air above," he added, with an almost mischievous grin. He had caring brown eyes that stared intently into mine as we spoke. I noticed tattoos on each side of his chest and his forearms.

"It's been three hours since our last stop, any bathrooms around here?" Marcus asked.

"Don't know." I said, and shrugged my shoulders. I pointed to a portable satellite I could make out near the field's edge. He just smiled. Jewel turned to me with a soft smile.

"I can wait," she said.

"It's only a few minutes to our place," I assured her. "I was expecting a whole orchestra," I turned and said to Marcus, with a grin.

"This is it. It's all we need," he replied.

I turned to Joey, "You get to visit the Great White North, too."

"I'm flyin' down to Holman Field in Saint Paul to hang out with an old Air Force buddy," he then explained.

"You're welcome to stay with us, we have plenty of room," I told him.

"Thank you. I appreciate that, but no. I'll just catch up when y'all are ready." He gave me a grateful smile, then turned and walked around the plane, looking it over once again. Marcus turned and began walking toward the outhouse.

"I've relieved myself in a lot worse places," I heard him say.

"Where's Kat?" Jewel asked, while looking as stunningly into my eyes as I had grown accustomed to.

"She left town," I smiled. "No, she's nervous. I don't think she knows what to expect."

"We'll take care of that." Jewel smiled with warm assurance, then she took hold and gave my hand a tender squeeze. Joey was taking their baggage from the plane now.

"We stopped at a place on the way up," Jewel explained. "We have two other places we want to look at."

"You're really gonna do it?" I said inquisitively.

"We don't know; if we can. I want to live on a mountain for a time. We've talked a lot about it. I dream about it, to see mountain sunrises. I can even foresee what it's gonna look like. We both know we're ready for new air to breath. Marcus finds contentment where we're at, but I'm convinced he needs this. He knows it, too." I just smiled at her. Marcus was walking back to us now. He heard the last thing she had said to me.

"She's lookin' to tip the edge off a summit's end. There's a mountain out there with her name on it, and she's going to find it. She has a full-moon-mountain-morning in her eyes," he said. Jewel gave him a funny look. It appeared to me that he wasn't all that convinced of the venture.

"My Jeep is right over there." I pointed. Joey picked up the two large bags he had set on the tarmac, and Jewel and Marcus each grabbed one of the two smaller ones. I motioned to Joey, then took one of the bags from him as we walked. He nodded gratefully. We threw everything in the back of my Cherokee.

"I'll call when we know something," Marcus said, turning to Joey.

"Good enough," Joey responded, then turned to me. "Good to meet cha."

"Good to meet you, too," I told him, shaking his hand again.

"Thanks, Joey," Jewel said, adding her sweet smile. He timidly smiled back.

"My pleasure; have fun up here." He turned, nodded to Marcus, and walked back toward his airplane. Marcus climbed into the backseat of my Jeep while Jewel sat up front with me.

I confess to restless anticipation as we drove that short distance to the cabin. Time seemed to take too long.

## CHAPTER 5

"You really do live in the woods!" Jewel exclaimed as we drove.

"There's 40,000 acres of state game refuge bordering our east," I told her, pointing in that direction. "We have federal scenic river way to our west. It's only a small strip of privately owned land in-between, we're lucky," I explained. "We stumbled on it about 20 years ago. We first saw it in the winter and without even knowing what the land really looked like; we fell in love and bought the place. It was a surprisingly added treasure when the snow melted and we got to see what we really had. I remember carrying Kat over the threshold the first day we moved in."

"How romantic," Jewel sighed.

We were coming to the driveway now. I turned in.

"Your semi sure stands out," Marcus remarked. I nodded and had to agree. We pulled up near the cabin. It was mid-afternoon now.

We had gotten out of the Cherokee and were taking the bags from the back, when Kat stepped onto the porch. She was wearing her usual blue jeans, with a thin, low-cut, light blouse. Her ruby necklace stood out, sparkling as it caught sunlight. Jewel smiled to her from that short distance. Kat stepped down and walked over to our picnic table near the porch, where she paused, waiting for us to approach. Marcus walked ahead of us, and directly up to her.

"Hi Kat," he simply said. I was walking behind Jewel, and in that moment, caught the extreme reaction. Kat's reddened face gave way to a wrinkled cringe. Her eyes widened, as she stared at him almost shockingly. She appeared ready to cry.

"I'm sorry," she said, looking at each of us, then she turned and briskly walked back into the house. Jewel awkwardly stood there. Marcus turned to me with a questionable look.

"She'll be fine, just give her a minute," I told them knowingly. "It's her moment of truth. It ain't like she'd just seen a ghost or anything," I lightheartedly added. That made them both laugh. The ice was breaking as smoothly as I could hope for. "Welcome to our oak tree ranch," I told them, as I stretched my arm, palm up, half turning, presenting to them of our surroundings. Then I turned back to them and simply told them, "Come on in."

As we stepped inside, Kat was seated at the piano bench, facing the door. She looked up at him again, trying to smile.

"A piano! You never told me you had one." Marcus said excitedly, and he set his bags down.

"Hi Kat, I'm Jewel." She set her bag down next to his and walked over to Kat, who stood up with a true smile. Her eyes were wet.

"Hi," Kat simply replied. She turned again to look at Marcus as if to catch that, "I can't believe what I'm seeing", second look. It was almost comical, but I kept a straight face.

"I haven't sat down to one of these in years, used to play all the time." Marcus explained, as he seated himself on the bench Kat had just vacated. He turned to the keys. Immediately he played what I recognized to be a 'C' chord, with his right hand.

"You remember anything?" I asked, as I reached over to our coffee table and turned on the tape recorder that was lying there.

"Oh, I think so," he confidently replied.

From what I could tell, he began to play and sing what sounded like a gospel song. It was something about a sweet spirit, although I wasn't concentrating. I was watching Jewel watching Kat who was watching him. I guess it could best be described as a parallel moment.

There were no more doubts to be had. A barrier had been virtually shattered; leaped over. Kat looked over to me; she knew now. I could see she still felt an element of shock, but she knew. I was sure she would acclimate soon. I tried to break the stiffness in the air.

"No, you can't take it with you on the plane," I joked to Marcus, regarding the piano. "We do have 10 acres we could sell ya though. We could be neighbors. You could come over and play it every day."

He smiled widely as he looked up at Jewel. She smiled back to him. He turned to Kat. She had a half smile as she tried to settle herself.

"Do you reach for soothing stanzas under her searching eyes?" he asked me, while looking up at her. "There's a glowing stillness in the radiance of that smile. What transpires in you?" he asked her. Kat and Marcus were looking at each other, I'd say intensely. She said nothing. He turned to me, "She will show you past turbulent shadows," he opined. Kat turned, eyes ablaze, as she cast a knowing look to me. The beauty in her face had sharpened. A fresh aura became pronounced. Her eyes had brightened to a sparkling glow. She was re-charged, revitalized, as she looked back at him. It was as though all the magnificence of his being had spilled upon her. She was swimming in his presence. The confused look that was on her face only minutes earlier, now replaced by blushing belief.

"I'm sorry I lost myself," Kat managed to say, still looking deeply at Marcus. She turned to Jewel with a "please forgive me" look.

"He's no ghost," Jewel said back to her with a smile. She put her hand gently on Kat's left arm.

"I know, it's just that…," Kat tried to say.

"You know now," I budged in. I gave Kat a quick kiss on her lips. Even her breath tasted different. She was ignited! Her feelings were, no doubt, ineffable.

He was fiddling with the piano keys. Kat and Jewel seemed to be sizing each other up with warm glances.

"Eddie's band's playin' yer Woogie song," he remarked, looking up at me. "It's goin' over hot at dances."

"Good, it was meant to be danced to," I replied, somewhat proudly. Kat looked over and gave me a smile.

I wanted things to settle in naturally now. The girls were alike in so many ways. I was sure they would come to get along immensely. They just needed a little space and time to warm up to each other.

"I gotta show ya something L; be right back," I told him. I went to our bedroom, quickly retrieving my best guitar from under the bed. I brought it out to the living room, where they were all looking at me.

"This is my other baby," I said, as I gave Kat a wink. "I had no intention of buying another guitar when I found her. She was just hangin' there, stunning me. Love at first sight. When I took her down and played her, I fell head over heels." I handed it to him as he was standing up to have a closer look. He smiled widely, while handling her the way guitar players do when they first meet such an instrument.

"Niiicce," he said.

Of my entire collection, this guitar, a Tacoma, made in Washington State, had the most beautiful appearance with the sound to match. It's dark sunburst in color, graduating from black to deep red, on to a golden, rich yellow, with a myriad of subtle tones and emblazoned gold in between. It has a lariat perforation, or border, around the outside of the face and sound hole; it's stunningly exquisite to an adoring eye. It has no pick guard, which to me, complements her appearance, as well as suits my finger picking style. I haven't used a pick since I unplugged from those early band days. I could see Marcus was in strong appreciation of what he was holding.

"Really light," he commented.

"Maple," I told him.

Jewel was admiring Kat's rings and bracelets. Kat was doing the same with Jewel's. They had sat down on the couch across from the piano. Marcus sat back down on the bench, positioning himself to touch off a tune on my guitar. To my delight, he played and sang an original I had never heard. He called it, *Great Plenty*. The girls watched and listened intently, and so did I. As one may guess by the title, it was a thankful song. It had to do with mixed blessings. It told how, when you think something bad has happened to you, it turns out to have happened for a reason, and actually improves your life — something that has a purpose one does not recognize forthwith. It was an amazing song. I had to think that only he, with that inner intrinsic mysticism, could have written it. As with most of his work, I had never heard anything to compare it to, both in melody and in the lyrics. I don't even have to mention his delivery. The girls looked at each other. Kat turned to me, then to Marcus.

"Where have you been?" Kat asked him in a stumbling, cheated way, almost with a scolding tone in her voice. It's the way I was beginning to feel most people would react if and when this thing ever came to light.

"Living a life of love," he calmly replied.

I got up, went to the closet near the front door, and retrieved my Martin guitar. Marcus spotted the name on the headstock immediately and repeated it aloud. This was turning into a "kid in a candy store" moment.

"Ohh yahh." he exhaled. I had tuned both guitars earlier that morning in anticipation of this opportunity.

"Can we do *The You in Me* for Kat?" I asked. For me this stood out as the greatest love song ever to have graced this earth. I couldn't wait for it to melt Kat. Marcus strummed the Martin with a couple of chords, a nod, then a smile.

"Sure, let's do it," he said.

We played it together, as I had taken intense care now to learn this song above any of the others he had written. It deserved to be played with the most passion and ability I could muster. He sang it better than the times previous. When we had finished, Kat was visibly stunned. Her mouth was slightly open. I don't recall that reaction from her about anything ever before. She was slowly shaking her head back and forth like she didn't believe it.

"Oh my," was all she could say. Jewel had a look of real pride as she smiled at Kat.

"This is an amazing guitar," he remarked to me.

"It's an HD28M, only made it in 1988. It has mahogany back and sides," I told him.

"It has a sound like I've never heard," he exclaimed. "I love it!"

I then shut the recorder off to conserve a dwindling tape and commenced to show off my entire guitar collection, bringing them forth from various hiding places throughout the house. There were two Epiphones, one acoustic, and one acoustic electric. There were two Takamines, one acoustic, the other a classical. Next was a blond acoustic jumbo Guild, then an old electric Rickenbacker twelve-string. I concluded with my old Fender Strat, and a well worn acoustic Gibson Hummingbird. In addition, I showed Jewel two banjos, my Roy Smeck ukulele, and a balalaika that my nephew had brought back to me from a trip he had taken to Russia. That instrument really interested her. All the while Marcus remained seated at the piano bench holding that Martin, almost embracing it, as he witnessed my exhibition.

Kat stood up now, and asked Jewel to come and see her oriental statuette collection in a glass cabinet next to our television. She showed her around our living and dining room, pointing out the paintings hanging on the walls that she had done. They were getting along famously. Marcus was trying a little finger-picking on the Martin.

"We need to show you your bedroom," I finally announced. I collected their two large bags, and with Marcus in pursuit holding the two smaller satchels, we strolled down the hallway to their guest room. Kat and Jewel were following not far behind. From there we continued on, showing them the entire cabin. We had added on two bedrooms years earlier when it became all too apparent that with our growing family, we needed more room. I had my small recorder turned on in my pocket, just in case.

"Dinner will be ready soon," Kat said as the tour was ending. We returned to the living room. Marcus had left the Martin on the couch and immediately retrieved it. I think he was in love. He was sure acting like it.

"Jewel reads palms," I reminded Kat.

"Can you read mine?" Kat immediately asked her.

"Of course," Jewel replied warmly, with a special smile.

They sat at the dining room table. Marcus was back at the piano bench, lightly strumming or, dare I say, flirting with his new-found love. I sat down on the couch and listened to Jewel. She was explaining some of the lines on Kat's hand.

"There's a strong center line with a star in the middle," I heard Jewel say. "I've never seen this, you're very different. Are you a gypsy?"

"My spirit is," Kat replied.

"Let's play something," Marcus said, looking at me. I got up and walked across the room to where I had left my Tacoma leaning by the fireplace, then returned to the couch and sat down.

"Got anything in mind?" I asked, leaning forward, retrieving a new tape from the coffee table drawer. I quickly replaced the old one and turned it back on.

"Nope, I'm mindless," he smiled, and began to play and sing, *Somewhere,* from the movie West Side Story. He never ceases to amaze me. His versatility seems endless. In some ways, his approach resembles mine regarding other people's songs. He would change their tempo, or sing their lyrics in a newly mixed pattern or presentation, always as vital and pertinent as they were in their original form. We sat and played cover songs from other artists for probably an hour. I lost track of whatever the ladies were talking about.

## CHAPTER 6

It was dinner time, and Kat had lit the candles. Through the windows of our dining room table the Wisconsin sun shown, settling between the trees. It was as picture perfect as anyone could hope for, another blessing bestowed.

Small salads were our starters, and Kat had baked a venison roast with wild rice and carrots. She had made warm buns, with gravy, and there was wine or apple juice to drink. She had baked a blueberry pie for desert. They all chose the wine. I had the apple juice; I'm not a wine drinker. The meal showed Kat's extraordinary way of pulling things off in true form, impressively delicious. Man, she's good at that. Jewel and Marcus praised her several times while enjoying their meal.

I had taken the liberty of bringing the pocket recorder to the dinner table. By now, I was taping nearly everything that transpired while being around them. I had missed so many things that were said before the recordings came into play. Now I obsessed at attempting to capture every pertinent word.

This was the first time they would notice the scars on my hands. I seldom wear my driving gloves when I'm at home.

"What happened here?" Jewel asked, as she reached across and softly touched my hand.

"Foolin' round with homemade rockets when I was a kid. One blew up in my hands," I told her. "Now they bruise easily. My gloves have become a second skin to me over the years." This always seemed to be an uncomfortable topic for Kat, and was most often avoided when we were around others.

"Grant was telling me about Clay and Hershel," Kat chimed in.

"Clay's like my brother, but really an uncle," Jewel explained with a grin. "Sometimes he can be so crass. When you meet him you'll find him to be inordinately charming; all women do."

Kat smiled back: "Grant told me how Hershel came to be in your life."

"You mean Hatty, don't cha?" Marcus winked.

"How cute," Kat replied, with a charming smile.

"Hersh comes with his encumbrances. He's just a child really, but with a heart bigger than most anyone. You'll love him," Jewel told her.

"This will be the longest we've ever been away from home," Marcus said, adding, "For so long I haven't wanted to venture out. I haven't wanted to know what the world is doing with itself, nature stacking their garbage against her shorelines. I can hear her buoyant tremors, waving in angry hallucination, being dragged by the undertow. If I had to watch, it would keep me afraid to sleep."

Jewel just stared at him, like he was engaging conversation not suitable for the present moment.

"You sound bitter," I interjected, wondering what Kat may have made of his statements.

"Not at all," he smirked.

"We have Clay watching over Hersh and the dogs," Jewel said. "I'm trying to control my uncertainty about it."

"Yah, didn't Clay once shoot a man just to watch him die?" Marcus asked her.

"I think you have him confused with a song by Johnny Cash, dear," Jewel said, humoring him.

"Oh yah," he said, with a "wasn't that a good one" sinister grin. We were all smiling.

"Tomorrow we'll have to show you our Ponderosa," I told them. "Do you guys have anything special you might wanna do?"

"I'd like to feel where the Mississippi River really begins — to experience it," Jewel replied.

"We could go there," I told her, as I looked across to Kat for affirmation. Kat nodded her approval. "How long can you guys stay?"

"We need to hook back up with Joey by Wednesday, two days or so I guess," Marcus replied.

"I'd really like to show off our St. Croix River," I told them. It's one of the cleanest rivers anywhere. We float it all the time. We have several boats. We could tie a couple of them together and just do a casual float tomorrow if you want, then leave and go to the headwaters Tuesday morning?" Kat smiled her agreeable smile at me.

"I'd really like that," Jewel replied. Marcus shrugged his shoulders as if to say he was willing to go along with anything.

The evening drifted in soothing comfort of friendship. It felt as though it had existed a lifetime. Marcus and I played songs he had written that we had been working on. They all sipped wine. I guzzled beer. I can't ever seem to sip anything, except for Thin Ice, but that's my only exception. I handed our best banjo to Jewel, and she played along on a couple of tunes, adding her vocal splendor. Kat was lit up, thoroughly enthralled the entire time. She had made new friends, something that doesn't happen often enough in the woods and dare I say, never friends like these. A true angel on earth, Kat's spirit could not have been higher.

We all began feeling fatigued right around midnight. It's too bad the best of times need to meet sleep. It's like my mom used to tell me as a child: "The sooner you go to sleep, the sooner you'll get there," and tomorrow was where we wanted to get. As for myself, I zonked out the minute my head hit the pillow.

## CHAPTER 7

I wasn't the first to awaken. Fact is, I was the last. The faint sound of a piano filled the morning air. I could hear women's laughter coming from the kitchen, which is right outside our bedroom. When I opened the door, the combined aromas of coffee, and sausage and eggs, overtook me. The girls turned to bid me a sweet good morning, all smiles. Kat must have slept well. She appeared chipper and bubbly happy. I turned to see Marcus seated at the piano, paper and a pen beside him on the bench. He was fiddling with the keys, not really playing anything, but appeared to be deep in thought. I surmised that he was at work on a song. For the longest time, he didn't notice me standing to his left.

Just then a car pulled into our driveway. We weren't expecting anyone. Marcus turned and saw me.

"Mornin' there," he said. A dimple stood out. I nodded back, but my attention was now on the new arrival.

"It's Lenny," Kat called out.

"Oh," was my resigned reaction.

Lenny is my nephew. He seldom comes around, but when he does, he just pops in unexpectedly and electricity often charges up the environment. I consider him the rebel of our family. He's loose, boisterous, vivacious, sometimes a bit crude, and once in a while, in trouble. I love him dearly, despite his overbearing, somewhat intense, nature. I went to greet him at the door.

"Hey Unk, how'd I catch you at home?" He nearly shouted; he's always louder than he needs to be. Perhaps he's hard of hearing.

"Hey Len, I'm on vacation. What's up with you?" I responded.

"On my way to a job site in Webb Lake; thought I'd surprise Kat."

"You always do," Kat responded from the kitchen. He and I both laughed; he more heartily than I. He almost always drops in when I'm out on the road; usually stops by when Kat is scurrying to get ready for work in the morning. Lenny has always been a "have toolbox, will travel" kind of a guy. He works any jobs he can find, but only in short duration.

"Hi Kat," he peeked into the kitchen. She nodded back to him.

"Len, this is Jewel," Kat said. He was already staring at her, probably hoping she was one of Kat's single girlfriends.

"And Marcus," I added, pointing toward the piano.

"Hey," Len responded. He turned to notice Marcus, then gave him a short wave hello.

"You're just in time for breakfast," Kat told him.

There, in that moment, it occurred to me that Lenny was much like Clay. He to, was a lady's man. He was good looking, and in great physical shape, very stalwart, and had tattoos emblazoned all over his strong arms. I think Jewel saw the comparison right off. She smiled back at him. Marcus turned to watch the proceedings. Lenny stepped over and plopped himself down at the dining room table. Then he jumped back up and went over to retrieve a guitar - my Seagull, which was leaning near the fireplace.

"Just got outta jail, I'm all dried out. Need to finish a job for a guy that I started, before I went in the stir a couple months back." He had a mischievous smile. No one responded. "Wanna play one?" he asked me.

"You didn't happen to bring back that Neil Diamond song book, did ya?" I asked him. Lenny is a novice guitar player, but enthusiastic. I had given him his first guitar, but the cops confiscated it a while back and he couldn't seem to trace where it went. He had inadvertently taken one of my song books the last time we sat down and played together, which had been over two years ago.

"Naw, I got it stored with my other music. I'll get it back ta ya," he said. He's been saying that for over two years. I picked up my Tacoma, and in an appeasing gesture, led off with the song *The Weight*, by The Band. It was one song, I would have to say, that we really play well together.

"Time to eat," Kat called to us after the song was finished. We all took seats as Jewel was placing plates and silverware on the table in front of each chair. Kat brought over scrambled eggs and sausages in two large bowls. We started passing food around.

"We have milk, orange juice, or coffee," Kat called from the kitchen. We all made our requests and she promptly filled them, then sat down herself.

"This is great!" Len said.

"We're goin' on the river this morning," I told him. Over the years, Len had made a few river runs with us.

"Sounds great; ever run the river before?" he asked Marcus.

"No, never have."

"Weather's good, you'll have a great time," Len told him, all the while not having an inkling as to whom he was speaking. This was an absolute testament to Marcus' scruffy looks. He definitely fit in with his backwoods appearance. Len could have taken them for our neighbors down the road.

"Where's Suzie?" Kat asked him.

"Ah, we broke up," he said, adding, "I still see her, but we don't live together no more."

It wasn't a surprise to me with Len's overbearing nature - probably drives all women a bit crazy eventually. But after a time, they seem to want to come back around to him.

Breakfast went by quickly, with light conversation. Kat told Jewel about what they could expect to see on our river float. The St. Croix River borders Minnesota and Wisconsin. She described a place called Sand Rock Cliffs. We would be circling through there between a large island and the shoreline on the Wisconsin side. Just past that is my favorite fishing (honey) hole. There lies a backwash where the current actually circles back up and around in a small, but deep hole. It runs a few hundred yards of shore length. In that area lurk some of the largest northern and muskie anywhere around — lunkers, the locals like to call them. They just lie there, not having to fight the current, waiting for food to float past. Of course, I had to brag to them about the ones I'd landed in my boat from that spot. All the while, Lenny kept uncharacteristically quiet, but of course his mouth was full of food much of the time. Come to think of it, he even ate like Clay.

Breakfast over, I began scurrying about. In overt gestures to Len, I tried hinting that perhaps it was time for him to think about leaving. Surprisingly, he stood up and walked over to give Kat his usual farewell hug.

"Gotta go. I think this guy wants me to get that work done. Good to meet you two," Len said, turning to each of them. Jewel and Marcus smiled back, nodding. Len never seemed to appear to know who Marcus might really be. When he walked out the door, I looked at the three of them and then laughed out loud.

"You are good at what you do," I told Marcus with a wide grin.

"Had a lot of practice," he replied with a smile, then he got up from his chair. The girls were smiling as they went about clearing the table. I saw Lenny pull out of the driveway. Now I had become antsy to show them around our place on this fine sunny day.

"Let's take a walk; I'll show you guys around the place." Marcus followed me to the front porch. We stood there for a minute. He was looking around at our yard.

"We've got 48 red oak trees just in the front yard alone," I bragged. "It could be a small fortune in veneer. We usually wait till spring to rake the leaves. Some don't fall off till then. We use that to haul them out back." I pointed to our old Nissan truck. "Usually takes a dozen loads or more with her before we get our yard cleared. It's a lot of raking," I said.

Marcus just shook his head as he stared at that little truck with no doors. I could tell he was trying to imagine all that I had said. "What's that on the roof?" he asked, pointing to the Nissan.

"A gas can; the gas tank," I grinned. "Gravity-fed," I added. My grin broke into a smile from ear to ear. "The fuel pump went out, so I just ran a line down. It works just fine. Only sometimes I gotta squeeze that ball you see on the line, to get the gas flowing at first." Now he was really shaking his head as Kat and Jewel joined us on the porch.

We have a path that starts on one end of our house and extends back into the woods, circling around 10 acres, until it comes out on the other side of the house. On the path we have a nine-basket Frisbee golf course. Playing it backwards after shooting the first nine turns it into a full 18. We put it together a dozen years ago. People who visit love to play over and over. They can't get enough of it, and it's great recreation out here in the middle of the woods. That, and an occasional billiards game, is the only exercise this trucker gets. Oh, except to walk from my truck to the buffet and back when I'm at truck stops. The course is a three par all the way, and we even have an electric golf cart that carries the beer cooler and extra Frisbees along the path as we go. We took them on the path while I explained. They gave fascinated chuckles as we went along.

At hole number five, I led them onto a side trail that intersects and departs over a small knoll. It then curves left, down into a small ravine where we've put together a gun-shooting range. There we've set up two clay pigeon launchers. They're erected on wooden stands, permanently cemented into the ground. When activated, they are aimed so they fling clays that cross in mid-air. I had also built a wooden target platform, located in the middle of the field. Marcus got excited when seeing all of this.

"I'm still into guns," he proclaimed with excitement. "Remind me to show you my collection when you come down. Man, next time I'm up here I'll bring a couple. I gotta try this."

"I want to try Frisbee golf," Jewel added.

"As long as you can keep the Frisbee on the path, you can usually make par. It's a lot of fun. Maybe we can throw a game when we get off the river," I suggested. The day was moving by. We resumed the walk that took us around and down the hill to our barn. There, attached along its side, is an open storage shed. Our boats and canoes are set on wooden stands there. As I showed them off, I explained how we would be taking the two wooden boats today, that they tie together nicely. Kat likes to say that they complement each other in color. The fact is, they are the most comfortable. I told them about the one I had purchased from an old fellow over 20 years ago. He built it himself. It has a raised floor so your feet don't get wet. The other one is what they call a McKenzie boat, made in Utah. It has a high bow, and also has a raised floor. Both are well suited for the river. Both had a fresh coat of green marine paint on them. We would float handsomely. One sits upside-down atop the other on our trailer. Both are light enough for two people to transport easily.

"We'll get the boats and stuff pulled up to the yard," I said. "Do we want to pack a cooler for lunch?" I asked Kat.

"We can put together some sandwiches, and something to drink," she replied, glancing at Jewel with a nod.

"Sounds good," I told her. Jewel bent down and picked up a blue jay feather from the ground. She reached up and slipped it under the band of Marcus' hat. They stared into each other's eyes in that moment, smiling. He gave her a quick kiss on her cheek. It's true their eyes do twinkle when they look at each other like that. She turned from him to walk with Kat back up to the house. One could tell the girls had begun a true friendship.

Marcus and I set about finding the oars and life jackets. We wouldn't need boat motors this time. The plan was to float from a place known as Norway Point, 4 miles up-river, to the Highway 70 state line bridge, 3 miles to the south. It entails leaving a car at the low end, where we eventually planned on finishing the trip. When our float was finished, two of us would drive back up river to where we began and pick up the Jeep and trailer. We would then both drive back down to retrieve the other two and all of our gear. I have it down to a 'hick' science. Our boats would float with the current, propelled briskly at about 3 miles an hour. The plan would be to take the time to get out and walk around on islands and sandbars along the way. We would tie the boats together like a raft, and drift our carefree merry way. In all likelihood it would take up the rest of this day.

I went to fetch the Jeep in the driveway and drove it down to the barn. There, we placed all the gear and an anchor in the back. We put the oars in the McKenzie boat and I backed up to the trailer, hooking it to the hitch. Boats in place, one upside-down atop the other, and we were ready to go. Marcus and I then walked up to the house to fetch the girls. They were busying themselves in the kitchen.

"Show ya my guns," I told him. He grinned, and without a word, followed me into our bedroom to the gun cabinet. I showed him my shotguns, my .30-30 Winchester, my Remington .22, and a sawed-off (barely legal) Stevens 12 gauge.

"Personal protection," I remarked as I passed it to him. He handled it with an air of sinister rebellion, pointing it at the outside wall from his hip. He was rather enjoying the moment.

"It's a mean killer, that's for sure," he said.

I showed him the assortment of pistols we own, none extraordinary, but he showed keen interest. There was a matching pair of .22 revolvers.

"These are for if Kat and I break up. It'll be a walk 10 paces, turn, and fire deal. I won't even bother ta pull the trigger - she's a much better shot than me," I joked. He gave me a grimacing look.

Just then Kat peeked in. "We're ready," she said.

"We'll be out in a sec. Showin' off the artillery," I told her. She just smiled, then disappeared from the doorway.

"Gotta try your shootin' range next time," Marcus repeated, as I was closing the cabinet. "I'll bring some of my own artillery."

"Yah, it's a blast," I said, lightly punching him on his left shoulder.

The ladies had put together some grapes, apples, and homemade Amish bread that I had picked up on my way home on Friday. We also had some good- old Wisconsin provolone and Swiss cheeses that Kat and I had picked up on Saturday from a store one town away, called Alpha. This place actually had won a "Best in the World" award a couple years earlier. In the cooler, they had stacked beer, orange juice, and bottled water. On the side, tucked half submerged beneath the ice, was a bottle of gin. Just in case of an emergency, I surmised. Now we were loaded and ready for bear, which turned out to be a pretty accurate depiction for what lay ahead of us. I grabbed my old Gibson from the closet near the piano, and that made everything complete. We headed out the door. As we walked between the house and garage, I abruptly stopped.

"Gotta show ya this," I said, leaning the Gibson against the house and walking over to open the garage door. They followed me in. Our garage has a built-on screened porch, where we've decorated it with old 78, 33 and 1/3rds, and 45 rpm records. They're assorted and displayed all over the walls in no particular order. Each complements another, intertwined between old music posters and memorabilia. We have a wicker table and chairs. Kat and I often have our morning coffee or early evening cocktails there.

"What a great idea!" Jewel exclaimed.

"Well, they're not gold like yours, L," I turned to him and said.

"Better off, they only serve to blind ya," he joked back.

"Eventually, we're gonna make all of this into a neighborhood bar and call it Boondocks," I told them. Then I opened a cabinet door and commenced to show them my vast coaster collection. I had been helping myself to a few from every bar I had been for the past, oh, 20 years. Some were real collector pieces, antiques. I guess they seemed impressed. Then I showed off my shot glass collection. I have at least two from every state except Alaska and Hawaii. Again, I believe I more or less caught their curious side. At the very least, they had come to recognize my compulsiveness.

"We're gonna knock out part of this wall and build a horseshoe bar. Part of it will be out on this screen porch, and the other half will be inside the garage, with a pool table right there," I pointed. "Then we're gonna add a small building to the back and put a door right there. It'll have tables and a small stage for the locals to come and pick. You'd be surprised how many pickers there are in these back- woods. Kat and I have met a few at a swimming hole called Fox Landing. I doubt I can get a liquor license, maybe beer, but it'll be a "bring your own bottle" and party with your neighbors kinda deal." I was rattling on and on, till Kat caught my eye. She motioned that we should get going. I think she likes to humor me about this project, and it may never get off the ground. It's a pipe-dream that keeps my mind occupied. That's what I'm sure she's thinking.

"This is going to be really fine," Jewel commented. "Maybe we can join you sometime." Wouldn't that be something, I thought. Marcus just smiled. I grabbed a pair of binoculars hanging on a nail, and we went back outside.

Throughout their visit, Marcus had kept uncharacteristically quiet. I later pinned it down to him being bothered by their reason for this whole trip. He genuinely enjoyed his stay with us, but the idea of them relocating seemed to be vexing him. I chose to sit down with him and talk about it another time.

Kat picked up the cooler, and I the guitar, with the binoculars strapped around my neck. The ladies got into the Camaro, while Marcus and I walked down to the Jeep, parked near the barn. We pulled up to the yard behind them, then followed them for the 3 miles down side roads to the river's parking lot at the state line bridge. As we were driving, I thought it might be a good time to confess something to him. First, I turned on the recorder in my pocket.

"Ya know, I never really thought much about you over the years, not even when you were at the top of your game. I liked your music you understand, but I was more of a Gene Pitney fan. Then it was all Beatles and that English invasion thing." He smiled.

"I sang the harmonies of a fretting heart - tried to sing my withering fears away," he replied. "Gospel was the anchor I needed to hold onto and still do. The rock and roll came on like some kind of fluke dream. It's all a daze to me now."

"Don't get me wrong, your songs were great. They'll live on forever."

"I know; mankind's funny that way. I never wrote those songs. They were constantly being presented to me. If I liked them, I recorded them. It's these songs now, the ones I've written since Jewel. She took me from black to colors I can't name. It's these songs that I really need people to hear. I don't even care about getting the credit anymore. It's the spirit of the thing. Those songs I did before are becoming a dry watering hole for tomorrow's cattle. It used to be where children reached for my garden. That purpose died for me before I even did. There's this new garden they need to find now."

This was one of those rare occasions when I actually understood what he was trying to tell me. I had to agree that these songs he had written were "out-of-this-world" special, and yes, he indeed needed to have them heard. Some of his songs we had been working on lately were so packed with insight. I bear witness to the fact that they astound. He wasn't interested in anything you'd call fame anymore. He had developed so much humility. I knew deep inside that somehow I'd be a part of what would make this happen for him. It was providence that had really brought us together, of that I am convinced. Then he slapped my thigh and brightened up.

"Old age was something I never really counted on. I can't turn back now, it's too late to die," he said with a grin.

"You kinda lost me again there boss," I responded. We laughed together.

We pulled into the parking lot beside the bridge then. Kat and Jewel had taken a stroll down on a cement boat ramp that led to the river's edge. We could hear the sounds of cars and trucks rumbled across the bridge from overhead, as we walked down to join them.

"There's Minnesota," I pointed across the water. There was a light breeze from out of the north and was approaching midday.

"Shall we get going?" I suggested. The conditions were about as perfect as they could get, but things could change, as sometimes happens. "It gets a little hard when the wind is out of the south," I explained, while we walked back up to the Jeep. "Your boat tends to spin in circles, or not go anywhere at all in this light current. It ends up resembling work when that happens, 'cause ya gotta row a whole lot, and you can't keep a canoe pointed straight. One time it was so bad, we stopped along the shoreline and I made my son walk home to tell Kat to come and pick us up two landings ahead of our planned trip. He was 12 years old at the time, and along the way a bear crossed his path. It scared him and I felt really bad about it when he told me. I was with a buddy, and for the first time in probably 10 years, I bummed a cigarette from him. I took a couple puffs while we sat along the bank recuperating from our struggle. It was the last time I touched a cigarette. I had been a heavy smoker in my younger years. But that's what this river can do to ya."

"I'm too old for that," Marcus proclaimed.

"Me too," I said. "Today the wind's perfect."

"Ya, we could tell you horror stories," Kat added. "We almost drowned our best friends," she said with a smile. Jewel and Marcus looked at each other and displayed grimacing facial expressions. We all chuckled, they perhaps a bit nervously. I could tell we were all pretty upbeat. Being in this forest and with such a great river sets ones inner being apart from whatever else the world might be doing at the time. It has a tendency to erase conflict within oneself. As hard as it may be to describe, I can safely say it makes me feel like I'm bonding with the water and trees. It's hard to depict what it was, what intended effect creation had in mind between nature and man in places like this. I only know that the pace of the rat race world out there pretty much misses what we were now sharing.

## CHAPTER 8

The drive up to Norway Point is longer than the actual river miles. Everyone was admiring the scenery, so we didn't talk much. It's all back roads that curve and zigzag in and out before reaching the landing road. That road is nearly a mile of straight gravel, before it winds down the valley and to the river. I felt compelled to tell them a far-fetched story as we rode along.

"North of here, there's a small town called Danbury," I began. "The world record largest whitetail buck was shot there, along the Yellow River. I think it was in 1911. The record still stands today. It has been recorded that a fellow named Jim Jordan shot it. To this day, it's come to be known as 'The Jordan Buck.' The interesting thing is, and it behooves me to tell ya, it was Kat's great grandfather, Eachus Davis, who really shot that buck. At least that's been the, shall I call it, family story that's been passed down. There's a surviving aunt who would attest to it, but the family has never chose to contest or quibble about it." As I related the story, Kat sat next to me, smiling proudly. "Eachus was hunting with Jim that morning. After he shot it, they tracked the animal to where it lay against the bank of the Yellow River. Eachus let Jim tag and claim it, having no idea it was a record breaker, and maybe he wouldn't have even cared. It was just a big old buck, tough meat, and Eachus was interested in bagging a more tender doe. He wanted good venison for his family. History books would argue this, but dats da troot, take it or leave it."

"That's a wild story, Hat," Marcus said, as our eyes met in the rearview mirror.

"The story goes, Jim sent it off to a taxidermist in Minnesota, but lost track of it for years. That's probably true. Someone discovered it in an antique shop I heard, measured the rack, realized what a prize it was, then traced it back to Jim.

"Should we be believing this or are you making it up?" Jewel asked politely.

"No, as far as the family's concerned, it's 100 percent true. But what I'm getting at, and it pertains to us now, is that history has skewed the facts. They even have a marker where the buck supposedly fell, and it's in the wrong place. Okay, what I'm getting at is this book I'm writing for you. Questions continually pop up in my head as to its possible outcome, how it'll be received. We're attempting to promulgate something that'll set the world on its ear. Maybe it's bigger than you guys imagine. Maybe it'll be perceived as something so unbelievable that no one will take it to heart: a canard," I added, as I turned to the back seat with wide eyes and a grin. "In a worst case, it will dishevel the aura this world has put around you." I turned back around. "It could have far reaching, negative effects. People could be really upset with you. Do you guys realize what I'm saying?"

"They need to know I was winding through dread and despair," Marcus replied back to me, at first calmly. "They were an abrasive flight over my tender wounds. I was fire starving for air, parched past loneliness. You're right, this book will be an insurrection out of previously unknown pages. Yours is not an arrow drawn by a reckless hunter. I really hope it'll be full of damaged edges, that it tumults many souls. It should be a storm flurry meant to twist and shout."

I had gotten Marcus somewhat riled up. I just stared at him through my rearview mirror for the longest time without saying anything, just trying to take in what he had said. I glanced at Kat, then back at Jewel. They weren't saying anything either. At least Kat got to hear how he is, what I had been telling her about his manner of speaking. Besides, my pocket recorder was getting it all.

"We saw a cougar on this road once," I explained, breaking a numb silence. "There must be a few that run through these woods along the river, but they're rare. It wasn't stopping for a photo opportunity. Dats da troot, too," I said with a chuckle.

What does he want from me? What does he expect me to be able to do? That's what I was asking myself, steering along that curved decline down to the river's edge.

At the landing turnabout, I backed the boat trailer to the edge of the bank. We all got out and set about wrestling the boats into the water. They put the cooler, lawn chairs, life jackets, seat cushions, and guitar in while I was tying the boats together.

"Look!" Kat exclaimed, pulling her river hat over her head and behind her shoulders, pointing upstream. From this landing, the river curves to the west, and there on the Minnesota side we saw a pleasant surprise.

A large black bear had just entered the water at a sandbar off of shore. In an instant, two small cubs followed. The sow slowly walked, then started to swim across to the other side where the river curves to the north. Her young ones followed. I scurried to the Jeep to retrieve the binoculars from between the seats. It was amazing to watch. The bears were quite far away and would reach our side of the shore, but far to the north, not causing us concern. They were oblivious to our presence as we quietly passed the binoculars back and forth to each other.

"Never seen that before," I muttered excitedly under my breath. I looked at Kat. We smiled at each other. We would be taking our guests on a worthwhile journey. We already had. The bears climbed onto the Wisconsin bank and disappeared into the woods.

"That was great!" Jewel said excitedly. Marcus lifted his hat and scratched his head, then turned to me with an appreciative gaze. Then he shook his head in a manner of disbelief.

"Yep, I guess we really are in the woods," he said. I turned to Jewel. She gave me an appreciative grin.

I then climbed in the Jeep and proceeded to pull the trailer to the parking area. I locked it up and walked back down to join them.

"Ready?" I asked. Marcus nodded. I let them climb in and get seated. For now, the ladies took one boat, while he and I would share the other. I stepped into the water. Someone usually has to get a little wet. The water was a trifle cold. I ventured to guess its temperature was in the low 60s at best. I'd become adept at guessing this over the years. Catfish generally don't bite until the water temperature reaches 54 degrees. Others say they don't bite until the buds on the oak trees are the size of a squirrel's ear. I go by water temperature.

I pushed and maneuvered our boat raft into a couple feet of water. Kat politely asked Marcus to lean the opposite way as I rolled myself up and in. I let my dripping jeans and river tennis shoes hang out over the edge of the boat for a minute. Our craft slowly took to the undulating current. Kat took an oar and placed it in the lock on the outside of their boat. I did the same to ours. We bring the oars along to steer clear of occasional protruding boulders. Although seldom the case, we occasionally need to position ourselves to enter what few small rapids exist, preferably bow first. There have been many times when we had no need to get the oars wet until steering for shore when the float was over. Both Jewel and Marcus seemed apprehensive as we set off down the river. I quickly arranged my cushion and a life jacket as pillows against the stern. I lay down on the slats of wood that were the boat's raised secondary floor. With my head resting against the stern, and feet up on the middle seat, I got arranged quite comfortably. It was my way of implying that they think about doing the same. This was it, time to relax. I pointed to the sky. The first of 11 bald eagles that we would see came to view. It was circling in the sky above us. Jewel watched through the binocs.

Kat was wasting no time. She poured a small cup of gin and orange juice, then motioned to Jewel. Jewel took the cup and Kat poured another for herself. Marcus and I both gave a "no thanks" with the flick of our hands.

We floated past the first small island, letting the current take us up to full speed.

"I've never seen river water this clear," Jewel called out to me. "Yet it has a distinct brown color."

"A lot of minerals," Kat told her.

"The fish are healthier looking than anywhere else I've ever seen," I added. "No pollutants flow in until it meets with the Mississippi farther downstream."

We passed Nelson's Landing, barely visible, with an island obstructing most of the view. I pointed out the landing to them. There were several tents pitched near the shore.

Next came Fox Landing, our favorite swimming hole. One can walk across the whole river from there most of the time. There's a long island running down the middle. We took the Wisconsin side. It's pretty much all sand bottom. There were people in the water and on the shore. We exchanged waves as we floated by.

Farther down, as we rounded a bend, we came upon our first set of small rapids. We could hear the turbulence of crashing waters over a mostly submerged rock bed. Marcus and Jewel had still not taken my suggestion to relax. In fact, as the sounds drew near, their backs straightened up. It reminded me of the time I saw my first alligator. I had to smile. Kat looked over to me. She smiled too. We breezed through the waves with the mere sound of a few light scrapes on the bottom of our raft, never tilting in the slightest. I never moved from my reclined position. Kat casually sipped her gin. If Marcus and Jewel were to remain this tense, they would be stiff as a board by the time our trip ended.

A pair of swans nestled along the weeds on the opposite shore. I pointed them out. Two canoeing couples paddled by nodding and waving to us. We were coming to a special place now. I motioned for Kat to man her oar. She knew what this was about.

"We can use a stretch," I said, as we steered toward the shoreline. There appeared a small clearing along the forest edge.

"This place is called the Old Paint Mine. I think you should see it," I explained, as our raft brushed against the shallows of a gravel and rock bottom, then glided up to the sandy shore. We got out for that stretch. I could tell Marcus was stiff, although Jewel slipped out of their boat with ease. I threw an anchor to the shoreline grass above.

As we stood on the shore looking across the river, I told them the story of this place. Around the early 1900s they mined the clay on the hill that was behind us. From it, they expelled the color terracotta - a dull red, but absorbing pigment. It was used for clay products that were sculpted, as with pottery that's baked in kilns. They also extracted it for paint. It had a reputation of lasting forever.

"Yah, they made it so good, they put themselves out of business," Kat chuckled. Jewel and Marcus found the comment humorous.

"Let's walk up; I'll show ya," I said.

As we walked up the hill, I pointed out the old tracks that were made from railroad ties, lying where we walked and off to our left, some almost hidden by deterioration amongst the underbrush and trees. At brief times, the tracks intersected with our walking path as we climbed the hill. They were extremely weather-worn and cracked, grown over with moss and other forms of vegetation. They long ago had served to guide the horse-drawn carts to and from the river below. There was a small stream meandering amid the trees that flowed down the hill, also to our left. We were deep in secluded woods.

"I believe it was sent downriver on boats to Stillwater or Hastings in Minnesota, but I'm not sure, maybe to Red Wing," I told them.

As we approached the top, I motioned to a path that veered to our left. We took it, and in a moment were next to an old wooden shack with a steel waterwheel attached. There was a stream running beneath the wheel, which was covered in rust and long ago had froze up from worn bearings and lack of lubrication. Nevertheless it was another picture postcard. Above it, not 30 yards away, was an honest to goodness beaver dam. It stretched across a fair-sized pond. It was so stable one could stand on it, even walk across the top of it, which Marcus did.

"This area is protected against trapping," I explained. "There've been beaver living here for who knows how long. We see them sometimes, and hear them slap their tails." I pointed to the clay along the bank. "We had a friend step in that with white tennis shoes. The color wouldn't come out of one of them. We teased him, saying he needed to step in it with the other shoe so they'd match."

We shared an enjoyably, reclusive moment together on that hill. Not much was said, except by the surrounding nature, as my tape will testify. It was easy to recognize the abandonment of this place by man. We began to walk back down to the river.

"There are no silent touches," I heard Marcus say, as if to himself, while we walked. I wondered what he was thinking, but I didn't ask.

Now the sky was intermittently filled with billowing clouds. In the distance, there soared an eagle or osprey. It was too far off to tell, and we didn't take the time to scope it out. I had been counting our eagle sightings - four thus far. It was an active day in the air. We got back to our makeshift raft, and I pushed us out in the same manner as I had done before. The next few minutes should be interesting, I thought to myself. Just ahead lay a rock shelf under the water, with an abrupt drop of maybe two feet where the water cascades over the rocks. It comes up silently and it's harmless, but can be a surprise. I didn't introduce it.

"Whoa!" Jewel called out. Marcus grabbed both sides of our boat with his hands. It only lasted a second or so. I caught Kat giggling to herself.

"Alright, I shoulda told ya 'bout that," I said. "No more surprises, I promise." Marcus looked at me and shook his head, but at least he was smiling.

"Strange misguided lamb, kicking at the flock," he stated.

Hmm, I grinned back, not at all understanding what he meant. I had gotten used to that. I looked over at Jewel. She too was shaking her head at me. Now I blew it; they'll never relax.

Surprisingly, after my promise of no more out-of-the-blue excitement, they did start to ease up. Jewel set a cushion on the floor, and using her life jacket as a pillow against the bow seat, she reclined. Kat did the same as I had done, and now the ladies were facing each other. Marcus loomed above us, high in his seat and cushion. He tried to appear comfortable.

Next we passed where the Snake River dumps into the mighty Croix. The water quickens here for a short stretch. We passed Soderbeck Ferry Landing, where I explained its significance.

"This was the site where they used to ferry the people and their vehicles across before the bridge was built farther down." So much historical data for one day; I was feeling like an old river-rat guide.

With a few calculated back-sweeps of my oar, the current then took us drifting across to the other side. There, between an island and the Minnesota shoreline, the waters became near stagnant. We were over a deep hole, and out of the current. I let us hold steady in one spot for a while. There were deer standing on the shoreline farther down. They had come to drink. An occasional bass or northern could be seen or heard jumping out of the water.

"This is nice," Jewel remarked with a sigh.

"The government has all the land along here. No one is allowed to build. What few cabins that remain were bought up, and the owners at the time were granted a 99 year lease. There's only about a half dozen of them. I don't know what will happen to the cabins when that time expires. It's all meant to go back to wilderness, eventually," I explained.

Marcus remained quiet throughout much of the afternoon, as did Jewel. We knew they were enjoying this respite, but they obviously had the true meaning of their trip still looming in their minds. It was the first time I had ever sensed any conflict between them, as slight as it may have been. It's just that Marcus' persona is so intense. And with Jewel so electrifying, they can make sparks without even trying. I could tell Kat felt it too, and she had just met them.

They were captivated by the bald eagles we had been seeing. As I maneuvered our boats back into the current of the main channel, we witnessed another first.

I pointed, and there, perched high on an overhanging tree branch, was a bald eagle with something gripped in its talon. Kat reached for the binoculars.

"Wow!" she shouted. "It's a turtle!" She passed the binocs over to Jewel. We drifted past quietly. It wasn't bothered by us. It knew we were there; Kat had made sure of that. We all took turns scoping it out. It was pecking at the meat beneath the shell.

"Never saw that before," I remarked in a low tone. "Never know what you're gonna see."

This was a nature-filled journey we were on today, heavenly reward of exceptional circumstances, and a lifetime memory. Each of us felt it.

We drifted on, and the current returned us to the Wisconsin side of the river. We passed a large, old cabin along the shore. The water was shallow now. We were lightly scraping bottom.

"Ya'll mind getting yer feet wet fer a while?" I asked, as we rounded another bend. We had prepared them that morning, how tennis shoes were called out for this day, and to be ready to get them wet. Bare feet are a no-no in the river. There are too many sharp variables, neglected broken glass, and occasional fish hooks, that could do you damage. Plus broken clam shells. Kat and I steered to an opening where a channel flowed apart from the main water. We were entering Sand Rock Cliffs.

As we parted from the main river's flow, our vessel dragged and then stopped dead in the sand. We all got out. The water was only a few inches deep. We each took to the sides and guided our craft into the channel. It took very little effort, mostly floating itself once our weight had been removed. This became necessary for 50 yards or so. The cliffs came into view up ahead. The water began to deepen, so we climbed back in. Barely moving now, we would again begin curving toward the main channel. A large island loomed several feet above us to our right, while picturesque sandstone cliffs soared high on our left. There was another eagle circling above. How perfect is this, I thought. I sensed that Kat shared that same feeling.

"They discovered a new species of dragonfly here not long ago," I told them. "People were all excited. They named it the St. Croix Snake Tail. Oooow a dragonfly, wow! hmmm," I added, almost sarcastically. I take that back, it was sarcastically.

"That is exciting," Jewel admonished back at me, smiling. I supposed she would think so. She can probably talk to them too, I told myself. I smiled back at her like some classroom child that had been caught throwing a spit ball.

"They have yellow at the end of their tails and a yellowish green back," I added.

She never stopped smiling; staring up at the rock formations we were passing by. All was then silent.

"There are campsites above that ridge, but it's awfully quiet. I don't think there's anyone up there," I finally said, as we drifted out to where the channel returned to the river

## CHAPTER 9

I look back now, at what a whirlwind, dream-like state we were floating in that afternoon. Maybe it was all that fresh air and perfect weather. Sometimes the fresh up north affects city folks differently. They get groggy and want to take naps when they come to visit us. It didn't appear to make Jewel or Marcus feel that way at all. Today, our trip seemed to have happened in one breath, an out-of-breath experience.

We were drifting slowly now over my fishing honey hole. I pointed to the water as we went by.

"Fish," I said with an affirmative nod. There were two men fishing from shore. Not much of a secret; they're just not goin' about it right, I told myself.

In a matter of minutes, we reached an island with a long sandbar that protruded north. We let our ship run aground. It was time for another break, and maybe a midday snack. I pitched our anchor in the sand, jumped out, then reached around Marcus for the folded lawn chairs. I came to realize there really wasn't much room for him to stretch with those there. I opened all four, setting them on the sand while they got out of the boats. Kat brought the cooler over and set it next to the chairs.

"Time for a nap," I teased.

Jewel brought the bag of food, while I went back to the ship and retrieved my guitar. I laid it down on the sand. We all walked around a bit to get the blood flowing in our legs again, and to explore our little paradise. We could see more canoes coming from upriver. A couple streamed by us paddling their kayaks. We went barefoot on the shore as we swished the sand and small stones from our shoes with river water.

We then began enjoying our little picnic. I remember wishing I had brought my ukulele. I snatched up the guitar and started playing an instrumental Spanish calypso number. Making most of it up as I went along, I used what I call "frayling" with my fingers. I'm not sure of its technical term.

It's when a player runs the back of his finger tips rapidly across the strings one at a time, small one first. "Ho lay! Here's to that Mexican hat dance stuff," I told them.

Jewel stood up, seemingly unable to resist. She began performing a very provocative, gypsy-style dance, twirling across the sand. It was exciting to watch. Marcus beamed with pride. We were all having a great time. I handed the guitar to him. Without hesitation, he began playing and singing, *Gypsy Woman*, by I believe, The Impressions, or maybe it was Curtis Mayfield. It was astounding! It should have been captured on video. Jewel danced lightly on, as if just for him. Kat sat with her wide-brimmed river hat, sipping gin and smiling with the beginnings of some sunburned cheeks. She tends to burn easily, hence the hat, which I think she should have placed on that pretty little head of hers much sooner.

The sun was attempting to stay afloat, settling above the western tree line as we departed that island. It had been a short, romantic interlude, one that happened without planning. Moments later, we could hear, in the distance, traffic crossing the state line bridge. Soon the bridge came into view. This float was nearing its end. We ran aground on the cement boat landing near the bridge pilings where we had stood hours earlier. I threw the anchor to the shore. We sat there in our raft for a moment, thinking it was over too soon. Where had the time gone? I sensed we were trying to reflect upon all that we had just been through as we sat there in our raft for a few minutes, not saying anything. It did seem to be over too soon.

It was decided that Kat and I would take the Camaro back up the river road to retrieve the Jeep and trailer. Marcus and Jewel would pull up chairs along the shore and watch things roll by until our return. I wanted to beat the sunset back to them.

As Kat and I drove, we shared with each other our thoughts on what had transpired.

"Oh, honey, I didn't mean to…" she began to say.

"It's okay," I interrupted, consolingly. I knew what she was about to tell me. I didn't need her to apologize for not believing in their existence, or in all of the stories I had piled on her. I knew it had been a difficult and a confusing time. The chain of events that had roared into my life were like a tidal wave. My trying to hold on, and trying to relate it, must have seemed to her like prattling at times. "No one in their right mind would have," I said to her affectionately, placing my hand on her thigh. Then we held hands.

I relayed to her a story. In my travels, I often had been working (more like struggling) on my book. Oftentimes it was at the end of my driving day, while having dinner in truck stops. It was on one such occasion; I think it was around Tonica, Illinois. I was eating a personal pan-size pizza. The woman who had just baked it for me was settling in on her break, and had just sat down to a hamburger and fries. We were the only two there at the time. I admit I was experiencing the doldrums, trying to balance disconcerted thoughts regarding my writing endeavors.

"Whatcha doin', homework?" she asked.

"Writin' a book," I kindly replied to her.

"Yah? What's it about?"

"How much time you got?" I responded.

"All kinds," she said in a full smile. I couldn't help but notice she was running a little late for dental work.

I began to relate to her the story of how I was rerouted just before Katrina, and how I had bumped into someone famous. Continuing, I explained how this person and I had hit it off, mostly because of music. Subsequently, we had become good friends. I told of visiting him, and of us playing guitars together. I explained that he asked me to write a book. Then I told her who he was. Her eyes widened. She abruptly stood up from her swivel stool at the counter and looked hard at me.

"I knew he was alive! I knew he didn't die!" she shouted, as half-chewed fried potatoes spewed from between the remnants of those teeth. It was quite enlivening. Her moment of displayed enthusiasm refurbished me from the labor I had been toiling under.

Kat laughed heartedly. It really was quite humorous. Then I told Kat how, that after finishing my pizza, the woman began singing that Elvis song, *Love Me Tender* from behind the register as I was walking out the door. Kat cracked up.

"If I ever finish this book, I want to try to find her again and give her a copy. I owe her a debt of gratitude for putting me back on course. My writings have come a long way since then, and now, even *you* realize he never died. You know we really gotta get down there and see them." I smiled earnestly at her.

"I want to," she replied, somewhat reserved, giving my hand a squeeze. Still holding onto a half smirk regarding my story, she was unable to control a brief laugh. Then she asked, "Do you think they had fun today?"

"Oh, I know they did," I told her. "But I can tell they've got a lot on their minds. I know they got to relax a little; that was good. You gotta know Marcus is fighting this thing about them relocating. Well, maybe not fighting, but there's discord, I guess you'd say."

"You sure?" Kat asked.

"I've gotten to know them fairly well," I assured her.

We were silent for a time, as we rode on. Kat soon suggested we order some Oriental take-out for supper. I agreed. Maybe they would too.

"I can't wait to meet these people you've told me about," she remarked.

"Wait till you see their place. I don't blame Marcus for not wanting to move. They have a paradise that'd be awfully hard to replace. Jewel's probably been through more than we realize. She takes on a lot of burden in this care giving she does. Maybe Jewel's thinking more in terms of an extended vacation; I don't know."

"Tomorrow should be interesting. I'm looking forward to going to the headwaters," Kat confided.

"Yah, these few days are some kinda adventure, aren't they?" I said to her.

We were pulling back up to the Norway Point parking area. I admit to having driven fast.

"I'll drop the car off at home; pick me up," Kat instructed. We would be passing by our cabin on the way back to them.

"Okay babe," I said, leaning over for a kiss and then I slid out my door. "I'll follow ya."

While making the return trip, I couldn't help but reflect on such a resplendent day. I hoped they felt the same. I realized Marcus must certainly be tired. He's used to his afternoon naps, and that river can really drag a lot out of a person. It would most likely be an early night.

When we got back to the bridge, they were seated on the chairs, looking out contently near the water's edge. I backed the trailer to the boats and we loaded everything in short order. They thought Oriental food was a great idea. If they were worn out, it didn't show. They seemed revitalized, spirited. I wondered to myself if they had reached some sustainable agreement while they'd had this chance to be alone. Maybe a compromise had been reached regarding this relocation venture. It didn't seem my place to pry. I only know their moods were jovial. I'd like to think it was due to our boreal milieu (northern air), and our magic river.

During the small chore of returning the boats and accessories to the shed, Marcus expressed interest in a game of Frisbee golf. The girls had gone to town to pick up our dinner.

"I have no idea how to throw those things," he told me.

"That's the beauty of it, you don't need to. Anyone can play. My son holds the course record at 16. That's 11 under par. That's a few holes in one. He's good, played it in college believe it or not, something called Ultimate. I can't throw distance, but I do alright."

"I'll drive the golf cart," he said with his smile. I grinned back.

It was getting late in the day; the sun had nearly set. We decided there wouldn't be time to make it around the course before it got too dark. We would maybe talk the ladies into a quick game in the morning before we set out on our trip to Itasca.

This night would blaze by gloriously. After a cozy, cordial supper, I showed them my vast collection of sheet music. I had been compiling this material most of my life. It encompasses many thousands of songs. We ended up playing a dozen of them or so that evening. Some of our own renditions had us laughing. Marcus played piano on a couple. He was quite accomplished with the keys. Even though playing had been in his distant past, he took to it with a natural love.

It was decided that when we got to the headwaters the next day we would both take notes, compare and combine them, and write a song about the experience.

"What flowers talk about while they bloom, before wilting," Jewel suggested.

That rang with enchantment. "Do you write songs?" Kat asked her.

"No, I just listen," she replied.

"To flowers?" Kat asked, smiling.

"They creep with need and I smile why," Jewel replied, smiling back to her. I wondered if Kat understood what she meant. Her expressions showed she did. I certainly didn't. I wondered at such florid thoughts. I could tell the girls had a sisterhood thing going on.

"We should bring a camera with us tomorrow," Kat suggested. Jewel and Marcus looked at each other for a moment.

"Sure, good idea," Marcus surprisingly concurred.

Such was our time together, sharing our cabin in the woods, as the night came to a close with its inescapable memories. Candlelight mellowing our reflections; it was a night like that.

## CHAPTER 10

Morning came suddenly. There were no piano sounds when I first opened my eyes. I had slept hard. I figured we all undoubtedly did. Kat arose before me. I closed my eyes for, what I thought was, just a minute longer. That's it, time to get with it I thought.

They were all having coffee in the living room when I walked out. Marcus had been exploring our bookshelf. Several books were lying on the coffee table in front of him. He was engrossed in a book called *Metaphysical Meditations* by Paramahansa Yogananda. He didn't even notice me in the room. The ladies were looking over some sketches Kat had done years ago while attending art college. They both looked up at me with smiles.

"Good morning to you, sleepy head," Kat said lovingly.

"I must be getting old," I replied.

"You work hard," Kat replied.

I looked out our bay windows above the bird feeders. The sky was overcast and gray; the leaves were wet from a drizzling rain.

"A little gloomy," I reflected aloud. Marcus had looked up from his reading.

"Might have to catch that Frisbee thing next time," he said to me. I nodded in agreement. "Interesting collection of reading material," he added.

"It's pretty diverse L. Kat and I have combined our collections, along with some of the stuff the kids left behind. Anything on Frisbees?" I smirked. He just gave me a smirk back.

We shuffled through our morning, taking showers, and packing for the trip. Kat whipped together some waffles, which filled us up. It was nearing time to go.

"It's a little over 200 miles to where we're goin'," I explained, gathering my things near the door. Marcus was looking at the piano. "No, ya can't take it with you. Move in next door, we'll work something out," I told him. He hastened a light laugh, then turned toward the door to join me.

Just before leaving, Kat gave Jewel one of her hand-made beaded purses, with earrings and a necklace to match. A beautiful set. I know the labor she puts into creating these things. It was a wonderful gesture. Now we were set to go. I set my bag out on the porch and hastened to grab the Gibson and Martin as we were making our way outside. I remember hoping to myself that they would be able to come back, as I closed the front door behind us.

Kat had booked two rooms at a place called The Pines Motel near Lake George. We were on a mission. It was approaching noon when we pulled out of the driveway. The ride to me seemed short. I'm used to driving six or seven hours without a break; it's embedded in my system. It may have seemed long to them. Marcus spent part of his time reading that book. Jewel silently watched things pass by. I wondered to myself if she missed that part of her past when she had spent time in the north during her youth. Kat was her usual quiet self as we drove. I usually have to engage Kat in conversation. If I don't initiate, things stay fairly silent.

"What would you guys think if we came down in the middle of September to see ya'all," I asked. Marcus looked up from his reading, peering above his glasses at my reflection in the rearview mirror.

"Can you come sooner?" he asked.

"That's when my next vacation is set up. It's the earliest we can do, L."

"That would be good." Jewel replied. "We'll have fun."

"It'll be a hundred starving fingers over a thousand lonely frets till then," he remarked. Kat turned and looked at him with a smile. I think she really enjoyed when he spoke that way. He winked at her.

"I don't know if I want her to meet Clay, though; I could lose her," I said, half-heartedly.

"Good chance," Jewel responded. Kat looked back; their smiles met.

"Great." I gave a resigned mutter. "Mister Stud Muffin," I said louder. No, in truth I wasn't really worried. She won't understand a thing he said anyway.

As the ride brought us near the park, we caught our first sight of the Mississippi, as it meandered under our roadway bridge. We pulled over for a stretch and then stood atop of the bridge as her waters passed beneath us. It was more like a small creek, only a few feet wide, dancing with the long grasses that swirled and formed her edges.

"This is amazing!" Jewel exalted. "I can't believe this!" She was bouncing about atop that bridge, displaying dance-like exaltation. It was what she had come for.

"The water acts like it has spent eternity knowing," Marcus remarked.

It was pretty cool, but hard to imagine this was the great river. The air was from the north and brisk, the sky overcast. It smelled like rain. He was looking over the rail at the water below.

"She flows like a scented dream, sweet undercoating of cooled summer breezes," he said.

"Sounds like a song. Need a pen?" I asked. He turned to me, his dimple showing, the same one that I presume had melted so many in the past. We got back in the Jeep then, driving those last few miles to the entrance of Itasca State Park.

We were on a paved road now, called Wilderness Drive. Our tour was clearly marked by wooden signs along the way. Sheeted above us was a canopy of large, virgin red and white pines, blocking the sky. We found out they were nearly 300 years old. First stop was the site of an 18,000-year-old bison kill, discovered through scientific excavation. We tried to imagine its relative significance with regard to time but it was hard to grasp. After passing a place called the Douglas Lodge, we came upon a spot named Preacher's Grove. Venturing a closer look, Marcus and Jewel walked over and sat down on a bench under some fire-scarred red pines that overlooked a lake. Then came our very first photograph of them, as Kat took the camera from her bag and stood with her back to the lake. She didn't even ask first, just turned and snapped their picture. They both smiled. The photograph shows that they were holding hands. As I look at that picture today, it beams with romance.

Anxious now to get on our way to the real destination, we passed a pioneer cemetery, and a 500-year-old Indian burial site, then we came upon a large parking lot. There were a dozen or more cars parked there. This wasn't going to be an exclusive experience. It was time to take a little hike. We passed a visitor center with a scale model of the river and its tributaries, mapping the journey it makes to the gulf. No intention of slowing down now, we'd catch it on the way back. We followed the path over a small walk bridge to an open area among the trees. There were quite a few people mulling about.

Spotting a tall sign that had been carved from a tree; I scooped the camera from Kat and took a picture. We were there. It said we were at 1,475 feet above sea level. Beyond the sign was a small lake. From it, an opening, where water peacefully tumbled, churning over and between a bed of rocks that lay stretched across what was no more than a small creek. Two people were walking on those rocks coming toward us from the other side. They had just stepped across the beginning of the Mississippi River. From that point it would wind its way 2,552 miles to the Gulf of Mexico. Each of us stood, staring at this marvel. There began a drizzling rain. No one paid any attention to the elderly-professor-looking gentleman that stood among us. I briefly tried to imagine this scene if they knew who he was. This serene touristy moment would turn and become a frenzied circus. He would be a surrounded animal in an imaginary ring. I stopped thinking.

"Small, whispering waters grow up to be a great river," Jewel quietly said. Her face held a dreamy, enduring serenity. I couldn't help but stare. There glowed from her an inner contentment. She wasted no time getting to those rocks. We all watched as she gingerly ambled her way, dancing along on 15 or 20 of them, with arms outstretched. She was humming some song, or more a Native American chant, spinning around at times, truly an enraptured gypsy. There was wonderment in her eyes. I snapped two photos. She winked at me.

"Ah, the clashing seminar of radiance. Mirror angling rivers are in her veins," Marcus commented. I wondered to myself; what on earth goes through his mind? At times there was such an insular quality about him — isolated, detached. He was an island unto himself. I looked at him inquisitively. "Our love is a river without banks, only the slightest of shorelines," he replied back to me and my stare. I just returned his smile.

He and I turned and walk down the creek side a short ways to where a flat log lay across and above the water, the river. It was a thin footbridge that extended to both shores. He took his shoes off and sat down on the middle of the log. With his feet dangling into the water below, he looked stoically in our ladies direction. I took another picture of Jewel. She seemed powder-loose. Then I turned and took one of him. Kat was standing along the shore near Jewel and the rocks, smiling. She had retrieved a small foldout umbrella from her bag. All of us were getting wet except her. I walked down to Marcus.

"L," I said as I neared. I snapped another picture of him when he looked up at the camera.

"Passion stretching for a roar," he said, pointing in Jewel's direction. I turned to look at her briefly, then back at him. "Easy to find where rivers go, but do we really know where they begin?" he asked me. I just shrugged my shoulders. I had a hunch that question was leading somewhere. "Endless in the true scope, the design of things," he added. "They keep going around in recirculation." It wasn't hard for me to fathom; I couldn't disagree. It was, after all, as I had once told him, where I wished for my ashes to journey.

Getting decidedly wet now, and with Jewel's dancing homage ended, it came time to make our way back. We spent a good hour in and around the visitor center, learning all kinds of interesting historic facts while we let our clothes dry out some. Plaques spoke of the early fur trader, William Morrison. And explorers with names like Brower and Nicollet. It is said Hernando

DeSoto discovered the Mississippi in 1541, and that it was the boundary of a peace accord in 1783. Henry Schoolcraft was said to have found this place with the help of an Ojibway guide named Ozawindib. He gave it the name Itasca, derived from syllables from Latin words meaning "truth" and "head."

Kat and Jewel seemed well within their element here. Theirs was the smoldering heritage within this air around us, this opulent land of wild rice and maple syrup. The expressions their faces held, the motions they made, were filled with reverie. Watching them, to me, made this trip worthwhile. I was surprised at the ease it took to coax them back to the Jeep. The day was waning, and I was hungry.

While we were making our way along the back roads, I turned the heater on low to dry our damp clothes. We were in search of our motel when we came upon a town named Becida. We saw no real town, per se, but we did spot a bar and grille, which we later learned happened to be much of the town. It seemed like a good place to stop to eat, maybe the only spot.

It turned out to be rustic and wonderful. There were maybe a dozen people inside when we entered. There was a family of six at a large table in back, and a few others seated at the bar. We grabbed a table along the back wall nearest the bar. As I can recall, we settled on walleye dinners, wine, and more than a few beers for myself. We were unwinding from, what was agreed by each of us, a glorious day. I remember suggesting how Hershel should see some of the totem poles we had passed along the roadway, and that maybe we should get some pictures to bring back for him. I was convinced he could carve a spectacular one, if he could see what they are.

About that time, I noticed a middle-aged gentleman seated at the bar. A few stools away from him were two men in cowboy hats. As I watched them conversing, it became apparent the single gentleman was the owner of this establishment. Having an admitted buzz on, and feeling uninhibited, I winked across to Marcus. He looked inquisitively back at me. I rose from my chair and approached the gentleman, and stood between him and the cowboys.

"Hey, how's it goin'?" I asked.

"Good, how's your dinner?" he replied.

"Excellent. Say, we were wondering. Are you the owner?"

"Sure am, name's Brett."

"Mine's Hatty Swiggs," I told him proudly. The odd name didn't appear to faze him. "We were wondering if you would mind if we brought our guitars in, maybe play a few while we enjoy some drinks."

"Go right ahead, anything you want," he said, most matter-of-factly. It was like he was asked that question all the time. He was a real down-to-earth, easy-going fellow. The cowboys both smiled.

"Know any country?" the older one asked.

"A little," I told him. "But how did I know you were gonna ask that?" I added. We all laughed. No one at my table could hear our conversation, but they were all looking at me. I turned and swiftly stepped out the door. I went over to the Jeep and quickly retrieved both guitar cases, then returned inside, in what was probably a heartbeat and a half. Marcus had a grin on his face. He had surmised what was going on.

"Yer something," he said, shaking his head at me when I approached our table.

"We've been hired ta do a gig," I joked. This was the challenge I was putting forth, for the two of us to play in public for the first time. I couldn't resist it. He didn't resist either. We set the cases on the floor beside us, pulled out the axes, and tuned them up. He adjusted his chair so as to face me and the wall, instead of the onlookers. Only the four of us knew that he must hide his appearance. I remember thinking; "At least he isn't holding aces and eights with his back to the door like that." I think strange thoughts sometimes. A new bottle of wine and a pitcher of beer were delivered to our table.

"Complements of the owner," our waitress said. We waved to him with gratitude from across the room.

"Did you take any notes?" I asked Marcus.

"Notes of what?"

"The Mississippi," I explained.

"Nope," he confessed.

"Neither did I," I replied. We all laughed.

I immediately began to finger-pick my slow version of the song, *I'm a Believer*, by Neil Diamond. I tried to sound as close to Waylon Jennings as I could, although Waylon is a much better crooner than me. I was just loosening us up.

For nearly two hours we played cover songs from other artists, to the applause of Brett and his patrons. A few other people had moseyed in and sat at the bar, but no one left. The atmosphere was warm, the setting cozy. The girls quietly chatted between themselves at times, as he and I played.

I was the lead singer that night. Marcus joined in on choruses, but ventured few solos. If he was uptight, the wine hid it. He was enjoying himself, and so were the girls. I noticed how, a couple of times, an elderly couple looked over at Marcus peculiarly. It was as if something inside of them sparked a long-forgotten memory. It was as though a part of them recognized him, but their embedded reality refused to identify with it. It was hard to describe, but there was a half of a recognition there.

After more than enough wine, beer, and adequate applause, we packed it in. We bid a goodnight to Brett and those around him, promising we'd be back someday.

When we finally got to our motel, the rain had stopped. The sky was breaking, with a few clouds under a hazy moon. For fun, we made up names for ourselves when we checked in. Kat had originally secured the reservation under her maiden name, suspecting we might wish anonymity. I decline to say what names we came up with.

It had been decided that we'd meet up in Marcus and Jewel's room after getting settled in. I brought my Gibson. Marcus had already uncased the Martin by the time we walked in. This being the final hours, our last night together for who knew how long, we were determined to make it last.

An amazing thing happened that night. What flowed from us, all four of us, back and forth to each other in the passing of musical notes — was as smooth as butter. There came the words and music to an amazing song. It was as though we had it inside ourselves all along. Or maybe it had been created that day, as if a painting from the brushes of memories. The strokes we took were as masterful as any ever put to canvas. The song created, *From a Whisper to High Water*, was about our modest and great river. Later we abbreviated the title to simply, *From a Whisper*. It was extraordinary — one we were all proud of. What a day and night in our lives this had been.

## CHAPTER 11

Speaking for myself, it was a blissful night of rest. For once, I wasn't the last to awaken. Kat lay soundly sleeping as I peeked out at the morning through a slip in the blinds. The sun was up and the sky was blue. I heard her rustling beneath the sheets; turning to her, she had been watching me staring out the window. The slightest sound can awaken her.

"Mornin, babe," she said, in a sheepishly sexy voice. I smiled at her when our eyes met, focusing deeply.

"It's another day," I said, sounding enthusiastic.

"How's the weather?" she asked.

"Sunny," I told her. "How's yer head?"

"Good," she responded. "How's yours?"

"I'm fine, could use some coffee and maybe a little breakfast," I told her.

"I saw a restaurant not far away," she replied. "Think they're up?" I shrugged an "I don't know" with my shoulders as I got myself dressed. I packed up my bag and guitar, then headed toward the door. Kat remained under the sheets as I stepped out into the morning air, bringing my things over to our Jeep that was parked just outside the door. Nothing was stirring from the room next to us. I decided I'd walk down to the office for a complimentary morning coffee. There I met Marcus. He had just poured a cup for himself. We looked at each other with our early morning grins; he blew into a Styrofoam cup to cool his drink. I poured one, too. We stood looking out the windows at the trees across the road.

"We must'a wore them out, L," I said.

"I believe so," he said.

"You guys up for some breakfast?" I asked.

"Will be. Joey's flyin' in at noon to Bemidji Regional. I told him we'd meet him there."

"Brunch then," I smiled and turned to him. He nodded.

"Don't s'pose you know when we'll be seeing you next?" Marcus asked.

"Wish I did. Soon as I can, I do know that. Kat says she wants to come down, but that wouldn't be till mid-September on our vacation," I told him. "I'll probably see you before that. In the meantime I'll be pluggin' away at yer book.

"Light is given to the servant soul," he said to me as he put his free hand on my shoulder and smiled. We turned and stepped outside. Kat was putting her bag in the Jeep as we approached our rooms.

"Hey doll," Marcus called to her.

"Hey yerself," she replied, with an awakened smile.

"I'll see if Jewel's up," he said to her as he passed by, then went over and unlocked their room door with his key.

"You got up quick," I told her. "They're taking off around noon." She just nodded. I knew she was as sorry as I was to see this end.

After checking out of our motel, we drove a short distance to a mom and pop café, where we ate quietly, a late morning breakfast. Things were pretty subdued between us, words dulled to near whispers, less than infused with thought. I could tell Jewel was feeling the aftereffects of our night before. She asked Kat if she had any aspirin, which Kat always does. After all, she has to put up with me.

"We'd like to come down in September and visit a couple days," I said, breaking a long silence, while looking over to Kat for her approval. I felt a need to cement this in. Kat gave me a "for sure" glance.

"Yes, please," Jewel replied, picking lightly with a fork at the omelet she had on her plate.

"We'll take a road trip in our Camaro, and see some sights along the way," I added. Everyone, although interested, again held subdued, yet earnest smiles. "So you're off to see a mountain, I surmise?" asking Jewel. It brought a bit of color to her somewhat pale complexion. There was no noticeable reaction from Marcus. He continued eating his breakfast.

"We have two more places to see before we go back," he remarked, not hinting excitement.

"I saw an Itasca moccasin store on the way here," Jewel said. I'd like to go back and have a look." Marcus nodded in agreement.

"Sounds like a plan," I told them.

From what I had heard, Itasca moccasins were known to be some of the best made. On our way, we stopped to take photographs of two totem poles we had spotted - souvenirs for Hershel. As it turned out, we all ended up with a pair of moccasins, with Marcus flipping the bill. Jewel got what's called the *teepee* type, which ties around the ankle and has fringe. Kat picked out a pair called the *dancer*, with a zipper up the back and also fringe around the ankle. Marcus got the *creeper*, a good hiking pair. I settled for the *canoe*, a low-cut, slipper type. Now we all had souvenirs. It was time for the ride to the airport.

Joey was waiting near a window as we pulled up to the terminal. This was as far as Kat and I would go. She knows I don't do goodbyes well, neither does she. Joey came out to greet us.

"Have a good time?" he asked.

"The greatest!" Jewel told him, and she turned to Kat. Slipping off one of her matching earrings, she put it in Kat's hand, closing it with hers. They smiled deeply at each other without a word, then embraced.

I reached in and pulled the Martin case from out of the back. Stretching my arm out, I handed it to Marcus. I had previously made my mind up.

"I give this to you," I said to him, with a welling tear about to form in my eye. I blame that on what I had just witnessed with the girls.

"No," he shrugged it off with the swish of his hand.

"It wants to go where it's loved the most, L," I said insistently. It felt as though he was gazing deep into my soul then. He took the handle. He put his other arm around my shoulder. Joey was looking on with a smile.

"I haven't been right about too many things in my life, but I was so right about you," he said. Then he squeezed me hard. None of us wanted to cry, but I believe we all needed to. I just happened to be the baby in the bunch, as I felt that tear roll down my cheek.

"Is he crying?" Jewel asked.

"Yeees," Kat admitted. They all looked at me with warm smiles.

"Okay, get outta here you guys," I said, handing Joey Jewel's bag.

"See you under new moons," Jewel said to us. She then turned to Marcus. He was smiling at us. He moved over to Kat, and they embraced. Kat couldn't fool me. She had a tear too, as Jewel and Marcus turned and began walking away. Joey smiled, nodded and turned to follow them.

"See you again," he said, turning back, then spun around to join them as they walked. Then, stepping into the building, they disappeared in an instant out of our sight.

"Let's get outta here." Kat turned to me and said. I nodded.

We took secondary roads back toward home that afternoon, stopping off at a couple of roadside bars along the way. We weren't prepared to let this end so soon. We started planning our next vacation over a couple of drinks.

"You know, I've always wanted to see Graceland. Do you think we could?" Kat asked.

"That'd be great," I assured her. "Wait till you get the feel of Louisiana."

As we sat drinking at our second bar stop, Kat was deep in thought.

"Do you think we should tell the kids about all of this?" she finally asked.

"You saw how they reacted last Thanksgiving. Besides, I'm not sure how Marcus would feel about that just yet," I had to reply.

"What do you mean?"

"It's just that we never discussed it. I know he doesn't want to jeopardize anything before this book is finished, not that it would. Right now the kids think it's just another of my Beanie, Jockum hallucinations. I think we should leave it at that."

I was referring to a true story about my childhood that Kat knew well. It turns out our kids had found out about it a couple of years back, thanks to my sister. She was having dinner at the casino where our daughter Lacey waitresses, when she let the cat out of the bag.

"Tell my brother to say hello to Junie, Beanie, Jockum, Miffum and Aikum for me," she told Lacey. Thanks Anne!

She went on to explain the story of the imaginary friends I had, and would talk to in the bathroom, when I was around 5 or 6 years old. She was dating her future husband, Stanley, when he asked her sincerely, "Is your little brother crazy?" My friends were several inches high, and looked like elves, or dwarfs. They chose to stay behind when we moved from that house and my imagination never brought them up again. I believe I had a healthy, rich, and lively childhood.

Lacey called me on my cell phone the day after she had spoken with Anne. I was on the road.

"I bumped into some old friends of yours yesterday," she said.

"Oh yah, who?" I asked.

"Junie, Beanie, Jockum, Miffum and Aikum," she responded, unable to control her laughter.

I played along. "Oh wow! I haven't seen those guys in over 40 years!" Lacey couldn't stop laughing, and eventually she told her sisters, brother, and my grandkids. Thanks again, Anne.

I decided to get Lacey and my sister back. The next day I paid them both with identical phone calls. I told them that as I was getting out of the shower at a Pilot Truck Stop, there they were! Two were seated on the sink, one on the back of the toilet, and one on the stool. Man, it was sure good to see those guys again! We talked about what we had been doing for all these years. Junie had passed away some 18 years ago. All the rest of these guys had gray beards now. Beanie walked with a cane, and Jockum had an oxygen tank about an inch high. Someone banged on my shower room door and said, "Only one person allowed in there at a time!" I told the boys to quiet down and meet me back in the truck, which they did. Now they travel with me always. I never have to be alone again. I thanked the girls for spurring them back to me. I think everyone is still laughing, including my little friends, wherever now they might be.

"Let's keep this thing to ourselves for right now, leave the kids out of it," I told Kat, as we drove closer toward home. She agreed.

It must have yet been at least 20 miles to the state line, when majestic thunderclouds gave us a lightning show we'll never forget. Those megaton-charged giants continued their flashing definitive bolts all the way past our river, until we turned north. There, the thickness of our forest joined by the approaching darkness calmly subdued them.

"Man, Ben Franklin would've gotten a kick out of that!" I said in exhilaration. Kat laughed, almost in an exhale, as though she had been holding her breath the whole time. We approached our driveway and turned in.

Home again, which always feels good. Yet this time there was a distinct difference. Through the dimness of a single lit desk lamp, we opened our cabin door and stepped inside. An electrically charged stillness had filled the room. It resonated of their presence, telling us that things would definitely never be the same again, in such a wonderful way.

I recall how the evening had ended so gracefully — music on the stereo, she and I holding to each other in a slow dance. We were swaying back and forth with the music, nearly falling asleep in each other's arms. I whispered in her ear, "Let's go to bed."

I lifted her head from my shoulder, gently using my left forefinger under her chin. She returned a whisper to me. "Yes."

# PART VI

## CHAPTER 1

I guess I should have known things couldn't go my way forever. I should have seen it coming. I mean, I've lived enough years to have expected such a fact. My relationship with Jewel and Marcus had been on an upward spiral. The calendar of events…dizzying. Somehow, that train was bound to jump the track.

Word has been spoken that as sure as anything, there is a basis throughout creation that necessitates the achievement of balance. Of this, I am referring to that age old argument which points to the existence of good and evil. It's the yin and the yang of things — what goes around comes around — karma, and the reap what you sow ideals. This panorama has ultimately fallen subject to endless debate.

Throughout the inner weaving of my memories, I only found to be true that indeed, ups and downs do come in waves. When things are going well, you can bet a fair amount of bad will settle on its heels. I don't know why this is, why there can't seem to be the prolonged existence of one, without having to give a turn to the other.

Some would argue there are those who live upon a bed of roses — born with a silver spoon, and that only good things happen to them. Then there are those who suffer the relentless torments of hell, only to pass away in utter misery. I can't believe that. I think there's calamity and joy, which dance through our lives in wavy patterns. Each of our tinted destinies absorbed in blacks, grays and whites.

My ins and outs have never revealed themselves in equal proportion. Maybe these things seldom do. The fact is, when I compare the makeup of my life's events, I'm not at all convinced that it wasn't just some dumb luck that often came into play.

The preclusive moment came with a phone call from Kat. Our wonderful vacation was over. We had danced and dined, relaxed in lawn chairs, and enjoyed our woods. Not to mention the special company that had come to visit us. As I recall, no substantial chores were completed, a perfect time off. I had been back on the road now for nearly a week.

"Hey babe, how ya doin'?" she began this call.

"I'm in Arkansas, passed through Hope a few hours ago. It's the birthplace of Bill Clinton. They've got a big sign on the freeway. Looks like there's a storm maybe comin'."

"You've got a letter here from work, it looks important. Should I open it?"

"Of course," I replied.

There was the rustling of paper over the line. She opened it and read the contents.

"Oh, I'll read it to ya," she said at last.

The balloon that had been floating aloft in my head began to deflate. Our company was curtailing its relief efforts to the Gulf region. The urgency had subsided, and we'd be winding things down. We were to remove the Hurricane Relief decals from our trucks as of August 1.

"What do they mean the urgency has subsided?" I caught myself nearly shouting in the phone. "Have they seen that mess?"

"They've given a lot to help," Kat reminded me in her quiet tone. That's her, alright, always looking on the plus side of things.

"Yah, but there's so much more! It looks like the cleanup has just started. Not enough has been done to appreciatively matter," I told her.

"Maybe they figure that now it will all come together in a natural progression. Dramatic things like that do tend to accelerate change," she assured me.

My, aren't we getting philosophical, I thought. I felt upset, rattled. She was just trying to calm me down. I couldn't blame her for that. It was about that same time that I lost reception on my phone. It happens more frequently than I think it should. Kat and I are used to it, and we take our conversation break. We'd talk again later.

I felt caught in the flames of consequence. My mind's eye was lapsing into a keyhole. I needed to talk to Darin. In a short while I would be coming into West Memphis. We have an operating center there and I needed a windshield replaced. There was a crack that had been running the full length on the passenger side, which is definitely not Department of Transportation legal. I had planned on spending the night there. It would give me time to think - to contemplate what all of this could mean.

Just out of West Memphis, my cell phone reception came back. I hopped on it. I felt like I was in a desperate hour. I dialed up Darin.

"This is Darin."

I quickly gave him my ID numbers so he could identify the driver he was speaking to. There was a moment of pause. He was punching me in on his computer.

"Grant, what can I do for ya?"

"Got the letter about Katrina Relief getting suspended."

"That's true," he affirmed.

"Does this mean no more shipments in that regard for New Orleans?" I asked.

"That's pretty much right. There will be occasional requests for deliveries, but nothing like we've been doing. It's pretty much over for us," was his response.

This letdown let my throat become dry. I said nothing for a brief second. Then off the top of my head, and without much forethought, I conjured up my battle line.

"I've got a perplexing problem. I've been writing a book about the hurricane and it's about half finished. I really need to somehow get back down there and get it done." There was an uncomfortable silence.

"You're writing a book?" Darin asked, puzzled. "I didn't know you were a writer."

"Trying to; it's coming along better than I had thought. This is my first attempt."

"Can I get a signed copy when it's finished?" he asked.

"Absolutely," I laughed. He had upped my spirits with that one. I didn't mind fudging the truth to him a little. At that point, I hadn't actually convinced myself the book would see its completion anyway.

"Don't get your hopes up. They're really drying things up on this, but I'll see what I can do. There probably won't be anything for a while, but I'll put you on it when there is," he said, promising.

"Thanks, man," I said, with as hopeful a tone as I could muster. By this time, I was pulling in at our maintenance facility, and our conversation ended.

While my truck was in the repair bay, I decided to take a walk. There's a small lake across the road from our O.C., with a hiking trail around it. Storm clouds were pushing in from the west. I needed to unwind, but I was going to have to move quickly. It turned into a brisk walk. I had doubled my usual pace and was panting for breath when I got back across to Beulah. I was told it would be a couple more hours. I retrieved my laptop from my truck and went inside to the cafeteria. I needed to see what I could do with the book in this, somewhat, state of duress. I ordered up a warm supper, and while I ate, I went about picking at my laptop keys. I found myself more at ease. The walk may have helped. As it turned out, thoughts and words flowed, another half dozen pages moved ahead.

Beulah's I.D. numbers were announced over the intercom, so I packed it in and went to find her. It was pouring rain. Loud clashes of thunder were being accompanied by half-blinding lightning bursts. I was getting soaked. Once back in my home away from home, I quickly changed into dry clothes. I felt more settled. Should I call Burton and have him relay a message to Marcus? I decided to wait. I was jumping guns in my mind. Maybe this wouldn't be as bad as I suspected. I settled in for the night, entering these latest events into my journal. I tried once more to add to the book. The rain beating on the roof made me tired. I nestled into my bunk and called it an early day.

## CHAPTER 2

Time edged on. There was a load to California, then a load of motorcycles from Pasadena back to Chicago. There were Canadian runs: Timothy Hay from near Calgary, Alberta, going down to Lexington, Kentucky, for the thoroughbreds there. Good miles, but discontentment had solemnly set in. I began to think of Darin's promise as incredulous. Maybe my mind was poisoned from lack of provocative input. Or was I simply missing those two? I struggled with writing; words became incongruous. Nothing seemed to fit into a story line, and the harmony wasn't there. I was limping along, at best, with writing. Upbeat feelings only came when I played guitar, going over the songs we had done together; his songs. There had been 14 recordings thus far, plus the song, *From a Whisper*, which we had all written together about the Mississippi River headwaters.

It was the middle of August now; I couldn't wait any longer. I had no Hurricane Relief identification on Beulah anymore. The closest I had come to them had been Atlanta, Georgia. It was time to make the call. Burton's secretary answered, saying that he was unavailable. I left a message for him to return my call. It wasn't until well into the next afternoon that his call was returned.

"Hello Hatty," he said lightheartedly, as though he enjoyed my new nickname.

"Hey Burton, how are things?"

"Very well. How've you been?"

"Okay, but there's been a problem," I said.

Explaining the situation, together with my anti-climactic expectations regarding Darin, I knew he could sense my frustration. He agreed to relay my disappointing news to Marcus and Jewel.

"Could you ask Marcus to call me when he can? My wife and I are planning a vacation to see them. I'd like to get that set up if we can."

"Sure thing. Cheer up. There are ways to make things happen. This is a minor glitch that we can work around. I know it's hard for you to see right now, but nothing's really changed. It's all good," he reassured me.

Just that conversation, Burton's way, made my life feel right again, almost giving me that back on track feeling. I had gigantic trust in him. He was like a confident big brother to me. I felt that the road would feel smoother under my wheels now.

There are some moments in life that invigorate, while others simply depress. It's those waves going by again. That sometimes fast, sometimes slow, roller coaster of life.

Another week went by without me hearing a word from anyone down South. Now I was at home again. It was Sunday afternoon, August 27, the day before my birthday, and the anniversary of my first having met them. Kat and I were sitting in the screen porch. I was once again imagining how I was going to make it into our little bar. The portable phone rang, and I picked up. It was Marcus.

"Well, hello there, Hatty." It was such a familiar voice now. It warmed me inside.

"Hey there, buddy," I responded.

"Burton told us about the situation. Sorry to hear it, but it's okay."

The afternoon was hot and humid as we conversed. It was small talk about what had been happening since we were together last, plus we cemented our vacation plans. Kat and I would road trip south in the Camaro, beginning on Saturday, September 16. We would do some sight-seeing along the way, and planned to arrive at Clay's place sometime in the early afternoon on Wednesday, the 20th. All was a go. We would stay with them until that Friday afternoon.

"You know how to get to Clay's place, right?" Marcus inquired.

"Sure do. I could get there blindfolded by now," I told him. He laughed.

"Not many people can say that," he responded. "Jewel wants to say hello to Kat. Is she around?"

"Right here." I handed the phone to Kat. She gave a brief hello to Marcus, then spoke with Jewel for probably 10 minutes. Again I could see a sisterhood thing going on between them. They had exchanged letters a couple of times since we were last together, enjoying their correspondence. They had been composing a song together through the mail and were calling it, *The Love of the Moon*. When this call ended, Kat and I gave each other wide smiles.

"It'll all work out," she said, trying to reassure me. Evidently my look had been a bit downtrodden prior to this call. "We've made great friends," she added.

"Let's plan the trip," I suggested. She nodded. "Be right back," I added, and went in the cabin to find my Rand McNally road atlas. When I returned, we sat close together at the porch table. "What do you want to see?" I asked her.

"You know the country, what should I see? Actually, can we see Graceland? I've always wanted to," she yearned.

"Now we have a goal, a direction," I told her with enthusiasm. I had toured Graceland several years earlier when I had been laid over in West Memphis for truck repairs. Even though the cab fare to and from was nearly $100, it was worth it. I spent the entire day going through the museums and gift shops. Being in the home itself was thrilling. I was sure Kat would find it that way, too. I was more than willing to do it again.

We studied the map with almost child dreamlike wonderment, as our fingers pointed out the route. We could make our way to Chicago and visit our son Nathan. Maybe he would take us out on the town. He has a stupendous job there, a big shot computer guy with a finance company based out of Europe. From there, we would go through St. Louis and show her the arch, the gateway to the west. It wasn't a big deal for me anymore, but having never seen it, Kat would enjoy something like that.

We have a nephew living in St. Louis who works for the government there. Maybe we'd have time to look him up. From there, it would be on to Memphis, fulfilling Kat's dream. And finally, we would push on through to New Orleans for as much time with them as possible. This entire plan took less than 10 minutes of finger pointing to finalize. We were gonna be happy campers.

Even though I would be back on the road on my birthday, our weekend together had ended on a high note. We both got stoked up, imaginations flaming. Now the waiting became the hard part. We needed to keep ourselves occupied. Before this vacation began, I would have one more weekend at home, then a short four or five more days of trucking. The company tends to keep me with local assignments that are close to home when the timing falls that way. It only helped to induce greater anticipation in Kat regarding our upcoming adventure. As one would suspect, those three weeks really dragged by.

## CHAPTER 3

While we thought it would never come, now here we were, throwing our suitcases in the back seat of the Camaro. Arrangements had been made for a friend to pick up our mail and check on the cabin while we were gone. Kat had made reservations, almost three weeks earlier, at the Heartbreak Hotel across the street from Graceland for Tuesday night. Nathan told us he'd be ready to show us a good time in Chicago on Sunday. We be road-trippin'.

Our youngest daughter Lacey had been enrolled in belly-dancing classes, having a great time with it. While we had been on the West Bank, recording *The Waggin' Woogie Boogie*, Kat had gone to a store called Global Village. There she bought a belt to add to Lacey's costume, as well as two sets of castanets - one for Lacey, and one for herself. In addition, she bought a set of Tibetan chimes called Ting Shah. Having gotten to know Jewel, Kat decided to bring the castanets and chimes along as gifts for her. I thought it was a cool idea. Now that she believed in all that I had been telling her, she also brought more large beads from her collection to give to Hershel. She picked out ones she thought might be most suitable to be incorporated into wind chimes. She was going to be a real hit with him, I just knew it.

We made it to Nathan's pad in Wheeling, Illinois, a Chicago suburb, on Sunday morning, having spent the previous night at a motel in Madison, Wisconsin. Nathan looked a bit worse for wear when he answered the door. He was wearing shorts and a wrinkled dress shirt with the tails hanging out. He was barefooted and his hair was total "bed-head." It was definitely not a "Sunday" appearance. I guessed that maybe we had arrived a little earlier than he expected. Always happy to see each other, we gave our hugs and Kat and I stepped inside.

"I have to jump in the shower; make yourselves at home. Hungry?" Nathan said in one breath.

"No, we had a great continental breakfast. We can go have a lunch after you splash some water in your face," I joked. Kat snickered.

"Sounds good. I was out late last night," he explained.

"We sorta gathered that," Kat said.

"Be out in a minute," he told us, turning and heading down the hallway.

Kat and I had never been to his new place. The last time we visited him, he was living in Palatine, another suburb. Both places are located northwest of Chicago proper. We could tell he was moving up in the world. This place was far more spacious, with a balcony and a good view. He had moved to Chicago with a friend shortly after graduating from college. He had since gained his Master's degree, and was taking additional night classes for who knows what. I think he's one of those career students who never really stops going to school. I remarked to Kat how he had come a long way from that first place with his friend Steve. Outside his old apartment were posters tacked on telephone poles, warning of city rat poisoning crusades. Nathan and his friends would shoot them with blow dart guns for fun, just outside the door. Yes, this new place seemed nice.

We sat on the sofa, amazed at his vast music and movie collections. His stereo was a major part of the living room, along with a very wide screen television. It was an entertainment center beyond our experience. We wondered about the cost, but weren't gonna ask. Kat got up and wandered over to the kitchen, which was small, and offset from the living room. It was a two-bedroom place. We joined each other at the doorway of one of them, which he had converted to an office. It was not at all tidy, as we peeked in. There were papers piled and scattered on a desk. A bookcase against one wall was haphazardly cluttered with books, folders, and an odd assortment of knick-knacks (paper weights?). A scrunched-up "fast food" bag and other things that I couldn't decipher were strewn about on the floor.

"He didn't get that from me," I smiled to Kat, as we turned from the door and went back to sit on the couch.

He's also a sports memorabilia collector. There was a glass showcase of signed baseballs and assorted items in the hallway leading to the bathroom. At the far end was the second bedroom, where he directly headed for when he came out of the shower wearing a robe and then he closed the door. He must have been in there 15 minutes, until he finally reappeared.

"I made up the bed. You guys have my room; I'll take the couch tonight."

"No…," I started to say, but he interrupted.

"Believe me, I'm used to it. I sleep on the couch half the time." He gave me that old boyish smile that I remembered from so long ago. "Go head and put your suitcases down there." He pointed to the bedroom. So we did.

His bedroom was well made up, with artistic taste much on the same level as ours. There were oil paintings hanging on all of the walls, I later found out they had been purchased over the years from his friends with art majors. All were done well, very tasteful. Some were done in a realism style, seemingly straight from studies of The Masters. There was a provocative Picasso-type piece, together with two charcoal drawings in much the same style, as well as a melting Salvador Dali look-alike. He had the beginnings of a pretty good art collection.

"You didn't have these the last time we visited." I was pointing to the paintings in the hall as we were walking down to meet him.

"Like them?" he asked.

"Yah, they're wonderful." Kat replied.

"I buy what I like when I see it," he explained.

"So, you're an art collector now too," I had to remark.

"Guess I am; probably going to be."

"Your place looks great," I told him. "Any rats?" We all laughed.

"How's work?" Kat asked.

"They're bugging me to move to Europe, or maybe Singapore."

"What? Why?" I found I had raised my voice.

"They're phasing out their Chicago offices. We're down to 14 of us now. I'm waiting to see if they offer me a severance package. That's what they've been doing. I don't really want to go overseas."

"So, if you get this buyout, you movin' back to the Twin Cities, or nearer to us?" I asked.

"You mean Twerp town? I think so, but one day at a time."

"Twerp town?" I inquired.

"That's what people from Chicago call the Twin Cities," he smiled.

I just gave him a dumb look. "Tell me about this playroom of yours. What's this stereo about?"

"If I crank the woofers on this baby it'll vibrate the nails right out of the walls," he bragged. "It's an Arcam CD player, with Rotel amp, B&W speakers, and HSU subwoofers." He obviously knew his stereo components. We had no idea. "Man, I have to get something to eat. You guys hungry?" he asked again.

"We could eat," Kat said, then added, "Your dad can always eat." I turned to her, meaning to smile, but I guess I didn't.

"Good, I'll drive," he said, tying his shoe laces.

"Everything fast-pace down here or just you?" I said, lightly chiding him.

"Everything," he replied. We headed out the door and into his built-in garage.

It was a short ride to a place called Walker Brothers, on Dundee Rd. It was a pancake house.

"I could do with some pancakes. You'll like this place," he said.

He was right; the décor was outstanding. The woodwork was wonderful, and the stained glass exquisitely crafted. Kat and I were very impressed. We couldn't get over the craftsmanship and the artistic designs. We were in pancake "awe," but we ended up eating very little. He went about his meal in a "having-been-starved" fashion.

It was decided over brunch that after we would take a ride along the shore to see some of the homes near the lake. This to us is entertainment. We enjoy seeing how the other half lives, if only to aspire in our future daydreams. It's fascinating to see what some have been able to acquire in their lifetimes, inspirational to say the least.

We meandered through side streets, and into the downtown area, marveling at The Sears Tower and the vast expansiveness of this town.

"Want to go up?" he asked us.

"Uh, no," I told him. "I don't do heights." He just laughed.

We made our way back to his place for some relaxation and to plan out the rest of this short visit. He would have to put in an appearance at his job in the morning. It was decided Kat and I would go to the art museum, which we had always wanted to see.

In true form, he followed through, pudding proof, the ferocity of this home entertainment system. Nine Inch Nails, Whoa! It was like nothing our poor ears, or minds, had ever experienced. After he knew he had sufficiently shocked us, he settled the system down to a special CD he had burned on our behalf. We thoroughly enjoyed that afternoon, drinking beer and wine, with light catching-up-type conversation. I rummaged through his music collection. We all sat on the couch together where we could benefit from the best sound perspective. All was relaxed and laid back. That is, until he asked THE question.

"So, where are you guys headed to from here?"

"Gonna go through St. Louis, then down to Memphis and see Graceland," Kat explained.

"Cool, I have to go there sometime," he responded.

"Then, down south of New Orleans, to the hidden bayous on the Gulf, south of Houma," I added.

"Where? Why? Still trying to find that alligator for TJ?" Kat and I sat silent for a moment.

"I take it your sisters haven't told ya?" I said.

"Told me what?"

So, as Kat sat quiet, I commenced to explain, in as delicate a fashion as I could, who I had met and where. I described the situation of our first having met. Nathan's eyes widened. He continued to stare at me, then he turned to Kat.

"And you're going along with this?" She could sense he was getting a little uptight with this conversation. She put her arm around him.

"I've met him, too. It is him. They even came and stayed with us a couple days." Then Nathan stood up, turning to me.

"Maybe when you're done, you can write about Jim Morrison, and then maybe Janis Joplin. I hear Jimi's hidin' out here in Chicago in some back alley, under a different name. He's shaved his head and has grown a long beard that's completely gray," he said, admonishing me. I realized I couldn't convince him. He was in the same frame of mind as the rest of our family. There was no use professing any farther.

"It'll all come out," I said in a resigned voice.

"Yah, okay," he scoffed.

"So, where's a good place for supper?" Kat broke in, trying to lighten this path we had stumbled on. He thought for a moment. His face lightened up from that toiled brow he had been displaying.

"There's a good prime rib place," he noted.

"Man, that sounds good," I told him. We were getting truly hungry by this time. Kat nodded her approval. "We're gonna have to make it an early night; we're old," I told him. He smiled at me. "We need to get heading south by noon or so."

Kat and I stood to go clean up and to change into something a little dressier. Nathan was in an improved mood when we rejoined him in the living room.

"Shall we go? I'm hungry," Kat said.

"Sure," Nathan replied, smiling at her. He turned, and we followed him out the door and again into his garage.

This time we drove to a place called The Blackhawk, where we dined on prime rib. They had a special way of presenting their salads there. It was called Spinning Salad, where it was brought to our table with a bowl on ice.

They then spun the bowl as ingredients were being added by a waiter - anything we desired. It was another unique experience.

Nothing more was mentioned about Marcus or Jewel during our meal. Instead Nathan hinted at his possible future plans of moving closer to us. We had gone back to relaxing and enjoying our time together. I wasn't about to say anything to change that.

After dinner, we drove back to his place. He lit a few candles and put on some Van Morrison. He knew our tastes, and what we enjoyed in music. It settled into a mellowing close to a fast day.

In the morning, we were all awake by 6 a.m. As Kat showered, I admired his sports memorabilia collection, while he proudly described each piece to me. Then he brought out his latest weapons. Did I mention he's a weapons collector also? He had a new Beretta 9mm semi-automatic pistol, and several strangely shaped knives that looked Oriental that I hadn't seen. He's easy to buy for at Christmas. For years I've been adding to his collection with swords and knives that I've found at or near truck stops.

After we all cleaned up, it was time to ready ourselves for getting out of town.

"You guys follow me, and I'll take you to a good breakfast and then show you the best parking at the museum. I won't have time to see the museum. Anyway, I already have, several times. I'll have to head for work," he told us.

We went to a place called Lou Mitchell's, where we had to wait in line to be seated. It seemed to be a popular "feed bag." The unique thing about it, as we had to wait, the girls were all given Milk Duds and everyone got free donut holes. All in all, during our visit with him, we ate our chubbys off.

Conversation over breakfast was light. He wanted to know the latest news regarding his sisters, so we brought him up to date. It sounded like he was looking forward to possibly moving back and being closer to them, and to his niece and nephews. He bought Lacey and her friend airline tickets to come and see him a few months prior to our visit. That was the only time any of them ever came down to see him in the entire eight years he'd spent in Chicago. I could tell he wanted to get back in their lives. He was the oldest, and two of his three sisters were now married. We just had to wait and see where his future plans would lead him, I guessed. Would he make the step to Twerp Town?

Later, it was a short jaunt to where he guided us to a parking place near the museum. As I locked up the Camaro, he stepped out of his car to bid us farewell.

"See you in the spring," I told him with a hug. It's been my favorite departing words to him every time we see each other, because unfortunately, it seems to be so long in-between..

He raced away in his new Civic Si, too fast for a parking lot. But oh, that's Chicago! Kat and I walked up the steps to the museum, where time seemed to then fly by and my feet got really sore.

Upon those walls rested many of the heavy hitters in art history. I had never been so close to the works of Rembrandt and Van Gogh. I could have touched them. I won't mention if I did. We were both enthralled by the experience. We couldn't even see it all. It was time to go, my feet showing little ambulation. I wasn't used to walking that much. We hoped to return there again someday. Kat bought a book featuring some of the works we had seen. I bought post cards, something I'm good at doing. We headed to the car and pointed her onto the street and eventually in the direction of St. Louis. Now, in our minds, we had bigger fish to fry.

## CHAPTER 4

It was a push to get to that Gateway to the West, but we made it as the sun was preparing to set. We parked near the Arch, walking toward it as the brilliance of sunset's reflection was exploding upon its shining steel. From one angle, it appeared gray in color. From another angle, light smoky blue. It was gleaming, a showing symbol, the prowess of man's pronouncement to his manifest destiny. This architectural wonder was screaming out to me.

I had tried calling my nephew, but to no avail. I was interested in asking him if any of his government agency friends knew of Marcus, that he was still around. I wasn't sure how I would have presented that question to him. It was meant to be, that we just move on, as I'm sure Marcus would have told me. We headed farther south, to a place called Cape Girardeau, where we grabbed some fast food, a low budget motel, and a good night's sleep.

Kat was bustling about early that next morning. It was time to get to Memphis. I rushed my shower, scarfed down my continental breakfast, lickety-split to the car, and southbound we went. Maybe when this vacation is over, I could get back to work, get some good rest, and slow down, I joked to myself.

We arrived in Memphis and to Elvis Presley Boulevard at around 10 that morning. I knew my way around the maze, and all of the buildings devoted to his legacy, which included his two airplanes that were parked near our Heartbreak Hotel. I saw no other place along that street where a person could stay overnight and still be within walking distance of Elvis' mansion. Across the street from our motel were those famous gates, and the hill leading up to Graceland. Museums and gift shops, unrelenting and endless, ran along our side of the road. As we were driving up, there already were crowds of people with cameras. Some were having their pictures taken in front of a Cadillac, or anything else that represented his fame.

After we checked in, it had been, pretty much, throw the suitcases on the bed and let's get going!

"Can I pee first?" I had asked Kat. She smiled at me, as I taunted her with the error of her ways. Our moods were near joyous, yet I tried to settle her down. It couldn't be done; it was out the door, as if we were late for something. We began walking up the block to where it all conglomerates. I remembered then how she had told me of growing up and listening to her aunt's 45's on Sun records. I realized this was a very special event for her. It meant more to her than I imagined.

"Let's go through the mansion first and then come back here for this stuff," I suggested. Having been here before, I thought this to be the best approach. We needed to buy tickets for all that we wanted to take in. Certain parts are added attractions for which you pay extra. I knew she'd insist on seeing everything. It all tied in best if we took the tour of his house first. I was certain, Lord knows, of having to carry all kinds of souvenirs around with us much of the day. She agreed to let me take the lead. I marched us to the ticket building. We decided on the middle of three packages, which pretty much would give us what Kat wanted. From there, we walked out to a rope-guided procession, where someone took our photograph, and another person handed us a set of earphones connected to a small box. With those placed on your ears, it can be a well-orchestrated tour, if one chooses to use it. I prefer the more rogue approach, letting my imagination be my guide. Kat listened to the instructions given, and put her earphones on. I did the same for the time being.

We got on a small shuttle bus and began listening to the guided program. We were then being driven across the street. His songs played as we approached the rock wall that connects to the entrance gates. The wall is filled with the splattering of fan written justifications, and they appear to cover almost every square inch of its rock and mortar. We continued through the musical gates and up the driveway to the mansion's front door. As we scrambled out, we were greeted by someone on the front step, welcoming us to his home. We listened to her brief introduction, as people's cameras were clicking away. Let's get on with it, I thought, while I leaned against one of the pillars.

Finally we were allowed through the front door. In front of us we could see the stairway leading up to the only section that is off-limits to the public. Up those steps, I understand, are his bedroom and bathroom, where he is said to have passed away. It was one place I felt compelled to sneak off to. It would be in my nature to try to do something like that.

To our immediate right was a white-carpeted room with white-painted walls, an extraordinarily long white couch, and two matching chairs near a fireplace. We had been listening to our headphones. I saw Kat put her set on pause, placing them down around her neck. She just stood there staring into that room, where toward the back of it were two stained glass windows depicting peacocks. They were facing each other, embracing from each side, an entrance to what is called "the music room." We could see a baby grand piano in there.

I nudged her finally, motioning for her to turn and look behind her. There was the dining room. It was smaller than one might suppose. It held a table that only seated six, placed over a black marble floor. An elegant and bountiful crystal chandelier loomed overhead. There were cabinets on either side, filled with dishes and other objects that I was unable to identify. We were only allowed to view all of this from a distance. No one was allowed to step past the ropes protecting these rooms, or even think about stepping one foot upon that white carpet.

Much of the trim in this area, including the staircase, was painted in gold. Our tour crowd had long since pushed ahead, and another one was overtaking us. I think Kat was trying to imagine more than the other people around her were. She seemed oblivious to anyone else being there, perhaps even me. Having taken this tour before, I motioned for her to, albeit slowly, move along. Our tour of the home itself, I would say, took about four times longer than it took everyone else. That was alright with me. She was getting her fill, letting all of its glamour overtake her.

It was on to the kitchen, and near to the infamous Jungle Room. That's also my favorite room, with its waterfall wall and Polynesian-type décor. There were monkeys as well as other wild life statuettes. I tried to imagine Elvis seated on one of the huge carved wooden chairs. It is well known that he rehearsed and recorded in this room. I tried imagining that too. Then we walked on ahead, pushing the "resume" button on our recorders as we went, only to pause them more often than not. We walked through hallways and down steps. At the bottom was the Television Stereo Room, painted in yellow, blue and white, with its yellow drinking bar. TCB (taking care of business in a flash), was emblazoned on the wall, emphasized with a lightning bolt. And there was the Billiard Room, with a tear in the felt of the table. There was a Tiffany stained glass light hanging over it. The walls were of fabric, mixed in busy designs.

Time had long passed us by when we, at last, found ourselves outside in the backyard, catching the heat of the day. It was very warm and muggy, with partly cloudy skies. There were other buildings to walk into: his office and his racquetball building, where, I've been told, he sang his last songs on the day he died. Then there was The Smokehouse, which had been used as a firing range. On the grounds and behind white wooden fences, horses could be seen grazing.

Finally, we came upon The Meditation Garden. The graves of his brother, mother, and father, as well as his grandmother, all lay in a semi-circle surrounding his resting place. All were covered by granite slabs, inlayed, and steel embossed with their epitaphs in what looked to be, yellow brass. Everyone around us was somber; the sounds of clicking camera shutters. With the eternal flame there burning, Kat and I looked over to each other. Why I'm not sure, but we both had the same expressions on our faces.

There was a large, white statue of Jesus standing before a cross, with small angels on each side. "Presley" was inscribed at the base. We couldn't resist asking a tourist if he would use our camera, the first and only picture taken that day, of Kat and I standing beside that statue.

We continued on, walking down a short driveway. All along the way were wreaths and display boards decorated by fans from around the world. Both sides of that driveway were filled with them. We read and admired each one as we made our way back to the shuttle pickup area, which was a canvass-covered, open-air tent with benches on each side. My poor trucker feet were pitifully sore. I'm used to sitting, not standing or walking for any length of time, a testament to how out of shape a driver can become.

It was time to go back across the street to the visitor center area. There was still a lot left to see, and oh, those souvenirs to find. We stopped to eat at a place called Rockabilly's Diner, then, with more museums ahead, we let them overtake us.

As I try to recount the day, certain things stand out in my memory. The car museum, with its purple Cadillac convertible, the black and red Stutz, and black Ferrari, were all vehicles I would love to own, if ever given the chance. There were his motorcycles, an interesting pink Jeep, and a Jetstar snow sled. It was the white Mercedes convertible he had given his wife Priscilla that Kat adored. Man, he must have lived it up, I was thinking.

I recall the hall of gold with seemingly endless awards and gold records. There was the big room, with Hollywood posters, more awards, and paintings of The King that his fans had created. Their wedding outfits were there, along with more than 50 of his stage outfits, belts, and capes. Almost all were covered with semi-precious stones of intricately ornate designs. Kat gazed at these for, what I considered to be an extensive period of time. My feet were goners. I remember seeing the Kid Galahad robe that he wore in the movie, and a karate outfit. There were his guns and guitars, and that famous TCB ring. It was decisively too much to absorb in any single visit. I realized how much I had unconsciously missed my first time there.

Before this tour was to end, we made it through his army museum, and sauntered around in both of his airplanes that had long since been retired there. The Lisa Marie was amazing. It had been converted into a hotel suite atmosphere. There was a small conference room, lounge, bedroom, and two bathrooms with wash basins adorned in gold.

At long last it seemed we had finished out this day but no, not true. We made our way in and out of every gift shop. To my surprise, Kat bought very few souvenirs. She found a sweatshirt she liked, a key chain, and a coffee cup.

I bought more post cards, intending to send them to our kids in the future. Now we were finished. I had Elvis coming out of my ears! Kat was on some kind of cloud 9. As I unlocked the door to our motel room, I turned to her and said, "Let's get back to the reality of us and now." She smiled, and we stepped into our room.

## CHAPTER 5

Wednesday morning, and in my estimation, we overslept. It was nearing 8 a.m. and I had to nudge her a couple of times. We had snacked on leftover pizza in bed and, as I can barely recall, watched a little TV. We slept well, but now it was me in a hurry to get going. We more or less shared the shower. Very little time elapsed before we had grabbed that courtesy cup of coffee, checked out at the front desk, and were driving down I-55 toward New Orleans.

We stopped at a truck stop in Pickens, Mississippi, sometime before noon for gas and snacks, and were nearing the devastation shortly thereafter. I dare say, the shock of what Kat was seeing wore heavily on her. When we drove through some of the hardest hit sections of New Orleans, she wept. I wanted her to see what I had seen, so I had driven out of route a bit. In retrospect, it was disheartening for me, realizing what I was putting her through. With such a subdued tone, she sighed; "One event affects so many; I feel connected to this somehow." She had been saddened in a way I hadn't anticipated, in a way that she didn't deserve.

Farther south now, and she had little to say. The scenes she beheld, coupled with the anticipation of our upcoming visit, lent weariness to her eyes. She had to have been getting tired. Our traveling thus far had been jam-packed as if in a condensed time capsule. Aside from all of this, it was hurricane season. She had mentioned that fact several times to me in the past few days, although the weather appeared perfectly mild. I only hoped she'd be able to relax once she became acclimated with their place.

Now we could hear, even feel, the grass scraping beneath the Camaro as we drove the open field toward the tree line. Clay's home came into view. I tapped on the horn a couple of times as we drove into the grove and pulled the car to a stop. I looked caringly at Kat.

"Here we are babe," I smiled.

"Clay's place," she surmised.

"Yep. We leave the car here. He'll take us up to them in his boat."

I could see Clay walking toward us from the house; he had a woman with him. Kat got out a little slowly, uneasily. I lumbered out in my usual fashion. This car sits low to the ground, and I have to admit, I'm not as spry as I once was. Clay walked up to us briskly. I turned on my pocket recorder. He immediately gave me a squeeze around the shoulders with that strong arm, while looking at Kat with his wide grin.

"Bon ami, ah lak dat un," he pointed to our Camaro. Then he gave Kat that debonair look. "Dis ur p'tite femme?"

"This is Clay." I introduced them. "This is Kat," I said to him. He nodded and tipped his baseball cap. A small woman peeked out from behind him.

"Dis ma 'tite belle, Delphine," Clay said. The woman smiled, and with a barely audible voice, said "hi." She was really small, I doubt five feet, with long straight black hair and bangs. She had a slender, cute face and a long nose. She was apparently shy, but she held a sweet smile.

"It seems like a long time," I told Clay, as I put my hand on his shoulder. Kat gave him a warm smile.

"Aye brudder, ah tink bot t'lung. Wilcum t'la Louisianne," he told Kat, using all of his charm. Oh, oh, I thought, here we go. Already trying, in that rakish way, to charm the pants off my lady. It may have been working, for all I knew.

"Nice to be here," Kat told him, with an equally charming pose.

"Dey're be'in way'in. Viens avec moi," he told us.

"What?" I asked. He motioned for us to walk to the boat. We retrieved our suitcases from the car. I didn't bring my guitar this time. I wasn't sure if this visit would be so much about music. I figured Marcus would have one lying around for me to use if we did get into it. I wanted this to be Kat's vacation, I guess, more than I considered it mine. She never gets a chance to get away.

All four of us settled into the boat. I pointed to Kat to look over at the opposite shoreline. There lay a fairly large alligator, sunning itself along the bank. It slipped into the water when Clay started up the motor. Kat gave me a grimacing look. I smiled back to her confidently.

As we began motoring up, I remember thinking how I had never seen Clay's house, never actually been invited in. I tried to imagine what it might be like, him being the bachelor that he is. Maybe it was a real mess. Maybe he had gator and snake hides all over the walls. Maybe he had animal skulls on the table. Maybe he didn't even have a table. I was having imaginary fun at his expense.

He pointed to another alligator lying on the surface of the water. It didn't seem bothered by us. I could tell Kat was nervous. She had a stiff smile. I noticed Delphine never seemed to stop smiling, like that was her permanent look. I later found that to be true. It never came up, or was indicated one way or another, if Delphine knew who Marcus really was. I don't believe she did.

As Clay cut his motor and took to the pole, it was the first time I had ever seen Marcus and Jewel waiting at the shoreline together, dogs included. We brushed along their bank, as Jewel waved and smiled at Kat. Marcus helped

Kat out of the boat first and then embraced her. Next, he helped Delphine, giving her a courteous hug.

"Arre'te, don do dat, mon jolie won dis coonass ta do dat," Clay told Marcus.

"As well you should," Marcus replied to him.

"Che're 'tite bete," Jewel chidingly said to Clay, while she was holding Kat's hand. I caught it on tape, but didn't know what she meant. He gave Jewel a mischievous grin.

"T'es trop grand pour tes cullottes," she retorted back to him.

I climbed out of the boat and gave a brotherly hug to Marcus. He still had the blue jay feather in his hatband that Jewel had found in our woods. Jewel looked captivating, her dress dazzling in nectar colors, layers of un-named hues, unearthly tones. They both showed genuine excitement in seeing us. I would guess they'd had very few visitors. The dogs never barked once, but went spastic with Clay once he stepped up on shore.

"It took forever to get back to you," I told them.

"Leaping over limbo? Pulses are the steps we take," Marcus replied to me.

Kat pulled the set of castanets from her purse, handing them to Jewel. "For your dancing," Kat told her. They hugged. Jewel slipped them on, then gave them a hollow clapping sound, while tapping her middle fingers and thumbs together. She raised her arms above her head and did a little dancing twirl. It was as cute as it gets.

We all began walking toward the house. Clay carried Kat's suitcase. I motioned for him to carry mine, and we both laughed. The soft radiance of the spring that I last remembered had now turned to a strong summer. The vegetation had become bolder, more fully dressed, covering everything in deep, darker greens. Kat and Jewel were conversing quietly, as the ladies made their way up to the porch steps. I glanced down at Hershel's cabin. He wasn't in sight. We stood on the porch briefly. Kat was looking around at everything.

"There's our bathroom," Marcus told her, pointing to their fancy outhouse. She smiled back at him. Delphine immediately stepped down from the porch and headed in that direction.

"No guitar?" Marcus asked me.

"Not this time. Thought I could bum yer old Martin, L," I said, kidding him. Although it would be a real treat to play it.

"You got it. Just don't scratch it," he said, a dimple protracting amid the whiskers of a half held-back smile. Scratch it? How could I? That old beat up thing had no room left for another scratch. I laughed and shook my head.

"Hersh around?" I asked.

"Oh, he'll appear, but probably not till tomorrow," Jewel said. "Come on in, I have supper ready."

"C'est bon," Clay replied. Jewel gave him a sisterly look. Delphine joined us on the porch, always smiling.

"You know your room," Marcus said to me as we stepped inside and had entered the kitchen area. The aroma in the air titillated my appetite. Clay followed me to the bedroom with Kat's things, dropped them at the foot of the bed, then hurriedly stepped out, heading to the kitchen. Jewel was showing Kat their bedroom with the attached greenhouse. I heard Jewel say something about a remedy for something, as she was picking up one of the potted plants and handing it to Kat. Then they began discussing paintings, as they stepped from the solarium and stood near the bed. The sun was escaping under the tree line, while I peered in on them.

"Yes, we already have birds," Marcus said to me from behind. I turned with a smile. "So far, not in the bedroom though," he added.

I patted his arm. "Better luck tomorrow," I grinned, then he and I stepped into the kitchen.

Clay was already seated at the table. Delphine was standing in the living room, paging through a book about Oriental rugs. She placed it back on the coffee table and walked over to us now as we all approached the table. We sat down cordially. The plate settings already in place, Jewel let the dogs back outside and began bringing over her serving bowls filled with those warm surprises.

Orange juice, apple cider and wine were the beverages. There are ham hock, grits, and okra-laced gumbo, she told us. I had tasted this before, and was glad to see it again. There was a huge bowel of broiled shrimp (Kat's favorite), complements of Clay, in addition, a new treat; crab etouffee, together with red beans, white rice, and French bread. For desert there would be blackberry pie, another absolute feast, more than enough food.

"Delphine and Clay are going dancing tonight," Jewel explained while she was passing the gumbo. I smiled at Clay.

"You're like my hero, man, you party animal," I joked to him.

"C'est ein affaire a' pus finir," he replied, caught on tape, but again, not understood. Jewel smiled at him.

"We visited Graceland on our way down," Kat said. Jewel and Marcus smiled, looking across the table at one another.

"I saw it once too," Jewel replied.

"I think everyone should see it once," Marcus grinned.

"Ah cane; t'far," Clay said. Delphine nodded the same.

"Outa the neighborhood, aye?" I teased him again.

"I tink fadder den grand bois, ah don lak ta," he replied, and he put his hand on my shoulder. Marcus simply continued smiling without a word.

We ate casually, with Kat commenting on Jewel's hair style. The two of them talked about the henna tattoos on Jewel's hands. Kat expressed interest in having one done on her sometime. Marcus just sat there, reserved, content. When the meal had concluded, we were gorged, except, of course, for Clay. Jewel asked if anyone wanted another helping, before pie.

"Mais oui," Clay responded, meaning one more time. "Merci beaucoup," became a mumble, as he went on cloying.

Kat was explaining how she had gone through her bead collection and brought down an assortment to give to Hershel for his wind chimes. She expressed hope that she could meet him.

"Probably not until tomorrow," Jewel said to her. "I fed him dinner before you came. He goes to bed early, but he's always up as the sun rises. He doesn't like the dark." That was something I had previously not known about him. "More?" Jewel asked Clay.

"C'est assez," he told her, seemingly satiated. She went over to the counter, and brought back the first of two pies. One pie would have been enough, but then there's Clay, bottomless. We stuffed ourselves even more.

The meal now decidedly finished, Kat offered to help Jewel clean up. Delphine stood up, gesturing to do the same, but Clay was in a hurry to get going.

"Ever't'ing s' bon, allons," Clay said, as he motioned to Delphine. They started toward the door.

"Bonne chance," Jewel said to them on their way out, looking over to Delphine. Jewel gave a wink.

"Mais oui," Clay said again, nodding to us with a wave goodbye. Then out the door they went. In that entire time, Delphine, never said two words. I knew she could talk, I think. She did faintly say "hi" when we first met.

"A party man," I said to Marcus, referring to Clay.

"Always has been," Jewel turned to reply. "Well, now you've met our famous playboy, so what do you think?" she asked Kat.

"I can't understand what he says, but I like the way it sounds, and I kinda understand what he means," Kat replied. Jewel was showing her the hand pump for water. They would soak the dishes for a time, while a large pan of water was being heated on the barbeque outside. The windows were open, a soft cooling breeze teasing its way in.

"Will I be alright going to the outhouse?" Kat asked. Jewel handed her a small lit lantern.

"You'll be fine; I'll walk out with you," Jewel assured.

Marcus was already in the living room. He was playing the guitar I had given him. He motioned for me to grab the old Martin in the corner. I was happy to. It was, after all, the sweetest-sounding guitar that had ever graced my hands. I checked the tuning and it was good. No, it was great!

"How's the book coming?"

"Well," I paused, after a few seconds, I replied; "I feel like I'm running on training wheels, playing with words like they were toys."

"You're glimpsing the vastness of that ocean," he said.

"It's hard," I confided.

"Everything is plastic that isn't sacrifice. Understand that what you write will bring frequent volley. You're a calmness amidst the angers that blight the sea," he said. I didn't understand a word of what that meant, and I let it go. I think he could tell it went over my head, so he added; "The way your dreams dare to desire will move your footsteps farther ahead." I still wasn't comprehending his meaning. There were things he has said that I can never understand nor try to explain. I just recorded them as they were spoken. I started finger-picking a progression in the key of "G." The girls came in from outside.

"Got a couple new ones for ya," he said. I was always happy for that. "Wrote this one about 20 years ago. It's about loving for fragile reasons." He started playing. I began following along by finger-picking. Kat and Jewel came and sat down. The song was called *Fragile,* but it came on like anything but fragile. It was strong acoustic rock and roll, with the chorus line, *Love just ain't enough; need devotion to back it up.* It was hard-core. I remember thinking as we played, this one should be done with electric guitars, drums, and the whole bit. The girls applauded when we finished. We laughed, and guess what? Marcus actually said, "Thank you. Thank ya very much." I laughed again, Kat just giggled. Jewel shook her head at him with a smile, as though he were acting corny. This man, having been so greatly privileged, having risen so high above his station in life, now was humbled, vulnerably tamed by his woman's mere glance. He looked back at her sheepishly; another precious moment for my life's memories.

He pulled another one out of that feathered hat. This one was called *Backstreets.* I didn't tell him that there already was a song with that name by Bruce Springsteen. It wouldn't have mattered, anyway. *Craze the backstreets, I'm goin' there / craze the backstreets, I was born there.* Whoa! Bruce could have written it. Marcus sang with such exuberance, I remember thinking he should have been on stage. It was rockin' with Springsteen style.

After that song was over the ladies went out to the kitchen for a short time, tidying things up. We continued playing, caught up in song — others that he had written, and songs we had gone over previously that Kat had never heard. When they returned, Jewel picked up the banjo and played along on a song we were doing. Later, she sang along on several others. We covered a few cover songs by various artists, my choices, while they polished off a second bottle of wine.

Kat and I were getting tired, and it may have shown. We started winding it down, in what may have actually been early. I didn't have my watch and Kat never wears one. We all agreed to call it an evening, get some sleep, and bring on our tomorrow.

# CHAPTER 6

We had slept well. The morning sun peeked through the familiar curtain crack as I first tried to open my eyes. The bed in their guest room was "cloud-soft" comfortable. Kat awoke before me but had continued lying there. I wondered then what she may have been thinking when her morning eyes met mine and that first smile moved our lips.

"Hey babe," she said.

"Hey. Did you sleep alright?" I asked.

"Slept good," she assured me. "I don't know how anyone else could have though, with that snoring of yours." Her smile had sweetened wide. I gave my sleepy smile back.

"Bet they're up already. Marcus is an early riser. I'm getting up," I told her. I looked over, but the wash basin wasn't there. "Need to go splash some water in my face," I said. Hurriedly, I got dressed. Kat sat up in bed, propping her pillow behind her head. Finally she seemed to be relaxed and rested. I opened our door and peeked out. Marcus was sitting in his chair, reading a book. Jewel wasn't in sight. There was the water basin, on a table just outside of our door, with two glasses, two hand towels, and a pitcher of water. I gave Marcus a smile and a short wave. He glanced over his glasses and smiled back. I lifted the small table, maneuvering it around our door and into the room. "Here we go," I told Kat.

"Oh my," she replied.

There was nothing left to be needed during my visits with them. I can't think of anything that was ever lacking, really. I went about my morning ritual. There was also, thoughtfully supplied, a spittoon-type jar for after one brushes his teeth. Kat was stirring, finding fresh clothes to wear.

"What to wear, what to wear, hmm," I said to her. "Yer in the swamp, you should wear yer swamp clothes," I joked.

"Yah, right."

"We could go naked 'cept for the bugs," I joked again. She just gave me a look.

I'll meet you out there," she instructed, as she saw me waiting by the door for her. I just nodded and stepped out of the room.

I looked at Marcus as soon as I opened the door. He had set his book down, and was looking toward the window. This morning's light seemed to be immersing his thoughts.

"There's a teasing dance that light plays, chasing dust around," he said with a grin, turning to me. "Sleep well?"

"We both slept good. Kat'll be right out."

"Jewel's in the garden with Hersh. She's gonna make flapjacks. Coffee's on."

"Great." I headed to the kitchen, retrieved two cups, and got one readied for Kat. "Looks like another nice day," I said to Marcus from across the room. He had picked up the classical guitar and was lightly strumming to something he was humming. Kat appeared at the bedroom doorway. I motioned to the coffee. Marcus looked up and smiled at her. She smiled back to him. I brought the cup over to her, as she sat down near Marcus on the couch. I sat down next to her. We sipped our coffee while Marcus surprised us with his rendition of an old Beatles song, *Till There Was You*. I hadn't heard that since the '60s, and never quite that way. I was about to go over and pick up the old Martin when Jewel came in.

"Oh, you're awake, good morning," she said to us.

"Good morning," Kat replied, and stood up.

"I'll get breakfast on, there's showers if you'd like" Jewel said.

"We're fine, can I help with breakfast?" Kat asked, walking over to greet her in the kitchen.

"Sure," Jewel said to her.

Marcus stood up and leaned his guitar against the chair.

"Check this out," he said to me, motioning with his head that I should follow him. We went into the art room, which had its repairs completed, new door and all. There were a large number of books on the bookcase that hadn't been there before. At the far end of the room was a painting easel, with a work on canvas in progress, and assorted art supplies surrounding it. There was a gun rack on the wall to our right, with two rifles and a shotgun. I noticed for the first time a shortwave radio on a stand against the wall to the left of the easel. I didn't ask, nor did he mention anything about it. I later took notice of a short wave antenna attached to the roof on the backside of the house. In addition, there were solar panels that had been installed over a new portion of the roof near their shower area. The black water tank still loomed overhead.

He stepped over to a tall cabinet near the gun rack, and from the top drawer, commenced to bring out several handguns. He proudly displayed them to me one at a time.

"I try to get out and shoot from time to time, when the urge hits me. Nobody's gonna take me alive," he grinned.

"I really like this one, L," I told him, handling an old Western six-shooter.

"Colt 45," he said.

None of these guns were fancy, not like the ones he had in the past. These were all basic weapons, well maintained. He still loves his guns, I told myself.

"Jewel's getting back into painting," I said, somewhat in the form of a question, as he put the pistols back and I pointed to the canvas.

"I hope so," he nearly whispered. Turning to me he added, "I so want it to be the way it was." He had a sullen look on his face. I knew Jewel wanted to move on to something different for their lives. I knew he didn't. I could find nothing in me to which I could respond to him. I just looked in his eyes and didn't say a word. He turned to leave the room, and I followed. The girls were busying themselves with breakfast. Marcus turned and stepped onto the porch. I hesitated briefly; Kat had her back to me. I caught Jewel's eye and gave a quick smile, then walked out to join him. It was going to be a warm day.

Just down the incline from the outhouse I saw Hershel with a wheelbarrow filled with rocks. He was stooped over, apparently adding a small rock-garden-type flower bed, adjoining an existing one. His back was toward us and he didn't know we were there.

"Gotta do my mornin' thing," I told Marcus, as I stepped from the porch and headed down Hershel's pathway. As I opened the door to the outhouse, Hershel stood straight up, turned and saw me, then smiled widely. I waved back to him. When I came back out, he was gone, nowhere in sight. I went back to the porch where Marcus was seated in a wicker chair drinking coffee.

"Hersh sure has a way a disappearin'," I said.

"Saw him go back to his cabin. He knows we've got company. Jewel told him you were bringing the Missus. He's pretty shy, ya know."

Kat's face appeared from the screened doorway. "Breakfast is ready," she said, then stepped onto the porch and made her way down the steps and onto Hershel's pathway where I had just been. I leaned on the post at the top of the porch steps.

"Hope he's not too shy to meet her," I said.

"Ah, he'll come around. We can always starve him out," Marcus laughed. I laughed back. Jewel stepped out. She handed me my coffee cup, freshly filled. I smiled just as fresh.

"We were talking about Hersh," I said. "I hope Kat can meet him."

"I'll be bringing him his breakfast soon; he'll come out," she assured me. "Kat gave me some Tibetan chimes. Wait till you hear them," Jewel excitedly said to Marcus. He smiled up at her, not saying anything. "They have a fresh ring to them," she added, metaphorically. He looked at her again, expressionless, but seemed to know what she was implying. Birds could be heard singing in the thickening air. The three of us were quiet there for a time. Kat was slowly walking back, carefully looking at each circle design along the footpath as she stepped. I had told her about these amazing art pieces. It was another reason she wanted to meet him. She has always loved art and those who make it.

"Those are wonderful!" she said, pointing back as she approached us from the bottom of the steps.

"Aren't they?" Jewel said. "He has some that are so fine, we won't even put them on the ground. They should be hung on walls."

Marcus then stood up. We all made our way inside for breakfast. Sure as anything, flapjacks were pancakes. They had several kinds of syrup, no doubt homemade.

"After we eat, let's go down to Hersh's porch with the guitars," Marcus said to me.

"I'm for that." was my instantaneous replied.

"I need to show you around," Jewel said to Kat. Kat smiled back to her.

It was still early, not yet mid-morning, but I was ready and willing to play music with Marcus anytime, anywhere. I had noticed how he seemed determined, maybe even in a hurry, for me to learn his songs the best that I could. I would later find out there was a reason why.

"I need to make some rounds in a little while. There are a couple folks that I need to treat. Would you care to come along?" Jewel asked Kat.

"Sure, I'd like to," Kat replied.

"When these two get together, they play music till a normal person's fingers would fall off," Jewel remarked, smiling at me. Turning to Marcus, she added; "No doubt that's what they have in mind for most of this day as well." Marcus gave her a wide-eyed loving look, his certain way of indicating she was right. Kat turned to me smiling. She knew all too well what this music meant to me.

No sooner had we finished eating - in fact, I hadn't quite - that Marcus retrieved the guitar that I had given him, from the music room.

Turning to me he asked, "You comin'?" His free hand was already opening the outside door.

"Yah, sure," I said as I stood up, still chewing. I went to the music room and picked up the old Martin. I would have had to run to catch up with him. I chose to lag behind. The girls were still seated when I walked by. "I think he wants ta play," I snickered, then I opened the outside door. He was already down by Hersh. "You wanna meet Hershel? Now might be the time," I told Kat, stepping out. Hershel was sitting on his porch, watching Marcus climb his steps.

"We'll be down shortly," Jewel replied.

I saw Marcus saying something to Hershel as he stood on the porch, then he took a chair. Hershel was looking at me with a bright smile as I approached. That smile could have been seen from a mile away. It had a way of brightening my day.

"Hey bud," I said to him, and I put my hand gently on his shoulder, then grabbed a chair and slid it close to him. Marcus and I began our ritual tuning-up procedure. The girls appeared from the house and started walking down to us. Kat had the box full of beads she had brought, and it looked like Jewel was carrying breakfast. She had a plate, covered with a cloth, a small hand basket with syrup, and a bottle of orange juice.

"Hungry?" Jewel asked, as she stepped next to Hershel. Kat was right behind her. Hershel was, I dare say, staring at Kat with a slight smile. His face became flushed. I believe he was blushing.

"This is Kat," Jewel said. "She brought you something."

"Hi Hershel. Thank you for the wind chime you gave us. It's beautiful. I brought you some beads," Kat said to him. His face brightened. Kat opened the box and stretched her arms out, offering it to him. He was beaming now. He made slight body motions as he examined the contents, like a child filling with glee. Kat smiled at him, and he gazed at her with a helpless, "love-at-first-sight" gleam. He then reached his hands up to hers, carefully taking the gift. He held the box closer to his eyes, as if staring into a treasure. Jewel set his food on the table next to him. Marcus already was strumming the beginnings of a song. I was pondering these events with deep interest. There came a true warmth from within me then, a coming together of what I had long been hoping would unfold — this moment, my treasure.

I followed Marcus' lead on a song I had yet to recognize. It turned out to be the song from the movie, The Wizard of Oz, *Somewhere over the Rainbow*. It was a rendition like I had never imagined. When he finished singing it, he said to me, "I took your lead and did a little changing of someone else's stuff."

"That was great," I said. "Fun to do, ain't it?"

"There's a million songs out there that can be made fresh this way. Think I'll try this more often," he replied. I smiled back at him.

The ladies had sat quietly, listening. Hershel just kept looking into the bead box, then glancing at Kat when he thought she wouldn't notice. Infatuation was occurring fortuitously. I'm not sure, in his diminutive understanding, that he recognized her to be my wife. He was deeply enthralled.

We played a couple of lively numbers, getting in a wakeup mode. Hershel was tapping his feet to the music, his face still beaming. He had not yet touched his breakfast. It seemed to me he was in his own "new world" experience. I had never seen him act this way. Extreme, it appeared to me his mood altered with an opposite magnetism, 180 degrees, when Jewel spoke between our songs.

"Jack will be here soon to take us. It's not far, and we probably won't be gone long," she explained to Kat. "You guys will have to look after your own lunch," she said to Marcus. He was strumming again, looking over to her with assurance. Hershel had turned almost pale, like he was about to get sick. He stood up with the bead box in his hands. Without looking at his food, or any of us, he opened his cabin door and walked inside. Then he closed the door behind him.

"Whoa," I remarked. Jewel just shook her head, almost motherly. We understood what had just transpired, but I could see bewilderment on Kat's face.

"I'll explain it to you later," Jewel told her.

"Got a bunch of songs we need to go over today," Marcus burst in.

"Good, keep you boys outta trouble," Jewel snapped back. His dimple reflected the soft sunlight.

Providence during that brief space in time, I felt filled with it. It was one of those "out of body" miniscule incursions that, at times overtakes me. It's like I'm looking down upon myself from somewhere else — a situation in which I recognize the universal significance of that moment as being a gift from above — a little weird, but not incredulous.

It wasn't long before the dogs began to bark. In a matter of seconds, the sound of a motor could be heard. That would be Mad Jack, I told myself.

"I need to gather up some things," Jewel said, as she rose from the chair. Kat got up to join her. The dogs were running toward the inlet. It was Jack. The ladies were walking up to the house while Marcus continued strumming and humming another unrecognizable song. I leaned back in a aimless pose, waiting for what would come next. It didn't take long for Jack to appear after the motor had silenced. He walked toward us when he saw where Marcus and I were sitting. He held to that pugnacious look of his, and I hoped to myself that he wouldn't scare Kat. I had told her about him, so I figured she'd be prepared.

"Good morning, sunshine," I daringly called out to him. His face cracked a smile.

"Good ta see ya, Hatty."

"You too, Jack. My wife's comin' with ya, so don't go stealin' her away from me," I warned.

"Who's gonna stop me?" he asked.

"Nobody, I guess," was my lighthearted response.

"Plan on startin' that project for the barbeque this weekend. Eddie'll be 'round ta help," Jack said to Marcus.

Leaning his guitar against the wall behind him, Marcus turned and asked him, "It's a good plan, right?"

"Yah, sure, it's gonna be great."

Looking over to me, L said, "We're fancifyin' her a new cookin' area. Gonna pull out all the stops." I could sense a need he was expressing, trying to keep Jewel fulfilled in this place. I didn't know what to say. I don't think he was expecting me to say anything.

## CHAPTER 7

Jewel had two separately beaded bags strapped on each side of her waist when they returned from the house. In addition, she had a larger, less intricately adorned bag strapped over her shoulder. Kat had an excited look on her face and didn't appear at all concerned about Jack when they were introduced. Jack was impressively charming. It was a side of him that I hadn't seen. Jewel appeared in a hurry to leave. "See you in a little while," she said to Marcus.

"See ya, babe," I told Kat. She gave me a twinkle. Her soft eyes sometimes sharpen to do that. "I'll be building calluses while yer gone," I added. Marcus smiled at me.

"We'll walk with ya," Marcus said, standing up.

We walked together to the inlet, dogs doing their little "dance-around." They weren't as spry with Jack as they were with Clay, but then again, Jack didn't pay them any mind.

"I'll be back with Eddie on Saturday morning and finish up those benches," Jack told Marcus.

"It's comin' together real fine," Marcus assured him.

As they were getting in the boat, Marcus surprised me by giving Jewel a kiss on the cheek. It was another "first" for my eyes. I held Kat's hand, settling her into her seat.

"TJ don't need no alligators," I kidded her. Jack gave me a quick smile, as he pushed off from the bank with the pole.

"I'll say!" she raised her voice to me with tightened lips, a bit chagrinned. I know she was apprehensive about alligators, as I had been. I confess that I still can't get used to them being around. I gave her an assuring laugh, as if it would make things seem all right. I waved to her, and they disappeared behind the marsh grasses. I left it to Jewel to better alleviate her gator anxiety. Maybe they won't even see one, I hoped.

Marcus and I stood silent for a time, the utterances of surrounding nature, protrusive. Suddenly, he calmly turned to me. He had an earnest look in his eyes as he pointed toward the main channel. "I watch the waters. The shoreline never waits. It knows what it can expect by now. It will become a ghost," he said.

I dedicated his words to my memory, standing there alongside him. I had left my table recorder on Hersh's porch, and had foolishly forgotten my pocket one in our bedroom. I tried to fit something into the moment.

"I've prayed that I can get this book done for you. The story is almost like a prayer for me now," I confided.

"The me of other years," was his first response. "All will continue on. It's at a gathering point in our lives where cares and concerns are being spent forth. You shouldn't worry. Pray, if need be"

It wasn't clear what he meant, or even if I'd remembered his words correctly. We began heading toward the cabin. Farther on, I heard him faintly say to himself, "Where time now has no time." What were his thoughts? I was perplexed.

"What was that?" I asked, as I caught up to his stride. We were stepping up to the porch now. I nearly lunged to turn on the recorder. It was clumsy.

"You're looking ahead of yourself for the purpose in what you're doing. When you do that, things become too delicate. Anyway, this thing may turn out more profound then you'll be able to tell. Sometimes things are not what they seem at the moment, nor are they controlled. You should know that. Time has everything to tell. Just go ahead with the story and don't worry about what has to be. It may never be. It's not all that serious. All these mindsets you put yourself through, worse nightmares to best dreams. Just know you're on the cusp of things, that's all."

Perhaps I would comprehend later. I only knew at the time I had captured what he was saying. It was, at times, a bit awkward trying to record, like I was trying to stop time for a brief second. Wait! Don't talk! Let me turn this thing on first!

Hershel had not re-appeared. Marcus again picked up his guitar as if on a quest that had no end. I followed suit, and as it was, we played that morning away. I recorded every song; almost all were exclusively his. A couple times I remarked how a particular song would sound good with such and such person recording it. For instance, I recall telling him how, on one song, it sounded like something Hank Jr. or even Hank III would do. He looked at me inquisitively. I'm not sure he knew who I was talking about.

On some of his songs we made changes, stopping in the process to reach favorable agreements. They were getting better each time we played them, resonance becoming clear, complete. The pride I felt endured, as if swelled beyond my own life form. I was more than I had ever been when I was in his presence.

Sometimes the bugs were a terrible annoyance, while other times, almost nonexistent. On this day, they seemed particularly bad. I worried about Kat. I knew she hated bugs worse than I do. I didn't remember her having any repellant. As for myself, I hate bug spray worse than bugs. A guitar player should know what an overspray can do to the finish of his instrument. It creates blisters, with having catastrophic consequences. I found out the hard way years ago, totally wiping out the face of a Guild steel string during a campfire songfest that lasted all night. I didn't notice the damage until daylight.

It was probably afternoon now; time flew like an anomaly. The dogs had begun their precursor bark, running toward the inlet. The next moment, I could hear the sound of a boat motor. The girls were back already. One thing about music, it pleasantly takes the time out of a day.

In almost an instant, they could be seen coming over the knoll, walking toward us, dogs dancing at their feet, but no Jack. Then in the distance, the sound of a re-started motor, which faded quickly away.

"How was that?" I inquired of Kat as they approached. A smile had her face illuminated.

"Wow!" was all she replied.

"Did the bugs bite?" She pulled a small squirt bottle of repellent from her bag, jiggled it at me with her fingers and raised her eyebrows confidently.

"Good deal. So you had a good time?" I asked her.

"An amazing time." She sounded excited.

"Let's go up to the house and I'll give you those things," Jewel then said to her.

"Be right back," Kat said, as she turned and they briskly began walking up the incline together.

Marcus was beginning another song. There was hardly ever a second wasted without notes being played when he held a guitar in his hands. It was clear to me he could sing all day and night, forever. The fact is, we had forgotten to eat lunch. Amazingly, I wasn't hungry. What kind of magic is this? *"The answer's in her diamond breath / the sighs she will be giving,"* Marcus sang. I gave an appreciative gaze, then danced my fingers across the frets in a race to catch up to its melody. He called it *Gypsy Lips.* How snuggled lips melt into one. I believe the whole song was about making love. I wished Kat would have been there to hear it. I knew the song would catch up to her eventually.

They were walking back to us now. Kat had a bag strapped around her shoulder.

"Look what Jewel gave me," she said as she handed it to me.

It was clearly made of alligator hide, even the strap. It appeared to have a large alligator tooth used for the latch. There were bead-shaped bones and shells hung by strings of braided hair off to one side. It looked old. I opened it. There inside were some smaller leather pouches. I looked inside one of them. It was filled with things I couldn't describe.

"I gave her some common cures," Jewel said to me. I was bewildered. "Peach leaves, hibiscus pedals, mamou root. You know, things people keep in their medicine cabinets." She had the cutest grin.

"Oooohh kaayee," I said, giving her a cockeyed look.

"You should see what she does," Kat declared. "Beyond amazing." I just smiled, believing it.

"You didn't eat?" Jewel said to Marcus.

"Guess not," he simply responded.

"We were fed well," Kat said.

"Oh yah, where's mine?" I asked.

"Poor dear, you're probably starving," Jewel said to me in a light, pitiful way, perhaps being a bit sarcastic. "We'll get a dinner thing going. Let's eat early; we have a surprise for Kat," she explained. Kat gave her a sweet sister look. Marcus was strumming still another song. My fingers were getting sore.

"Don't you take naps anymore?" I joked to him.

"Not so much when we have guests."

"Well, can I go take one?" I asked with a laugh.

"Sure, go ahead," he answered, though he knew I was kidding. I wouldn't lose these moments to sleep, not if I could help it. Jewel gave Kat an expression, a sign of sorts, and they briskly walked back up to the house. It was odd to me, how Hershel had just vacated the scene and not returned. What was his world, really? It was common nature for Jewel and Marcus how he performed these vanishing acts, only to reappear almost mystically. Marcus was playing an original now that had become familiar to me. I was becoming encased in a wardrobe of music that was all his own. I began wondering if there was something more being expected of me. There were times when I felt tutored. It would all come to light in due time.

It was then he surprised me with a new rendition of two of his songs. Combining them into one - super-transposed is the way I'd put it - he took *Stealin'* and *The You in Me*, and made them into one song, appropriately named, *Blend to One.* At once, an enchanting recipe of love had been put to music. And again, he had astonished me.

In a mode like there would be no tomorrow, we went on to play heartfelt songs, so inspiring it put new beats in my heart. I reflected on this briefly to myself, but intensely. With all his new music, there had become an astonishing new "him." Every instant, each insert of time we were sharing, was a restorative exploration of the universe of our souls, his and mine. I hoped I was bringing to him even a small portion of all that he had been giving me. To my benefit, I had the knowledge of his past, the star that he was, comparing it now to this phenomenon he had become. Even if he were to burst on the scene today, having never had a past, the venerable eminence, this anachronism he can't help but exalt, would open Earth's gates with light beyond dreams. These gifts from our creator, given unto such a humble man, continue to marvel me each new day. I can't begin to say enough about what he has to offer or what he has given me.

I caught myself just staring trancelike at him as he played. My admiration was distracted only when I caught a glimpse of Jewel from the corner of my eye. She was waving for us to come up to the house. I motioned for Marcus to look in her direction. He did, nodded, then went on with his song. Kat appeared from near the barbeque. She was holding a large pan with what looked like oven mitts. Marcus stood up when his song was finished. I stood up with him.

"I suppose we had better get up there," he said. I nodded. We took the guitars and stepped from Hershel's porch. Judging by the position of the sun, it may have been past mid-afternoon. As we were about to reach their porch steps, Jewel came out.

"Dinner's ready. Clay radioed and he'll be coming by later for a visit," she told us.

"He can't have her!" I said, referring to Kat, with a jousting-like pose. We all laughed. Jewel gave me that look; why would I even worry. It's this mere mortal's inkling of insecurity, I imagined. I smiled my boyish smile to her. She turned and went back inside, and we followed.

Inside, it was smelling great again. Now I was hungry. It was shrimp and deviled eggs gumbo, a new surprise, never failing to amaze me. In addition, broccoli soup, another great meal was set before us.

We ate our dinner, I would have to say, hurriedly.

"There's something we're eager to show you," Marcus said to Kat. She looked up from her plate and smiled, first at him, then at Jewel. I guessed in my mind it had something to do with "the place with no name," and the island.

"Feel like taking a walk?" Marcus asked Kat.

"Let them finish," Jewel told him, as she prepared another plate. "I'll meet you down there." She walked out to bring Hershel his supper. He had to be hungry, I thought. From all accounts, he had chosen to skip his lunch.

"I'm stuffed. I need a walk," I said, leaning back on my chair.

"It was wonderful," Kat said to Marcus with her sweet smile. She pressed a napkin to her lips. After a moment she took one last bite, pushed back her chair and stood up. She delicately picked up her empty plate, setting it on the counter behind her. Turning back to us, she said; "I'm ready." I knew her well enough to see that she was eager, too.

"We can take care of the table later. Let's try and catch the rest of the sunlight," Jewel had told her moments earlier. The three of us were standing now. Marcus led the way to the door. Jewel was just coming out of the cabin as we were walking down. The four of us neared the familiar path at the edge of the thicket.

"Watch for snakes," Marcus turned and said to Kat, who was following directly behind him as they entered the path. She turned to me and I just shrugged. I hadn't seen a snake in all the times I'd been there - lizards yes, but no snakes. Marcus caught a glimpse of our expressions and added, "Once bitten twice shy."

"Those are snake flowers," Jewel said, giggling from behind me. We looked back at her. She pointed to some orange flowers alongside the trail, cosseting a small brook. "Those pink blooms are mimosa trees," she pointed further on.

We soon stepped into the park-like clearing, familiar to me now as a place beyond any name. Beautiful, serene as ever. Bedding themselves along the shallows were cypress trees with light green moss blanketing their bark. Over what appeared to be an endless pond, partially covered by sheets of bright algae, all lay calm. Nature was now profusely showing off her bushy mangroves and swamp maples, intermixing with her oaks and palms. Jewel had educated me about the tupelo gums, honey locust, and dwarf palmettos. They were all seemingly encompassed as one, hugging together by those now familiar embracing vines. They formed and hung there in altar-like splendor.

"These are wax myrtle," Jewel pointed out to Kat. The marsh grasses stood golden against the late-afternoon sun.

This place always led me to new imaginative affirmations — nature with her lioness, innocuous purr. Each time, it evoked such magnificence. I could see egrets and ducks. There was a blue heron, half hidden, in the tall grasses of shallow water.

"What are those?" Kat asked, pointing toward the shore of what she now recognized to be an island.

"Black skimmers," Jewel replied.

"What a wonderful island," Kat remarked, gazing longingly across the water. "What a beautiful gazebo."

"Cool bridge, huh?" Marcus pointed. She nodded back at him with a smile.

"It should be, it's all yours," he said to her, capturing her eyes in his.

She had a sincere, melting look, although she must have thought he was making jest.

"Can I move in?" she asked, putting her hand on his arm, giving him a most gorgeous smile in lightly pursed lips. I heard Jewel laugh.

"Grant said you always like to take your vacations on islands, so we built this for you. We've named it Kat's Island. Now you have a new vacation getaway," Jewel told her.

Kat put her hand over her mouth now. Clearly, the surprise had sunk in. Her eyes were welling up. I took her hand. She was becoming sentimental. I pointed out the bench under the willow, off to our left.

"That's their place of solitude," I told her.

"Romantic interludes, I'll bet," she nearly whispered, squeezing my hand in hers.

"Shall we m'lady?" Marcus asked. And with bended arm, he wrapped it around Kat's. Elbow to elbow he began escorting her to the bridge, and then across. Jewel and I followed, smiling to each other, no, giggling.

There were two birdbaths made of porcelain, complementing the pond's edge, off to each end of the island. They had been filled with fresh water. There were nearly a dozen assorted trees, with one lone palm. Flower beds along the ground encircled the gazebo's screened outer walls. It was another perfect calendar picture. Marcus opened the door. Each of us eagerly stepped inside. There were benches around the inner circumference. A small table had been placed in the center, with four wooden chairs; they appeared handmade. Kat and Marcus sat along the bench, while Jewel and I took our places at the table.

"Well, what do you think? Does it feel like a vacation?" Marcus asked her.

Surprisingly, she turned and leaned to him, and with both arms embraced him, kissing him on the cheek. Then she belatedly looked over for Jewel's approval and mine. Our smiles were intently upon her.

"You really did this for that reason?" she said, turning to Marcus.

"We thought it was a great idea," he replied.

"It's a great addition to our home, don't you think?" Jewel asked her. Kat was smiling widely.

We sat relaxed, conversing in small talk. It went from the ambient beauty of where we were to talking about our lives. We each had tidbits of life's experiences we were sharing. No real course or direction was taking precedence, that is, until Kat turned the topic to Marcus. With genuine interest, she began asking him about his past. He seemed comfortable with her curiosity, and began exploring deeply into his recollections.

He told us about how he briefly grew a mustache in 1957. He reminisced about the first time he played out in public at a dairy show. He used to listen to The Grand Old Opry on Saturday nights. He really liked a group called The Statesmen back then. He mentioned that his family had relocated a number of times when he was a kid. The conversation progressed to his late teens and what he called Louisiana Hayride days. He really started to open up then. None of us interrupted. Kat occasionally spurred him on with any detailed questions she could find. She was digging for treasures.

"Musta played 50 shows for them," he told her. "We drove an old Chevy when we first started, couldn't even afford to eat."

He spoke admiringly of his band members and about how he met his drummer. He told us about meeting someone named James. I could sense he was skipping around a bit, yet with genuine affection and some regret about the way things turned out. He talked about Johnny Cash and recalled the last hayride, which he thought was around 1956. He mentioned a group called The Jordanaires. I wasn't sure if he was keeping things in sequence, or for that matter, perspective. Kat urged him further. My tape player was reeling with every word.

My voice could be heard saying, "In the South, I once heard a trucker talk about 'The Tupelo Tornado'." I'm not sure what I was driving at with that interjection. I remember Marcus just smiling.

The tape goes on, revealing him telling about how he went on to act in major motion pictures, how they kept him cooped up in motels. He said he was never able to get back home. Then he told of the places he had owned in Hollywood, about a house in Bel Air and something about a monkey. But it didn't appear to be a happy time for him back then. He was surrounded by buddies, but hardly ever ventured out on the town.

"Made a lot of movies for 'em. I fancied myself an actor, but there was no depth, nothing real of me," he confessed.

He was telling us about touring. He spoke dearly of someone named Charlie. He spoke admiringly about a group called The Sweet Inspirations and another called The JD Sumner Quintet. We were enchanted during this recollection ride. Whether accuracy played in part, or as a whole, we had no way of knowing.

Enlightening us, he told of the time he was about to go out on tour once again, yet deep inside, he knew he just couldn't do it. He had kept that to himself at the time.

He explained more fully how he and Jewel first met. During that time, there had come the realization of how he had been wasting his life and what he needed to do about it. There was shown to him a true light. He told of the deciding moment when he knew he had to get out, and how it had to be done. Of this, at his request, I must now spare any details. I am confident that this will come to light, addressed at the time of his choosing. Too sacred are those moments for me to reveal in these writings. I leave the timing up to him.

It was at this time I made out a faint buzzing sound or bell, coming from near the willow tree. Jewel looked at Marcus.

"I'll go," he said to her, and stood up.

"I'll come too, L," I told him, wondering what it meant. We briskly crossed the bridge, passing through the thicket along the path, and to the clearing of their yard. The dogs, barking, ran toward the inlet. We were near the house when the barking ceased. He stopped at the bottom of the steps and waited, not saying a word.

"It's Clay," he finally told me, and within a matter of seconds, sure enough, Clay appeared, dogs dancing at his feet. Delphine was with him. It was nearing sunset as they came closer. I could make out in the twilight that he had a 12- pack of beer in one hand and a can of beer in the other. I could hear the faint sound of music coming from a boom box she was carrying. Marcus didn't seem all that enthused.

"I'll go get the guitars," he said to me, climbing the stairs up to the door and briskly stepping inside.

"Ca va," Clay hollered to me, Delphine holding that smile of hers.

"How's it goin'?" I said to them.

"Whattaya t'ink a bow a beer mon ami?"

"Sure."

"T'ought dis coonass brng p'tite. Bonheur ta ever'body! Laisseez les bons temps rouler," he nearly shouted. I later found that to mean, "Let the good times roll." He set the 12-pack on the ground, reached in, and handed me a warm beer. He appeared more than half drunk. Marcus came out holding the guitars. He nodded to Delphine, then to Clay.

"Bon poonah," Clay said to Marcus in a toned-down voice.

"We're headed for the gazebo," Marcus told them. Delphine had switched off her radio. Marcus handed me the old Martin. He seemed now to exclusively prefer playing the Martin that I had given him. Clay offered him a beer but he declined. Marcus said something in French to Clay as we walked. My pocket recorder didn't pick it up and I can't remember what it sounded like, but it caused Clay immoderate laughter.

"I s'pose," was all Clay said.

I followed them back onto the path. Clay was in front of me, moving sidled and ungainly. I surmised that he must have started drinking early this day. Moving across the bridge, Clay waved to the girls, while scuttling in some dance-like fashion. Acting a bit ludicrous, he stumbled his way through the gazebo door.

"Still partying, I see," Jewel said to him.

"Oui oui, c'est vrai," he told her, then laughed.

"Hi Del," Jewel said.

"Ello," Delphine replied. She can talk! I became convinced.

Marcus sat down next to Kat on the side bench and almost immediately began strumming the guitar. Jewel was seated on the other side of Kat now. The rest of us took places at the table. I leaned the guitar against my leg, while holding it by the neck. I wasn't ready to play. Sometimes I can't just jump into it like that. Besides, I was enjoying my beer. Clay was awkwardly cajoling Kat and Del, slurring that Cajun tongue of his.

For the most part sounding of gibberish, he was telling a tale of some loup-garou, or werewolf that lives in the swamp woods. How it was blue and had yellow eyes that mesmerized you. Kat and Delphine were finding it humorous, but his prattling didn't appear to affect Jewel in the same way. She gave him a look, as though he were acting out of line. I decided to mess with him a bit.

"So, Clay, why you s'pose wolves howl at the moon? Think maybe they believe it's alive, since it's always changin' shape? Maybe they're afraid of it. Or maybe they think it's a god, a deity of some kind, and it's just their strange way of worshipping it."

He looked at me with glazed over eyes and that smile of his. Without a word Clay then moved over to the bench and took his shirt off. Propping it up as a pillow he turned, and straightened out his legs, reclining backward. He lay there, looking up at the ceiling, still smiling. My little statement had its intended effect. He never said another word. Then again no one did. About that time, Delphine pulled a large bottle of peach Schnapps from a denim bag that had been strapped around her shoulder.

"Oooo," Jewel remarked.

"Wansm?" Del asked. Jewel nodded approvingly with a wide grin.

Del then surprised me when she also pulled out a ukulele. She handed it over to Jewel without a word. Jewel then handed it to me, saying, "I heard about you and islands; let's christen this one." I smiled appreciatively as I took it from her hand. I heard Marcus laugh.

Let's hear something," he said.

I quickly tuned it to the guitar. "Well let's see, I suppose," I announced. Then I began strumming an old classic, *When the Saints Go Marching In*. I was trying to make it light-hearted. Marcus sat sternly, taking the song to heart. He then suggested another old song, *Oh Mary, Don't You Weep*. I wasn't familiar with it, but he instructed me on the chord progression and what tempo to play it in. When I began, Marcus stood up. One could see strong belief in those illustrious candle-lit eyes. As he began singing, it took on the relevance of a gospel sound, deep with passion. His voice was smooth, yet as honey poured over sandpaper. I got shivers. When it came to the chorus, he motioned for each of us to sing along. Slowly, obligingly, it built to exuberance. All of the ladies and I were smiling, our voices blending harmoniously. Even Del's lips were moving, although it may have just been pantomime. I could hear no sound coming from them. Clay just lay there with his grin. We were having so much fun with this, we probably extended the song far past its original format. I recall farther on, between our guitars playing, I picked up that uke one more time. It was for a song that I think was written by Leadbelly, called *Midnight Special.*

Therein lies what would become of that dwindled afternoon, sustaining into the night. That bottle found its way around, back and forth to each of us, even Marcus. Mixing it with my beer was a real treat. I'm being sarcastic; they didn't mix well. Maybe Clay has a steel stomach, but I'm not that lucky. The fact is, between the songs we played that night; I had to literally run out near the water's edge to vomit, disgorging on two separate and memorable occasions. It seemed an acceptable procedure, as were the use of bathrooms that were located between the trees, any trees. I did my best to keep up with the festivities, which included playing the Richard Thompson song again, trying to keep Clay from passing out. It had fast become his favorite biker tune, and I could tell he had bragged about it to Del. She seemed excited when I mentioned I was about to play it.

We probably played for hours. Again my fingers were sore. It got to the point where I politely, gently, leaned the old guitar against a chair and stood to take a stretch. To my surprise, Marcus set his down too. Things got quiet for a time.

"Mouche a' feu," Clay broke our silence, pointing up at a firefly just outside the screen.

We noticed that they had become abundant, flittering all about. The evening had long since dwindled into darkness. By then, Clay was besotted, clearly comatose drunk and stupefied. I, for one, wouldn't have trusted him in a boat of any kind at that point.

The girls werc seated around the table now. Under the candlelight, they were looking through the CD music Del had brought along for her boom box. Kat picked one out and Del got it started. I was somewhat surprised at Kat's choice. I would never have guessed, but there we all were, sipping peach Schnapps and listening to Julio Iglesias under the stars. Marcus must have felt inspired. He stood up, took Jewel's hand, and began a slow dance with her. Kat gave me a longing look. I stood up, took her hand, and we moved about together on this new dance floor, dancing on, into that warm Louisiana night. Del sat pristinely illuminated against the glimmering light of a single candle. Clay was, for the most part, a goner.

After that brief romantic interlude, we were all showing wear, agreeing we would take this night to bed. Clay was laying flat out, mouth hanging open, producing sounds like I'd never heard before. Del tried rustling him from his self-induced state.

"Let the gators have him!" Jewel exclaimed. Kat glanced her way with concern. "Don't worry, he always carries a gun in his boot," Jewel assured her, as she lit a lantern. Kat turned, blowing out the remnants of what had once been a tall candle. Del pulled a long flashlight from her bag, aiming the beacon straight into Clay's eyes.

"C'est moi, viens avec moi," Del said to him, as she bent down near his face. He grinned widely, his eyes still closed. All the while, Marcus sat quietly, appeased in his mellow mood. It looked like he had, at long last, found Clay's antics amusing. I saw him wink at mc while we watched Del struggling to raise Clay to his feet.

"Che're 'tite bete, em jus de tete dure, il a pas d'esprit," Jewel said to Del. She then offered her help, extending his legs from the bench, and fitting his boots to the floor. Each of them took an arm and lifted him to what, almost, resembled a seated position. He half-opened his eyes, still grinning.

"There's hope yet," I blurted, as we watched the endeavor. I looked to Marcus for a shared chuckle and got one. Kat sat at the table, taking it all in.

"You guys will be spending the night," Marcus said to Del.

"I say we set him adrift," Jewel laughed, pulling him to his feet. He was able to stand, sort of. After all, he is a professional.

To make a long story short, we all made it back to the house. Jewel handed Clay a pillow, helping him take his place on the floor. She was humorously upset. A moment earlier he had stepped (stumbled) on one of the dogs as he made his way onto the porch. There had been a loud squeal, but no apparent damage to the dog. A makeshift bed was laid out for Del on the couch. We called this one a night.

Too hot to sleep, head still spinning, with my stomach not at all itself, I stared up at the ceiling. Kat had no trouble with slumber, my arm under her head; she rested against my chest. I couldn't really align any thoughts, mini-ideas pounding through my mind. I knew we had to leave tomorrow, but I felt a sort of contentment.

## CHAPTER 8

I didn't recall having fallen asleep, but I was grateful that I did. Clay's distinct voice protruded through the door, forcing open my eyes to the light of a new day. The sun was shining strong against the curtains. Kat laid with her back to me, sleeping soundly. Disquieted, I tried abstracting the events from the previous night, restlessly impounding my memories for fear of their losses. The tapes, blessings again bestowed, were assuredly filled with uncloseted revelations. There would be much to sort out. I so needed to make it all balance.

We must have lain there for some time. Voices had silenced from outside our door. I rose out of the bed, decidedly needing to know what was going on. I freshened up some, leaving Kat to her, hopefully, pleasant dreams.

It was Marcus, once again seated and reading a book, that treated my first focus. I had found him in this same pose a number of times during these morning moments. He looked up to me over his glasses in that familiar way.

"Mornin'," he said quietly, as indeed, the whole house seemed now to be.

"Mornin'," I replied. "Thought I heard Clay a bit ago."

"He had to get Del back. She works in the office at an oil company."

"Did he make a full recovery?" I inquired.

"Oh yah, like ridin' his bike," Marcus assured me. Just then Jewel came in from outside.

"Hey there," she said to me.

"Mornin' star shine," I caught myself saying.

"She still asleep?" Jewel asked about Kat. I nodded.

"What time might it be?" I asked.

"Quarter to eleven," Marcus replied.

"I should get her up," I told them.

Just then her voice was behind me, "I'm up." I turned and stepped back into our room. She was sitting, head propped up by both of our pillows, sleepy-eyed. She always looks beautiful that way. I, on the other hand, look like warmed over death in the morning. My hair usually sticks straight up, horrifyingly, and known to scare people. I don't know how she consistently does it. Then again, I don't know how I consistently do it either.

"You look no worse for wear," I told her. She smiled at me.

"Jewel's gonna do henna on me today," she said.

"Really?" She nodded back little-girlishly, so cute.

"Better get up then. We need to leave right after lunch," I reminded her. As it was, we wouldn't have much more than two days to get home. I needed to be back with Beulah and on that road first thing Monday. She must have begun to realize our time limitations, as she rolled from the bed, sauntering about the room, readying herself. I left her to her preparedness, closing the door behind me.

I went over and sat on the couch. "We have to leave soon," I said to Marcus.

"I know," he replied. I could see Jewel, her back to me in the kitchen. She was preparing what would be brunch. "I have more songs for you to hear. You'll need to hurry back," he added.

"I'll do what I can," I replied. "Don't always have a choice."

"There's time," he calmly replied.

"I've sure got a lot of writing to do," I confessed.

"Call 'em as ya see 'em," he responded brashly.

"Not a simple thing," I added. He tipped his head and looked earnestly into my eyes from above his glasses, not saying anything. Kat opened the door and stepped out. Jewel turned, and their smiles met. Kat turned to look at Marcus.

"Whatcha reading?" she asked him.

"Mark Twain's Joan Of Arc," he replied. That surprised me, but I wasn't really sure why. He probably reads everybody and everything, I told myself.

Jewel had put together some patties to be fried outside on the barbeque. They were made with ground shrimp, garlic, onions, spices, and peppers. She had seafood-stuffed potatoes already baking; she was planning to send us off with bellies flaming full. She had laid some things out on the table. She would do the Henna tattooing on Kat before finishing her cooking. The two sat down at the table after the coffee had been poured. I wandered over to catch a glimpse of what this was all about.

"I believe it dates back to the Egyptians," Jewel explained. She was mixing a dark paste-like substance in a small bowl. "It's mixed with eucalyptus oil. When I finish the design, I'll cure it with sugar and lemon juice. Then I won't want you to wash it for the rest of the day," she instructed.

It evidently absorbs in the skin like a stain. She was using a small brush and a small splinter of what looked like bone or ivory. She began creating intricate wave designs along Kat's fingers and atop her right hand, then encircling part of her wrist. At times she painted with the brush, then switched to delicate blotting or dotting it on with the splinter.

I walked to where Marcus was now seated on the couch. I turned on the table recorder. He had been writing. There were several pieces of paper scattered on the coffee table. I sat down next to him. He reached for the paper nearest him, handing it to me. It appeared to be fresh lyrics.

"Tell me what you think of this," he said. I set my cup down to read. It was in poetic verse. "Sometimes I do the music first. Sometimes I do them both at almost the same time. Sometimes I do it this way. Whatdaya think?"

"I like it, it's different. You'll set it to music then?"

"Already have it in my head," he said. "Still need to get the tempo figured right."

This was going to be another exercise in grandeur, I could see it. I couldn't wait to hear it.

"I'll have something figured out by the next time I see ya," he assured me.

The girls were giggling about something in the other room. Marcus got up, grabbing both the guitars that had been leaning in the corner against a chair. He brought them over and handed me the old Martin, then sat down without saying a word. I started playing the first song I had ever done for him, *Let It Be Me*, by the Everly Brothers. He had that grin as he strummed along. As I sang, I noticed the girls had stopped what they were doing and had turned to watch us. I doubt that it was me; it's just that it's such a great song. When I finished, Marcus applauded gently. The girls went back to their Henna. He began strumming an unfamiliar arrangement. He wasn't singing, but was motioning for me to join in with whatever I could offer. I tagged along, awkwardly at first, but catching on to what he was alluding to. We began making new music. There evolved a wonderful melody with an intriguing back beat, another exciting new sound. Was this where he was looking to go with those words he'd had me read? It's his amazing way of sparking new horizons. My guess was correct. He was writing the chord progression down on that same sheet of paper, together with some side notes.

"Does it have a name yet?" I asked.

"Yah, *Royal Spattering*," he blurted and laughed aloud. The girls turned with wonder. Now I started to grasp those lyrics. This song was his attempt to cast dispersions on that which he had been. He was defaming his myth, laying discredit to what they had imposed on him in that life. Man, this was heavy! I sat amazed to be a part of its creation. And although it seemed only half written, I knew this would become a masterpiece. I applauded him after my realization. He smiled widely, knowing I got it. "We'll get it finished next time," he winked.

"Can I take some pictures?" Kat asked from the kitchen table. There was a brief silence, and I studied Marcus and Jewel's expressions from across the rooms to each other.

"Sure," Marcus finally said. "Of what?"

"You guys, and maybe the island," Kat replied.

"Sure, sounds like a good idea," he said.

Jewel showed no disapproval, appearing to be completing her artistic endeavor. "It should last well over a month," she was telling Kat. "When it wears off, come back and get another one."

I stood up now, looking at Marcus earnestly. I went over to resituate the guitar where it had been. I was getting antsy with the thought of so many driving miles ahead of us.

Perhaps sensing this, Jewel got up from the table. "Lunch won't take long at all," she said.

"I'll help," Kat told her.

"We need to let that get some air," Jewel added, pointing to Kat's hand.

Marcus stood and walked over next to me. He didn't say anything. We shared, that instant, in the rewarding air around us, the knowledge of what we had just created musically. There was a lot of satisfaction being felt in the room at that moment. It felt like we were wrapping things up. Now the ladies were stepping outside.

"*Royal Spattering*," Marcus repeated. "No more room to lose," he expounded, giving me his pronounced smile. Then he slugged my shoulder lightly with his fist. He must have been experiencing a profound humor in that. I think it was helping him bury the past somehow; soothing to him in a way that he had been searching for. He acted deeply relieved from something. I hadn't previously seen such a mannerism in him. A mere minute had passed, when Kat came back inside. I retrieved a fresh tape from my pants pocket, reloading the recorder in my shirt.

"Need to get the camera," she said, as she passed us and headed straight to the bedroom. She reappeared just as quickly, and practically flew out the door. Marcus turned and smiled at me.

"Clay'll be back soon to take you guys," he told me. I nodded without a word. I knew the time was nearing, but I seem to feel the same way every time it gets near my time to depart. There was a closeness between him and me, ever stronger when we got to this point. It would seem like eons before I would see them again. It always felt that way. It was at this juncture he availed to me a purpose he had all along intended. He was about to present me with a shock.

"My music will be yours," Marcus confided. He put his right hand on my left shoulder as he spoke. "I have no intention of ever recording them myself. I don't really much care about even gettin' the credit for 'em. I need you to think about who, out there now, could do them justice. Maybe you'd be interested in doin' some yourself?"

I looked at him most startled, having trouble comprehending at first. Was he giving me his songs?

"I'm no professional singer," I told him modestly, yet convinced.

"They need to get out there. They need to get out of my hands. I want them heard in the best possible light. No hurry, but I just want you to start thinking about it, thinking about my songs in these terms."

Therein lay the reason, he had so emphasized, that I dedicate his music to my memory — how we had gone over and over, almost labored, subjugating each song to all the ins and outs, until we were both satisfied with their best possible outcomes. He had been planning this all along. More than ever, I couldn't find my next words. I'm sure I just held that faraway blank stare.

I could make out, through the screen door, Hershel sitting down on his porch. Kat had asked Jewel earlier if she thought he would let her take his picture. Jewel told her she wasn't even sure, with his modicum of intelligence, that he knew what a camera was.

"I'll need to say my goodbyes ta that guy," I told Marcus. I pointed through the door. The music thing was dancing in back of my head with real sugarplums. I had to absorb this, but I really couldn't focus.

"Let's go down," he suggested.

"Yah," was all I could manage to respond.

We stepped out to the porch, paused, and just stood there for a moment. It promised to be a hot, sultry, sunny day. Again no words were said. My recorder was reeling on in my shirt pocket, brand new tape with plenty of room. Then Marcus stepped down from the porch, making his way to Hershel's cabin. Maybe dazed, it took a second for me to convince my feet to follow. I scrambled to catch up. He was halfway there before I could. He did have a tendency to walk faster than me.

Same old Hershel. Same face-wide smile. For once he wasn't really doing anything, just sittin' there. We stepped up to greet him. Marcus put his hand on Hershel's shoulder. I simply said, "good morning." We took chairs beside him, letting the silence glow peaceful. Not a word was spoken for minutes. It was great company.

We could hear a rustle in the bushes, off to our left; the girls were approaching. They started laughing about something, then saw us there. Kat was smiling as she approached us. Without hesitation, she drew the camera up from her side, snapping a picture of the three of us seated there. I looked over at Hershel. I do believe he didn't know what had just happened. At the sight of Kat, his face again blushed. He stood up, turned, and went inside. The girls had stopped at the foot of the steps. He came back out almost immediately, walked over to above where Kat was standing, and handed something down to her. He went back and sat down. It was a smaller version of one of his footstep carvings.

"He's giving it to you," Jewel explained.

"Oh wow, thank you." Kat brightly replied up to him. "Look," she told me, handing it up. It was a carving of two turtles, side by side, with designs around the edges, very impressive art work, sophisticated. It made me ponder just how intelligent this man might really be. What did he actually know, or did the creator merely instill in him this great artistic ability.

The dogs sat up, turning their heads. In a flash they were barking, running to the inlet. That, most likely, would be Clay. We could hear the motor now, and in another instant it shut off.

"Let me get a picture of all of you," Kat said. Jewel stepped up on the porch and stood next to Marcus, who remained seated. Kat snapped a photograph.

"Let me take one of ya'll," I said, motioning for Kat to take my place. I took two quick photos and then went up to Kat and half whispered in her ear. She needed to put the camera away before Clay saw it, I explained. I had told her earlier about his phobia. She then slipped it into her pocket.

Our timing couldn't have been more perfect. Clay and the dogs appeared in the clearing. He saw us immediately and came walking down.

"Ca va?" we heard him say.

I found out a while back that it meant, "How's it going?"

"Mornin', or is it afternoon?" I asked him jokingly, because the truth was, I really didn't know for sure. I guessed it to be around one in the afternoon.

"De pomme?" He had a small bag of apples and handed one toward us to see if anyone wanted it. Hershel stood and took it from Clay's hand. Clay brought out another and thrust it toward us.

"We're just about to eat lunch," Jewel said. "You're just in time." No one else went for his apple.

"C'est bon," Clay replied.

Jewel suggested we head up to the house, as she was about to retrieve her hot potatoes and quickly fry up those patties. Kat and I had some last minute packing we needed to do. On the way up, Kat decided she would help Jewel, so I told her I could manage to get our stuff gathered together myself.

Clay acted uncharacteristically refined. His demeanor was, well, subdued. I wondered if he felt embarrassed over his behavior of the night before. It hadn't bothered Kat or me. We were quite used to drunks. During lunch he hardly said a word.

As the ladies were bringing in the food, I heard Kat ask if she could bring Hershel his lunch. Jewel had no problem with it, so Kat scurried down to the cabin. Hershel was still seated on his porch. I watched from the door, her handing him his plate. She said something to him, then put her hand on his shoulder. He looked up at her, no doubt smiling. She then stepped down from his porch to return to the house.

As we ate lunch, I gave the usual "hope to see ya soon" jargon. My conversation was half-intended to entice them to see us again. I reminded them we still owed them a game of Frisbee golf. I offered the option of visiting us in the winter, informing them of a friend of ours who raises sled dogs.

"Bet that's something ya ain't tried yet," I told them. Marcus smiled, but gave no response.

"I do miss the snow sometimes," he finally said. Jewel looked at him and then said that she did too, just a little.

"We could tour the north shore of Lake Superior, or maybe stay on Madeline Island," I added. It was Kat and my favorite place for a short vacation excursion. "We could spend an evening, maybe play guitars at a place called Tom's Burned Down Bar," I said, explaining that it was a bar on the island that had burned down. Instead of rebuilding, canvas was put up for a roof. It's probably one of the most unique places on Earth, with its makeshift additions, and an old car was parked in the middle of the haphazard table settings…hard to explain. They looked at me with that "you from another planet?" inquisitiveness in their eyes. They found it an entertaining tale. "You'd need to see to believe," I added.

Time had, as usual, flown by. We needed to get going. With our bags on the porch, we started saying our goodbyes. I tried to make it as least painful as I could for my poor mind, but it always seemed hard. Hershel had vanished from his porch now, and we began walking toward the inlet. Clay insisted on carrying Kat's suitcase, but once again, wouldn't take mine. The girls held hands as we neared where the boat was moored. Everything was then placed on board. It's these last few minutes that I almost wish could be avoided, the interactions between such good friends. Goodbyes are hard for me. Yes, I had a tear welling up during my brotherly embrace with Marcus. He once again told me to "stay alright." Jewel saw my watering eyes when we gave each other our farewell hug. We would find a way to be together again soon, she promised. When we shoved off, all became silent. The only sound heard was that of the disturbed shallow water, disrupted by Clay's pole. Just before the bend, just before the tall grasses erased our view of them, Jewel raised her hand high in the air and waved. "See you soon!" They were the last words we could hear. Marcus said nothing, but I'd like to believe he was smiling.

The float back felt arduous. No gators spotted, and not many words were spoken. Standing on Clay's dock, I tried to lighten these last few moments.

"Say goodbye to Del for us," I told him. He quietly, sheepishly, said he would. "Ya need ta get yerself another dog," I told him.

"Nay, ba I can jes yea," he responded. He turned, giving Kat a farewell embrace, then he shook my hand heartedly, saying, "C'est ein affaire a' pus finir bon poonah." I guessed it meant something good, as I responded with how we would miss him and hoped to be back soon. Kat told him how happy she was to have met him, then we made our way over to our Camaro. I turned off my pocket recorder, gave him a quick wave and squirmed inside the car.

While we were making our way from the grove and out to the clearing, Kat said nothing. There had been a lot to absorb in this short time. Sometimes, in the past, when I had left there, there had been this incredulity to my thoughts, like it had been some sort of a dream. Maybe Kat was feeling it now, too. For the sake of the book, and for future experiences there, I now felt the need to maintain discernible, my emotions with all I encountered. Kat, I do believe, still had that element of shock in her thoughts.

Ideally, I had hoped that by this time to have driven through New Orleans in the dark, wishing to spare Kat from more scenes that might haunt her memories. As it was, she may have been exhausted, or chose to spare herself.

She laid, head back, eyes closed, through most of that, still obvious and disturbing devastation.

I drove until nearly midnight that evening, anxious to get some of the road behind me. It would be two nights in motels during our trip back. I drove to "beat the band." It's what I do best, after all. I am a driver.

During our conversations, Kat told me how Jewel had confided in her how badly she wanted to move to a new place. She told Kat that Marcus wasn't in as good of health as he appeared. Out of her concern, she thought a change would do him good, a new climate with high-altitude air. She was seeking to revitalize him, while sparking herself at the same time.

"She wants to go," Kat said. I had a concerned look. I knew I did when she told me these things.

"It can't be his lungs that are the problem," I thought aloud. "The air is thin in those places." Kat had nothing to say to that. I felt a little helpless about these things she was telling me. There would be nothing I could do except wait things out.

In another conversation along our way, I teased her about Hershel. "You break hearts wherever you go, don't cha?" She just smiled, gazing out the windshield.

We talked about the pictures she had taken of the island and gazebo. She took one of the bridge, and of the bench under the willow, which she thought was exceedingly romantic. The only hurricane she would encounter would be the whirlwind tour that this vacation was on. My only regret was her not having had an opportunity to try Thin Ice, but there would always be next time.

She talked about her adventure the afternoon she accompanied Jewel on her rounds to visit her patients. Jewel carried various elixirs with her, and spoke highly of garlic oil. She also explained to Kat of the great healing powers of a Native American herb or tea with red clover and several other ingredients, called essiac.

The first person they visited was an elderly woman, who was very upset because she felt she had been "crossed" by a neighbor, whom she considered a conjure man. He had uttered execrations at her. She felt that an imprecation, a curse or spell, had been placed upon her by his conjuration. Jewel treated her with blue lily, as well as chanting some incantation to wash away the affliction. Kat said it was like something out of a fairytale, mysterious and eerie, even scary. On the second person Jewel had used what she called la pre'le, or horsetail, to treat his prostrate problem. She boiled it with sugar, as a drink. He fed them crab dinner afterward, along with his fresh garden vegetables. Their final stop was to visit a young boy with asthma, which she treated with alligator grease, again reciting another incantation. The one she had used on the old woman sounded like a faraway chant. This one was more of a lullaby. You've got to believe that what she was telling me sounded a bit wacky.

"They love her. She gets total respect, and they swear by her - she really heals," Kat said to me. Of this I had no doubt. She'd healed me in more ways than anyone could imagine. Then Kat told me of that bag Jewel had given her, that it was full of remedies, complete with written instructions for their proper use. To tell you the truth, I haven't been eager to be "under the weather" since our trip.

"I wonder if they found their mountain during the trip up to our place?" I asked.

"We talked about that," Kat replied. "I asked her, and she told me that they may have, but it was all she would say."

At last we were home again. There's really no feeling that compares with pulling into your own driveway after being gone a while. It was Sunday evening, so we indulged ourselves in one more short excursion downtown before I had to get back on the road. We stopped in at Smokey Joe's for a couple drinks, where Kat proudly displayed her new tattoo. By then, the tattoo was turning a burnt orange in color. Never letting anyone know the true identity of our southern friends, we skimmed over the adventures we had been on. I chose, for the time being, to keep to myself that discussion Marcus and I'd had regarding his songs. It would require Kat's opinion during some future quiet dinner, maybe at a candlelit table, maybe the next time I was scheduled to be home.

# PART VII

## CHAPTER 1

When time is the element I focus my value on, and its essence sets out to confound, I get truly paralyzed. The cure for me is in the partaking of any new adventure. This is when I can find myself in search of a new beginning, much like a flower turns to water for life. When my waters become stagnant or dried up, my moods cripple. Dull, mundane broadcasts take over and rule in and out of my mind.

It had been another six weeks gone by. Now we were entering into November. I waited, to no avail, for the assignment that would bring me back to them. My writings were trudging up hills, going around in insignificant circles, banalities to me. I was losing interest, feeling dispirited. Writing only two or three unconfident pages a week, insipid words lashed back at me before the ink even dared to dry. I somehow felt lost; directionless.

I don't know why, but thus far, I had felt disinclined to contact Darin - to have him make good on his promise to me. I was certain he could have been doing more. Surely, there had been shipments coming and going from that region. Had he forgotten? I fully understand why people scratch walls. I was almost there, but I grabbed the phone instead.

"This is Lee on Darin's line."

Totally unfamiliar to me, my reaction was, "Who?"

"Lee, with the support team. With whom am I speaking?" I gave him my driver number.

Darin had been the director of dispatch on my board for as long as I could remember. Support team members are all of those who work under the director. They do much of the grunt work.

"Lee, is Darin available?"

"Darin has taken another position with the company," he replied. Whoa, now that was news!

"When and who's in charge now?" I nearly blurted.

"His name is Ken. No one told you?"

"No, but I'm thinking maybe they should have."

"You should have gotten a memo messaged to your qualcom," he explained.

"Well, I didn't."

"I can have you talk to Ken if you'd like."

"That'd be great, thanks."

It took a minute for Ken to retrieve my call. I wasn't sure what to expect, but this pretty much explained everything. I was taking back all the bad thoughts I had about Darin. A driver just has too much time to think. It's not always a good thing, nor what I do best.

When Ken came on the line, he seemed like a nice enough guy. I introduced myself, while politely asking if he had a few minutes to spare. He said it wasn't a problem, so I commenced to explain the previous arrangement that I had with Darin concerning the Katrina relief efforts. I told him, without elaborating about the details, of the book I was in the process of writing. I said the subject matter took place in the South, particularly Louisiana. I asked if I could buy him lunch sometime when I was in his area and further explain my project. He agreed, so I popped the question. Could he send me down that way as often as possible? Without hesitation, he said he'd be glad to. To best define the effect of what my newfound jubilation released on me that night, I wrote like some enchanted witch!

Journal entry: 11/7/06, 10:30 P.M.

*"I write on relentlessly now, as if trying to overpower some shadow that can never be captured."*

The book was moving again, dawdling words had ended. Round pegs were fitting into round holes, slipping through the other side and calling themselves yesterdays. I was conveying my thoughts to paper in some conveyor belt of time. Pages were telling it right. I hadn't even noticed that another two weeks had gone by. Journal entries came at all hours of the day and night.

I was out on the road, and it was nearing Thanksgiving when the dispatch came for me to pick up a load near Tyler, Texas. Don't even ask me where I was previously; it's a blur. I was to take this load to a drop lot in Reserve, Louisiana, a suburb of New Orleans. There I would pick up another relayed load waiting there and bound for Gary, Indiana, positioning me to make it home for the holiday. Ken was doing me right. I would have time for an overnight. I needed to make the call. Burton was the man.

"Hatty Swiggs to speak with Burton," I told his secretary. I wanted to see where that would go. He came on the line almost immediately.

"Well, if it isn't Hatty Swiggs?" he said with a laugh.

"Hey bud," I responded, then went on, excited to explain my travel plans. "Be in Reserve tomorrow, on the 20th around noon. Got time for an overnight, if it can be done?"

"Can you call back in a couple hours? I'll try and have an answer for ya."

So it was agreed, and I did, and so did he. Everything was set. My trip plan would allow me to rendezvous with Credence at noon. Jack would probably be the one taking me by water. Clay might be indisposed, I was told. Excitement building again; it always did, I called and told Kat. I noted for the first time that she seemed excited for me, with a special "say hello from me" instruction.

It was hard for me not to get riled up when it came to these highly anticipated visits; I shouldn't. I remember hooking up to an empty trailer at one of our customer locations. While pulling out, I wasn't paying enough attention, my mind was elsewhere and I scraped against another one of our trailers that had been parked alongside me. There was hardly any damage. It did, however, mean I would need to schedule myself for a "remedial" at one of our operating centers. This entails having to take an hour-long computer course on slow maneuvering, plus going out with an instructor for a short ride to see if it had been an isolated incident or a sign of acquired bad habits. This is a "must" company policy. All of which is time-consuming and of no monetary advantage to the driver. It was the price I had to pay for getting ahead of myself, or at least trying to.

None of that mattered to me now. I was on US 61, and as I passed the town of Gramery, crossing over the Blind River in St. James Parish, I knew I was right on schedule. Credence met me at the drop lot in Reserve. He most assuredly knows his way around. I hadn't seen him in a while, so our ride-time was spent catching up, me telling him about Kat, and all we'd been through. He was glad to hear things were working out so well. He had always assured me that they would.

Mad Jack was sitting on a deck chair at the dock smoking a cigar when we broke through into the grove of Clay's yard. After a hearty handshake greeting, Jack and Crede exchanged some small talk while I set my bag and guitar case in the boat.

"Where's Clay?" I asked, rejoining them up in the yard.

"Rough weekend," Jack said with a sigh. Credence laughed, which caused Jack to laugh with him. He turned to Crede, saying; "He danced so much swamp pop, Roxanne and Ramona are having to nurse him back." Then Jack gave Crede a light jab on his shoulder, as if to say, "you know what I mean."

"That's reassuring," Crede remarked, still smiling.

"I thought he was a professional?" I resounded. They both laughed again.

"Professional what?" Jack asked, adding, "He's an amateur all the way." Now we were all smiling on the same page.

"See you here tomorrow, around noon I understand," Credence said to me.

"That'd be great," I told him.

"Have a good time. Say hi to 'em for me," Crede told me, then turned and started walking to his Chrysler.

"Will do," I yelled to him. He was already yards away, and seemed in a hurry to keep going.

"Ready?" Jack asked. "I've got Eddie up there workin', so we best get on with it."

"What ya got goin' on this time?" I asked, as I stepped into the boat.

"Finishin' up that barbeque deal, you'll see."

The ride up was racy. I think he gets off on torque. Soon, very soon, we were entering the inlet, and there he was. "This is more like it," were Marcus' first words to me.

"Been longer than I would have liked," I responded, while setting foot on their shore. "How's it been goin', L?" I asked, firmly shaking his hand.

"Been fine, but need'n those magic fingers a yours." He put his right arm around my shoulders and gave me a hug, warming me instantly. Jack held the guitar case and handed my bag to me. We turned to walk. Their home quickly in sight, the activity appeared to be around the barbeque area, which I could hardly recognize. I did make out Jewel; how could I miss? She was working with a spade, putting in another one of Hershel's carved foot path circles. It looked like she had several more she intended to put down. It would be a new route, to what amounted to a small pavilion hovering near the barbecue. Eddie was inserting tiles on the pavilion roof. The dogs were jumping with recognition all around me now.

As things opened to my full view, I could see two half-circle picnic tables under the roof, near the outer edges. An intricately designed wooden table stood between them in the middle. There were no chairs yet, but the tables were situated on a bed of stones, a patio-type surface, with room between the cracks for the grass to grow. The entire setting was unique to me. A great deal had changed around that old rock cooker and its vine-wrapped chimney. Smoke now rising, I could smell food being prepared. All of this construction was a work in progress that I was sure Jewel continually would be adding her charm to. I pictured flowers and vines in my mind, capturing the whole setting under the splendor of her artist's touch.

Marcus pointed to Jewel as we approached, "She's the angel threads that keep it all going," he said. Out of reflex, I reached in my bag for the pocket recorder and turned it on. I could see in all of this, Marcus' last-ditch protracted efforts to keep her here. I wondered to myself, why was it that I understood more than he did, that it wasn't gonna work? She smiled up at me, as we walked up to her. She had been bent down on her knees, patting the dirt around the circle she had just settled in its place.

"Hello lady," I said lovingly.

"We missed you; how's Kat?" she asked, as she stood up, brushing the dirt from her hands. Those eyes were melting into mine.

"Good. She told me to say hello. She wants to see you guys as soon as we can find a way."

Jewel's smile ignited, adding to the sun's glimmering reflections. The brightness firing up moved amazing colors in those dazzling eyes of hers. I was caught again, absolutely spellbound. A butterfly was hovering around her as she stood there. I'm aware I just stand and stare during interludes like these.

Eddie had climbed down from the roof to greet me. He gave me a "Hey," when he walked up. He was never much for words.

"How's the band coming?" I asked him right off, shaking his hand.

"Playin' out every weekend," he answered proudly.

"You guys must be pretty good. Have ta hear ya sometime. Marcus says you call yourselves The Patty Melts."

"Naw, we changed it to The Farm Fresh Eggs." I couldn't help it; I laughed out loud. "But we're thinkin' a changin' it to Splash In The Pants," he quickly added. Marcus and I gave each other a confounded look. We both burst out laughing. Contagiously, Jewel and Jack immediately followed suit.

"Told ya he was a lot like me," Marcus said, slapping my shoulder with the back of his hand. We couldn't stop laughing. Eddie grinned, happy to have created such hilarity.

"Sounds like something Clay woulda come up with," Jewel remarked, adding to the levity. Man, it was great to be back!

## CHAPTER 2

In the midst of all this activity Jewel had prepared an overly generous helping of lunch for her troops. There was salad made with crabmeat and avocado, together with seafood jambalaya. Jack had furnished a cooler of beer, while Jewel and Marcus would simply sip their orange juice. We used a stack of folding chairs that had been resting against a tree, and we all sat down at the new tables.

"Years ago I woulda had a fireworks war over an occasion like this," Marcus revealed. I think he wanted to celebrate, but Jewel turned to a less festive subject while we ate. She talked about how the bayou was being lost, blaming greed and the oil companies. She and Mad Jack engaged in heavy conversation. They talked about some Coast 2050 plan. They were in agreement on how the navigational channels and pipelines had disrupted the course of water flow, increasing the land's disappearance. Jack was getting riled up. I tried to inject a little light into their darkened subject.

"Maybe they'll find a way to stop it, or maybe find profit from a different angle and save it that way," I said, admittedly a bit naive.

"Greed don't die easy," Marcus said, sighing deeply. "I'm tired of the pains I feel in others and the world," he added abstractly, then leaned back in his chair. He was, evidently, trying to turn them away from the topic.

It was during this chit-chat that I started paying more attention to Marcus' appearance, since Kat had told me what Jewel had said. It was true, he did appear drawn, tired. There were pronounced "worry wrinkles" on his brow and around his eyes that I hadn't noticed before. He always wore that hat I had given him, at least around me. Sometimes he would push it up as he talked, and this time I took careful notice. In addition, his color wasn't good, not like I'd remembered it to be.

With Hershel conspicuously missing, I saw an extra plate set aside. We finished our meal and Jack was ready to keep moving. I'm sure he knew that Marcus and I wanted time to ourselves. He instructed Eddie to square off and gather his things. They'd be back tomorrow, he told us.

"I'll leave the beer for Hatty," he said with a wrinkled, and dare I say, a crusty smile. Then he began picking up his tools.

"Awe, you don't have to Jack, well, maybe just a couple," I said.

After bringing their things down to the shed, Mad Jack left the cooler with what beer remained, and he and Eddie headed toward the inlet. I knew time would fly by. I appreciated Jack's thoughtfulness. We'd see them again in the morning.

Jewel put together a plate of food for Hershel and headed down to his cabin immediately after Jack and Eddie were out of sight. Marcus and I were still seated at the table.

"How's yer writing comin?" he asked.

"You mean songs? Nothing. The book, about the same. It's gonna take me years, or more like forever to write this thing." I was feeling addled, disenchanted.

"Why's that?" he asked.

"Maybe I haven't convinced myself that I'm a writer, and nothing I've written so far has really told me any differently. Although, in the past month or so, some things have sparked, I'll admit. But there are times I just wanna give up."

"If you want to stop being a gunfighter, you'd need to stop carrying your guns," he said to me. Sincerity livened up in his eyes. I just gazed at him, dumbfounded. What did that mean?

"Walk with me a bit," he then told me. Oh, oh, I immediately thought. We got up and started walking toward the inlet. The sound of Jack's boat motor faded in the distance.

"Are you putting demands on yourself again?" Marcus asked. "Because I'm not putting them on you, or at least I don't mean to. Time is really not an element here. This is merely a documentation you're drawing. You don't need to make it more than that." He was trying to explain, but it wasn't sinking in. We stood on the bank near where the boats land.

I took a deep breath, then I said, "I thought I had the steps figured out, how to tell it, but I keep backing up. Sometimes I don't even know where to go, or how to get there," I sighed sincerely. He said nothing. "Words are sometimes culled soon after I write them. Are you really sure you want me to do this?" He gave me a look from above his glasses that spoke volumes. I knew I'd never ask that question of him again.

"There's a method to my madness," he said, trying to explain. "What the new life becomes for us depends in part on the rectitude you're subscribing to with your writings."

"Well that's just great!" I blurted, misinterpreting what it was he was referring to. It didn't help our moment. I think I came off a bit sarcastic.

"As reality often deals in fiction, let fiction play its hand in reality if you must," he said. I gave him another puzzled look. What did he mean by that? Maybe I was missing all of his points. It wouldn't be the first time. I could tell he knew I didn't get it. An egret or tern walked through the water into our view. I stared at it for a time.

"Oh, I'll keep pluggin' away at it," I finally said to him in an inane fashion.

"Stay with me before the fire's gone, burning us in air," he quietly responded. "When they bury me to ashes, all the things of me, you will know." Now he was looking at me with sullen eyes. I didn't know how to respond. He put his hand on my shoulder again as he was turning, then he began walking toward the house.

"I found your birthplace," I told him, catching up to his stride. I guess I only brought that up because I hadn't understood any of the last things he had just said to me. "The neighborhood probably don't look the same now," I kidded.

"What neighborhood? As I recall, our place was about the only one around," he said, laughing. We stepped onto the porch. Jewel had not yet returned from the cabin. The sun was low in the tree leaves. We both knew what I had come to do. My guitar and bag were gripped in my hands.

"Does she need help cleaning up?" I asked, referring to what remained of our lunches under the pavilion.

"Dogs'll get that wrapped up, she'll see to it," he said, opening the door to the house and motioning for me to come inside. He lit a lantern on the table near the front door. "You know, word has actually leaked out over the years of me being alive, and even of me living down here somewhere. There have been breaches in our security; it tethered us for a time. It's all been rectified now. It would be difficult for anyone to approach this place anymore. We have far more security here than meets the eye, literally. I'll never be shot in the back like Jesse James."

He offered me no details, and I didn't ask that he expound on what he had just said. I believe he was trying to reassure me of something, but I wasn't sure what. After I threw my bag on the bed in my room, we went about our ritual of tuning up.

After a time, before we started playing, he leaned his guitar against the couch. "In the end, I need them to know what really happened to me," he said, almost manifestly. "You've got to pull this thing together."

"Yah, and what set of wings would you like me to fly on?" I briskly asked in an improved mood.

"Pledge faith," was his response. "Like I said, I don't care how long it takes, maybe the longer the better, even if it turns out to be labeled as fiction," he confided. "It's not obscurity I treasure so much anymore; it's fulfillment. Anyway, they're gonna wanna know how we pulled it off, the details. They're gonna wanna know who's buried there. That's the knot that's gonna be hard for me to untie." He picked up the guitar and started strumming an unfamiliar chord progression. I tried following along, but I wanted so much to interject, ask him who, who was buried there, or what?

Since we first met, I had run the entire gamut of possibilities through my mind, trying to solve that puzzle. There were any number of ways it could have been accomplished. I contemplated everything from a wax effigy of his likeness, all the way to the opposite extreme of blowfish poison, with a few other ideas in between. I had heard how blowfish poison could slow the pulse and heartbeat down to an indistinguishable rate, giving the appearance of someone deceased. Later, as it wore off, the body would revitalize. I chocked that idea up as too far-fetched. Who would go to that length? But how did they do it? I say "they" because there had to be others involved, paid off maybe. Could Jewel have worked some magic?

For those who were close to him and duped by the scheme, it was cruel. I surmised that it had to have been nearly unbearable for Marcus to go through with it. Then again, it would have been the only way he really could have gotten out. The only way he could have been allowed to live this life with Jewel for all these years was for the world to believe he had died. I figured he'd give me answers in due time, if he really wanted me to know. I decided to waste no more energy thinking about it.

He was going into a song he had written, called, *Can't Catch a Thing.* It had a funky sound. He even thumped his hand on the guitar in keeping with the beat as he played. Drawing a parallel to fishing, it transposed itself, to going after things one wants, as opposed to what one needs. Kind of like that Rolling Stones song. I immediately thought of Jerry Lee Lewis, and how he could really make this song "zing." It was as if it had been written just for Jerry Lee, and I told Marcus that. He just smiled.

"Call him up!" he then blurted out with a laugh.

Jewel came in the door. It had become dark outside. He looked over at her as she went about putting things away in the kitchen. She must have washed the dishes outside by the pavilion. I knew there was a hand water pump near the barbecue.

"I was always the proud stallion on the outside, but I had a lot of damaged edges before she came," he said while watching her. She turned and looked across the room to him, then smiled softly. He went on, "Misty sensual, shimmering haunting eyes — heaven sent. They meet mine in this deepest hush. It's the highest value, only sparkle represents. She has visions, you know?" All the while they were staring at each other while he spoke. Then he turned to me, smiling. A dimple, transfixed along a beam of moonlight that had slipped through the window shade, blazed from his cheek. Jewel came over then, carrying that good, old bottle of Thin Ice, along with three small cups.

"Oh no," I gently admonished. "I gotta drive tomorrow."

"I dreamt of you," she quietly replied, sitting down next to me. "We found each other in the dark," then she calmly filled the three cups.

"Okay, just one." I weakened.

We lifted and toasted a round, with Jewel saying, "We who dance together can never more dance alone." We downed the shots in cowpoke fashion.

Then Marcus told her, "This writer is looking to kill dead conversation, the unacceptable wreck within himself," referring to me. She smiled at him, then at me, without saying a word. I was pretty sure he was talking about the writer's block I'd been experiencing. To be honest, I can never quite be sure what he's talking about, but I've come to live with that. "I've found blessings are based on the attraction," he said to me, then he began playing another song.

I decided, at that moment, trying to take in that which he was attempting to give me was impossible. They were way ahead of me. This was a pilgrimage only lent to me. Maybe, with a little luck, these special qualities that emanate from them might somehow rub off on me. I could only go on with hope.

He was playing the song, *Sugar Cookie,* which we'd worked on a while back. He had changed it considerably. That's what I like about music, you can do that. We only had the one drink that evening, but true to form, we played dozens of songs. Jewel joined us — as raptures were required and were definitely fulfilled. Therein, comprised, no, composed, a very spiritual evening. As corny as that may sound, the heavens were glowing down on us, and we knew it. I remember thinking to myself at the time, who is this woman that took him away from the world? Everyone is gonna need to know.

Journal entry: 11/26/06, 2:30 A.M.

*"Difficult to describe, the place I now find myself. This perfected music we've almost toiled over. Sometimes we go over the same song 20 times, changing some little thing, in search of what it is he's trying to achieve. What is he trying to achieve? I know them all by heart now. Something in me yearns for new daylight."*

## CHAPTER 3

The next morning Marcus was in his usual stance; he was reading something by the author, O. Henry. Jewel was nowhere about, and it seemed Jack had not yet arrived. I walked over and stood near him. In a determined pose, I handed him my journal with the cover open.

"Do me a favor, throw your autograph on here for me wouldja?" I asked boldly, handing him a pen. He looked at me with a grin. Then, without demur, he commenced to sign his real name. I was shocked at first. It was what I was hoping for, but I didn't think he'd do it. For me, it was the tangible affirmation I felt I needed. It was his dedication to me, and from that moment forward, there would exist an undying dedication to him. We looked at each other, and understood. He never said a word.

I glanced, and saw Jewel through the back door. She was doing something on the porch. I turned and walked out to greet her, clutching my now priceless journal.

"Good morning," I said softly, opening the screen door.

"Well hello there," was her sweet smiling reply. She was dressed more plainly than I was accustomed to seeing. She was wearing a cream-colored dress, stained and smelling of fresh dirt. Her hands also were dirt-covered. She was laying out some freshly picked, I don't know what, on a table. Over her shoulder I saw Hershel, tending to his rock garden, just down from the outhouse, where I was about to go. I set the journal on a chair next to the table, hoping, I suppose, that she might give it a look.

"Back in a minute," I told her, as I limberly bounded from the porch steps. There was that morning mission to fulfill. I gave a short wave to Hershel as I stepped into the art house, it really was an art house. Over a period of time Jewel had completed a number of unrelated artistic endeavors throughout its interior walls. Some could be considered art deco, while others were just plain modern art. There were border designs around every edge, including the window and door frames. So much to look at, one could not do it in a single sitting. I'm sure it had been fashioned to be examined and appreciated during many sittings.

Hershel was engrossed in his project when I came out, so I let him be, returning to Jewel on the porch. She was sorting her plants one by one, laying them out to dry. There were a number of different kinds. I didn't ask her to explain them.

"Has Kat cured you of anything yet?" she asked, as she looked up at me with a grin.

"Haven't had any ailments," I told her. She just kept smiling, and so did I. She hadn't touched the journal, nor did she ask about it.

"It's nearly lunch time, so guess what I've got prepared for you?"

"Gator?" I quipped.

"Close, and almost as good. It's frog legs and eggplant, complements of Hershel." That stunned me nearly as much.

"Yumm," I said. She gave that little giggle as Marcus came out on the porch.

"Elbow'll be comin' soon; I suppose Eddie too," he said.

"No school?" I asked.

"He's done with that. Gonna be a big rock star," Marcus replied with a grin; no, more of a smirk.

I turned to Jewel, "Does Hershel know he's coming?" referring to Jack.

"Yah, they've pretty much been coming every day. When he hears the boat, he'll be gone."

"I'm gonna go say hi to him now then," I said, as I stepped from the porch and headed his way. He was subjugating his rocks in tiers, with oval designs around a small handmade pond. I wasn't sure how he planned to keep it filled with water, but I knew he would work that out. What a landscape artist, I thought to myself. There was his usual bigger-than-the-moon smile, and his face beamed when I walked up to him.

"Hey, buddy." I put my hand on his shoulder. "This is great," I pointed. He looked down at his project, then back up to me and nodded. His smile never subsided. "Will these be filled with flowers?" He nodded repeatedly. "Wow!" I exclaimed, and again I put my hand on his shoulder in a gesture of respect. I think he knew my meaning. "I gotta go soon, but next time we'll play some songs for ya," I told him. He nodded again. I took his hand and shook it. He seemed a little timid when he gave me a parting smile. "See you next time," I assured him, then I turned to rejoin the others on the porch. Marcus was sitting in the chair where I had set my journal. It was sitting on his lap.

"It's sorta like a diary, a journal my daughter gave me to keep track of things. It's helping me in my writing of the book. You can look at it, if you want," I told him.

"Oh no," he replied, handing it to me. "This should be your more private thoughts. I would like to read anything you've got so far in the book though."

"I'll bring something down next time. It's still rough around the edges, not really put together the way I'm hoping it will be."

"That's alright, I'll get an idea where yer goin'," he assured. "Maybe I can offer some destructive criticisms," he said, laughing. Jewel looked over at him, shaking her head.

There went the dogs when they heard the sound of a boat motor. Where had the time gone? We all looked at each other. Marcus stood up and stretched his arms out.

"Will we see ya anymore before the holidays?" he asked.

"Unlikely. I have a few extra days they owe me, but I'm sure I'll be spendin' 'em with the kids and grandkids. You guys still gotta meet them."

Jewel smiled. "Lunch is ready, I'll get it set up," she told us. They knew by now that I had a timetable to keep. There would, most assuredly, be an assignment waiting for me back in Beulah's cab. I still had at least a half a day of work ahead of me. Marcus went back inside. Jewel grabbed my elbow. "No matter how he tells it, he was my salvation as much as I was his," she said to me sincerely, then smiled and let me go. I smiled back, not saying a word, yet wondering what that story was about. I would choose another time to ask her more about it. I went inside to gather my things.

Marcus was standing in the music room, looking at some papers when I walked by. I went into the bedroom and picked up my stuff. When I came back out, I set my guitar case and bag on the floor near the coffee table. "I don't hold much stock in material things," I told him. "Everything I value would fit in a paper bag and a guitar case."

"I can see that in you," he replied. "I've been looking over my old songs, you know, from the other lifetime." He set the papers down on the table. "In Hawaii, I've heard they still light torches," he said with a smile. He had mentioned that to me once before.

"You'd be surprised by the music today. It's become diluted, hard to filter out the good, like panning for gold," I told him.

"Full-circle changes," he remarked. "Music, yah, it killed me, then rolled me into this new set of bones you see I'm living in now."

I laughed. I thought he was being funny. He was really trying to seriously explain.

"I get all the answers that I need to know now. I was leaning walls of insecure before, pitted on edges, like you seem to be with your writing actually," he said, sounding earnest. There was a knock on the door. It was Mad Jack. Marcus turned slightly to acknowledge him, and Jack came inside.

"No Eddie?" Marcus asked.

"I'll pick him up on the return trip. He was out late last night, him and that band of his," Jack growled.

"Jewel made a big lunch," Marcus told him.

"He can eat cold," Jack replied, matter-of-factly, regarding Eddie.

Jack always seemed that way, never really riled, just gruff. He was an easy-going, steady guy, once one got past that mean persona he tended to show everyone.

Over lunch, the conversation got interesting. I had inquired about how they kept up with the news of the world. They insisted there was no interest. Of the things important to them, Clay would keep them up to date.

"He told me John Cash had died," Marcus said.

"June too, and Carl Perkins and Waylon Jennings," I said. He knew that too.

"Jerry Lee's still kickin' hard as ever. He's got a new double release out called Last Man Standing, with a bunch of artists joining him; it's great!" Marcus smiled, as if from inner reflection. I pondered how this may well be the only news important to them. The world had come to a standstill in their lives. With this book, I wondered if they realized they would be grabbing hold of that merry-go-round once again. What effect would it have on Jewel and Marcus? Culture shock came to my mind.

Time had once again gone by. His parting words to me, as they often had been: "Stay alright." Jewel had given me another bag of health food treats.

## CHAPTER 4

Now the holidays had passed, sated gratefully for me in a mellow love. I know Christmas may be stressful to some, but it never seems to be with us. Everything slows down; it's time for hugs, eggnog, and gingerbread men from Grandma Kat's oven for the grandkids to decorate. I wondered to myself, as I may have done before, did Marcus and Jewel sing carols? I pictured how Marcus would do that. Kat had sent them a Christmas card. Jewel had written her a letter a week earlier, expressing her desire that we all get together again soon. I remember Kat looking at her hand where her henna tattoo had long since faded and disappeared. She was going over the photographs of our visit to their place. She asked me if it was just a fairytale dream, or if we had really been there. I got a kick out of that. It was too early to plan our next vacation, but it most assuredly would include them, our new best friends. We have our old best friends, like Rick and Mae, and that will never change, but Jewel and Marcus were our new ones.

I had taken extra time off, with plans to go back on the road on Wednesday, the 3rd. Now it was the morning after New Year's Day. I was standing, pajama clad, sipping my second cup of coffee. I will never forget that I was staring out the window, daydreaming over at our used, and all but forgotten, Christmas tree. It stood just outside the house, stabbed into a snow bank. Where strands of worn tinsel had danced — now they were snarled, instilled within and around the tree's needled branches. They trailed off directionless by tormented winds.

This morning was calm; almost weather-less. The sky was filled with pillow-soft clouds. I glanced over at Beulah; her electric extension cord lifeline was trailing off and then disappearing into our snow-covered front yard. It had been a normal winter so far. Then the phone rang.

"Can you answer the phone?" Kat called out to me from another room.

"Yah, I got it." Taking me by surprise, it was Marcus.

"Hatty, it's Marcus. I've got bad news."

"Ohh-kay," I cautiously replied.

"Hershel's gone. He's passed away."

"What?" I nearly shouted. It was a hairpin-trigger response. I put my hand on the back of a chair to steady myself. "No," I responded precipitately. "What are you saying?"

"We found him in the garden Saturday. We tried to revive him, but he was gone."

I sat down then. "How? How?" I managed to ask.

"We took him down to Clay's. His uncle and cousin took him to the morgue. We still don't know. We think his heart just gave out. Jewel's crushed. Burton's with us right now, and so is Clay. We wanted you guys to know."

"Can I call you back," was the only thing I managed to say.

"Sure, son. Call on Burton's cell phone. You got the number?"

"Yah, sure, let me call you back in a few minutes," I reiterated, ending the call.

I had practically folded in the chair, my legs turned to rubber binders. Head down now, elbows on my knees, hands clasped and suddenly moist, it started to sink in. I knew I didn't dare try to stand. I knew I couldn't. I could hear Kat walk into the room.

"What, what's the matter?" I was obvious to read.

"That was Marcus. Hershel died."

She said nothing, but quietly took the chair next to me. After a time I looked up at her, and our eyes met despairingly. My right hand now behind my neck — tears were drowning my eyes.

"What did he say?" she asked softly. I told her what Marcus had told me. We sat there quietly, staring blankly at nothing. "It wasn't a snakebite or anything?" Kat finally asked. I simply shrugged my shoulders, not having any answer.

"His heart was bigger than it had to be," I managed to mutter, then I started to cry out loud. Kat couldn't help it; she started crying too. We reached across to hug each other now, sobbing on one another's shoulders. The lack of our discourse had taken firm hold. I bawled like a baby. Moans unheard before poured from my heart. Tears streamed unmanaged from a depth of terrible loss. All meaning escaped me. I stood to stagger about the room. A numbness prevailed. I could find no focus, eyes blurred by tears.

"Are you okay?" came her soft, soothing voice. I couldn't answer. I was beyond consoling. A best friend had been taken from my life. I walked almost in circles. Kat has always been stronger than me. She understands the universe and its facets better than I do. She would come to grips and somehow help me do the same. For now, my tears went on and on.

I wondered about his last moment alone. Was he afraid? Was there any calm before he passed? Did he remember me? Was there ever a last smile? There would never be another. I feared my life would take a backseat to the sorrow I was drowning in.

After a time, I simply said, "I need to go down." Kat had no reply. I couldn't reconcile how, my mind jumbled, but I felt compelled to go.

"I can't go," Kat said. "We're in the middle of a huge case."

She works in a law office and I never ask what they deal with. It's not that it wouldn't be interesting to hear about sometimes, but I've never been inclined to do so. She doesn't volunteer information; "client attorney privilege," I guess. Anyway, my mind gets clogged up enough with my own dealings. As much as I've been able to, I've always tried to erase that which isn't simple. That is, until I met those guys, and the book. Now I had to face this.

In the weeks leading up to that tearful morning, I had found myself overly fastidious, touchy, and hard to please. I knew that it was due to my writing. It was always so easy to just write songs, tunes popping up in my head to go along with any old words. Now my words had to do more than just make simple sense. They had to deliver a story of fact, whether I fully agreed with what was being told or not. My inner self had been fighting against this all along. In my mind, the book was taking on the semblance of a lit stick of dynamite. I was running around with it in my hands as though it could unleash the secrets that might destroy their world. That evening I drank whiskey, which I hardly ever do, and, judging from my journal writing that night, Marcus's thought processes must have been having an effect on me.

Journal entry: Jan. 2nd/07, 9:30 P.M.

*"Drained to this stubborn work of clay, my day has been stirred muddy by broken rudders. Pilfered hours so wasted in rage. Do I hear the sour sounds of an unforgiving night?"*

Kat knew I had to go. We talked about it in bed when the lights were off. It was decided I would leave as soon as possible. I never did call Marcus back that day. I just couldn't manage to compose myself. Kat had wanted to speak with Jewel. The best she'd be able to arrange with her job would be to go in late tomorrow. I would call Marcus after I confirmed some time off with my company. Kat fell asleep in my arms, my head resting against her shoulder. I must have slept too.

There are never any doubts in a mind that has been set by a broken heart. The clearness of intent will not waver. I arranged an emergency leave from work by 7 a.m. that next morning, not having to return to duty until the 10th.

Tears having subsided, daybreak brought little in relieved comfort; grief would not shake off. I made a simple plan. With the choice of flying or driving, I chose the "rocket." After all, I am a driver. With the distance being some 1300 miles, the Camaro would get me there in two and a half days. Nibbling on a piece of dry toast and forcing it down with coffee, I made my mid-morning call. Burton answered.

"Hey Hatty."

"Hi Burton. Is Marcus around?"

"No, I'm in my office right now. What's up?"

"I wanna drive down. Can I catch a boat ride when I get there?"

"I'm sure you can. Got any timetable?"

"I'm gonna leave right after lunch today and plan to be at Clay's sometime before sunset on Friday," I assured him. "I'll need to leave for home again by Sunday afternoon."

"We can make that happen, and oh, they need you, ya know?"

"We need each other," I reflected aloud.

"Just so ya know, Jewel's beside herself. I've never seen her this way. Maybe you can help."

"I haven't really come to grips myself." I told him, with a recognizable sigh.

"I know. It's hit all of us hard. Call me back before you leave if you want. I'll radio Clay, but consider it set."

We ended the call knowing full well I would go there if I had to swim. That being just a catch phrase, since I still feared alligators. My determination was no less compelling. There would be no rest for me until I could be with them during this.

"I wish I could go, but I just can't. I want to," Kat explained.

"I know babe; they'll understand," I assured her.

"I wish there was something I could do," Kat added with such a resigned look, my heart broke even more.

"They know you're with them," was all I could say to comfort her.

I felt tears making a comeback. We held each other then; a lover's embrace intended to keep us from falling. That's what lovers do: transfer their strength to lift each other from weaknesses.

Kat and I managed to hide our sorrow long enough to smile, as we parted in the driveway. Our embrace had been one gone over hundreds of times before. We would do all of our catching up when I returned.

With her driving the Jeep, I followed her out to the road in the Camaro. We turned south and made our way to the first stop sign. She turned left, with the blow of a kiss reflecting from her side mirror. Gesture returned, I went straight ahead to the highway and started crying again.

## CHAPTER 5

Best described as a time warp, wrapped up in the music blaring from my radio, I made my way to Louisiana as fast as I could. Pulling off the road for catnaps at rest stops when needed, the only night I spent in a motel was Thursday. I needed to shower and freshen up, and perhaps get some decent sleep before I got there. In one of our cell phone conversations, Kat told me Jewel had called her.

"She doesn't sound good. I could hardly get her to say anything," Kat said.

I arrived in Clay's grove shortly after 3 on Friday afternoon. He must have heard me pull in. No sooner had I gotten out to stretch, I had a strong arm around my shoulder.

"Hey bro, how's it goin'?" I reacted, although I knew the answer to that.

"Ca va mal," he replied. I didn't know what that meant, but from his expression, I could gather the gloom.

"What was that?" I asked.

"Ici on parle francais," he smiled, although unenthusiastically.

"Ohh kayy," I told him. I knew he was saying something about French.

"Allons ta da boot," he said, motioning toward the canal. "Iz goood ta see ya ageen mon ami," he said as we walked. My tape recorder was already working overtime.

"How are they? How's Jewel?" I asked, as we neared the water.

"Che're 'tite bete," he said, although he knew by now I didn't understand. "I cane elp beaucoup, ah tink cuz you bean ear, she ge t'rough. We ge t'rough t'gedder." He turned to me with a languid expression. I gave him a long caring look. He appeared bedraggled, worn out. I threw my bag in the boat, put my hand on his shoulder, and gave him my bravest smile. He returned what he could of one back to me.

"Ya ne'da shrimp wit me, is da joie de vivre," he said, just before he started up the motor.

Although I didn't understand, I replied consolingly, "I know." It was the only words shared between us during that brief excursion, of what I had come to realize was upstream. The ride was somber.

Hersh would have been 48. Why was he called? I wondered to the gray sky as we made our way. Even the darkening water seemed portentous. Waves lapped at the bow, exasperated. At last, Clay cut the motor and poled for the inlet. No one was there to greet us as our boat silently glided in. The sky was growing dark. I could see no moon. I heard no dogs.

"They know I'm coming, don't they?" I half whispered.

"Oui oui, dey do, dey're bot tared ta mort," he replied. I shrugged my shoulders; he nodded an affirming "yes" to my question.

When their home came into view, it all looked dim, the air lonely. Turned-down lantern lights could be seen in their windows. The dogs started making their fuss now. By the time they recognized me, Marcus had opened the door and was standing on the porch above us. Even in the deepening darkness, from the faint glow of the kitchen window's light, I made out his smile.

"No guitar?" I heard him say, breaking the night air. I shrugged and shook my head. "The music never stops," he pined. We climbed the steps, gathering more light. He put a warm hand on my shoulder. "You know that, don't you?" he asked. I just smiled, but I again wanted to cry. "Supper's on," he said, then he led us inside.

Jewel was seated at the table, not really doing anything. She looked up at me right away. There was a destitute aura about her. She seemed a tarnished jewel then, her heart wrung out. When our eyes met, I gazed into hers as deeply as I could. They had always been so filled with exciting nuances before, a myriad of delicate and graduating colors. Now they were sorrow soft, swelled, sagged and half-closed. They were retreating as they looked into mine, saline washed from unabated tears. Now a fogged-over light green, gold burned away, their dazzle had disappeared.

"I needed this many years to cry," were her first words to me. Her voice was broken, rattled, and almost apologetic. Clay sat lethargically next to her. She appeared totally inconsolable. The atmosphere was hung rueful, heavy with weariness.

Marcus then told me that the funeral had taken place a day earlier, and that they had buried him near his mother. It had turned out to be heart failure, a heart attack. Standing at the end of the table in the light, Marcus' face appeared gaunt, complexion sallow.

"Grief will subside and lay a comforting blanket over despair," he then said, looking at me. Then he looked down at Jewel.

"Any world that breaks apart will fall together again," I heard myself reply. I was trying to quote a Steely Dan song, as best I could remember. Racing head-on to make sense, these things have a way of just coming out of me. Jewel looked up, and to my relief, although for but a brief instant, she gave to me one of those delicate smiles. Desperately now, I yearned for ablution from this downward spiral.

"Are you hungry?" Jewel asked in a weak voice, looking at me, then at Clay.

"I could eat," I said.

Clay gave a hint of his old self, "Oui," he said, as his face showed signs of his light.

"It's just alligator balls," Jewel said nonchalantly.

I must have immediately looked dumbfounded, as everyone started laughing. Jewel and Marcus caught each other's glances. There was a grateful glimmer showing in their eyes in that instant. Maybe it was the first time they'd taken a deep breath in days.

"Alligator balls, is that anything like other balls?" I confoundedly asked, although partly in jest. We all laughed together.

"Actually, it's just crawfish etouffee and crackers, but almost as good," Jewel said. It turned out to be a delicious soup. There was garlic bread and coleslaw to top it off. The moment of levity was short lived, not carried over at the dinner table. It would be accurate to say that Jewel and Marcus just seemed to pick at their food in slow half-filled spoonfuls. Clay never had a problem with any pabulum. He downed two large bowls. Actually "ate" or "devoured" wouldn't be an accurate description. "Gobble" may best describe how his eating habits go, or "inhaled." Lassitude held its grip. No one was saying anything, deep in mournful thought.

"It's times like this that make me realize the fragility of life," I said quietly, trying to impose against the silence.

"I'm sorry," Jewel said. "I don't mean to be so inward. It's just that I've had this ringing in my ears, sounds of explosions where I never meant to fall."

"Sounds of thunder when you're growing old," Marcus said to her with a smile.

I was thinking to myself, how close a pair they really were. They think, talk, and pretty much breathe a shared space. Always set apart from everything around them, it seemed too deep for anyone else to ever comprehend. It was at that moment I realized the depth of which I adored them.

"Hell answers to the wicked," Jewel said out of nowhere. "Thank God, he never has to listen to that." There was distance in her voice.

I knew then that her swollen eyes had been just as much an angry cry. It was just the way she expressed herself. She was grieving, yes, but almost seemed mad at herself. I tried to clear things in my own stumbling way.

"It's a long way between what we hope for and what is to be," I said.

"What man scribbles in darkness, the devil reads clear," Marcus said. "And Hersh was never a scribbler."

Clay remained quiet throughout the meal and the conversing. I'm not at all sure he was grasping what was being said. This somewhat morbid conversation was getting hard for me to take. I excused myself for a moment, telling them I had something they needed to see. I went back to the bedroom and retrieved from my bag a rough draft manuscript of what I had written thus far in the book. I had promised Marcus earlier that I would let him see where it was headed, so here it was. Deep inside, a part of me was hoping he'd read it and then say it wasn't what he had in mind. Maybe he'd relieve me of this duty, scrap the idea, and stay dead. Most of me realized that was not gonna happen. I reached across the table and handed the roughly bound pages to him.

"Are you gonna make me as famous as Mark Twain?" I scoffed, off the cuff and with a sinister grin. I sat back down. He only smiled at me. I winked across at Jewel. She winked back. It tingled.

"Is it the past, future, or how it is right now?" Marcus asked me, as he brushed through the pages with his thumb.

"I suspect it'll be a bit of all three," I replied. "Read it when you want. It's just a rough first draft, only gotten started. You can let me know what you think next time I come back." He agreed and set it down beside his bowl. He patted the top page with his hand.

"Unrehearsed depth, demanding art to be unconcealed," he said amusingly, almost talking to himself. I shrugged my shoulders and turned my head to the side, raising my eyelids as if to say I didn't know, but hoped he was right. We had finished dinner now, even Clay.

"Well, it isn't the past or future, but it is right now," Marcus then said, standing up from the table. "There are sparks in our play. And when I'm hot, I stick to fire. Lightning can't even catch me. Ready to make music?" he asked, looking intently at me. He was the only one showing any enthusiasm.

"Sure," I replied. "I guess."

Clay, more or less, excused himself. He said he had to get going, telling us he'd be back on Sunday to pick me up. Jewel quietly rose and went about clearing the table. She was moving in a sluggish, slow motion sort of way, unanimated as I had never seen her. Marcus and I went to the music room. I hadn't brought my guitar. I thought it might be inappropriate for some reason. I preferred his old Martin, anyway.

After the usual tuning session, accompanied by the hodge-podge of mixed strumming, we settled in. I remember thinking how I wished Clay had stayed a while longer. I would've liked to have played *1952 Vincent Black Lightning* for that motorcycle madman. Maybe it would have livened him up.

As it was, this session would show little semblance to any previous. The passing of Hershel weighed hearts heavy. The air was overhung from a disconsolate impediment. What I'm trying to say is, the power of sorrow held strong its grip over our whole evening. It was seeped in dread.

Jewel never came over to join us. Instead she chose to retire to her room. We were all drawn out, tired, but Marcus tried to make a go of it. We worked on two songs, *Broken Down Memories,* and *My Last Addiction*. Unable to sway in our usual, creative way, it became a real struggle. Realizing we'd reached an impasse, and needing to wrestle this gloom away, we relinquished the night.

Tomorrow would bring a new beginning light — fresh breezes to shake this stark dust from our bones.

Journal entry: 1/5/07.
*"I so need to turn this into just growing pains, and maybe even some promises from a friend called 'hope'."*

## CHAPTER 6

The day broke quietly, not a sound heard anywhere. The sky shone gray through that crack in the curtains. I expected Marcus to be sitting in his usual pose, reading from some prolific author. He was nowhere to be found. I had to get to my morning routine.

As I approached the "art house," I focused on the short distance down the hill to a small wooden cross that had been erected amidst the rocks that formed around Hershel's garden. It must have been where they found him, I thought, then I opened the outhouse door. I later found out that it was Eddie who had found him, lying amongst those tiers of rocks.

When I came back out, I walked immediately to the cross. It was plainly built, just two simple pieces of wood. There was an inscription burned into it: "Playing your heart with love, peace came sooner than the music you had left to give." I stood over that spot for the longest time, and for the first time since I'd been at their place, I felt a cold wind.

I turned back toward the house, expecting at any time to see one or both of them. I stopped at the bottom of the porch. Could they still be sleeping? A few steps back, I looked to my left. The pavilion appeared to have been completed, but it stood silent, no one there. If they were still in bed, fine, I wouldn't disturb them. There was one place left that I knew of to look, and I needed a walk. I made my way down past the cabin and meandered on the path to the right, on to Kat's Island and "the place with no name."

Reaching the clearing, seated there beneath their willow, her head swayed slightly upon his shoulder. I stopped. They were looking out at the water with their backs to me. The glow over them, radiant — a subtle, yet ardent love.

"It's the chance for our moment, you and I," I heard her say to him.

Quietly watching, I suddenly became over-run, fraught in vicissitudes of new emotions. What was happening here? What on earth was I doing? How would they ever be able to stave off the inestimable consequences my book would cause if it were ever published and believed? It would destroy this Eden that had been created just for them. At that point I became burdened by the thought that I may be his own personal Judas. The only thing missing was the 30 pieces of silver. I scolded myself in my poor mind. Now there was a lowly feeling in my blood, tearing my heart where my soul cried, as if it were wrapped in barbed wire.

I must have made a sound. Jewel turned to look at me. Maybe she knew I was there all along. She gave me a warm smile, turning back again to rest her head in their natural repose. Hands in my pockets, I walked over to the right and in front of Marcus. He smiled up at me.

"Were ya gonna let me sleep all day?" I asked with a smile, trying to shake off those previous thoughts. Jewel winked at me; her eyes were swollen and red.

"Looks like it's gonna rain; good day to sleep," Marcus replied.

"Yah but there's notes out there waitin' to be captured," I said.

"Yer right. Did ya bring a net?" he responded.

"I did!" I replied, trying to spark excitement. Jewel lifted her head from his shoulder. They looked at one another and smiled.

"There could be music in this day," he softly said to her. She nodded, melting again onto his shoulder. "There's more I want you to hear," he said, turning to look at me. Trees were singing in the wind just then.

"Can you hear that?" I asked.

"They're begging in prayers for the gospel sounds to come along," Marcus replied. Even though I hadn't brought my recorder, I remembered his words. Trying, even to this day, to decipher their full meaning, I simply found them to have been beautifully spoken at the time.

After this brief reclusive moment, we began making our way back to the house. We talked about the cross as we walked along the path. It turned out Jack had built it. I found that to be ironic, since Hershel was always so afraid of him. The inscription was burned onto the wood by Jack's hand also, with Jewel's guidance in the words that were chosen. I remember telling them how Hershel's dream would forever smile. I sensed that ease had been restored. It was the making of a new day.

Once back in the house, Jewel made her way about the kitchen. Marcus and I, once again, settled into the music room. I could hear rain beginning to fall upon the roof. As my table recorder whirled, we played songs we had worked on earlier. Under Marcus' direction, we repeated songs that I believed had previously been satisfactorily recorded. It was becoming redundant. Unless his intentions were for me to memorize these songs so well I could sing them in my sleep, it seemed superfluous to me. I already sang them in my sleep.

Jewel came to join us, carrying a heaping bowl of shrimp, and two different dipping sauces. It would be shrimp cocktail to hold us until supper. As we dipped and munched, Hershel's funeral came up in conversation. They wished I could have been there, knowing how much he meant to me.

In actuality, I hate funerals, and I try to get out of going to them whenever I can. I didn't tell them that, but instead told them how I would want mine to be. I explained how, in the word funeral, the first three letters spell "fun." I wanted mine to be a "FUN-eral," with munchies, and songs of my own choosing being played. Instead of flowers around my coffee can, I told them, I wanted guitars. Let a minister say a few words, but for the most part, I needed it to be a pleasant experience for all those attending.

"In fact, the first 100 people through the door will get a free Hatty bobblehead," I told them. Now I really had them laughing, just like the good old times. I went on to tell them another far-fetched idea. I would have my ashes pressed into clay pigeons and have all my friends take potshots at them.

"Oh that Hatty, he was a real so-and-so. Pull! Bam!" I said.

Marcus piped in, "Oh that Hatty, promised he'd write a book for me. Pull! Bam!"

He and I were having too good of a time with this. Jewel shook her head, giving us the look of a mother having just caught two 10-year-olds trying to out flatuate each other.

I calmed things down a bit. "The full culmination of my life's wishes would be to have Jackson Browne show up. If he would play piano and sing, *For a Dancer*, that would be my life completed." Marcus wasn't familiar with the song, but assured me that he would do everything he could to make that happen.

"If I go first, I need you to do something for me," he then said, and therein, he began playing a familiar trilogy number. In it were the songs, *Dixie* and *Glory Halleluiah.*

"Could you learn and play that at mine?" he asked me sincerely after he had finished singing. I assured him that I would.

"There's one more," he added. Then he explained it to be a song that Frank Sinatra had made famous years earlier, called *My Way*. I agreed to learn it, so he decided to teach it to me right then and there. I'm glad he did, because the way he wanted it done, chording and melody, were selectively varied. It was not exactly as I had heard it performed before. It was enjoyable to learn, but we discovered that I couldn't hit the high notes on the last few words. We opted for a soft finale.

With all of this, including going back over some of his songs again, the afternoon had flown by. Jewel had long since departed our musical workshop. With the warm comfort of their wood stove, she'd been cooking up another lavish dish in the kitchen. The rain was subsiding. Our dinner would be chicken gumbo, butter bean roux with white rice, and tea cakes. It would be impossible for me to describe those delectable tastes.

Hours that had previously seemed iced over were now thawed; we were warm together again. Smiles were abundant, and the air clearer, as we talked further about the music.

"Can a song ever be about nothing?" I heard myself asking on the tape.

"My spirit can't handle limp words," Marcus had replied. "In my songs, I borrow the heart out of love."

"Some songs seem to be about nothing; the artist somehow lost from himself," I told him.

"It would confound me and expire my soul to write that way," he replied. "When I write, words are the seeds lured by my spirit." It seemed we were exploring deep theology with regard to making music.

After we finished dinner, it would be more of his songs we'd play. My fingertips, long past the tingling stage, had turned to real pain. I went on for the sake of delicate moments. I realized we may not pass this way again. Each new experience seemed to be gaining more value to me. This day had given us constructive healing — its teachings, immeasurable. I gratefully took it all in, my life becoming further enriched.

On this visit to be sure, some of my moments with Marcus and Jewel had proved daunting. There were times that were near colorless, adding listlessness to our days. It was during those moments that I had felt racked in torment — meat being hammered by a butcher. I felt like a brittle sheath, attempting to wrap and hold a corroded blade. Anything and everything tore at me, grinding at my very nerve endings, infecting the blood in my pulse.

Overall though, time distills, and my memory will ever glisten to its finer warmth. There had been a true healing brought unto us. We helped each other take new breaths. We made each other smile to get stronger.

I recall walking to Clay's boat after lunch on our final day together; the four of us, brothers and sister. I remember the words Marcus said to me just before I departed. I play it back on my recorder, over and over again, trying to comprehend.

"You know the mind tends to wash clean that which we have soiled, or that which may have soiled us. In that, this escapade called time heals everything. There's always emphasis on what brightens our lives. The conscience battles any corruption of our souls, keeps us from diluting our true reasons."

# PART VIII

## CHAPTER 1

So many things he has said, I've been left to ponder. While researching the development of this book, I came across something one of my tapes had captured. I can't recall the instance, time, or even the place. Although I'm adequately certain, it occurred in "the place with no name." A few of the tapes got scrambled. By this, I mean I neglected to label them with date, time, and location. I taught myself as I went along how to better organize my writing processes to best secure accuracy for the sake of this story.

Our conversations together, as often as not, drew profound and exhilarating explorations, call it insights, about life and living. Sometimes we'd talk about where we were in the universe, in time and space. He had studied existentialism and a number of religions. He modestly admitted it was hard to speak of things anew, that it had all been said before. Yet I firmly believe his poetic interpretations could not have come from any other soul. His affinity to kindred spirits of the past, he would say, were purely on a molecular level. I think it's a touch more than that.

I'm getting cosmically carried away here now, and for this, I apologize. But it has something to do with this space he has brought me to. I'll try again, for our sake, to get my feet back on the ground. But for now, I feel obliged to include this quote from Marcus: "Time burns us so eloquently, we can't help but run in its flames. Our lives are bought and sold by the reasons we seek to douse it. Right up to our last days, we're made to believe some gentle force will extinguish that which dares to consume what we have left." Like I said, I am left to ponder.

As mild as the weather seemed to have been that winter, it lay taxing on my mind, how time was dragging me along. Marcus had long since lit the wick to the flame in my life that begged for more air. It was turning late February now. Kat had received a letter from Jewel. It wasn't the usual full-of-sparks correspondence. In fact, it appeared flavorless. All it indicated was that they were getting on with things. I interpreted her words to mean that the aching in their hearts had somewhat subsided. She spoke in generalities, no specifics. It burned at my desire to get back to them.

An assignment came across that would finally route me to within range of a possible meeting with Ken, my dispatcher. I had been eager to introduce myself and present this situation to him. I viewed it as one step closer to getting back in the swing of things with Jewel and Marcus. I was holding onto high expectations.

With a phone call, it was arranged. I would buy lunch and introduce him to my book. I wanted to impress upon Ken my needs regarding Louisiana and explain why it was so important. I was willing to tell him as much as I had to in order to enlist his help. He chose Applebee's for our meeting place. "I'll be the guy with long hair, goatee, and wearing a beret," I told him.

We met in the entrance. He walked straight up to me, introducing himself in a polite, professional manner. He was a young man, maybe half my age. He was quite tall, slim, and with short, cropped black hair. He was dressed semi casual. We probably looked like the odd couple as the hostess led us to a table.

Our conversation began with small talk while we were looking over our menus. Talk consisted of "getting to know you" questions like where we live, if we're married, and our families. Things seemed to be acclimating nicely.

"So tell me about this book," he inevitably inquired. He had told me earlier that he would be honored to be included as a character in my novel.

Maybe I blindsided him by getting straight to the gist of things, I pulled no punches. I told him about the hurricane, and how, by a twist of fate, I had met someone famous — someone who the world presumes has long been deceased. I told how subsequently we had become good friends, and that my intentions were to write the story about him. I must have been bursting at the seams to reveal things, and I pretty much blurted out who Marcus really was.

The inevitable disclosure had turned his expression to what can best be described as cock-eyed. He abruptly set his fork down in his salad, leaned back, and pushed his chair slightly away from the table. He gave me a look that made me think he wished he wasn't there. Positioning himself back at the table, he picked up his glass of tea and took a short drink. All the while he said nothing. A minute turned into forever. He looked at me sternly, eyes intensely studying my face, then he squirmed about in his chair. He didn't appear comfortable anymore. The least he could have done was laugh; maybe take it as a joke, but it didn't hit him that way. I tried to further explain how Marcus had met Jewel, and what led him to be down in the bayou, but I could see Ken was no longer listening.

"He's dead, Grant," he finally said, beaming into my eyes with a disbelief, like I was laying some kind of big sham on him.

"That's what he wanted the world to believe," I replied. "It was the only way he could have done this!" I declared resoundingly, with a truth that pled to be brought forth into the light. It even sounded to have echoed in the restaurant.

"Grant, he's dead," he reiterated emphatically.

"But Ken, he's really not. I see him all the time, we play music together." I went on to try and explain, now with a touch more fervor.

"He's dead!" Ken retorted, interrupting so vehemently, it gained other's attention and set me back ajar. I looked into his eyes with stunned disbelief at this ineradicable position. We were no longer anywhere near common ground. Different worlds had hence collided, and it shook me up.

There was no other choice but to swiftly, and as gracefully as I could, accept his interpretation, and try to settle this matter down. Using what psychology I could muster up from my college days, I merely simplified the topic.

"Well, I'm writing a novel, and at least I can say I did that in my lifetime," I conceded disparagingly.

There was no resignation in his stance, though he did go back to eating his lunch. And from then on, his looks at me were sardonic, disdainful, with no sign of acceptance. How can I best describe it? It turned out to be one of the most acrimonious, harsh and biting, moments of my life. It stung like I had been doused in acid.

The rest of our time together offered little comfort. I was careful in the few things I tried to talk about, but they turned piffle, met by his aversive wall. He acted disagreeable and delicate to a fault. Every interaction between us made us more squeamish. In short, the meeting was an utter fiasco. Afterward, it led me to wonder if I had walked away with anything. I was drenched in fatigue, soaked with sour sweat.

I knew that nothing within me had been extinguished, I would remain resolute. I couldn't let this encounter lower my spirit in any way. I would not lose heart. The image of completing the book had become utterly attainable to me. Knowing what I had come to know had impacted so much the person I was growing to be. Still, it gave me sordid thoughts as to how the book might be perceived. What would the world gather from this notion of him having been out there somewhere all this time and now making a comeback? I began to consider the word "fiction" more earnestly. Otherwise, could my work really be afforded the wounds of such discrediting? Ken had actually been a valuable lesson.

## CHAPTER 2

Trying, I admit unsuccessfully, to convince myself that I may have needed this time away from them, the month of March was creeping along. I was going over what work had been done thus far in my writings, considering its credibility. Their story was as much about Jewel as it was about Marcus. Having not yet ascertained how Jewel might want all of this depicted, I recalled her once telling Marcus - how she wanted nothing more than his most tender wishes. At that, I saw her kiss the palm of his hand. "Thy will be done," I finally told myself, so on my writing would go. Nothing flows like a gypsy, and that, I happen to be.

Tuesday, March 27, I had just delivered in Dallas. To my amazement, an order came through to New Orleans. The timing would be tight, but it looked like I could assume a quick overnight with them. I'd take whatever I could get. I had to wonder if this assignment was a fluke, or if Ken was having any kind of change of heart. There was no way of knowing. I made a call to Burton and set the wheels in motion.

My jubilation was short-lived. On I-635 headed to I-45, my trailer tires on the passenger side locked up and my rig went into a skid. I must have laid rubber for a quarter mile before I could find a safe place to pull over. With traffic barreling in on me from all sides, I had to settle for a thin strip of shoulder nearing an exit ramp. Having then put out my emergency triangles, I made a call to company maintenance. They would arrange to have someone sent out as soon as possible. That "soon as possible" turned out to be nearly three hours. My positioning amongst traffic was precarious. For a time, I sat out in the ditch, fearing some cannonball would rear-end my rig. The air was cold. I had to wait out some of the time in my cab, my nerves on edge. When help finally arrived, he determined that a brake valve had failed, and in addition, he would need to replace both tires. This immediately caused grave concern about my best-laid plan. I put in another call to Burton.

"He's in a meeting, can I take a message?"

"Could I have his voicemail please?"

After listening to his prerecording, I left these words: "Burton, Hatty here, disregard last communiqué. I had an equipment breakdown. I've pretty much lost my window of opportunity on this one. I'll call back when my luck changes."

That was all I could really say. Disappointment was setting in as I watched from my side mirror, this intrepid repair man working in traffic. When might be the next time I would get the chance again?

Our last time together had been one of sore, opaque, darkened days. We had become so fragile. I had witnessed their frayed world seem like a frightened fawn, cornered. I had no answers, no comfort or cure. Their illustrious glow had melted away. I remember having prayed for light to return to their faces. I yearned to get back to where one can never fully return.

Spring was fast approaching. Believing in all that gives and takes, I was writing relentlessly now. Many nights I lay robbed of sleep. Even during my time at home my focus was on writing, much to Kat's dismay. There was a battle shaping up in my "out of shape" plans. Did I care what was depicted as fact or what would be interpreted as fiction? I had to quit trying to find a reader's separation of the two. It had to cease to matter so much to me. With every spark in my spirit's flame, I just wrote what I knew. Forget about the torpedoes and full speed ahead.

Letters between Kat and Jewel were infrequent, existing of wishes to get back together soon and the like. The song they had been writing together through the mail may have gotten lost in abandonment. In one letter, Jewel vaguely hinted of another location, something about finding a mountain. She offered no elaboration, but it sounded as though they were busying themselves somehow. Contacting them by phone had proved fruitless. I left messages with Clay and Burton to have Marcus give me a ring sometime. Nothing panned out.

April was burning by, and soon I would need to make my yearly vacation requests with the company. While speaking with Sharon, my driver services representative, about an unrelated matter, a thought came to me. My regard for Sharon is with the highest esteem. She's a one-of-a-kind angel who has helped me with all the incessant problems that arise for a driver. Her untiring dedication cannot be outdone. I decided to lay it all on the line, to tell her about the book, yet without detailing my subject matter. After hearing what I had to say, she sounded excited. It was time for me to ask a favor. Would she have any influence on Ken? I needed to get back down there. I asked that she talk to him, to see if he could send me any assignment that would get me back to them. I wasn't asking for any opinion change from him, only help. She assured me she'd see what she could do, but could offer no promises. I would try to give her time to work her magic. Time elapsed.

I have my ""I will" and "I won't" days. Although hesitant, I briefly conceded aloud my project a work of pure, mitigated fiction when I contacted Ken once again. I was at the point where I would stoop to beg. Sounding still irritated, he reluctantly said he would see what he could do. For me to have committed myself to him at that point, it surely crossed my mind that my insanity now prevailed. Then again, I had learned a few things about miracles, and if Marcus didn't mind how the book would be thought of or labeled, I shouldn't either.

"I needn't worry about such matters. Time has a way of working out the truths," he once told me. "It won't be written like that which has ever been written before; that's what'll make it shine." So I wrote on, seeking out the better me, to be more. This work would continue to be *my truth*.

The month of May was at hand, and putting off my vacation request, I was languishing over every assignment given to me. Just as I was certain that Ken's position would not change, it appeared to be premature. With a 70-hour restart in my favor, I was assigned to deliver a load to a company called Georgia Pacific in Zachary, Louisiana, just outside of Baton Rouge. Delivery was set for Wednesday, May 11. I could be in the area by mid-day Monday if I hustled. This was gonna work. "Oh Sharon, you veritable angel," I said to myself aloud. "I owe you one big hug."

I made the "must" call, and Burton made the "must" arrangements, to be finalized when I got closer. Planting old Beulah at a truck stop near Laplace, in St. John's Parish, my visit was then solidified. Holding my pace at an even keel, with no more scratching trailers by trying to get ahead of myself, I got there by noon on Monday.

While waiting for my rendezvous with Credence, it occurred to me, in an eerie congested thought, how perhaps I had matured. I was taking things more in stride now, with the premise of "what will be will be," or as Clay would put it, "Que sera sera." I wasn't getting myself all worked up about things as much anymore. With Jewel's insistent help, I had lost some weight, and maybe my blood pressure was more in check. Never having been that easy-going, always finding things to be half empty rather than half full, a light went on in my brain: I had changed. For the first time in a long time, something, that thought, actually cheered me up.

When I spotted the Chrysler pull in, I pulled the curtains closed around the inside of Beulah's windshield. This time, I would bring the Gibson along with my overnight bag. I was looking forward to a restored musical experience.

"Hey, old-timer," I called out, as I walked up to his open driver's side window.

"Who you callin' old?" was his response.

"Me," I said. "I always talk to myself." He laughed aloud. It was good to see him again, although old Crede appeared to have aged some. "Still got this town in the palm of yer hand?" I had to add.

"Ever known me when I didn't?" he grinned. I had to shake my head "no." "I hear they're excited to see ya. A lot of things have been shaping up."

"Good things, I hope?" I said, more in the form of a question.

"I'd bet yah, but I'll let them fill you in," he replied.

Nothing was mentioned about Hershel's passing during our ride. I chose not to bring it up. I so needed this visit to move on. Somehow, I thought Hershel would have felt the same way about it. Again, we conversed disgustingly about this poor city, how restoration was near a snail's pace.

"If this were Washington everything woulda been spiff by now," he said. I had to agree with him. "So many people not gonna come back here, got nothin' to come back to," he added bitterly. He was so right. Too much had been taken away, and for those people, there has shown no glimmer - no offer of hope. Very few tangible uplifting reasons could be seen on those sad streets, appearing sacrificed and forever devastated. Barren death had painted its drab brush strokes on this landscape, on these neighborhoods of once-flourishing families. Imagining how much had actually been lost was almost incomprehensible. Even unto the country sides, the scenery will remain shaken throughout our lifetimes and beyond. I thanked heaven that my mind had a far better place to go.

So familiar to me now, almost like coming home, we wheeled into Clay's grove. Fresh tapes and new batteries for the recorders were the order of the day during each of my visits. I always made sure they were in place by the time I reached this point.

"Where's our boy?" Crede said aloud, as we stepped from the car and stretched a bit.

"Out gallivanting, no doubt," I replied.

The sky was clear. All was quiet, if one can call Mother Nature quiet. Sounds of breezes through the trees, mixed with insects and bird music, filled the air. As I gazed at Clay's home, again I realized how I had never been given an invitation to go inside. My imagination began to go to work again. Confessing to be tilted by a little humor, I concluded, maybe he had thought it best not to disturb the indigenous roosting of those chickens on his kitchen table.

"Well, I can't leave you alone in this unstable environment." Crede interrupted my thought with a grin. I had come to understand Credence wasn't much of an outdoorsy type. "We can wait in my car," he then added.

I could hear the faint sound of a motor coming from down-stream. It grew louder quickly. I smiled at Crede and walked over to the water's edge, casting my eyes in that direction. It was Clay, all right, big smile, and that rough carefree style. He gave a wide wave with his arm raised high above his head. I waved back in the same manner. His boat was moving fast. In less than a minute he cut back his speed. Crede had joined me by the dock. Clay's boat skimmed the water near us, then bumped his wharf more than softly, and slammed up against the shore near Credence.

"Orimomo!" Clay yelled in his stentorian fashion, louder than ever. "Eye padnat!" he said to Crede, with equal volume. "Bon Poonah!" he yelled to me. I walked over next to them. "Dis pauvre boot," Clay exhaled.

"Comment ca va?" I said to him. I had learned that it meant, "How's it going?"

"Ca va mal," he replied. "Ah g'ah leek, a ole en de ba'm, mon ami." he pointed near his feet. His tennis shoes were under water up to his ankles.

"Whadja hit?" I asked. He just shrugged.

Clay jumped out, and the three of us pulled on a rope that was tied to the bow, getting the boat halfway up the bank. It was as far as we could manage to get it. The weight of the water the boat had taken on would give way no more to land.

"Don dere, sum pou carencro ga' dis coonass" he said, adding a couple of expletives in between that I sort of recognized, as he was pointing in the direction from which he had come.

"We gotta scoop this water out before she'll move up more," I explained.

"Oui, oui, vite," Clay responded and he jumped in the water. He unfastened the motor from the back, brought it up on shore and then he went back in the water. He pulled a bucket from behind the stern's seat and poured its contents into the water: crayfish. He started vigorously bailing the water from off the floor of the boat.

"Got one for me?" I yelled. He stopped, gave me a wide grin, and motioned to the boat tied on the opposite side of his dock. I walked the dock to that boat's stern and spotted another bucket tipped upside down near the middle seat. On my knees now, I reached in and grabbed it by the handle. I sat down to take off my shoes and socks. Clay called over to me, and from what I could decipher, told me not to take them off. He said something about the clam shells cutting my feet. I understood. Credence was chuckling aloud now, though he may have thought it was just to himself. There would be no way he was gonna get his dress pants wet. Those spiffy shoes were staying dry and right where they were at. I climbed into the water on the other side of Clay's shipwreck and bailed gung-ho.

Every so often Clay and I would stop, and the three of us would give another winded attempt at landing the boat all the way up on shore. Clay and I would push from our positions in the water, while Crede tugged at the rope from dry land. We had to measure our progress inch by inch until finally, she rose out of the water and slid on to the grass.

We shared a tired but well-deserved laugh. Clay was retrieving three beers from his Styrofoam cooler that had been sitting on the floor near the bow seat. He brought them up to us and he sat down on the grass. He handed one to me and I took it, exhausted, plopping myself down beside him. The ground was damp from recent rain, but that mattered not. Water had splashed all over us anyway as we worked to save his sinking ship. He lifted a beer to Credence but got motioned off.

Standing over us now, Crede said, "Done my good deed for the day; catcha tomorrow." I looked up, unable to contain another laugh as I nodded in affirmation. He lifted his hand to us in a "so long" gesture, then turned and walked away. Clay and I gave each other another look and we both laughed again. Crede turned back to us, but turned his head away again, shaking it as he continued to walk on. I lay down on my back.

"Ah ge de udder boot. Ever't'ing bon," Clay said, then got up and walked over to a small shed near the water. He retrieved a gas can, lantern, and two life jackets. He walked the length of the dock and set everything in the other boat. Then he climbed in and hooked the gas can line to its motor, as I sat on the shore just watching. He looked over at me.

"Ready?" I asked.

"Mais oui," he replied.

I arose quickly, gathered my bag and guitar case, and headed to the dock. Setting them carefully on the floor near the front seat, I climbed in. It took a couple pulls with that strong arm of his, but the motor kicked in, and with a smile at me, he eased her into the main channel. My destination was now only heartbeats away.

The waters were as familiar to me now as the place from which we had just embarked. The only thing I sensed different was that the shorelines had maybe gotten smaller, the canal maybe wider. I couldn't say for sure, but I was giving way to wonder. As I looked down at my soaking-wet socks and shoes, there came to me a comforting realism of how I belonged in this place. It was no longer someplace else, or as it had been the first time, a surreal, nearly primitive and unworldly dream. I would forever be a part of where I was now.

Reaching the inlet, there again, I spotted Marcus walking toward the bank we approached. The dogs were scampering around him, barking at us. Again our boat skimmed the shore weeds until it rested. He smiled down at me.

"Many moons pass Amigo," I said to him, returning his smile.

"Been walkin' the craters on the edges of each of 'em," was his reply.

As Marcus reached out his hand to help with my things, I handed him up the Gibson, wondering what he meant by what he had just said.

His hair and beard were decidedly longer, his complexion much improved, a far cry from how I had left him last. Clay was briefly explaining his boat situation to him. As Clay spoke, I noticed a boyish goodness showing through on Clay's old manly unshaven face.

"Better get to it then," Marcus told him. "This setting sun tells of what will be tomorrow."

"Yea righ, Yea ye righ," Clay replied. He laid my bag on the ground beside me, put his hand on my shoulder and gave it a squeeze. Smiling, looking deeply into my eyes, Clay then turned and stepped into his boat without another word.

"Tomorrow then," I called to him. He nodded and pushed out with the pole. Marcus and I watched silently as he maneuvered out of sight. Then came the familiar sound of a motor starting. I turned to Marcus, asking earnestly, "How are you? How's Jewel?"

"Faith has been our teacher," he said. His eyes shone that old familiar warmth. "She's with Elbow right now. She was called to help someone, should be back any time."

I picked up my bag and we began walking toward the house. "Been getting a lot of writing in," I told him as we made our way. I wasn't sure what to expect in response, if he had read that which I had left for them.

"Needin' to talk to you about that," he said, then he stopped walking and turned to me. "We read what you gave us."

A moment of uncomfortable silence transposed, troubling me. If instant sweat could talk, mine was screaming. What silence may have indeed been brief seemed deathly quiet far too long. At last he spoke.

"You're gonna leave Mark Twain in your dust," he softly said, then adding his smile.

I exhaled, not realizing I had been holding my breath. Then I gave a short, indiscernible sigh to myself, blithely responding, "Here I thought my only claim to fame was gonna be that I shook the hand that shook the hand that shook the hand of Abraham Lincoln." I was attempting humor, a release from those everlasting seconds of pent up tension I had just experienced. He gave me one of his once famous smirks, tilting a side of his lip.

"You write like ink were the gold in your pocket," he insisted, with strong and earnest sentiment. Now he was taking me by surprise and my face must have shown it.

"Yet it's all spilt if it has to exist on anyone caring or believing," I hastened to reply, not actually taking the time to think of how best to respond. He set my guitar case on the ground; put his hand softly on my shoulder, then, as I came to realize later, he commenced to quote old "Honest Abe" himself.

"Under all this seeming want of life and motion, the world does move nevertheless. Be hopeful. And now let us adjourn and appeal to the people." Then Marcus gave me, what transpired to appear as, an old-wise-man wrinkled smile.

He went on to counsel me with chastely. "Your writing will no doubt be cast into the sight of clogged men's minds. They can't see past the patches on their pilgrim jeans. You can't let their collective bargaining blight your way. I wouldn't change a thing. It's far better than I imagined it would be. Just keep your cool lines open; finish it. You're headed where you need to go and you're nearly there. It's being told." Now he was looking sternly into my eyes as he spoke. "The only thing," he paused. "The only thing is, you need to out-and-out say *who* I am."

"They'll hunt you down!" I instantly blurted out, in an excited, uncontrolled, and fairly shocked protest. He looked again at me.

"All eventualities have been prepared for," he calmly replied.

"But I just can't bring myself to go that far." I tried expressing this in a manner to show him how exhaustingly this had tried my soul. But did I obtrude; go past where he had expected? He didn't reply; instead his eyes widened, then picking up my guitar, he continued walking. I half expected to be admonished.

"I would have thought you might have spelled my nickname differently," he mentioned casually as we walked along.

I hoped my last words had not been an affront to him - to have insulted him somehow. He had lent his countenance to my work. Why couldn't I just take that final appeasing step he was asking of me? Was I quibbling over something he'd be able to keep under his control? It was a question that has yet to have its answered day. He once told me that no one has ever really walked in anyone else's shoes. He had always been charmed, always had, and is still leading his fortunate life.

## CHAPTER 3

As soon as I stepped onto the porch, I set my things down, explaining to Marcus that my shoes were soaking wet and how they had gotten that way. I didn't want to go inside with them on.

"Walk with me," he said. It was becoming one of his favorite things to say. Every time he said that, my life would move toward new beginnings. What twist would this one take? I followed him back down the steps. He had stopped for a moment, looking in the direction of Hershel's cabin. I still pictured Hersh sitting there on that porch. "She hasn't cleaned anything out of there yet," he said, pointing down to the cabin. Then he looked at me. "Well, the title's right. And when I said the truth needed to be told, it was meant to be more than about me. You're writing it right. You're making the message greater than just 'my' story, whether you know it or not. I'm sure others have written myths and legends about me, but you're doing it right, let's walk."

We started down the hill toward the cabin. I was smiling to myself as we made our way. It humbled me somehow, that he really thought I was navigating my writing properly. I'd been looking at it for some time as being offbeat, and a losing proposition. Like I had thrown all of my marbles out the back door before I even walked in to play the game. It felt to me like I was chopping Jewel and Marcus' heads off.

This time, Marcus and I traversed a different pathway. We walked around the left side of Hershel's cabin. Glancing up the hill, I stopped, and took a moment to look at the cross in Hersh's rock garden.

We walked around to the back of his cabin, where there was a well-worn trail going into the thicket and down a slight ravine. We walked for maybe another 20 or 30 yards. Breaking into a clearing, there lay the shoreline of a large swamp, maybe a dozen yards in front of us. We stopped walking. Near the shore were a couple of old wooden chairs, alongside the beginning of a small dock that stretched into the water. To the right was a dilapidated-looking shelter, set on poles, protruding from the water. It had a roof but no walls. It appeared to be a boat shelter, for nestled quietly in its shadows was an anchored old wooden rowboat. Spanish moss of silver mist, with hinted tints of soft green, hung everywhere. Entangled convolutions of vines, creeping through the foliage, captured all that had been manmade. There were flowers everywhere, in whites, pinks, and reds. This had been Hershel's hideaway, his safe haven, his sanctum.

"Watch for snakes," Marcus said once again, for what must have been the 20th time. I must have scoffed a bit, as though humoring him. "Are you watching?" he then added. I assured him I had been. "What about that one?" he asked, then he pointed.

This time it was real. He pointed to tree branches directly above the two chairs. There, on one low overhanging branch, my eyes now focused on a large snake that had wrapped itself amongst the twigs. I stood frozen, staring.

"It's a water moccasin. You don't wanna get hit by that," Marcus said. This time I nodded more sincerely. Marcus moved a few steps closer to it. Both he and the snake were acknowledging each other's presence. The snake then slithered around the branch, slightly uncoiled and then just dropped to the ground. Within seconds, it began making its way into the tall marsh grasses toward the water's edge and disappeared. I didn't want to move, but Marcus made his way cautiously toward the chairs. He motioned for me to come and sit with him. Yah, sure. I didn't move a step. He motioned again insistently. "It swam away by now," he assured. I nervously joined him there. The mosquitoes were noticeably annoying. Perhaps it was my instantly profuse sweating that had gotten them stirred up. When at last I began to relax, I noticed what must have been Hershel's boat. It was so similar to one I had back home, it was almost uncanny.

"There's not a ton of time left. The clock runs like I've never seen before," Marcus finally said to me. "I say to you again, it just needs to be told. You don't need to prove anything. It's the soul I need rested, not my ego filled. You're documenting it in the right light, and that's what matters to us. History will write its own pages. We just want you to be assured you have our support on it all the way. Finish it where you find it best. Set fire to everyone's tail." He smiled broadly at me and I smiled back without giving him a response. "Only a couple of good-time minutes left to go," he then added.

"Are you goin' somewhere?" I asked.

"We all are," he replied.

"Anything I should know?" rephrasing the question.

"The changes will all explain themselves. No need for us to ask, or try to answer questions," he said with a grin. He was talking in riddles, and I guess I just wasn't in the mood to try to follow along.

"Kat and I need to make our vacation plans for this year. She'd like to come down again, unless you guys maybe wanna come up?" I said.

"You won't be able to make your plans around us for a time," he replied.

Now I knew something was up, but I didn't want to think too hard about it. Letting his remark ride; I knew he'd tell me what I needed to know when the time was right. I didn't pursue it. I went back to our discussion about the book.

"So, do you have any idea what kind of backlash this book could cause?" I asked. I was trying to spur him. "A lot of people could be upset with what you did. Some may wish you'da stayed dead. Maybe this whole thing will wind up in some publisher's wastebasket, anyhow. I've surrendered to my anxiety over public reaction. You coming out in the public eye, it's leaving a bad taste in my mouth. It's been testing my resolve."

"Faith brother, God will see this through," he replied calmly. "It's whatever is meant to be, just as it always has been. I have everyone to answer to, don't you see? But I can't waste my time on their high-powered ethics. I can't hold to the chasms they'll put me in. I can afford to stave all of that off.

"There could come an onslaught of sorts. Some may think it scandalous." I interrupted.

"I don't expect that you'll understand this, but God is bringing wind to the wild side of my moon. For years I've known this to be coming," he said.

"But can you discern the hearts of men?" I asked sarcastically.

"I leave that up to you and Mark Twain, son," he replied. He smiled widely then as he lightly slapped my knee, then he stood up. The baying of dogs could be heard coming from near the house. "I knew a book could be written to dramatize the meaning of it all - the impact it's had on my life. Soon I will come out of a world that cost me so much to get to," he declared, his tone emphatic.

"I'm trying to understand," I said, as I stood up next to him.

"We're all going where he wants us to be, dear friend. It's the start of another beginning. I've had the best, now I need the rest."

Where on earth was this conversation going? It kept circling in profundities. Perhaps I could unravel some understanding when I played back the tape later. The dogs had ceased their barking.

"It's my lush vagrant angel," Marcus said. "She's the light tingle that tears the ground, my sweet shadow." He started walking the path back. "Live a day, die a day. I can't seem to catch up to living, like living catches up to me," I heard him say. I quickened my pace to catch up to him. "Anyway, news travels faster than it's made. It won't be up to us to itemize the truths you've come so far to explain."

I tried to expound on what he was saying by awkwardly adding as off the wall a comment as I could muster. "So you're trying to bestow upon this poor humble head, the weakness of a nation, of a misconstrued world," I pronounced boldly. I wasn't really sure what I had just said. He stopped and turned to me.

"Still, you'll be around to take other chances," he said, giving a quick laugh, then continued on his way.

"What just happened here?" I asked myself. I continued to follow behind him.

We came around the corner of the cabin and I caught sight of Jewel nearing the house. She was alone.

"Life smiles on her as if she only dreams in purples," Marcus said.

When she saw us, she turned to walk in our direction. As we neared, she appeared as though she had just been through an ordeal, yet, I could see the colors in her were returning. Her luster had endured, was revitalized. Always as candy to my eyes, she dazzled in all she captures from what is most exquisite. Her dress was of agate design, seemingly infinite in patterns of earthly colored lines. Worthy I thought, only to be draped around such a sublime goddess. An equally colorful medicine bag hung at her side from a shoulder strap. Do I make too much of her eloquence each time I see her? I think not. I shall stand forever enthralled.

Coming upon her, I gave a half-bowing gesture of reverence. Then within my hand, I gently pressed her petite fingers. Extending them up, touching them upon my lips, so gallant a kiss I gave; her smile paid me back with an added blush. What had gotten into me had been there from the very beginning.

"Oh, Grant," she exhaled. Flames danced with animation in the colors of her eyes.

"Just a little something about missing you," I softly, and oh so charmingly had to admit to her.

After a Mona Lisa smile, warm enough to set fire to the heart, she asked, "Now what've you boys been up to?"

"Dodging snakes," I replied with a grin, trying to be cute. She gave Marcus a concerned glance. With a smile he nodded it to be true. She sought no further elaboration.

"I've got grilled shrimp salad on ice, you hungry?" she asked, looking back at me.

"Of course," I told her. She turned and we followed her lead back up to the house.

Somehow the day had burned by. The sunlight danced between the tree limbs, softened to a purring yellow. Hints of orange scarlet flushed the sky in what could be seen of the horizon. The mosquitoes had all but disappeared, which is something I've never been able to understand. I have a theory about barometric pressure, and another about their energy and sleep cycles. I have absolutely nothing to substantiate any of it, so it deems no further exploration.

Back on their porch, I took my soggy shoes and socks off, explaining to Jewel how they had gotten that way. She and Marcus just smiled at one another, then we all stepped inside the house. Jewel set about preparing my highly anticipated dinner. Bustling about in the kitchen, I stood to watch her briefly, then went and retrieved my guitar. Marcus was already sitting in his favorite music chair, playing his favorite mahogany Martin. I quietly joined him and tuned up.

I will ever aspire to have the diligence in music that he has shown he has. On top of that, his music continuously casts shadows over the mediocre, always on new edges. This time he was about to astound me once more. It was a song he had just finished writing. He called it, *She Always Wears White Dresses*.

I fumbled along; following with a finger picking pattern I tried to make suitable to the arrangement. He continually invents chords I can't find names for - more like partial chords, forever on the move. The song's theme was as untraditional as one could imagine. I take that back, unimaginable. It told of a cosmic woman, encompassing all women, in a mystic Mother Nature realm. I guess I find it hard to explain. Basically, it's about a woman's protection of a man, unseen yet unrelenting, most powerful. I asked him when we had finished how in the world he came up with it.

"Ideas slap against my mind's walls and coat the conscience into an awareness dream," was his reply.

Huh? "So your ideas are never-ending explosions?" I asked, trying to comprehend.

"Until time lets fall its hold," he replied. "When my wine turns to turpentine, and I can't see beyond the bars," he said, then continued, "Jesus is my poet laureate."

Marcus had such a calm manner, it could have nearly rubbed off on me - that is, if I hadn't been so flustered, trying with my mind's eye to figure out what in the world it was he meant. All of the things he was saying confounded me.

Jewel brought dinner over to us. There were three large empty plates and an enormous bowl filled with shrimp salad. There was orange juice, tea and wine, whichever we preferred. We leaned our guitars against Marcus' chair and took a break.

"At least I can say I sang my life away," Marcus said, as he scooped salad onto his plate, then he reclined back in his chair. Without trying to presume anything, I again brought up the past, my tape recorder whirling. I asked if he missed the sumptuous, largesse-prone lifestyle I had read about that he had once lived. I told him I had heard how he lavished so many gifts on everyone around him. I asked if he thought they were grateful, or if he felt he was just buying their loyalty.

"I was pretty much full of myself," he began explaining. "Friends were marking me up. Some were true, others, well maybe it was just me being too generous. It was all so easy for a long time." Then, true to form, he got off on another tangent. "I don't concern myself with the flesh anymore, got the best of me much of my early life." He mentioned an awkward moment concerning an incident he'd had at his mother's gravesite. "Emptiness can await the scholar, like truth awaits the defeated. No one should really be able to blame me for ending up here, especially if my last hurrah ends up with them. I knew some time ago what it would take to save the rest of my life. I've been racing to keep finding it."

Was I catching a hint of something between his words? I blurted out the question of the century. "Are you thinking of coming out?"

There was a silent pause. He and Jewel looked at each other, expressionless. I knew they were reading each other's eyes.

He turned to look at me and said, "When my dust is all gathered, eternity will scream, asking was he worth it. Far better than blank sorrow, time will answer. Was he asking to be found? In every breeze that whispers, Heaven will pronounce."

I sat there astonished at his answer, or lack thereof. I think my mouth may have been gaped open again. Then, at last he tried in his own way to answer the question.

"I've heard they're really pushing my old image out there now. Everyone trying to score. All the way from impersonators to golf balls; impersonated golf balls," he laughed.

"Would you have expected anything less?" I asked, trying to urge him to continue.

"No, I've tried to make blame, even blaming dreams. There's so much to blame — blaming the dangers, blaming Mount Everest, blaming my mind for blaming me. I finally quit blaming," he said.

Now I was really knocked out of breath. I just sat there staring at him. "Come on, out with it," I was thinking. Had he said what I'd wanted to hear, or at least in part?

"If they caught wind of my consideration of coming out, I profess no worry over the impact. Anyway, it would need to be a pictorial exposé. Maybe a devout issue of Life magazine. Maybe make my own version of This Is Your Life," he said.

"You could always jump out of a cake," I joked, attempting to make light of my confusion.

They gave an unsparing laugh, then he gave me a strange look. I didn't know where my comment had come from in the first place, so I shrugged my shoulders and gave him a stupid grin. With that, he laughed again. Jewel giggled a little.

"It would need to be a slow pace resurgence, so as not to overwhelm. I don't know how it can be done. I guess I really don't want the world to know the "how" and "why" of me," he concluded.

I needed to speak my mind: "You could tell the world how you feel, you speak so profoundly. There are so many things askew out there. The world needs you back. Restore yourself to them, whether they embrace you or not." I wanted so much at that moment for them to agree. It would have made my life so much easier.

"Either that or I'm gonna have to change my name again after your book comes out," he said.

My bubble burst. "The book can have no real ending!" I retorted almost irritably. "It's a composite; a You and Me story, and that's it."

"What's it gonna take to make it more than that?" he asked sincerely, possibly sensing my blood pressure had spiked a bit.

"It scratches surface truths!" I further convulsed. "It's a hard sell."

"You want me to make it happen?" he asked.

"Both of you somehow," I told him, almost pleading. "Right now you either come out, or I fade you into a sunset. As it stands up to this point, I have neither one. For an ending, conclusions elude me. There's a huge blankness. Do you know what I'm trying to say? You're the only true King that America could ever have. There, I said it."

His response: "Never so rich that you can defy any price."

What? What was that? End of topic evidently. Jewel rose to clear our dishes. She knew I was upset. Marcus picked up the Martin and began singing, "People get ready, there's a train a comin'."

I interrupted. "Where is all this going?" I asked them, uneasy, my stance implacable. I was trying not to be upset, but I was antsy for that conclusive answer.

"Where it's meant to be, son," he replied, and he continued strumming. I peered at him, frowning. He stopped playing. "Love makes light, and it'll all be reflected."

"The love of the moon for the sun reveals the need to shine," Jewel called out from the other room. It was a line from the song she and Kat had been writing in their letters to each other.

"Mirror angling rivers are my veins too," Marcus gently offered up in conclusion.

Now I was fit to cry. Would there ever be a way he could talk to me in a language that needed no defining? Not thus far. I felt a scream building inside of me. I searched to calm myself.

I thought of him then, how he had been like a father to me, a teacher, a poet. I really am just a humble tool for something that's far above me. I needed to just ride this out. It's a far more wicked world out there now than the one that he had left. I consoled myself in the belief that he was being guided by something larger than life, bigger than I knew — something that knew best.

Then he filled in my thoughts, temperately stating, "When are you gonna dream for me, take off those pre-supposed wraps? Bend those tribulations, and love toward the light?" For some reason, he brought out a smile in me, my arrogance admitted ignorance.

We played on that night. As I warmly recall, Jewel got teary-eyed over a song I sang, called, *Boulder to Birmingham*, by Emmylou Harris. I was a bit taken aback by her sensitive response. Was there a more hidden meaning for her in the lyrics?

Much of the remainder of that evening was, once again, set on recapturing the essence of Marcus' songs. Most of them had been recorded on tape a number of times by now. I needed another safety deposit box for storing all that was accumulating. To my surprise, as his final song that evening, Marcus played an old number by, I believe, Eddie Rabbit, called *Cold Kentucky Rain*. He sang it with incredible feeling.

Jewel had retired moments earlier. Marcus began looking drawn, tired now. I myself, exhausted. No doubt we were all sleeping soundly long before midnight.

## CHAPTER 4

As a new dawn once again teased its way through that familiar crack between my curtains, all was quiet. I lay in bed for some time, having no desire to climb out and get dressed. I was thinking about all that had happened the day before. What actually had transpired? Did I somehow miss some important meaning in all that he had said? Were answers being given to my questions? When he attempted to explain himself, all it seemed to do was cast such shadows in my mind. Had it all gone over my head? I needed to bear down on those tapes from yesterday. I would be giving them close scrutiny.

Finally I rose and got myself dressed, including a pair of clean, dry socks. No one was around as I peered out my doorway. I expected to maybe see Marcus reading, but he wasn't there. I would search further, after my morning pilgrimage. When I stepped out on the porch, Marcus was seated on the bench swing. We bid each other a good morning, and excusing myself hurriedly, I moved along. When I returned, he was still sitting there.

"And how are you this fine morning?" I asked.

"Real good. Go help yourself to a cup a coffee." I did so, then went back and sat beside him on the bench. I noticed someone had hung my dirty wet socks over the porch rail. My shoes sat on a stool in the sun, just a few yards out into the yard.

"Jewel's with Clay. She's acquainting someone to her people; someone who will be able to help them from now on," Marcus explained.

Man, if that didn't beg questions. I was a little gun-shy from yesterday, so I failed to respond at first. Finally, I half-jokingly found a way to ask.

"Is she planning on retiring?" I smiled.

He didn't sense the humor. "No such thing for her," he replied. He was staring out over and above the tree line. "You know, I can't seem to recall any days without her now. Every day has been a blessing light. It's in her eyes, and it shows the world to me. She's always led me to those soft pillow sunsets of promise. I lavish her hold all over me."

This guy's in love, I thought to myself, amused. Then I shot the question straight out. "You guys are leaving this place, aren't you?" To my astonishment, he answered straight out.

"Yes."

I stopped the movement of my giggling foot. "When and where?"

"Well, it's a little too early to presume. There's a couple places we've found that really interest us. I think she's made up her mind. I'm waiting for her to convince me with those Popsicle charms of hers," he laughed. "That's why I told you not to plan your vacation around us. I think it will come to pass soon. Not to worry, chief, you'll be kept in the loop. We've got a lifetime of plans for you." He lightly slapped my knee again. I figured it was all I was gonna get out of him for the moment.

"Even falling stars tell her something," he then said, his train of thought shifting back to, guess who? He was thinking deeply about her. "There's a stillness in my love," he sighed. "Two hearts beating against each other, that's what God meant, a heart love beat tango."

Man was he floating out there somewhere. I hated to disturb his cloud, but that's me sometimes, Mr. Clumsy.

"Ya know, there are a lot of songwriters out there these days that would bore the pants off you," I told him, trying to change his thought pattern back to music. It worked.

"Once I gave a benefit concert in Mississippi for some storm victims. I was trying to show that I was just a regular guy and I could relate to their weariness."

"You're more like a poet or philosopher now. Great songs are coming out of you," I assured him.

"I cry almost every day, mostly in the morning," he admitted. "Don't get me wrong, it's a happy cry. I'm as happy as a man could ever be. I'm just overwhelmed by it all. I sometimes think of the people I had to give up for the sake of my selfish sanity, for my survival. My songs can never change those things I had to do." For a second, I figured he was anchored in self pity. I wasn't about to commiserate.

"Let's give a big hand for courage," I ended up telling him. That brought out a strong smile to his face.

"There will be new chapters coming in our lives, brother," he then added, "I have something for you." He rose from our bench and retreated inside the house, leaving me sitting there for several minutes. I found myself encompassed by a sorted daydream. I was staring at the same tree line, their branches swaying to the wind, my mind seemingly unable to construct any real thought structure.

At last, he came back out. There was a large manila envelope in his hand. Standing over me, and without hesitation, he handed it down to me.

"I give this to you," he said. I gave him a bewildered look when I reached up and took it from his hand. I bent open a metal clasp that held it closed and pulled out the paperwork from inside. Astonished, more than bewildered, I was looking at his songs. All of them had been typewritten. I looked up at him, I suppose wide eyed.

"What's this?" I asked.

"They want to go where they're loved the most," he said, winking at me.

He rendered me speechless. This would have been a perfect time to have said something profound.

"I'd like to see them go as far as they can. I know you can take them there," he said. I immediately felt bowled over with love.

He had mentioned something about this sometime ago, but I never actually pieced together what it would come to. This was why he had, so gruelingly, taught his songs to me over these past months. He had planned on giving them to me all along.

"Too bad Roy's passed on, I sorta owe him one," he said. "Do this for me, and no real hurry. Find the right people out there that can do these songs justice. Even you, you could record the ones you like."

"Me? I'm no star," I exclaimed. "And besides, I was in a band years ago - it was a rag-tag affair. It's hard to hold a group together. There's always egos and personality conflicts that tend to get in the way. For me to try to put a band together these days, well, it would turn out to be a real fly-by-night outfit. Whoever does these though, most assuredly, will become famous. Just you having written them will be enough."

It still had not transposed my senses what had actually just happened here. I failed to fully grasp that indeed, these treasures were being granted unto me, the endeavors of my future.

"There's no copyrights on any of 'em. I don't care about that. I'm entrusting them to you now," Marcus explained. "I've had my day. I just want them heard, mostly for the beauty of it all. I think they can add to God's wonder. After all, he's the one who gave them to me."

I began slowly paging through them. These were songs that he made sure I had memorized and taken to heart. There were 19 total in the package. On the corner edge of five of them, he had noted the word "female," and on three, the word "duet." As I pointed that out, he explained it was how he would prefer to have them sung.

What sprang to my mind immediately was now there would be a need for yet another safety deposit box. The others were filled the tapes, filed under the words, "High Test Love Songs." They were a priceless musical treasure trove in waiting.

Looking at these titles he had just handed me, I recognized that he had included his latest song, now more simply retitled, *White Dresses*. I hadn't really had the chance to work on that one.

"Can we go over some of these?" I asked.

"I was hoping you'd say that," and with a blink of an eye, he turned and started back inside. I rose to follow him, papers in hand. I left my coffee cup on the porch.

Our guitars leaned, as we had left them the night before. I placed the papers on the coffee table and started sorting through them, choosing the ones about which I still had questions. Making sure both recorders now picked up every note and vocals, I diligently rehearsed with him, as if we were about to go onstage.

Excitement building, tantamount to this virtual libretto he had placed in my care, I lost all track of time. With the dogs wildly rustling about, Jewel and Clay came through the front door. I snapped back to Earth. I didn't even realize we hadn't eaten anything. I glanced at my watch to see, it was 3 in the afternoon. Marcus and I gave each other the look of knowing we had now subjugated all of these songs to our satisfaction. It was time for me to pack everything in. I would need to get back to Beulah, take a shower at the truck stop, and get a good night's sleep. I had to deliver my load the next morning. Marcus knew what my timeframe was all about. He rose from the couch, walked over, and leaned his mahogany Martin in the corner near the window.

"I don't see any dirty dishes," Jewel admonished. "You didn't see the crabmeat avocado dip and chips in the cooler?" She turned to me. "Will you have time for me to cook something up?" she asked.

"Avocado would be great. No, I need to get going soon," I replied.

We munched on chips and dip, which were wonderful. Clay and I drank a couple cans of beer each. The conversation was light. Jewel seemed to be aware of Marcus' intent regarding the songs; papers strewn about the coffee table. She sat poised; her pleasing looks in my direction, as I gave the appearance of having taken up the challenge. Several times, Jewel and Marcus gave each other contented looks. I told myself, that for the time being, I would need to place these songs in a secured place. One thing at a time, I had to concentrate on completing the book.

We seemed to especially savor this last no-frills meal together. Again Marcus went on, emphasizing how he wasn't concerned with any time element. He knew I would need to put my writing through an editing process and all that, coupled with the complications of finding publication. He expressed full confidence it would all come to light.

"I don't care if it takes 10 years." he reiterated. It was agreed; we would talk about the disposition of his songs after I had thought about them for a while. "There but for the grace of God," he concluded. I assured them his work would find their intended audience.

As for my writing, well, precious little made by the hands of man can be spared a hint of sin. I never confessed it to him, but I swore and cussed plenty while I toiled over what felt like years of banging on those laptop keys. To be sure, it was always a labor of love.

There on the bank, next to the boat, Marcus dropped another surprise on me as I was about to leave. "You're an author now," he said. "I don't picture you being able to stop. Besides, this book is merely a tome. There'll be much more to write about."

"You mean a second book?" I asked. He just gave me that dimpled "glory be" uplifting smile. "To write much more I would need to know much more. What I have will pretty much fill in this episode." I said this, baiting him, hoping perhaps he would surrender his stance, maybe come out in the open. Was he asking for the testament of his life from me? He didn't bite, didn't say anything. He didn't even add anything to my conjecture. Instead, Jewel handed me another goody bag full with things that I trust would make me live on forever. "You gotta quit trying to make me immortal," I teased her. "We're meant to pass away; it's what makes life matter so much."

It was then, and with much ardor, she leaned over and gave me an ever-so-gentle, pulsating kiss. She didn't say a word. Those warm lips, pressed briefly upon my cheek, brought beatific rhythm to my heart. I do believe my knees may have been shaking.

"I wish you enough. God's speed," were Marcus' last words to me.

I left them on the bank that afternoon, each of us seeming to understand that a phase of our quest had somehow been completed. This time, even when Clay shook my hand goodbye and gave me a brotherly hug, it felt much more like an honest-to-goodness *real goodbye.*

## CHAPTER 5

Over a quiet dinner, I brought Kat up to date on what I supposed were their impending plans. She is less inclined to speculate than I am. Her world dwells more on what is real right now, never getting too far ahead of herself. I wish I could be like that. My thoughts are full of conjecture and fantasy worries. An old man once told me that he had wasted so much time and energy in his life worrying about things that never happened. I saw myself in him, and still do. I just can't seem to change those ways about me.

One can imagine my surprise when only a few weeks later, an assignment came through for me to deliver to a New Orleans warehouse. Ken had a change of heart? Maybe he just wanted to see his name in print, as I promised it would be if my novel ever saw the light of day. More likely he was touched by an angel; less likely it was just circumstance. Cards don't often get dealt this way. I tried not to make a judgment. I just thought of Sharon, and was glad to be heading back South. I made the call to Burton.

"They're not here, but they've instructed me to have you stop by if you find the time. Clay's with them; he's helping them for a while, they're relocating."

"Where at?" I asked politely.

"Jewel's mountain, is what they told me to say. Jack's watching over their place till they come back for more of their things. It's my understanding he's gonna be living at their old place semi-permanent. Eddie is staying at Clay's till he gets back in about a week."

I told Burton I would be there on Monday the 11th, around 1:00 P.M. I had questions, but they wouldn't transpose verbally. My questions were snarled, colliding into each other with half answers. What sort of furtive flight was this that Marcus and Jewel were taking anyway? An exodus from what? I couldn't find any focus in my speculation. I needed to wait it out. Marcus had always assured me that I would remain in the loop. I wanted to get down to their place, maybe clear my head a bit. I had been writing incessantly, studying the interview tapes as I went along. This would be a short stay. I would need to be back to Beulah before noon on Tuesday.

As it was, Credence seemed less talkative. Maybe his thoughts were scrambled too. He would remain in New Orleans under Burton's employ. I asked him if he thought they would be getting a new driver for up there on that mountain. He didn't think they'd be traveling much once they settled. It sounded to him that they may be staying up there for quite some time. He would go and visit occasionally, once they got all "homey," as he put it. His voice hinted of despair. A couple of times he had taken deep breaths. He mentioned how there would be new landscapes for Jewel to paint.

When we arrived at Clay's, Eddie came out of the house to greet us. He assured us Jack was on his way, so Crede gave me a rather swift, "so long" handshake. I didn't feel he was ready for any sort of long-term "goodbyes."

Eddie and I exchanged small talk. I told him that I had heard Jack was gonna be living at their place now.

"I guess we both are," Eddie explained. "Jack's place don't have land anymore. Gulf dun swallered her up. His boat floats over his driveway now. Gator's been waitin' fer him ta walk in his sleep."

Then Eddie surprised me — took me back. He looked hard into my eyes and declared, "I know who he is."

He had a pretentious haughtiness about him, a bragged swaggering to his tenuous form. He appeared arrogantly proud of himself. My inner reaction was at first defensive, to say aloud, "Took ya long enough!" But I held my tongue, thought hard, and stood there holding a blank expression to this contemptuous moment. I gave him a look as though I didn't have a clue what he meant. His words had a troublesome effect on me. My lack of reaction may have had its intended effect. He just turned away, saying he had to take off. "Maybe I'll see ya later," he said as he jumped in his dented, rusty, old Mustang. Letting the dirt fly, he fish-tailed his way out of the grove.

"Hmm, that was interesting," I said aloud. I tried to make sense of what those few seconds could really mean, my nerves suddenly becoming solicitous, filled with concern. Could this be a harbinger of things to come, an omen of sorts? Then I asked myself, who knows what will play out? I have since come to reconcile that moment in the same way that Marcus would have.

Everything happens for a reason. The truth, after all, will be known when everything is said and done. I couldn't bring myself to worry any longer about what damage the book may cause. Still I questioned their judgment, leaving Eddie here to help take care of things. Had it been a prudent thing to do? Maybe people would track this place down. It wouldn't be that hard to do. Maybe they'd pick the place apart. At that instant, I pictured in my mind the Biblical fall of Eden. Would there be an infernal reckoning? "Where the devil and God meet at the brink of a last career," I found myself saying aloud, shaking my head. The statement was caught on tape, even though I wasn't absolutely sure what I had meant by it. Marcus had made me this way — making statements from off of the tip of my tongue, off of the tip of my mind somewhere. Standing there alone, my thoughts were trapped in the momentum of some outskirt cloud. My thought process had definitely taken a sharp turn, from discourse to the obscure.

A boat was coming, the sound of a motor ever closer, it was Jack. He bravely waved as his boat coasted up to the dock.

"Hey, old-timer!" I shouted.

"Hey, old-timer to you!" he shouted as he drifted in. Tying her off to one of the posts, he not-so-limberly climbed up on to the dock. I grabbed his hand, as he appeared unsteady, and helped him to his feet.

"Ain't as young as I once was," he admitted. "Just wait, you'll get there," he warned.

"I know; sometimes I'm there already," I smiled. He smiled his rough smile back at me.

"Good to see ya," he told me.

"You too, Jack. How's the elbows?" I joked.

"Wanna find out?" He made a quick gesture like he was about to strike. I could tell by his posture there would be no doubt the damage he could still inflict on someone. I pictured myself airlifted into the water about 20 feet, just by the appearance of that sheer might. I made a cowering gesture in return, and we both laughed.

"How much time ya got, are ya stayin' over?" he asked.

"Like to, but gonna need to get back in the morning."

"No problem, could use a little company. Don't know how they stand ta be alone out there so much. I like people around."

"Well, they've got each other," I told him.

"Yah, I guess."

"How come you ain't married, Jack?"

"Wife passed away some 14 years ago."

"Oh, I didn't know. I'm sorry."

"Sha we header on up?" he asked, motioning in the direction of their place. He made no further comment about his wife's passing, so I just nodded that I was ready to go. I left my guitar with Beulah, but brought the tape recorders. I wasn't about to miss anything that could help me along.

During the ride up, Mad Jack said nothing except, "Aye," as he pointed to an alligator on the shoreline. We were up to their inlet in no time flat. As we scraped the shore, already things felt somewhat empty. I could hear no songbirds, and the wind was picking up. The shrubbery was soaked by a recent rain, and it felt like it was about to rain again.

"Got some jambalaya on the cooker; ya hungry?"

"Sure, but looks like rain, mind if I take a little walk first, case I don't get a chance later?" I asked.

"Go head, I'll take yer bag up ta the house. See ya when ya get back," he replied.

I thanked him, then turned in the direction of where I had come to realize was my favorite place in all of Louisiana. I took more care to watch for snakes, but I impetuously, anxiously, pushed ahead. When I broke clear from the path, I stood in that virtual park, The Place With No Name. I listened quietly, but could hear no sounds. It was already starting to rain, a storm was imminent.

I scanned my view over to the island. It appeared distinctly smaller; the water had swelled. This lake had risen to where it was now within mere yards of reaching the gazebo on the island's far side. I could see no flowers. The birdbaths were all but buried beneath menacing waves, waves that now were lapping the underside of the bridge walkway. I could see what appeared to be a kingfisher on the island. The wind had picked up, a storm nearly upon me. I would need to scurry to keep from being caught up in it and drenched. Yet there I stood; stilled in this place that surrounded me with cold, tranquility departed. It overtook my senses, as if by the blustering wind itself. I fell under the auspices of this ever changed and all too vivid picture. Eerily missing was that copiously enhanced Eden. Was I witnessing an ebb? I became overwhelmed by the truth of certain separation from this world where I now stood. I felt in that self-effacing instant that I would cry. Was this Eden soon to be transposed? Was it not to be his final resting place after all? That which he had confided, standing as I recalled, so confident. Warmth was washing away from this place. The air chilled me, winds marking dynamic promises where contentment once stood. A heavy squall came upon me now. I hurriedly turned my back, retreating to the path that would take me away from being witness to a dying dream. Words would never explain how those few minutes had sucked me to empty. The only blessing would be if I never had to confide this aloud to anyone. I would need to heal this wound by myself.

Running up to the house, I was too late to beat the downpour. Reaching the porch, it was as though I had been in the shower with my clothes on. I was soaked to the gills, and even my tennis shoes would have a tough time getting over this by morning. I slipped them off without bothering to untie the laces. I threw my socks on the porch floor and went inside.

"Got caught good 'ey?" Jack remarked, viewing my condition. He threw a towel at me.

"I'll say!" I caught the towel, then quickly took the recorder from my shirt pocket and dried it off. My hat lay flattened, drowned about my head. Its brim had lost all signs of life. I stood with water dripping all around me on their kitchen floor.

"I gotta get outa these," I told him, referring to my clothes.

Jack nodded in agreement and pointed to where he had placed my bag next to the coffee table. I made a short dash to the bedroom. Throwing my wet things in a laundry duffel bag that I retrieved from a side pouch of my travel bag, I quickly changed into dry clothes. I'm never without a spare hat, and this time it would be a blue beret.

Rejoining Mad Jack in the kitchen, he had just dropped the ladle for his jambalaya on the floor. He picked it up, wiping it off on his shirt. Dinner was about to be served; I just smiled.

"Zat military?" he asked, pointing to my beret.

"No, just beatnik," I replied with a grin.

With a couple cans of beer in front of us, it was now time to eat. Not much for conversation while he dined, he reminded me a little of Clay. I caught a glimpse of Jack looking at the scars on my hands. He made no comment, choosing not to waste any time while scarfing down his meal. I simply followed his lead. The cooking was pretty good. It was the first opportunity for us to spend any amount of time together. I think we were both working on being comfortable.

"No dogs?" I asked between swallows.

"Naw, took 'em with 'em," Jack said, adding, "Oh, they left somethin' for ya." He stood up still chewing, and walked behind me over to the art/library room. I turned to watch him. When he came out, he had one of Hershel's wooden circle disks in his hand. He laid it down next to my bowl. "They wanted you ta have this." It was slightly over a foot in diameter with a thick, lacquer finish. I studied it for a minute.

"Wait a sec, it's a Mandela, the circle of life!" I resounded.

"Yah, guess so," Jack replied.

It was exquisitely carved, far more intricate than any previous pieces I had seen; truly of museum quality. I ran my fingers over the design, lending them to my imaginative interpretation. Jack looked at me like I was trying to read Braille or something.

"This is outstanding! He never said a single word aloud, but spoke so many in all that he touched. This one is almost like a Biblical testament. It speaks volumes!" I said, nearly rejoicing. I sat there astounded, relishing this gift.

"There's a note 'er somethin' on the back," Jack said, scooping another bite with his spoon.

I picked it up and sure enough, taped to the back in the center was a small, folded note. I gently pulled it loose from the wood and opened it. Having previously seen handwritten lyrics, I recognized it to be Marcus' handwriting. It read: "And the winds now blow deep on our vested walls. With the soul, sparks send life to gather the breath that never ends nor disappears."

I reread his message, maybe half-dozen times. I thought I understood what it meant, but with Marcus, meanings are in the mind of the beholder. I remember him once explaining to me, referring to Jewel, "She brought me back from the dead, after all." So, depending on the context, time and place, one must decipher accordingly.

Jack, picking up his bowl now, stood up from the table. He was finished. I still held the Mandela in my hands. Marcus' note lay beside my spoon. This was all too much. My food was getting cold. Setting the artwork by the side of my bowl, I proceeded to scoop up what remained. There, finished.

Seeing me rise from the table, Jack retrieved two more beers from the cooler on the floor near the cupboards. I put my dirty dishes in the pan of water he had filled next to the sink.

"Got a place I can dry those shoes of yours out by the barbeque," he said, as he headed for the door.

"Think you could dry my gloves too?" I asked. He stopped and nodded. I quickly retrieved them from my room as he waited.

I followed him out, and sat down on the porch swing while he made his way around to the back of the house. The rain had lightened to a drizzle. The humidity was thick; embracing this stifling air, sticking to my skin and overloading my lungs. I labored with each breath. My dad used to describe air like this as "close." I sat there, waiting for Jack to return.

"Don't remember it getting this hot," I remarked, as he came from around the corner.

"Gets that way. Hey it's summer; enjoy it," he replied.

"Yah, okay, the beer helps," I told him.

"Plenty more," he assured me, and we walked back inside. He brought out a couple more beers and handed me another one. Although I was hardly half-finished with the can in my hand, I took it anyway. He went to the music room and plopped down in Marcus' reading chair. I went in and sat on the couch. We were quiet there for a time, just me and Old Elbow.

It should be noted that from what I could see, none of the furniture had changed. Wherever they moved to, they hadn't taken anything large with them. The guitars and banjo were gone. "That's to be expected," I told myself, maybe aloud. I later noticed cardboard boxes in the art/library room, piled high in a preparatory state. There were no books left on the shelves. None of Jewel's jar remedies were there, and the art easel was gone. The following morning, as I peered through the glass from outside, the greenhouse looked nearly empty. It all appeared to have been done so stealthily, as if in secret.

"They didn't take any furniture," I remarked, sipping my beer.

"Had no call to, I guess," Jack replied.

"Their new place must be furnished," I added.

"Don't know, ain't seen their new digs."

We were warming up, like two new friends. When I explained the reason why, he didn't seem to mind me turning on the table recorder. I told him about my family, my kids and grandkids. I told him the story of how I first met Jewel and Marcus, how it all came to pass over a silly baby alligator. He got a kick out of that, and began opening up to me. Sharing fragmented stories, he spoke with the veracity and richness that must nurture itself straight from out of this delta soil. I sat listening, mesmerized. He told of people he knew in the area, and about the silly idiosyncrasies that encompass their lives. We shared much laughter.

Then, turning his leg half to the side and lifting his shorts a few inches, he again pointed out his scars. They looked to have been serious wounds at one time. "Got a Purple Heart for this, from being strafed by friendly fire," he said with a grin. He had told me some of this before, but must have forgotten. Embellishing as he went along, he explained how Burton, Clay, and himself were all been Vietnam vets. He had met Burton over there, but not Clay. "Still gives me trouble sometimes," he added, as he patted his thigh with a smile and then straightened out his shorts.

When this thoughtful conversation wandered to the times he was on patrol, he started talking about booby traps and tunnels; how he had seen friends die. Then his words abruptly stopped. It was as far as he apparently wanted to go with those memories. I sat, relieved. His emotions had built up. We drank in silence for a while.

As he settled back, more at ease, he spoke about his wife's passing, how she had died of cancer. They had raised two sons, now grown and moved away. He boasted about how rowdy he had been during his married years.

He had become "more suitable" to his fellow man, as he put it, after his wife got sick. "I got religion back then," he explained. "Those same guys I had scrapped with, they came to our need. We were plenty bad off back then. I had problems with my back and was out of work. That was around the time Burton came into our lives. It was at a vet reunion. Not long after, he got me hooked up with Marcus, and well, here I am."

He claimed it was Marcus who led him to the Lord, but he didn't elaborate. He mentioned again how he had never met Clay, but had heard about Jewel. "She's legendary in these parts, so was her dad. Jewel gave Annie a lot of comfort back then, I owe her a debt of gratitude. I'll never be able to repay her for what she did for my Annie."

I'd swear, if he wasn't so bad-billy-goat-gruff looking, I would have to say that I depicted a tear. I suspect he was more than capable of crying, relating those things to me. It only served to intensify my perception of what I had already come to know in his regard. Whatever Elbow Jack was in his sparing years, he had indeed evolved into a gentle spirit. His morose outer texture washed away, he showed me who Mad Jack really was. All was brought to bear for him, I imagine, by the complications of life's lessons, both in sadness and in wealth. There are so many more stories I'm certain he could tell. I hoped to someday hear them.

"So, you think Clay'll move with them?" I asked.

"Not a chance; the ladies need him here. They'd never let him go," Jack grinned. I laughed aloud, then thought more seriously about what had become apparent to me; Jack was aware of who Marcus really was. In fact, Marcus had once told me so. But Eddie, well I don't think he was really a part of Marcus' plans.

"Eddie knows who Marcus is. He told me at the landing today," I said to Jack.

"He'll keep quiet; he'd better," Jack sternly replied. I gave a doubtful look. "It's all good, everything's good," Jack assured me, detecting my concern, and adding how tractable Eddie was for him. I sorrowfully doubted it, but I let it pass. It was hard for me to imagine Jack's control over him. I tried not to think about what havoc it could wreak. It gave me cause for apprehension. I feared for what might come to pass.

The night had settled in, and we relaxed. I inquired about how long he thought he might be staying at their house. Sadly, he reflected, there really was nowhere else for him to go. His home was in a region that had been rapidly swallowed by the Gulf's waters. His belongings were in storage somewhere. His age showed, as he explained his losses to me. A feebleness came through that outer mighty appearance. He was growing old right before my eyes.

"Maybe they'll stay on the mountain. This place could be yours someday," I told him.

"She'll never let go of this place; too much here for both of 'em. I know 'em that well," he said.

We had gained a closer friend that night, a bond that would last. Moments had given way to hours, although it was still early by most standards. I admitted to him that I needed sleep. It would be a full truckin' day tomorrow and I would need to start out early. Thanking him kindly for the beer buzz, I bid him a goodnight. Arrangements had been made with Credence for me to be picked up around 9:00 that next morning.

Journal entry: 6/11/07

*"Too hot to sleep. The skies were once so much clearer here. I remember thinking back then, would there ever blaze brighter stars?"*

It had been a whirlwind visit. A scrambled egg breakfast, dried tennis shoes and gloves, followed by a hastened boat ride back down to Clay's place. All the while, my hands lovingly clutched the Mandela.

Eddie was nowhere around when we reached Clay's dock, but his Mustang was there. Credence, prompt as ever, sat in his car until we stepped up on shore. The "so long" from Mad Jack was completed with a sturdy handshake and his genuine wrinkled smile. Crede, on the other hand, acted more like we would never meet again. It seemed like a real goodbye when he said it to me. I assured him I'd be back. "Life is long," were my final words to him. Both he and Jack reassured me that Marcus had conveyed to them that he would be getting in touch with me as soon as they were settled. After an early morning rushed load of laundry completed at the truck stop, it was back to my "gung ho" driving.

My writing can best be described as ever-more-feverish since the visit. It is becoming paramount for me to wrap things up. In the back of my mind, stand convincing thoughts in terms of music. They brazen of bigger fish I need to fry. I have all of these songs, a whole world of opportunity. It pulsates my voracious mind with the rising sun of each new day. I've begun writing two more originals, calling them, *No Shoulder to Cry On* and *Fly by a Blue Moon.* I'm becoming excited to play them for Jewel and Marcus.

## CHAPTER 6

So what was needed to be told, I have told. To write more, I would appear to be rambling. I've probably done enough of that already. Like I tried to explain to Marcus, I would need to know more to write more. I expressed to him how this book might not be well received. I fear it may not come across in the same way he appeared to me to have pinned his hopes. He may understand and accept that scenario, I don't know. With regard to any negative backlash regarding these writings, "Tell them to go propagate their species," I recall having once been his response. "That was kind," I thought at that moment, and I remember laughing.

It's the Fourth of July now, and alas, I find myself right back to where this story first stumbled upon its beginnings. Seated at the table I now amuse myself. I'm thinking maybe it's time for me to get back to that deck of cards. I could certainly use a little solitaire. Kat and I are enjoying a week of vacation, with no real plans other than to appreciate our woods and maybe do a float on the river.

How does one find a suitable ending to this story? Postulating that I've told all he wanted told, what more could I add to his interminable legend? How may I expound or elaborate? What words, appertaining to such an ardent spirit, might I further draw upon? It has always been tantamount for me to express reverently, yet without exposing his real name, who he is and where he now stands. I grasp to marshal my thoughts, feeling stretch marks on my brain. Posing staunchly, I am compelled to abide by his guidance: "To God the glory be," he once told me, and so it must.

Marcus is someone suited to all times. His epitaph will no doubt reflect and resound throughout the ages. I wonder what history, with its saddle-sore years, will pronounce? And what will the world do with him now? To me, he has admittedly been a fiery poet, a philosopher, my teacher, and of course, my dear friend. He diligently immersed himself in the music whenever I was with him. Always gracious, unwavering, he never once doubted me or my ability to complete the task he had set forth. There were times I had given him plenty of cause to doubt. He was always with an erudite manner toward me, always polite and in control. Why, when I looked in his eyes, did it never fail to bring me closer to a realization of God's existence in our lives? His voluble words, though perplexing, always expanded my energies beyond their accustomed borders.

He had confided in me, that when this story reached its inevitable conclusion, he likely would be changing his name again. The resiliency of a Phoenix rising up from the ashes. Feeling compelled to close these writings, although pensive, disquieted, my mind fights toward ease now. I wrestle to be assured I've fulfilled my promise of faithfulness, loyal to this obligation brought forth by the brother of my heart. At this very moment, I play back his voice on my recorder.

"Verily I say to you, nearest to infinite are the words at your disposal."

So have I elucidated all that words can do? Rest assured, I could probably go on forever. Trying to stave off a barrage of unneeded attention, that is why I've omitted his real name from these writings. I allude only to his true essence.

Believe me, it didn't feel half as far going there as it now does coming back. And as for a synopsis, a plot? I can't answer that. Dramatic, enticing, compelling intrigue? Yikes! Does a book really need all of that? I guess it'll depend on what one makes of it as it is read.

I sense much editing ahead. Where do all these commas go anyway? I will need to come back to all of this after I allow my mind to clear for a time. There are these hours of tapes I still need to pore over. Then there are my journal entries, filled with enduring memories, and admittedly, some gibberish. And rest assured I will continue the writing of them. Why do I get the feeling he's saving the best for last?

It's been some time since I last saw or heard anything from them. I'm still waiting as patiently as I possibly can to find out about their latest endeavor. I'm becoming restless to move on with this music that has been bequeathed to me. I'm sure there are so many more pages, volumes that will someday be written. New chapters, unimagined, will yet unfold. Still, this writing's time has drawn nigh.

I can hardly wait to relate to them a dream I recently had, more of a nightmare. I'd be interested in his take on it. It could stand some interpretation. I don't recall the location, just another truck stop somewhere. I was in a deep sleep, dreaming I was in an abandoned house with no furniture. The setting sun shone through a large living room picture window. I went to pull a string hanging down from a light on the ceiling, but the bulb had burnt out. There came from around the corner of the next room an apparition, an ethereal shape. It was that of an old man, definitely dead. He was floating off the ground toward me. It scared the be-geebees out of me! It was coming closer, pale, a ghostly pale white face. I wanted it to get away. "Aaahhh," I sounded out in its direction. It continued floating closer. "AAaahhhh!," again, I cried out even louder. Then it was upon me, not much more than a foot away. It opened its mouth, as if about to say something. "AAAAAHHHHHH!," I screamed, horrifically loud. I know it was out loud, because I'd awakened myself from the outburst. My heart was beating against my chest like the drum solo from *In a God a La Vida,* by Iron Butterfly.

"What was that all about? What just happened here?" I heard myself gasp aloud.

The truck driver parked next to me had turned off his engine, probably trying to better hear what was going on. I bet he thought I was being murdered in my bunk. It was a warm night and I had my small vent windows open over my bunk. I'd say the entire parking lot heard me. It had mortified me, shaken my wits to no end. Even now, writing about it, when I conjure up that image, shivers run through me, I get the chills. It was a nightmare too uncanny, too enhanced, to be unreal. When I told Kat about it the next morning she told me to just shake it off, that it had only been a dream. "Never so real," I recall telling her.

It wasn't until two or three weeks later, as I was about to pass through Hannibal, Missouri, that I came upon a billboard on the outskirts of town. The sign read, "Visit Mark Twain's Boyhood Home and Museum." There was a large picture of him staring down on us passersby. I nearly jumped my track. The realization stormed over me. It had been him. He was the specter in my dream. I had been haunted by Samuel Langhorne Clemens.

I pulled into the only truck stop in town, went inside and asked the guy behind the counter, "Is Mark Twain buried there?"

"No, somewhere out East, I heard," was his reply.

I had made up my mind that if he was, I would unhook my trailer and bobtail old Beulah right to his gravesite. I was more than ready to apologize for ever having boasted that my writing could better his, or even compare. I wanted this slate wiped clean. Kat instructed me later that if it happened again, next time I should try not to be so afraid. Maybe he was trying to tell me something — that I should hear what he had to say. What could I ever hope to extrapolate from Mark Twain's ghost? Could it really become a recurring visit? I would really like Marcus' opinion of this. I'll bet Jewel might have something hypnotic to add.

With the Mandela lying on the table next to me, I find my fingers playing over indentations where his benign fingers had been. My thoughts turn to Hershel, I can't help it, and it's beginning to rain. Kat had been submerged in this assiduous intricacy that Hershel had created. Where was his mind? It had to have been beyond what anyone could pre-suppose. We decided this piece will be exhibited above the mantel of our fireplace. It would become the centerpiece of our home, displaying the celestial order of life, expounding on untold truths. Someday I hope to contact the curators of an art museum. I'd like to see if they would be interested in having us loan such art as this to them, to be shown for a period of time. I'd venture to bet they would agree.

I stare out the window now, beguiled, glazed over by afternoon's way of turning thoughts to introspection. I'm witnessing Beulah being rain-washed; she sure can use it. But how tired she looks. Even this bath doesn't seem to bring out that old shine anymore, 800,000 big miles on her now. So many loads she has put her back into, so many countless tons. All of that patience she had given me, although she sure has a mind of her own at times.

Maybe I need to write a song about her because her fate has now been sealed. I found out from a mechanic two weeks ago, that from what he could see on the computer, she was slated to be sold in Mexico. Our fleet was being revamped, eventually to be overtaken by automatic transmissions. No more mashing gears, inevitably making me lazier. I'll bet they won't even speak English to her down there, that's what I'm thinkin' to myself.

"There, this is it," I catch myself muttering, trying to focus on my laptop screen. "Let's put an end to this story."

Admittedly, I find melodic thoughts interfering. They're giving out discombobulated musical memories, mixing half arrangements, the songs of my past with those in my future; a music-go-round. Notes are playing ping pong between my ears. This poor brain, having been waltzing circles for who knows how long, as if to the harmonic rattling, the echoing of these bouncing raindrops on the window.

Okay, now I'm watching a finger awkwardly leading my hand, requesting the pleasure of this last dance toward the "print" key. Oh, for that good, old-fashioned rumba drama of final pages being played out by an awakened printer. From our couch in the living room, Kat's calling out to me, "Can you answer the phone?"

Made in the USA
Charleston, SC
15 July 2011